KILL YOU TWICE

Chelsea Cain's first four novels featuring Archie Sheridan
have all been *New York Times* bestsellers. The first two,
Heartsick and *Sweetheart*, were listed in Stephen King's
Top Ten Books of the Year in *Entertainment Weekly*. Also
the author of *Confessions of a Teen Sleuth*, a parody based
on the life of Nancy Drew, and several non-fiction titles,
she was born in Iowa, raised in Bellingham, Washington,
and now lives with her family in Portland, Oregon.

BY CHELSEA CAIN

Chelsea CAIN

KILL YOU TWICE

PAN BOOKS

First published 2012 by Minotaur Books,
an imprint of St Martin's Press, New York

First published in Great Britain 2012 by Macmillan

This edition published 2013 by Pan Books
an imprint of Pan Macmillan, a division of Macmillan Publishers Limited
Pan Macmillan, 20 New Wharf Road, London N1 9RR
Basingstoke and Oxford
Associated companies throughout the world
www.panmacmillan.com

ISBN 978-0-330-51284-8

Visit www.panmacmillan.com to read more about all our books
and to buy them. You will also find features, author interviews and
news of any author events, and you can sign up for e-newsletters
so that you're always first to hear about our new releases.

For Carolyn Keene. I refuse to believe that you aren't real.

Sweet as sugar
Hard as ice
Hurt me once
I'll kill you twice.
—*Unknown*

1

Archie Sheridan slept with the light on. The pills on his bedside table were Ambien. A year before they would have been pain pills. Vicodin. Oxycodone. A cheerful skyline of amber plastic bottles. Even now the table looked empty without the clutter. Just the Ambien, a cell phone, a week-old glass of tap water, and a red gooseneck lamp from IKEA.

His kept his gun in the drawer. On the nights the kids weren't there, he slept with it loaded.

The Ambien prescription was untouched. Archie just liked to know it was there. Sleeping pills made Archie groggy, and groggy wasn't a luxury he could afford. If the phone rang, if someone died, he needed to go to work.

Besides, it wasn't getting to sleep that was the problem. It was staying asleep. He woke up every morning at three A.M., and was awake for an hour. That was how it had gone since the flood. Now he just figured it in. Went to bed an hour earlier. Compensated. He didn't mind it. As long as he controlled his thoughts, kept his mind from wandering to bad places, he was fine. Focus on the present. Avoid the dark.

The gooseneck lamp stayed on, its red metal shade getting hotter by the hour.

Three-ten A.M. Archie stared at the ceiling. The apartment was sweltering and his bedroom window was open. He could hear the distant grind of the construction equipment still working to clean up the flood damage downtown. They'd been at it in swing shifts for three months, and the city still looked gutted.

If it wasn't the noise from the construction, it was the trains he heard at night: the engines, the whistles, the wheels on the tracks. They traveled through Portland's produce district around the clock.

Archie didn't mind the noise. It reminded him that he wasn't the only one awake.

Everyone had a cure for insomnia. Take a warm bath. Exercise. Drink a glass of warm milk. Eat a snack before bedtime. Drink herbal tea. Avoid caffeine. Listen to music. Get a massage.

Nothing worked.

His shrink told him to stay in bed.

Don't even read, she said. It would just make getting back to sleep harder.

He just had to lie there.

But his pillow was too flat. The used mattress he'd bought groaned every time he turned over.

The heat made his scars itch. The new skin was tight and prickly, reminding him of every place her blade had sliced his flesh. His chest was knitted with scar tissue. Patches of dark hair sprouted around the thick pale pink gashes and pearly threads, unable to grow through the tough flesh.

That sort of itching, in the middle of the night, can make a person crazy, and sometimes, while he slept, he scratched his scars until they bled.

Archie ran a hand along his side, the scars pebbly under his fingers, and then over his chest, where his fingers found the heart-shaped scar she had carved into him with a scalpel. Then he made a fist with his hand, rolled over, and pinned it under his pillow.

❖

Four-ten A.M.

Archie's cell phone rang. He turned over in bed and looked at the clock on his bedside table. He'd been asleep ten minutes. It seemed like longer. His eyeballs felt gritty, his tongue coated. His hair was damp with sweat. He was on his stomach, naked, half his face smashed against the pillow. As he reached out and fumbled for his phone he knocked over the bottle of Ambien, which toppled and rolled off the bedside table and clattered to a stop somewhere under the bed.

Archie brought the phone's glowing LCD screen to his face and immediately recognized the number.

He knew he should let it go to voice mail.

But he didn't.

"Hi, Patrick," Archie said into the phone.

"I can't sleep," Patrick said. His voice was a strained whisper. Probably trying not to wake up his parents. "What if he comes back to get me?" Patrick said.

"He's dead," Archie said.

Patrick was silent. Not convinced.

The official report had been death by drowning. A half-truth. Archie had held Patrick's captor's head underwater, and when he was dead, he had pushed his body into the current of the flooded river.

The corpse still hadn't surfaced.

"Believe me," Archie said. *Because I killed him.*

"Will you come and visit me?" Patrick asked.

"I can't right now," Archie said.

"Can I come and visit you?"

Archie rolled over on his back and rubbed his forehead with his hand. "I think your parents want to keep you close right now."

"I heard them talking about me. They want to give me medicine."

"They're trying to help you feel better."

"I have a secret," Patrick said.

"Do you want to tell me what it is?" Archie asked.

"Not yet."

Archie didn't want to force it. Not after what Patrick had been through. "Okay," he said.

"Will you count with me?" Patrick asked. It was something Archie had done with his own son. Counting breaths to get to sleep. Patrick and Ben were both nine. But Patrick's experience had left him changed. He was mature without being sophisticated.

"Sure," Archie said. He waited. He could hear Patrick getting settled and imagined him curled on his side on the couch in his family's living room, the phone held to his ear. Archie had never seen that couch, that house, but he'd seen photographs in the police file. He could picture it.

"One," Archie said. He paused and listened as Patrick drew a breath and exhaled it. "Two." Archie sat up in bed. Patrick yawned. "Three." He put his feet on the floor. "Four." Stood up. "Five." The windows in his bedroom were original, made up of dozens of factory-style rectangular panes. If Archie ran his fingers over the glass, he could feel tiny waves and ripples on the surface.

"Six," he said.

He made his way to the window. "Seven." The light was on inside, and it was still dark enough outside that Archie could see his own mirror image in the glass. As he got closer, his reflection faded and the city appeared. Out his window the Willamette cut a curved path north, slicing the city in half. A sliver of light along the silhouette of the West Hills marked the first hint of dawn. The river was almost lilac-colored.

"Eight," he said.

It was the truck's backup alarm that caught his attention. The window was open, hinged along the top so that it swung out horizontally. Archie's eyes flicked down to the street below.

"Nine."

The streetlights were still on. The produce district had wide streets, built big enough for multiple trucks full of apples and strawberries. But the trucks didn't run much anymore. The warehouses were now mostly home to used office supply stores, fringe art galleries, Asian antique stores, coffeehouses, and microbreweries. It was close in and cheap, as long as you didn't mind the trains that barreled through the neighborhood every few hours.

"Ten."

The truck down below had backed up to the loading dock of Archie's building and stopped. A black sedan pulled up beside it. Two men got out of the cab of the truck and walked around to slide the back door up. A woman got out of the black car. Archie knew she was a woman the same way he knew that the men in the truck were men. It was how they stood, how they moved, the dark shapes of their bodies in the yellow glow of the streetlights. The woman said something to the men, and then took a few steps back and watched as the men started unloading large cardboard boxes from the truck.

A U-Haul.

Someone was moving into the building. At four in the morning.

Archie had stopped counting.

"Patrick?" he said.

The other end of the line was silent.

"Good night," Archie whispered.

He ended the call. It was 4:17 A.M. The bed beckoned. He could still get a few hours' sleep before he had to head in to the office. As he stepped away from the window, he thought he saw the woman look up at him.

Jake Kelly only drank fair trade coffee. It guaranteed a living wage for coffee farmers, who otherwise might be slaving away for a price less than the cost of production, forcing them into a cycle of debt and poverty. Jake needed a cup. He needed the caffeine. But the center only had Yuban. He could smell the nutty aroma of French roast wafting from the brewing air pot. Was he tempted? Yes. But then he thought of the indigenous people of Guatemala, working for pennies in the coffee fields. Every choice a person made, what to buy or not to buy, what to eat and drink, had the power to change lives. You were either part of the solution or part of the problem.

He focused on the task at hand.

The trick to cleaning a griddle was kosher salt. Jake let the griddle cool and then scraped it with a plastic spatula. Charred pancake batter collected in satisfying little clumps. He'd brought his own yellow rubber gloves. The center didn't have any, and it didn't seem right to ask them to spend money on that sort of thing. He'd brought the kosher salt, too. It was Morton's, in a blue box with the girl in the yellow dress carrying an umbrella on the label. He sprinkled some salt on the griddle. The coarse white granules bounced and scattered on the cast iron like hail raining down on a sidewalk. You didn't want to use soap or detergent. Jake scrubbed the griddle with a pumice brick, grinding the salt against the surface until his fingers ached. Then he used a damp cloth to wipe up all the salt and muck it had loosened. It took five passes with the cloth until the surface of the griddle gleamed.

He wasn't done. He unscrewed the plastic cap of an economy-sized bottle of vegetable oil and drizzled a thread of it on the cast iron. Then he got yet another cloth rag and used it to work a thin coat of oil over the entire surface of the griddle. More oil. More rag work. Small circular motions. Start at the center. Work your way out.

He was bent over, eyes even with the surface of the griddle, inspecting his work, when Bea, the center's director, walked into the kitchen carrying a plastic laundry basket piled high with dirty linens. She was a sturdy woman, old enough to be Jake's mother, with the wild hair and anxious eyes of someone who has just stepped out of a very fast convertible.

"You're still here," she said.

Jake glanced at the oven clock and realized that his shift had been over for an hour.

"I'm seasoning the griddle," he explained.

She smiled. "You don't have to do that."

"I don't mind."

"The last volunteer just used paper towels and 409," she said.

"I'm sure they did what they thought was best." He hadn't known how to take care of a griddle, either. But he'd seen it on his orientation tour of the kitchen, and afterward he'd looked it up. He'd taken notes, copying down bullet points from various Web sites. People could get pretty passionate about the proper care of griddles. After reading some of what he found on the Web, Jake began to wonder if it wouldn't be easier to just make the girls' pancakes in a skillet. He thought about suggesting that, but he didn't want to make waves.

"I wish we had more volunteers like you," Bea said. She blew a stray piece of graying hair off her forehead, adjusted her grip on the basket, and headed for the back door.

Jake peeled off the yellow gloves, tucked them in his apron pocket, and ran after her to help. "What's with the laundry?"

"Washer's broken. I was going to put this in my car so I don't forget to take it home tonight."

Jake didn't even hesitate. "I'll take it," he said.

She frowned and raised an eyebrow. "Really?"

Jake took the laundry basket from her hands. It was heavier than it looked. Or maybe she was stronger than she looked. "Let me take it home. I have to do laundry anyway tonight. I can bring it back in the morning."

Bea crossed her arms and shook her head with a smile. "You're a blessing, Jake."

Jake beamed. "I'm happy to help."

"You want some help getting it to your car?" she asked.

"I've got it, thanks."

Bea opened the back door for him anyway, and he lugged the basket out to his car. The center had a small parking lot, five spaces, just enough for staff and volunteers. Three of the cars in the lot were silver Priuses. Jake took the basket to his silver Prius and set it down on the pavement so he could open the trunk. He paused to look up at the sky. The morning sun on his face was warm and the cool summer breeze tickled the hair on the back of his neck. A white butterfly spiraled lazily through the air, dipping in and out of view. Not a cloud in the sky. Jake closed his eyes and put his face up to the sun. In the Pacific Northwest, days like this were precious.

He smelled something—sandalwood? cloves?—and opened his eyes. The butterfly was gone.

Then he heard a thud, like a baseball bat hitting a melon, and felt a searing pain in his head that knocked him off his feet. It took him a few seconds to realize that the two sensations were related. As he lay there on the concrete, slipping into darkness, the last thing he saw was the laundry basket beside him, a fine mist of blood settled on the dirty sheets like dew.

3

Human meat had a particular smell. It was blood and
flesh, metallic and salty, feces and fat. Like the slaughterhouse
stench of butchered animals, but different.

Sourer.

It was a smell that Archie had trouble describing, but always
knew immediately.

The dead man's wrists and ankles were bound with rope and he
was dangling from the lower branch of a cedar tree, his hands tied to
the branch so he hung like a sick Christmas ornament, his bare feet
a few inches from the ground. He appeared to have been skinned
from the neck down. The beefy red muscles of his chest wall gave
off a bloody gleam, and the lacelike threads of exposed yellow fat
looked almost pretty against the raw meat of his flesh.

The weekend summer sun was high and bright, and there was a
cool breeze that belied the late afternoon heat to come. Rays of
sunlight pierced through the cedar boughs. The corpse's light hair
fluttered gently along with the leaves. He looked to be in his mid-
thirties, average height and weight. But it was hard to tell.

At the corpse's feet, already marked with an evidence flag, was a
wilted white lily.

Cedar needles covered the ground beneath the body, and where the cedar needles gave way to earth, the dirt had been raked clean with a branch, obscuring any footprints.

Archie bent his ear to listen to the distant sounds of children playing echoing through the woods.

Henry had arrived at the scene first, and his shaved head was already glistening with tiny beads of sweat. He looked off into the distance. "Playground," he explained.

Archie knew the park. Ben and Sara played there.

They were on Mount Tabor, which was less of a mountain and more of an impressive hill with high aspirations. It rose up on Portland's flat east side, a dormant volcanic cinder cone, its slopes covered with elegant historic homes nestled among ancient conifers. The top of Mount Tabor was a wooded park. There were hiking trails. Tennis courts. Picnic areas. A crenellated stone water reservoir. A popular playground. Every August hundreds of adult Portlanders built soapbox cars, dressed up in costumes, and raced from the top of the park, down the winding road to the bottom of the hill.

"I'll clear the area," Henry said. He turned and headed off toward one of the patrol units on the road. He still walked with a limp, though Archie could tell that he tried hard to hide it.

"How is he?" Robbins asked once Henry was out of earshot. Robbins had his medical examiner's kit open, and had bagged the body's hands. Now he stood with his fists on the hips of his white Tyvek suit, studying the corpse like a butcher sizing up a cut of meat.

"Still weak," Archie said.

"Physical therapy?" Robbins asked.

"Yep," Archie said. Henry was supposed to work with a therapist twice a week. But it was hard to keep appointments as a cop. Homicides had a way of cropping up at inconvenient times.

The soft bed of cedar needles on the ground under the body was soaked with blood, and as Archie inched closer to the victim he was careful to stay on the outside edge of it. Blood draining from a victim who is still alive will coagulate. It's what stops people from bleeding to death every time they nick a finger slicing a bagel. Assuming you don't open an artery, an open wound won't gush; it will pour something red and thick and sticky, like honey. Coagulated blood still hung from the corpse's feet in viscous strings.

Standing there, Archie was almost eye to eye with the corpse. The killer had suspended his victim at that height intentionally, Archie thought, so that they could stand nose to nose. It put the killer at around Archie's height, five-ten.

It had not been an easy death. A makeshift gag had been stuffed in the dead man's mouth, forcing his jaw so far open that his chin nearly touched his neck and his cheeks bulged. Rigor had caused his lips to peel back, so that his teeth and gums grinned madly around the gag, making his mouth appear all the larger. His face was frozen with pain, forehead muscles contracted, dark brows raised, crow's-feet splintering into his hairline. His eyelids had contracted, revealing a flat, fixed gaze. With the exception of his head and arms, his entire body was glazed in blood.

"Take a close look," Robbins said.

Archie leaned forward. He could make out brown body hair on the dead man's shoulders. He let his eyes travel down the body and saw the same fine hair on the man's thighs, thicker and curlier around his genitals. Walking in a slow circle around the corpse, cedar needles crunching under his feet, Archie saw, amid the rivulets of blood, freckles, patches of skin, surrounded by red. The man had not been completely skinned from the neck down. The killer had taken his pound of flesh only from the man's chest and abdomen. The victim had then been allowed to bleed. A lot. Slowly.

Archie was aware of Henry stepping back beside him. Archie had to fight his instinct to nursemaid Henry now that he was back on the job. He didn't ask how he was doing every ten minutes. He didn't ask if he was making his physical therapy appointments, or try to help him get out of the car. No special attention. That was how Henry wanted it. Now Archie gave his old friend a few moments to survey the scene. It didn't take long for Henry to come to the same conclusion Archie had reached. Henry scratched the stubble on his head and adjusted his sunglasses. The bloody corpse was reflected in his mirrored lenses. "The amount of blood on the ground," Henry said. "He was still alive when he was tortured."

"The wounds look premortem," Robbins agreed. "He's been dead four to six hours."

Archie batted away a fly. Cautious people didn't kill in public places. Cautious people killed in rented apartments and on lonely roads and in the backs of stolen vans. It took a special kind of someone to commit murder. It took a special kind of special to commit murder in a public place, and to take time doing it. It didn't bode well. People who didn't make logical choices were hard to predict, which made them hard to catch.

"Park closes at midnight, opens at five A.M.," Henry said. "So if they came in a vehicle it was last night or this morning."

"You're assuming they came in together by car," Robbins said.

"Maybe the victim came of his own free will," Archie said. "Maybe they met in the park. Maybe they walked."

"Or cycled," Robbins said. "On a tandem."

Henry ignored him. "No one matching his profile has been reported missing today," Henry said.

"Do they sweep the park at night looking for cars?" Archie asked.

"They're supposed to," Henry said.

It was a big park. A little recon to discover which areas of the park weren't swept on that final patrol, and the killer could have driven his victim in, tortured and killed him, and then driven out after the gates went up in the morning.

It was one forty-five P.M. The body had been found an hour before. Archie could make out the scars in the dirt where the cyclist had lost control and skidded ten feet before wrapping his mountain bike around the trunk of a cedar. The bike was still there, on its side, one wheel bent. A cracked rearview mirror had snapped from the handlebar and lay on the ground a few feet away.

Underneath the darkened canopy of conifers, Archie counted the mounted spotlights of at least three television news crews. The cameras winked, light reflecting off the lenses. The police tape perimeter had been generous, but with a zoom lens and some creative angling, those cameras could get a shot of the body.

"We need to get him down," Archie said.

"Just waiting for the word, boss," Robbins said. He dug into his open ME kit, snapped out two pairs of latex gloves, and held them out to Archie and Henry.

Archie stretched the gloves over his hands. Even after a year, the left one still looked wrong without a wedding ring.

A few flies buzzed around the corpse's head. One landed on his open eye, fluttered its wings for a moment, and then flew off.

Robbins unrolled a white body bag on the ground and then unzipped it. Body-bag zippers did not sound like other zippers. The big plastic slider grinding against all those plastic teeth, down the side and across the bottom in a J-shape, carried a special menace. Robbins flicked open a medical-looking blade and handed it to Archie. "You cut," he said. "I'll catch."

"What about me?" Henry asked.

"You stand there and if I shout that my back has given out, help me. Otherwise, try not to contaminate my crime scene."

There was a white plastic step stool already set up near the body, and Archie climbed up on it with the knife in his hand. The rope around the corpse's wrists didn't look remarkable, and neither did the knotting, but Archie still hesitated.

"Photographed it from every angle," Robbins said.

Robbins was the best ME Archie had ever worked with. There was no more discussion. Archie gripped the branch with one hand and started to saw at the rope with the other. Robbins stepped behind the body and placed his gloved palms on the dead man's back. When the rope gave, the dead man dropped an inch to the ground. He did not slouch back or crumple in a heap. He dropped straight down, like a lawn dart, his arms frozen straight up above his head, stiff with rigor, his toes pointed. Robbins eased him back into the waiting body bag, like a piece of furniture.

Zip.

Robbins stood up. His latex gloves and the arms of his Tyvek suit were smeared with blood. "Hands look okay," he said. "I should be able to lift a good set of prints."

Archie unwound the rope from the branch and stepped back to the ground.

"We've searched the immediate area. No sign of his clothes."

"Check the trash cans throughout the park," Archie said. "And see if anything's floating in the reservoir."

Henry held out an evidence bag and Archie dropped the rope in it.

"Not exactly a cornucopia of clues," Henry said.

"There's one more," Archie said. He squatted alongside the body bag, and pulled open the zipper to expose the dead man's head. Then he reached into the corpse's gaping mouth, dislodged the gag, and pulled it out. It was a fist of white and yellow rubber, caked with dried saliva. Archie had to use both hands to carefully tug the ball open, turning it inside out and separating the two parts, the rubber peeling apart with a final sticky snap to reveal a pair of yellow kitchen gloves.

Archie held the gloves out to Robbins. "Print them," Archie said.

S usan Ward gave a great hand job.

It hadn't come easy. She had read books. She had practiced. It had been, at times, a slog. But she had overcome her general lack of manual coordination and mastered the technique.

She pressed her palm flat against the fly of Leo's slacks and held it, feeling the heat of his body under her fingers. He was wearing a skinny black Italian leather belt and she unbuckled it and unhooked the tab of his pants and slid her hand underneath his boxers.

She loved this part, the promise of it—the control.

He started to say something. "Shhh," Susan said.

The hallway to the bathrooms was dark. But Susan had positioned herself so that she could see back into the restaurant bar where they'd been sitting. She could see the massive dark wood countertop, the TVs above it, the lunch crowd perched on tall chairs, downing their tapas and wine. She'd see anyone coming. Then again, with her bright orange hair—a shade of Manic Panic called Electric Lava— they'd be sure to see her. That was part of the thrill, the tension that came with the possibility of public humiliation. It made Susan's face hot and the arms of her skin prickly.

Leo's breathing quickened.

God, he was pretty. He was the prettiest boyfriend Susan had ever had. She gazed up at his face, his pale smooth complexion and his dark hair, those eyelashes. She licked her lips and kissed him lightly on the chin, feeling a warm flutter move through her lips, down her neck and chest, to her center.

She kept her hand moving—green glittery nails, bitten to the quick—teasing him. His face didn't change. She liked that, his self-control. He watched her with his dark eyes, mouth turned up in a slight smile, his expression registering only the tiniest amount of surprise. But he was alive under her hands, his body responding to her touch. She used one hand to free him from his trousers, careful not to break rhythm, listening to her own internal metronome.

Leo's breaths came long and slow now, like he was concentrating on them, but his expression did not change.

It took two hands to execute a hand job. She ringed her thumb and forefinger around the base of the target. A gay friend had taught her that. It heightened engorgement. But mostly it made the target look bigger, which, Susan had learned, was incredibly important to every guy on the planet. The other hand was trickier. Twist. Roll. Twist.

It was not an easy maneuver. The first couple of times Susan had tried it, her arm cramped up and she'd had to ice it. Nothing breaks the mood like a freezer gel pack.

But she had practiced since then, and could now Twist Roll Twist like a concert pianist, which is to say, elegantly and by body memory. In fact, she had found that it helped to not think about it, and to just let her hand Twist Roll Twist on its own.

She breathed in Leo's smell, the spice of his expensive aftershave, the tobacco of his occasional cigarette, the starch of the shirt. She felt light-headed and content. Leo swallowed hard and flattened a palm on the wall behind her.

She could feel his rhythm. The target was on course. There was no turning back. He was all hers.

Susan leaned her head contentedly onto his chest, her eyes just above his shoulder, looking out toward the bar. Making a guy come gave her an inordinate amount of satisfaction. She was pondering the psychological significance of that when the "Breaking News" graphics on the TV caught her attention. It had only been three months since she'd been fired from the *Herald*, and she still had a Pavlovian reaction anytime she saw those two words. Her pupils dilated. Her heart rate increased. Her muscles tensed.

Leo put his hand on her breast.

Susan pressed herself into his palm, still keeping one eye on the TV.

Leo's eyelids were heavy, his lips open. Twist. Roll. Twist. But the TV news headlines kept calling to her. Murder. Torture. Mount Tabor.

There was a helicopter shot of a thicket of trees. Then a ground shot, taken from a distance, of a blurred body hanging from a branch. She saw Lorenzo Robbins next to the body, recognizable with his dark skin and white Tyvek suit.

Leo came, catching her by surprise. His stomach muscles clenched and a spurt of hot semen shot between them through her hand.

And at that exact moment, Susan saw someone else she recognized on TV. He was also standing next to the body. Something in the woods seemed to catch his eye and he looked up, right at the camera, right into the restaurant, right at her, standing there with Leo Reynolds's dick in her hands.

"Archie," she said.

Archie stood in the parking lot feeling the sweat congeal on the back of his neck. It was midafternoon now, and the heat was starting to radiate off the asphalt. The Life Works Center for Young Women was located in an old three-story house in Southeast Portland, in a neighborhood full of rambling old wooden houses, most of them long since converted to apartments. The front of the house was painted pastel pink, but the sides and back were lemon yellow, as if whoever had been painting the house had gotten busy, or distracted, or just forgot to come back and finish the job. The house had a big covered front porch, a front yard planted with overgrown vegetables, and a neighboring lot that had been paved over with black asphalt to create off-street parking.

The blood-splattered basket of laundry was in the parking lot, between two silver Priuses. Priae? Archie didn't know.

Blood spatter came in three categories: passive, transfer, and projected. Passive bloodstains were caused by gravity. Blood dripping off a butcher knife, blood pooling around a body, blood dribbling down a chair leg. It was relatively neat and contained.

Transfer blood spatter occurred when wet blood was transferred from a primary surface to a secondary one. Then it got tracked around on the nice clean carpet leaving boot prints, or smeared from a palm onto a windowsill, or wiped on someone's jacket. Transfer blood was ugly and messy, but it meant clues—fingerprints, shoe size, a bloodstained item of clothing in the killer's closet.

Projected blood spatter was much more interesting. It was created by force, by impact, something greater than gravity, like, say, a fist, hammer, baseball bat, or car windshield. It spurted, gushed, sprayed, and misted—it made art.

It told a story.

The bloodstains on the white sheets in the laundry basket were projected spatter. Tiny drops of various sizes created a constellation of red on the white sheets, like paint flicked from a paintbrush. The drops were elongated, with rounded tips and tails, revealing the direction of the blow. The crime scene investigators would measure the length and width of the bloodstains, plug the results into trigonometry equations, and use a computer program to reveal the point of origin and the exact impact angle. Archie didn't remember the trig he took in high school being nearly that interesting.

The bamboo that formed a hedge between the house and an adjoining property swayed gently in the breeze, and the hollow stalks knocked together softly like a wind chime. The garden had been freshly composted and the air carried a faint smell of sun-baked manure. Overhead, the clear sky was streaked with jet contrails.

"We haven't touched it," Bea Adams said. "If that's what you're thinking."

Archie had been quiet for too long. He did that sometimes. He knew it made people nervous, but he couldn't help it.

"Of course," Archie said.

Bea Adams was the director of the Life Works Center. Gray hair sprang from her head in electric spirals, and she wore a pocketed linen smock over a turtleneck even though it had to be ninety-five degrees. Her glasses had red plastic frames with orange stars on them. A red kabbalah string encircled one wrist. "Is it him?" she asked. "I heard the story on public radio. The body in the park. I thought Jake had gone home. Then I came out here and found this." She fluttered a hand at the basket and then lifted it to her mouth. "God, he's not dead, is he?"

The blood spatter was significant, a hard blow, but not a fatal one. The body on Mount Tabor had skull damage. "When did you last see Mr. Kelly?" Archie asked.

"A little after eight," she said. "He volunteers in the kitchen for the breakfast shift. He stayed late cleaning up. I told him he didn't have to."

Archie gave Henry a look, thinking of the rubber kitchen gloves they'd found at the crime scene.

The time frame fit. Archie checked his watch. It was almost three P.M. "You didn't notice his car was still here before then?" Archie asked.

She looked around at the three silver Priuses in the parking lot.

"Right," Archie said. Every other car in Portland was a Prius or a Subaru.

Archie heard his name and looked up to see Henry motioning for him to come over. "Excuse me," Archie said to Bea, and he walked over to where Henry was lurking in the shade of the bamboo. Henry held up his cell phone and said, "Kelly's not picking up his phone." He added, "And I sent a unit over to his house, and he's not answering the door." A patrol cop came over and handed Henry a DMV photo printout. They could do that now—enter data in a dashboard computer and out spits a photo. Archie and Henry both looked at the image off of Jake Kelly's driver's license. The laser quality wasn't great, but he could have been the man in the park.

Archie scanned the eaves of the house for cameras. The center was a nonprofit group home for teenage girls. Some were court-referred for repeated minor offenses—shoplifting, fighting, property damage—others had been expelled from every high school in town, some had been kicked out of one too many foster homes. They were all, in one way or another, difficult. The center offered the girls a chance to get their GED and the possibility of a life that might not include prison.

"Any surveillance?" Archie called to Bea.

"No," she said.

Archie didn't ask why. No money? A gesture of trust? It didn't really matter. It was the same result: no photographic evidence. Robbins was comparing the corpse's teeth to Jake Kelly's dental records right now. But based on the evidence so far, Archie was fairly confident they'd have a match.

"You do background checks?" Archie asked Bea.

"Sure," she said. "We get state funding. It's required." Kelly would have been fingerprinted for the check, but the state destroyed fingerprint cards after the applications were approved. Still, the forms would provide a wealth of other information. Next of kin, past jobs.

Archie's phone rang. It was Lorenzo Robbins. "Go ahead," Archie said into the phone.

"The dental records match," Robbins said. "It's Jake Kelly."

Archie slid a glance at Bea. She was pale, her gaze fixed on him. She fully understood what the content of the call had been. "I'll call you back," Archie said to Robbins. He hung up and put the phone back in his pants pocket. There was nothing good to say at this point, nothing that made things better. He had learned that a long time ago.

"Well, shit," Bea Adams said.

"A re you mad at me?" Susan asked Leo. She took a sip of red wine, and let the pinot glass rest against her bottom lip.

"No," he said. "Guys love it when you say someone else's name as they're ejaculating."

Susan set her glass down on the wood bar. A half-moon of dark purple lipstick marked where her mouth had been. "It wasn't like that," she protested. "I saw him on TV."

Leo lifted his palm at her. "Just stop talking."

Their lunch had come and gone and Leo had barely said a word. Mostly he talked on the phone. He said he was working, but Leo was a lawyer with only one client—his father—and as far as Susan could tell his services mainly involved checking in on several strip clubs his father's company had acquired. She took another swig of wine. It was the most expensive pinot they had by the glass on the menu— fifteen dollars, which seemed crazy, but Leo was paying, and he could afford it. Leo's family was rich. And they'd made their fortune selling a product more addictive than lap dances. Seeing as being a drug dealer was one of the few professions from which be- ing a lawyer was a step up, Leo had that going for him. Susan took another swig of wine. It didn't taste any different from the stuff she bought for nine dollars a bottle. She'd wanted a cocktail. But it had seemed too early for vodka. If they stayed at that bar much longer, it wouldn't be.

There was a mirror behind the bar and Susan caught her reflection in it. Her hair was highlighter orange and it gleamed in the mirror like something radioactive. In the last two years she'd cycled through turquoise, violet, and pink. But the orange was different. It looked like an accident, like she had gone into a salon asking to look like Lucille Ball and had come out looking like one of those traffic safety cones. People didn't understand she was *going* for traffic safety cone, that that was the point. She had almost died. She had lost her job at the newspaper. She was barely able to eke out a living as a freelancer. If it hadn't been for her book about all the kooky ways people died, she would have starved. But she was alive. Archie Sheridan had saved her life just three months ago, when he'd pulled her half dead from the floodwaters. It had been two years since they first met, when she'd been assigned to profile him for the *Herald*— the cop who had caught serial killer Gretchen Lowell—and her life had not been the same since. She had told Archie Sheridan things that she'd never told anybody. And he had trusted her with the secret that had nearly destroyed his life. Yet somehow, every time they were together, one of them nearly ended up killed. She wanted her hair to say, *Danger Ahead*. Instead strangers on the street pursed their lips sympathetically and assured her that the color would fade. Susan thought about redyeing it. But that meant bleaching her hair out again, and her hair was already getting sort of fuzzy from all the dye jobs. She wanted to wait at least a month before she put it through another color change.

"What are you thinking about?" Leo asked.

"The Middle East," Susan said.

She let her eyes fall on the TV above the bar. The local news had cycled back to the murder in the park, and there was the helicopter shot again, the crime scene from above. The trees were mostly evergreen, with deciduous trees sprinkled between them. As the shot zoomed in, Susan could make out a sliver of crime scene tape, a clutch of people, and something else. . . .

"The trees," Susan said.

"What?" Leo said.

"I have to make a call," Susan said.

"Let me guess," Leo said. "Archie."

Susan dialed Archie's number. It went to voice mail. It went to voice mail a lot when she called Archie. "It's me," she said. "I saw you on the news." She could have told him what she'd seen. But she decided not to. If he wanted to know, he could call her back. "I noticed something about the crime scene," she said. "Might be important. You know how to reach me."

Archie's phone buzzed against his thigh. He usually carried it in his jacket pocket, but it was too hot these days for a jacket. The vibrating phone tickled his leg. He ignored it and followed Bea Adams into the living room, where she'd gathered the nine teenage girls who currently lived at the center. Like most places in Portland, the house didn't have air-conditioning. A variety of ancient fans blew warm air noisily from points around the room. The sun coming through the window illuminated a billion specs of dust that swirled slowly in midair.

Archie sneezed.

"Gesundheit," one of the girls said.

He looked up. A fine mist of his saliva floated in front of him, sparkling in the light. Beyond it, on the other side of the sunbeam, was a couch, and on the couch sat four girls. The girl who'd spoken sat on the floor in front of the couch. The facial piercings were gone, and her hair had grown out and was bleached blond, with two inches of light brown at the roots. A colorful Indian skirt pooled around her legs. Tiny mirrors were sewn into the fabric and they reflected the sun, projecting bright spots above their heads onto the plaster ceiling, like a disco ball. Her thin round shoulders pushed forward and she smiled at him.

She'd Tasered him once. The fifty thousand volts of electricity had dropped him to the floor.

"Hi, Pearl," Archie said.

She was supposed to be in Salem, back with her foster parents. Archie wondered how long that had lasted before she'd run away again. A month? Two? She'd been sixteen when they'd met and already an epic pain in the ass. Archie was guessing that a year had not mellowed her.

"You look old," she said.

Yes, still a pain in the ass. "I feel old," he said. He cleared his throat and glanced around at the other girls. They gazed sullenly back at him. No tearstained cheeks. No histrionics. No loss of innocence at the violent death of someone they knew. These girls had already seen the bad the world had to offer. So they weren't surprised. It would be different, Archie thought, if they had seen Jake Kelly's mangled body hanging from that tree.

Pearl was tapping a plastic pen against her front teeth, tap, tap, tap. The fans whirred and heaved. Archie's eyes felt dry.

"I'm Detective Archie Sheridan," he said, for the rest of them. He skipped the usual get-everybody-comfortable small talk. It was too hot in there. "Did any of you see anything out of the ordinary this morning?" he asked.

The girls shook their heads or shrugged, or stared blankly, which meant the same thing.

"Did any of you see or talk to Jake Kelly?" Archie asked.

More head shakes. "He works in the kitchen," a girl with an orange Mohawk said, like it meant something.

Bea Adams took a small step forward from her position against the wall and said, "The girls aren't supposed to fraternize with the volunteers."

Especially the male ones, thought Archie.

Pearl was chewing on the end of the pen now, working it between her teeth at the corner of her mouth like a dog with a strip of rawhide.

"None of you saw him this morning?" Archie said.

"I shuttled the food in and out of the kitchen," Bea said. "The girls weren't back there at all."

Archie returned his attention to Pearl. She caught him looking at her and stopped savaging the pen. "What?" she said. She lowered the pen to her lap, holding it between her first and second fingers, a substitute for the cigarette she really wanted.

"Can I see your hand, Pearl?" Archie asked.

She looked down at her hands and then back up at him, mouth uncertain. "Why?" she said.

Archie smiled. "Just a hunch," he said.

Pearl considered this for a moment and then threw a defiant look around the room and shrugged. "Whatever," she said. She held her left hand toward Archie. As she shifted forward, the disco lights reflecting off her skirt spun dizzily around the room.

She'd been holding the pen in her right hand.

"The other hand," Archie said.

Pearl hesitated; then extended her right hand, palm up.

Archie stood, walked over to where Pearl sat, and knelt in front of her. Then he took her hand in his. It seemed tiny, the nails bitten to the quick. No rings. A tattoo on her inner wrist consisted of a single plainly printed word: *lucky*.

"The news said that you saved that kid," Pearl said. "Someone kidnapped him and you saved him. Patrick somebody. I heard about that."

Archie lifted her palm to his face. Her veins pulsed against the pale skin of her inner wrist, the tattoo still black, relatively new. He could feel her hand tense. She pulled it away. But not before he caught a whiff of what he was looking for.

It was a bright, spicy scent, and instantly recognizable. "Cloves," he said.

Pearl tucked her right hand under her left armpit. "So what?" she said.

"You can't buy cloves anymore," Archie said. "They're banned. Along with all flavored cigarettes."

Pearl smirked. "I know a guy."

The smell was fresh. "You smoked this morning," Archie said.

Bea's arms were crossed. "It's not allowed in the house," she said.

"So you went outside," Archie said to Pearl.

"They're not allowed to smoke on the front porch," Bea said.

"We're not allowed to do anything," the girl with the orange Mohawk said.

Archie leveled his gaze at Pearl. "If I go to the side yard, by the parking lot, I'm going to find your cigarette butts. I'm guessing you're the only one around here who smokes cloves. And I'm thinking I'll find butts from this morning."

Pearl turned her head away. "I didn't see anything. I saw him go by with the laundry."

A warm, dust-thick tunnel of air oscillated past from the fans, and Archie sneezed again. This time no one said gesundheit. They were all watching Pearl.

"Then what?" he asked.

"I came back inside," she said.

"What time?"

She had the pen in her hand and was gripping it so hard, her slender fingers looked like they might snap it in two. Her arms had goose bumps. Everyone else was sweating. "Search me," she said.

"Pearl," Bea said. "You need to tell him what you saw."

Pearl looked away. "I saw Jake," she said. "I liked him. I talked to him sometimes. But I didn't talk to him this morning, because he didn't like me smoking."

Tears slid down her cheeks. She reached up and rubbed them away, and when she lowered her hand her face was smudged with ink. The pen had leaked.

"Do you believe me?" she asked Archie.

Sure, she had Tasered him, and when he'd come to he'd found himself hanging from meat hooks, but then again, she'd helped rescue him, too. Good times. "Yes," he said. Pearl's face relaxed. Inky tears streaked her cheeks. When Archie's daughter was four, she got into his wife's makeup, and ended up with eye shadow and mascara all over her face. She'd cried, too, that day. It was something kids learned to do when they wanted to get out of trouble. Archie leaned back and caught the attention of a patrol cop standing in the foyer of the house. "Get a CSI in here," Archie told him.

Pearl's eyes grew large. "Why?" she said.

"I want you checked for blood spatter," Archie said.

Pearl's tough façade faltered. Archie tried not to smile.

The light was on in Archie's apartment when he got home. He could see it from outside. It made him feel like he was coming home to something other than an empty place in a half-developed wasteland of warehouses and low-overhead retail. It was almost nine P.M., and still light. Daylight hung on hard in the Pacific Northwest in the summertime. The short dark days of winter unspooled into days that started early and stayed light long after dinnertime. It was still light out when kids were sent to bed, and already light out when the alarm went off in the morning. Everyone stayed up late and got up too early. Everyone was tired.

Jake Kelly didn't have a family. Archie had called his closest relative, a cousin in Iowa, and broken the news. So far they had turned up no leads, no witnesses, no trace evidence. The only clue they had was the flower.

Archie looked up at his building from where he'd parked across the street. It looked a lot like every other building in the riverside produce district: six stories of weathered brick, with big factory windows and an old loading dock in front. The old glass reflected the dusk, so the building seemed to shimmer in and out of existence. Only a few lights were on inside. The developers were carving livable apartments out of the brick warehouse one apartment at a time, and only a few were occupied. When Archie saw the blonde, for a moment he thought she was inside his apartment, standing in his window, looking down at him. He had to remind himself that Gretchen was locked up. Then, after a startled second, he realized that she was standing in the window a floor below his. She was five stories up, but when she stepped back suddenly he was certain that she'd seen him looking up at her.

It made him feel strange, like a peeper, when in fact hadn't she been looking down at him?

Another blonde. That was the last thing Archie needed.

He kept his eyes on the ground and hurried across the street. It had been three months since the floodwaters that had damaged much of downtown had receded, but the smell of it still lingered, a wet rot that crawled down Archie's throat and settled in his clothes. The heat only made it worse.

The building had been built as a produce warehouse, with offices upstairs. Back in the thirties they had distributed apples from Oregon farms. Truckers from California would load up their trucks and then race back south. The first few loads got paid the most. After that, the novelty passed and the price dropped. Truckers died all the time on that route. They fell asleep at the wheel or took a turn too fast. These days most of the world's apples came from China.

Archie went through the oversized door on the loading dock and took the old freight elevator up to the sixth floor.

His cell phone started ringing again as soon as he opened the door to his apartment. He pulled the phone out of his pants pocket, but didn't pick up the call. Instead he set it on the table inside the door. He glanced at the screen as he walked away. He had twenty-two missed calls.

Archie walked around his apartment turning on fans and opening windows. It was a familiar routine, the same order every time. The feeling of air moving gave, at least, the impression of the temperature dropping. The stink from the flood was bearable up here. He unbuttoned his shirt and walked down the hall to the living room, and stood looking out his window. He wondered if the blonde was still standing at her window, one floor below. Outside, the sky was layered in pastels and the Willamette River looked almost lilac. Portland was a city painted in bold colors—deep green trees and stark white mountaintops, red brick and blue water. Then you'd blink, and it would all go pastel—pink sky, lilac river, silver skyline, a French Impressionist Portland. It was this Portland that somehow always ended up on postcards. It didn't help that the second tallest building in Portland, at forty-two stories, was a big pink glass skyscraper.

Archie smiled. Portland. Known for its blush-tinted scenery, and its serial killers.

Beyond the roofs and old wooden water towers of the produce district, Archie could see the twin glass towers of the convention center and the ribbon of interstate that paralleled the river. Straight ahead, beyond it all, was Mount St. Helens, an hour north in Washington State. The mountain had erupted back in 1980, and killed fifty-seven people, and still spit out a plume of steam once in a while just to remind everyone she was there. An old coot named Harry R. Truman had refused to leave his home on the mountain when authorities came calling. They never found his body.

The phone rang again. Archie glanced back at it. He could only avoid the calls for so long. He felt a pain under the scar on his chest, told himself it was just in his head, and walked over to the table and picked up the phone.

"You don't give up, do you?" Archie said.

There was a pause on the other end of the line. "Detective Sheridan?" said a man's voice uncertainly. "This is Jim Prescott at the Oregon State Mental Hospital."

"I know who you are," Archie said as he walked back to the window. He had listened to the first few voice mails Prescott had left. Archie had thought that if he didn't call back, Prescott would get the message. He'd been wrong.

"I've been trying to reach you," Prescott said.

Archie knew all about Prescott. He had an undergrad degree from UC Davis and an M.D. from Harvard. He'd ended up on the psychiatric staff of the Oregon State Hospital right out of med school, and he'd clawed his way to chief shrink by the tender age of thirty-five. Archie had read all of Prescott's reports on Gretchen. That was the arrangement. One-way access. Emphasis on *one-way*. No one outside the hospital administration, including Prescott, was supposed to know just how involved in Gretchen's care Archie really was.

"I've left messages," Prescott said.

At thirty-five, Archie had been running the Beauty Killer Task Force—combing crime scenes, interviewing relatives, observing autopsies.

"I'm one of Gretchen Lowell's doctors," Prescott said.

Archie scratched at the scar on his neck. Traffic was backed up on the interstate. The parade of red taillights headed north as far as he could see. Too late for rush hour. There must have been an accident. "I'm not coming down there," Archie said. "You can tell her to go fuck herself."

There was a pause. Finally Prescott said, "She's been making progress. She's been quite adamant about needing to speak with you."

The white headlights heading south were slow now, too. Gawkers. Human nature. Everyone had to look. "She's playing you, Doctor," Archie said. "There's no shame in it. I've been played by her." That was an understatement. "Epically. But trust me, whatever she's telling you to make you think that you calling me is at all appropriate in any universe, she's lying."

"She says she has a child," Prescott said.

Archie's body went numb. He swallowed hard, trying to recover his voice. "That's impossible," he said.

"She thinks this child is in danger," Prescott said. "That you are the only one who can help."

Archie had seen Gretchen's medical records. Her tubes had

been tied. The scars were old; the doctors who'd examined her thought the surgery had been done when she was a teenager. This was all part of the game. The sky was darkening and the traffic on I-5 looked pretty, a festive ribbon of red and white. Archie shook his head slowly and laughed. "This is insane," he said. "This is what she does. She manipulates people. You know that. She's convinced people to kill for her, for Christ's sake. She fucks with people's heads for entertainment." He would not give her the satisfaction. Not this time.

"What if it's true?" Prescott said.

"I would not save Gretchen Lowell's child if it was dying right in front of me," Archie said.

"What if you're the father?"

There it was. Archie had always wondered why she hadn't said anything. The waiting had made him crazy at first. Knowing at any moment that she could go public to a lawyer or a reporter or a cop. Archie had told a few people some of the truth. But no one knew the whole story. No one but Gretchen. Maybe Prescott didn't know anything. Maybe he was fishing. "That's impossible," Archie said definitively.

"Is it?" Prescott said.

Archie's mouth was dry. "Don't call me again," he said, and he ended the call.

Blood throbbed in Archie's throat. His chest ached. Acid rose from his stomach and made him gag. He tightened his fist around the phone, walked deliberately back into the hall, and then slammed the phone hard against the exposed brick wall. It made a satisfying cracking sound and split into three pieces and fell to the floor.

Archie's hand pulsed with pain and he lifted his bleeding knuckles to his mouth. But the impact had splintered away his anxiety. He was in control. It felt good, actually. He was starting to think about giving the wall one more punch when he heard a knock at his door.

Archie's spine stiffened. He didn't move. Every cell in his body was telling him to draw his weapon. He wasn't expecting anyone. But so what? People answered doors all the time without an overwhelming feeling of dread. Then again, it had been a long time since Archie had. Sometimes he forgot that there were people who moved through the world unaware that someone might slam a hammer into their parietal lobe at any moment. What would those people do in this situation? They would answer the door, he decided. They wouldn't even hesitate.

He was reaching for the doorknob when he remembered his hand.

He looked down at it. The knuckles were skinned raw, the folds of his finger joints filled with blood. He turned and looked behind him. The phone lay broken on the floor.

Another knock.

Archie stuffed his wounded hand in his pants pocket and cracked open his door.

The woman in the hall on the other side of the door was smiling. But Archie could see the smile falter a little when she saw him. He could imagine what he looked like then: shirt unbuttoned, sweating, red-faced, and baffled. He never should have opened the door. He wanted to go back inside. He fumbled to button his shirt with his left hand.

She smiled harder.

She looked to be in her late twenties. She was wearing a ribbed black tank top, cut-off gray sweatpants, and teal rubber flip-flops. Her skin was bronzed. She was younger than he'd thought when he'd seen her through the window.

"Hi," she said. "I'm Rachel."

She held out her hand. Archie hesitated. He pushed his right hand deeper in his pocket. Then offered her his left. Rachel looked confused.

"Sorry," he said. "Injury." It seemed too vague, and he searched for a more satisfying explanation. "I have a cat." He groaned internally. A cat?

But she seemed to buy it, and she held out her left hand, too, and they shook. Her handshake was firm and friendly. Archie made sure he let go first.

Even in the light of the hall's compact fluorescents, her body glowed. She was a picture of health and youth. Rosy cheeks. White teeth. Wide blue eyes and a broad smile. Her shiny blond hair was either natural or very expensive. The smile widened, earnestly. Her tan was all one shade of unblemished golden honey. Even her teeth looked expensive.

"You're not from around here," Archie said.

The smile faltered again. "I'm your new neighbor," she said. "I just moved in downstairs."

He'd made her nervous. He hadn't meant to. His hand was starting to hurt now. He wondered if it was bleeding through his pants. He didn't want to draw attention to it by looking.

"People here don't tan," he explained.

Her eyes fell to his belt and he saw in the tiny jerk of her brow that she had noted the gun holster on his hip.

"I'm a cop," he said quickly.

Rachel's eyes brightened. "Oh, that's you," she said. "I heard there was a cop in the building."

The building manager. Archie wondered what else he'd told her about him.

"I saw you come home," she said. "So I thought I'd introduce myself." She paused, waiting.

Archie wondered how someone got a tan like that.

She said, "It's customary to share your own name at this point."

Archie cleared his throat. "Sorry. Archie." Sorry Archie. That was him, all right.

She peered past him. "You live here alone?"

His kids came every other weekend, but that seemed too complicated to get into. "Just me," he said.

Rachel seemed to be waiting for something. Was he supposed to invite her in for a drink? Offer her a Welcome Wagon basket? Archie was bad at this sort of thing. He could solve a homicide, but social obligations left him mystified.

"Do people not do this here?" she asked. "Go around and meet the neighbors? I'm from San Diego, so if this is weird, tell me, so I don't continue to make a total idiot of myself."

"Do people do it in San Diego?" Archie asked.

"No," Rachel said. "But I thought that Portland was friendlier."

"We are," Archie said. "But we are also socially awkward. I think they cancel each other out."

"So if I need to borrow sugar or a spark plug or something . . . ?"

Archie thought for a moment. "I don't have any of those things."

Her smile faded and she glanced back down the empty hall. "I haven't seen many people around the place."

"Not many people live here," Archie said. The one-two punch of the flood and the economy had left his building in development limbo. All the better, as far as he was concerned.

"Well, it will be quiet, then," Rachel said. She sighed and her breasts lifted against the tank top. "Nice meeting you," she said. "I'll see you around."

Archie had the urge to say something, but he couldn't figure out what. So he settled on saying, "Welcome to the building."

She gave him an awkward little wave and walked off down the hall toward the elevator. He watched her for as long as he could get away with.

10

S usan's feet hurt. She had bought a pair of red Frye motor-cycle boots with her last *Herald* check and they were killing her, but she was determined to break them in. It was August. She should be in flip-flops. But flip-flops did not look as awesome with a short black skirt as red Frye motorcycle boots.

Still, she needed to get off her feet. Now.

She banged on the door to Archie's apartment. If he wasn't going to answer her calls or return her voice mails, then he could at least tell her to get lost to her face.

She shifted her weight from foot to foot and banged again.

The door opened, and Archie peered out. He lifted his eyebrows and blinked at her, like he was surprised. That wasn't weird. It wasn't like he knew she was coming. But he looked surprised in a different sort of way. Like he was expecting someone else.

"Hi," he said.

"Who were you hoping I'd be?" she asked.

Archie glanced behind her, down the hallway. Susan looked, too. There was no one there. She hadn't seen anyone on her way up.

"My neighbor was just here," Archie said.

Whatever. "Now it's me," Susan said. She bent over and wres-tled off a boot.

"Hi," Archie said.

Susan wasn't in the mood for Archie's bullshit. "You said that," she said. "Now let me in." She squeezed past him into the apartment, carrying one boot, and immediately began tugging at the other one.

"Let me guess," Archie said. "You were in the neighborhood."

"You didn't call me back," she said. The boots were off. She set them side by side near the door and wiggled her toes on the floor. Her socks were mismatched and stank of sweat and funk and heat. There weren't many people she felt comfortable enough around to reveal that level of personal fetidity, but Archie was one of them.

"I had a lot of messages," Archie said.

She hadn't been to Archie's new place before. When they had first met he was recently divorced and was living in a sad apartment in North Portland, then he had moved back in with his family in the fancy house in Hillsboro. Then there was the psych ward, a stay with Henry Sobol, and now this. He had neglected to invite her to the new place. With Archie, she sometimes had to take things into her own hands.

She moved inside, looking around, and he closed the door behind her. She saw his phone lying on the floor in pieces and glanced over at him, but he didn't offer an explanation.

The apartment was nicer than she'd been expecting. Exposed brick walls. Massive factory windows. Hardwoods. High ceiling with exposed wood beams. Archie didn't have much furniture: a few bookcases, a simple black couch that looked brand-new, a couple of chairs Susan recognized from the house in Hillsboro. The kitchen was open to the living room, and full of midrange steel appliances. She couldn't see the bedrooms. She assumed there were at least two—one for him, one or two for the kids. There didn't appear to be overhead lights, just floor lamps and desk lamps, all of which were on. A couple of standing fans were furiously redistributing the apartment's warm air.

She took a step closer to the window. It was twilight and the city was all sorts of shades of ash. It was an impressive view. She could see Mount St. Helens. There was nothing Portlanders liked more than old-growth wood and a mountain view. This whole part of town had smelled funny since the flood, but still, he'd done all right for himself.

"This is nice," she said.

"Don't sound so surprised," Archie said from behind her.

She remembered then that she was mad at him.

"Did you listen to my voice mail?" she asked, turning around to face him.

"My phone's broken," Archie said, glancing at the pieces on the floor.

Susan noticed his hand then. He'd had it in his pocket when he'd answered the door. It was wrapped in a few feet of toilet paper, but bright crimson spots of blood were soaking through the Charmin over his knuckles.

She looked at the broken phone. So maybe hers hadn't been the most notable call he'd gotten today.

"Do you have a first-aid kit?" she asked.

"I'm fine," he said.

"You're bleeding," Susan said. He had kids; he had to have a first-aid kit. Where would he keep it? "Bathroom?" she asked.

Archie nodded.

Susan walked to a hall she could see on the other side of the living room and found the bathroom. She opened the cabinet under the sink and pulled out a canvas bag with the words FIRST-AID KIT stamped on the side. It still had the price tag on it. Susan set it on the side of the sink and looked in the mirror. Her skin glistened with sweat and her eye makeup was smeared under her eyes. Why didn't men ever mention that? You could spend four hours with a guy and have makeup all over your face, and he wouldn't say a word. Then, when you confronted him, he'd deny having noticed it. How could you look at a face for four hours without noticing that kind of thing? Men were infuriating sometimes.

41

She tore a piece of toilet paper off the roll, folded it, got it wet under the faucet, and cleaned the liquid liner off her cheeks the best she could, which wasn't saying much. Now she looked like she'd been crying. She tossed the toilet paper in the toilet, flushed it, and checked back in the mirror.

Not just a mirror. A medicine cabinet.

Don't snoop, she told herself.

It's none of your business.

The last time she'd looked in one of Archie Sheridan's medicine cabinets it had been full of painkillers.

But that was before he'd almost killed himself and ended up rehabbing on the psych ward.

A tiny peek.

That's all.

A smidgen of a look.

Susan kept the water running to stifle the sound, and she opened the cabinet.

She held her breath. The three glass shelves were stocked with amber pill bottles of every size. She glanced at the bathroom door. She didn't have the time to go through all of them. She would have to be fast. She started twisting the bottles around, looking for labels, scanning names, looking for medicines she recognized. What was all this stuff?

The door to the bathroom opened. It was her fault. She hadn't locked it. Why would she have locked it? She was just looking for the first-aid kit.

Archie stood in the doorway looking at her.

His medicine cabinet was wide open. Susan had her arm extended, her fingers on one of his pill bottles.

"I'm looking for an Advil," she said.

"That's Prilosec," Archie said. "For my stomach. I'm off the pain meds." He scratched the back of his neck and gave her a tired look. "But if I wasn't, I wouldn't keep them in there."

Susan slid her hand away from the pill bottle and closed the medicine cabinet. Her reflection stared back at her from the mirror, her face scarlet. Her eyeliner was starting to run again. Susan could feel it leaking down her face. Why did she even bother? This was so classic. She barges in, sweaty, with her frizzy orange hair and raccoon eyes, and then gets caught going through his medicine cabinet. This was the problem with Archie. She didn't know where the boundaries were. One minute he was saving her life, the next he wasn't returning her calls. She had been dead. She had been clinically dead. And he'd saved her, and now she was alive. So what was she supposed to do with that? Put it in a box and tuck it away somewhere? Bury it in the backyard?

Susan turned toward Archie and nodded at his hand. "Have you washed that?"

He looked down at his toilet-paper-bundled hand. "No."

"Put it in the sink," Susan said.

He watched her for a second and then unbundled the blood-soaked toilet paper from his hand and held the hand over the sink.

She could see the extent of his injuries now. The skin of his first and second knuckles was smashed raw, leaving dime-sized open wounds. She held his hand under the faucet, but every time she moved it from the water, dark blood filled the wounds and snaked around his wrist and then trailed down the bowl of the sink. If it hurt, he wasn't showing it. It must have been a hell of a phone call.

"Did it help?" she asked. "Breaking your phone and smashing up your hand?"

"Actually, yes," Archie said.

"Sit down," she said, and she guided him to the toilet seat next to the sink. "This might take a minute." She shot him a quick wry smile. "I wrote an article about first aid once, so I'm practically a paramedic."

She turned off the faucet and pressed some toilet paper against Archie's wounded hand to stop the bleeding while she found a tube of Neosporin in the first-aid kit. Then she lifted the toilet paper and squeezed out some Neosporin gel onto the places where Archie's skin was open.

He could do it himself. Obviously.

She was kind of amazed that he was letting her. Maybe he felt bad about not returning her calls. Maybe he felt embarrassed for her, catching her snooping like that. Maybe he felt bad . . . generally. She didn't know. He seemed distracted, but that wasn't exactly breaking news. He was always 15 percent somewhere else. Plus, it was a hundred degrees in his apartment. Her forehead was starting to sweat. How he got any sleep in this sauna, she didn't know.

The Neosporin slowed the bleeding a bit. Susan found a roll of gauze and pressed the end of it into Archie's palm and then began wrapping the gauze around his hand.

"I noticed something that might be important," she said.

"Right," Archie said. "The local news."

So he had listened to her message. That was good. At least he wasn't deleting her messages on sight.

"Local news is often very revealing," Susan said.

"What did you notice?" Archie asked.

Susan moved his hand from the edge of the sink to his lap, and knelt in front of him, still circling his hand with gauze.

"The trees," Susan said.

"The trees on Mount Tabor," Archie said.

The roll of gauze was smaller now, most of it forming a misshapen white mitten on Archie's hand. Susan leaned her face close to the bandage, took the gauze in her teeth, and ripped it. "The guy, your victim, he was tied to the tallest tree."

"The tallest tree."

"Not *the* tallest tree. That would be a sequoia named Hyperion in Redwood National Park. It's over three hundred seventy-nine feet." Susan caught herself. "Sorry." She had been a newspaper feature writer for so long that sometimes these facts just bubbled out of her. "Yes. The tallest tree. In the crime scene area. On Mount Tabor."

"And you know this because?"

Susan took the end of the gauze, where she had torn it, and tucked it inside the rest of the bandage. "Because I saw it on the local news. They had aerial footage of the scene. Review the tape. It's taller than any of the trees around it. It's the tallest tree."

Archie was quiet.

"So that could be a clue, right?" Susan said.

"Maybe," Archie said. "Or it might be a coincidence." He was slouched forward on the toilet seat. Susan was sitting on the floor. She was suddenly aware of how small the room was, and how close their bodies were. His shirt was buttoned wrong. She found that weirdly charming. It was really hot in there. Archie reached his good hand toward her face, and grazed her cheek with his fingertips. Susan couldn't move. "Your eye makeup is a little smeared," he said.

She touched her face. "Oh," she said. She could feel her cheeks warm. "Thanks."

Archie stood.

"Why don't you ever call me back?" Susan asked.

"I have a lot on my plate, Susan," Archie said.

"Is it because of Leo?" she asked.

"I'm too hot in here," Archie said. He left the bathroom. Susan stewed for a second and then hopped up and stomped after him. She found him sitting on the black couch, his bandaged hand in his lap.

"So?" she said, standing.

"Thanks for stopping by," Archie said.

It was evening now and the apartment seemed strangely bright compared to the dark sky outside.

"I know you don't like him," Susan said.

"I do like him," Archie said. "We have a history."

She knew all about that. "You helped catch his sister's killer," she said. She sat down next to him on the couch, careful to leave a respectable eighteen inches between them. "It's not the ideal way to meet," she said. "But you of all people know what he's been through. He thinks the world of you." It was more complicated than that,

Susan knew. Archie and Leo's father went way back, and Archie knew exactly how Jack Reynolds made his money. "His father is hinky," she said with a sigh. And by *hinky* she meant *a drug kingpin.* "Okay. I'll give that one to you. But"—and she lifted her finger for empha-sis—"he's not like his father." She reconsidered this. "I mean, he's not perfect. But he's not Scarface."

"You don't need my permission to date Leo Reynolds," Archie said.

She didn't. Certainly. That was ridiculous. Why would she? Still . . .

"What if I wanted it?" Susan asked.

Archie looked at her for a moment, and then rubbed his eyes with his good hand. "There are things I can't tell you."

"No duh," Susan said. "You are like a walking vault of things you don't tell people. People who have secrets should pay you to hold on to them for them. You could be like a secret bank." She rolled her eyes. "There are things you can't tell me?" she asked. "Worse things than the things I know already? How is that even possible?"

Archie didn't answer.

She wanted to remind him that she wasn't with the paper any-more, that he could trust her, that she was his friend. She wanted to tell him that she wouldn't betray him. But mostly she wanted him to know it, without being told.

"So you won't get dinner with us?" Susan said.

"Susan." He could make her name sound so long sometimes.

"We could just swing by a food cart," she said quickly. "No pres-sure. Some Belgian fries and a Korean taco or two."

Archie crossed his arms and looked at her. "I saw Pearl today."

Susan immediately lost her train of thought and tucked her socked feet up under her on the couch. Pearl? Here? If Archie was lying, it was verbal kung fu par excellence. "Seriously?" Susan said.

"She lives at the halfway house where the victim was a volun-teer. She may have been the last person to see him alive, besides the killer."

It had been a year since they'd seen Pearl. "I thought she was back at her mother's in Salem," Susan said.

"Foster mother. I checked. She ran away again. The state put her in the house while they look for new placement."

"How does she seem?" Susan asked.

"Like a defensive smart-ass with a chip on her shoulder," Archie said.

"That's called being seventeen," Susan said. She'd liked Pearl. Pearl hadn't meant to Taser Archie. Well, she'd meant to Taser him, but how was she supposed to know that her then-boyfriend was going to drag Archie away, suspend him naked from meat hooks, and try to hack him up with an ax?

Hadn't everyone had a bad boyfriend at some point?

Pearl had made some bonehead choices, but she had a good heart.

"She lied to me today," Archie said.

"A teenager?" Susan said with faux surprise. "Lying to an authority figure? Impossible."

"She told me that she was smoking outside, and that she hid when she saw Jake Kelly go by because he didn't like her smoking," Archie said. "Claire took a team to his house this afternoon. Said it smelled like an ashtray."

Susan was feeling self-conscious about the pack of American Spirits in her purse. "So he smoked," she said. "That doesn't mean he was cool with her doing it. Maybe he thought she was too young."

"Or maybe she lied to me," Archie said.

"Do you want me to talk to her?" Susan asked. "Use my teen interrogation skills?"

Archie smiled. "You two do have a lot in common."

Susan suspected that wasn't a compliment. "Maybe we can go get piercings at the mall," she said.

"I'll pick you up tomorrow morning at ten."

Susan studied him. He looked tired. "This is supposed to get me out of your hair, right?"

"Yes."

"Okay," she said.

She stood up, and as she did, her phone rang. It was in her purse, which was more of a velvet sack with very long straps, and which Susan wore slung across her torso. She dug out the phone and glanced down at the number. It was that guy from the Oregon State Hospital again. They'd been playing phone tag all day. She wondered if Archie had gotten a call from him, too. Then she glanced over at the pieces of Archie's phone and answered her own question.

"Need to get that?" Archie asked.

She knew that she should tell him that she had accepted Gretchen's invitation to meet with her for an interview. He would want to know. He would want to talk Susan out of it.

Scratch that. He would want to forbid it.

And then Susan would have to go see her anyway, and then Archie would be disappointed and worried.

That was the thing Archie didn't know about Susan. He was always working so hard to protect her that he didn't realize that she was just as interested in protecting him. Archie had nearly killed himself getting out from under whatever spell Gretchen had had on him.

She wouldn't tell him. Not yet.

Susan turned off the ringer on her cell phone, already looking around for her beautiful, painful boots. "It can wait," she told Archie. "For now."

Archie Sheridan wasn't the only one who could keep secrets.

I t was the noise from the construction crew this time.

Part of the esplanade walkway had buckled under the flood-water and they were using earthmovers to finally haul away what was left of the broken concrete. It sounded like giant metal teeth chewing on boulders. Archie gave up trying to sleep and sat up in bed.

He looked at the clock. It was 2:59 A.M.

His neck was stiff and as he reflexively reached up to rub it, his fingers found the scar across his neck where Gretchen, with a draw of her scalpel, had sliced open his throat.

That was the thing that Henry and the others didn't under-stand. Why Archie could put himself in her path again and again after what she had done to him. He knew she wouldn't kill him.

Not on purpose.

Even as he'd fallen to his knees, the blood draining down his chest, he'd known it wasn't a fatal wound.

Archie sat on the edge of his bed. The fan tickled the hair on his naked body. Sweat crawled down his back. The air felt thick and warm, concentrated, like it was pressing in on him.

He kept his hand on his throat, the scar a fissure under his fin-gers. They had stitched the gash closed, and each stitch had left its own scar, very Frankenstein. He could feel his blood beating in his fingertips. She had felt his pulse, too, when she had cut him, would have used it to gauge the location of the carotid artery, careful to miss it as she pulled the blade through his flesh.

Life was a series of near misses. Car accidents dodged by quick reflexes. Railings that broke falls. Antibiotics. Seat belts. Helmets. We should all be dead a hundred times over.

Archie had tried to kill himself with pills. Slow suicide, the shrinks had called it. Archie wasn't sure he believed them. He had a gun. He knew how to put a bullet in his brain.

He hadn't taken the pills to die, he'd taken them because they were the only way he could stay alive.

His artery throbbed.

He could feel the scar under his fingers.

She had missed his carotid by one centimeter. About the width of an average shirt button.

Lucky, they had said.

But bleeding out from an artery was not a bad way to go. He'd seen it. Death came quickly. He'd watched a young man die after Gretchen took her scalpel to his femoral artery. No centimeter reprieve that time. She'd cut clean through it. That man's life had seeped away in minutes.

Another person Archie hadn't saved.

The screech of metal against concrete echoed through the open windows and Archie stretched his head to his shoulder until he heard a satisfying crack. Then he lowered his hand from his neck and inspected it. His palm was wet with sweat where Susan had wrapped the gauze. He unwound the bandage, now specked with dry blood, and then got up and walked into the bathroom. He tossed the gauze in the trash and ran his hand under the cold faucet for a few minutes, until it stopped throbbing, and then he splashed some water on his face.

When he looked up, he was faced with his reflection in the medicine cabinet mirror. His curly brown hair, gray flecks at the temples.

Crooked nose. Skin scattered with broken blood vessels. He'd gained back the weight he'd lost during the two years he'd spent on medical leave after Gretchen had tortured him, but he'd never look the same as he did before. The deep wrinkles on his forehead and at the corners of his eyes made him look ten years older than his forty-one years. Even his pubic hair was graying.

Pearl had been right. He did look old.

Archie smiled.

He wondered what Gretchen looked like. Right then. Locked up at the State Hospital.

He hoped she had a mirror, too.

Archie lingered on that thought. The water from the sink ran in rivulets down his face and along his neck. His hair was damp with water and sweat.

Patrick's kidnapper had been drenched—his hair matted with blood—in those last moments when they grappled with each other in the floodwaters.

Archie turned away from the mirror, pulled a towel off a rack, and dried his face and hair. He could still feel the resistance of the man's head as Archie held it below water, his hand knotted in the dying man's hair.

Archie slung the towel around his neck and felt for his pulse in his throat. When he found it he dug his fingers into his neck and kept them there. He counted to ten.

There was something comforting about that throbbing. His heart was still pumping. His body hadn't given up on him yet.

After a few moments, he was able to look in the mirror and see only himself, hair disheveled, face a little raw from the towel-scrubbing, but still Archie. He was still here, wasn't he? She had marked him with her fingerprints, the scars, literal and figurative, but he was still himself, he was still in control.

He opened the medicine cabinet and removed four large prescription pill bottles.

The labels on the pills read *Prilosec* and *Prozac*. He opened one of the bottles and tapped out a few white oval pills onto his palm. The sound of the pills tumbling out of the plastic bottle made his mouth water. Each pill was stamped with the letter V.

Vicodin.

When Archie had agreed to check himself into rehab, Henry had gone through his apartment, gathered up every last painkiller he could find, and flushed them all down the toilet.

Henry knew Archie, knew to go through all of Archie's pants pockets, his jackets. But Henry had never thought to look for Vicodin in Archie's other pill bottles. Where better to hide them?

Now Archie eyed the Vicodin in his hand. He still ached for them, for the bitter chalky taste, for the flush of pleasure that came ten minutes later.

He liked to take them out and look at them. Sometimes he lined them up on the back of the toilet tank, counted them. He liked knowing they were there. But he was already letting the pills drop from his fist back into the Prilosec bottle when he heard his phone.

He screwed the cap back on the bottle, put everything away in the medicine cabinet, and returned to his bedroom, where his phone was ringing insistently on the bedside table.

When he'd broken it, he'd knocked out the battery and split the casing into two pieces. He'd put the battery back in and secured it all together with duct tape.

Apparently, it still worked. There were some advantages to not having a smartphone.

He picked it up and sat down on the bed.

"Hello, Patrick," he said.

"Did I wake you up?" Patrick asked.

"No," Archie said, rubbing his eyes. "I was already up."

"I'm seeing that counselor again," Patrick said.

"I'm glad," Archie said.

"Can I come visit you?" Patrick asked, and Archie could hear the pleading in his voice.

"Not right now," Archie said.

"Are you mad at me?" Patrick asked.

It broke Archie's heart. "Look," he said, "even if your parents agreed, I can't take care of a kid right now." He couldn't even take care of his own kids with his schedule. If he got a homicide call in the middle of the night on a weekend he had the kids, he had to bundle them up and take them back to their mom's. They'd go to bed at his house and wake up at hers, which wasn't ideal for anyone.

"Archie?" Patrick asked.

"What?"

Archie could hear Patrick breathing.

"I think my parents are scared of me," Patrick said.

"They're just scared," Archie said. "Not of you. Just generally. They're worried about you. And they're worried about saying or doing the wrong thing."

"Really?" Patrick said.

"Yeah," Archie said.

Archie heard Patrick yawn. "I'm tired," Patrick said. "I'm going to say good-bye now."

"Talk to your counselor, Patrick," Archie said. "Okay? Tell him what you told me. It's okay. He can help you."

"Uh-huh," Patrick said, and then he hung up.

Archie set his phone back on the bedside table.

His knuckles were still raw, the fresh scabs ringed with pink. His hand had been wet when he had poured the Vicodin into it, and the pills had melted a little, leaving a white chalky residue.

Archie lifted his palm to his mouth and licked it.

The next time Archie's phone rang his bedroom was filled with the milky light of early morning. He was still half asleep when he picked up the phone.

"Look out your window," Henry said.

Archie sat up and wrapped a sheet around his waist. "Which one?"

"West."

He walked to his bedroom's westward-facing window. A warm breeze came in through the open window, along with the sour scent of rot from the flood. The west side was ablaze with morning. The jagged tree line of the West Hills was bright against the sky. Windows winked at him. The river sparkled. It took a minute for Archie to register the smudge of gray against the sky to the north, and then trace it back, to the west side of the Burnside Bridge, where several fire trucks and at least five patrol cars were parked, emergency lights blinking. Traffic was backed up across the bridge.

"Can you see it?" Henry asked.

Portland didn't have many visual landmarks. Its blush skyline. Mount Hood. The twin spires of the convention center. And then there was the fifty-foot neon PORTLAND, OREGON sign erected on an Old Town rooftop. For much of its existence, the sign had advertised White Stag sportswear. Archie remembered it from his childhood trips to the city, an outline of the state of Oregon with a white stag leaping over the company's name. Back in the fifties, someone got the idea to add a red Rudolph nose to the stag every Christmas. The sign was bought and sold, and the product being advertised changed. But anytime anyone talked about dismantling it, Portlanders rallied. They loved their composting, renewable energy, and recycling, sure, but they also loved that gaudy neon sign. The city had finally acquired it a few years ago, and had changed the lettering to PORTLAND, OREGON, leaving the stag and state outline intact, ensuring that Rudolph would visit Portland's children for generations to come.

Now the sign was smoldering.

"There's a body," Henry said. "And another lily."

"I'll be there in fifteen minutes," Archie said. He lifted his face to the sun for a moment before he turned and headed into the shower.

12

S usan Ward parked her Saab in a visitor's parking spot outside the Oregon State Hospital. She had a knot in her stomach,
and the start of a headache. The hour-long drive down to Salem
had been brutal. She had thought she could beat the heat by going
early in the morning. No such luck. Her air-conditioning had been
broken for years, and even with both the front windows rolled down
she had sweated through her T-shirt. The thermos of hot coffee
she'd downed on the way probably hadn't helped. She flipped down
the visor and inspected her reflection in the mirror. The wind had
done a number on her hair. She tried to get her fingers through the
tangled thatch of tangerine, wincing as she worked out the snarls.
Her lipstick was rubbed off on the mouth of the water bottle she'd
been sucking on to keep hydrated, so she wiped the rest off on her
hand and reapplied a shade of orange that almost matched her hair.
Then she added mascara. She inspected her reflection again. Better. She saw a tiny coarse hair between her eyebrows, took hold of it
between her thumb and forefinger, plucked it out, and flicked it out
the window.

She squinted out of the car up at the main building. It had
opened in 1883, and looked like an asylum from a gothic horror
movie. They'd filmed *One Flew Over the Cuckoo's Nest* here, which

pretty much said it all. The state had given it a coat of cream-colored paint since then and refurbished some of the structures. During the remodel they stumbled across a storage room stacked with what looked like copper soup cans. Turned out they were the cremated remains of more than five thousand former patients.

The hospital had done a lot of PR gymnastics in an effort to get out of that one.

Susan was satisfied that there were only a few people around, prowling the paved paths that knitted the hospital campus buildings together, and no one was looking at her, so she peeled off her T-shirt right there in the car. It felt good, the sting of air on her sweat-dampened skin, and she sat there for a moment, outside the nut-house, topless except for her purple bra, before she tossed her sweaty shirt in the backseat and pulled on the clean one she'd brought to change into. She smeared a new layer of deodorant under her arms and checked her reflection one more time.

She was ready now.

She got out of her car and trudged up the curved path to the hospital's main entrance. A frigid blast of air-conditioning hit her when she pushed open the door, and Susan shivered. The entry opened up into a lobby. The carpet was an alarming shade of electric blue. The walls were incredibly white. All the moldings and other original architectural accents appeared to have been long ago ripped out or painted over. Ahead, a large set of thick wooden double doors led into the main hospital. The doors were behind a formidable L-shaped counter. Two women sat behind it. One was on the phone. The other one looked up at Susan with the bored forced smile endemic to medical receptionists everywhere.

"I'm here to see Gretchen Lowell," Susan said.

13

Archie, in the course of his job, had gotten used to a lot of things. The smell of decomposing bodies didn't bother him anymore. He could watch a medical examiner use a bone saw to remove a brain from a corpse, the blade grinding into the bone, the blowback of fine white powder that looked like sawdust but was actually pulverized skull. That, he could handle. But he had never gotten used to the smell of charred human flesh. It was stomach-turning and sweet, rank and meaty, putrid and metallic. It was the smell of something wrong, something that should not have happened; something that was disturbing on a primal level.

Once you smelled it, you never forgot it.

The roof of the old White Stag building was wet, not from rain, but from water from the fire hoses. Some of the firefighters were still gathering up equipment, their heavy jackets peeled off, their helmets set in a neat line near the stairwell access door. The morning sun was already warm, but there was a promising breeze coming off the river. The West Hills were lush and green to the west, the mountains were crystal clear to the east, and from the roof of the White Stag building the city could not have looked prettier.

The body, or rather the charred husk of what remained of the body, lay in a dirty puddle in the shadow of the PORTLAND, OREGON sign. The sign, more massive up close than it seemed from below—the letters were as tall as Archie—was soaked with water from the fire hoses. But it appeared to have escaped the brunt of the fire damage.

The body had been the source of the fire. The sign had been collateral damage.

The corpse was still smoking. Thin wisps of gray rose from the cooked torso and then quickly dissipated into the clear heat of morning.

It was impossible for Archie to tell if they were looking at a male or a female. The hands and feet had crumbled to ash, leaving the corpse with jagged charcoal stumps at the elbows and knees. The hair and facial features had melted away, leaving only an open maw of perfect bone-white teeth where the mouth had been. Any clothes were now ash. The body was curled on its side, shoulders pinched forward, arms and legs horribly twisted. The flesh looked like tar, with something raw and red underneath, like undercooked steak, spotted with shiny tapioca patches of melted fat. The lily lay a few feet away, soaked with water and then crushed, most likely flattened by the heel of a firefighter.

With the body in that position, fetal, mouth agape, anyone would think that the victim had died in agony. Archie had to remind himself that fire causes the muscles to contract like that and the body to go fetal. It did not mean that the person had been in excruciating pain. Necessarily.

The breeze from the river had already started to erode the remains, lifting tiny particles of ash into the air. Everyone up there had probably breathed in a piece, some speck of a burned-up hand, some bit of thumb. If a local news helicopter got too close, half the body would go up in a gritty dust storm and they'd all be brushing ash out of their teeth for days.

"Where's Robbins?" Archie asked Henry.

"On his way," Henry said, his aviator sunglasses reflecting the cerulean sky. "Calls started coming in about six. Early commuters saw the fire and thought the sign had gone up. Firefighters responded.

Fire burned fast and hot. They didn't even know there was a body until they put it out. Must have used an accelerant."

Archie stepped back and looked up at the PORTLAND, OREGON sign.

"Could be suicide," Henry said. "Self-immolation."

"How about spontaneous combustion?" Archie said. "Could be that."

"Lightning strike."

"Fell asleep with a lit cigarette?"

"Could be murder."

"I guess we shouldn't rule it out," Archie said.

Henry reached into his pants pockets, pulled out a pack of gum, and offered it to Archie. He took a piece. A lot of cops chewed gum at murder scenes. It helped to ameliorate the smell. It was not a habit that Archie had ever embraced. Something about it had always struck him as disrespectful. Cops who wouldn't dream of chewing gum in church would stuff a wad of bubble gum between their teeth at the first whiff of decomp.

Facing the smell of roasted human flesh, Archie could see the wisdom in it. He put the gum into his mouth. It was spearmint, and unsettlingly warm from being in Henry's pocket.

Henry also had a piece of gum, and the two men stood together taking in the crime scene as the human remains continued to smolder at their feet.

Only the center of the sign was blackened, a few of the letters partially melted, some of the support scaffolding tarry where it had been singed. Archie guessed that the victim had been tied to the sign. The fire must have burned through the rope or cord, and the body then dropped to the roof. He redirected his attention to the remains.

Henry, who must have been thinking the same thing, pointed out a snake of ash that could have been the remnants of a burned ligature. "Right there," he said.

Ozone concerns aside, the PORTLAND, OREGON sign was a city

treasure. Vendors sold postcards with that sign on them, and silk-screened mugs. This wasn't some grove of trees in an out-of-the-way corner of Mount Tabor Park. This was public. Which made it risky.

"Why the change in venue?" Henry said. "Nature not his scene?"

Archie heard a ruckus and he and Henry turned to see Robbins, who had just come out the stairway door and had apparently accidentally kicked over several firefighter helmets, which he was now trying to gather up.

Robbins was wearing a new Tyvek suit, which, in the bright sun, was so unsoiled and so sparkling and so white that it was nearly blinding. After a few apologetic gestures to the remaining firefighters, he made his way over to Archie and Henry, carrying his ME's case. If the smell bothered him, he didn't show it, but he did give the ledge behind them a leery look. "I don't like heights," he said.

"I thought you rock-climbed," Henry said.

"When I rock-climb," Robbins said, "I don't look down."

Another gust of wind blew over the roof, and more ash swirled up into the air and seemed to hang there above them.

"Heights," Archie repeated softly to himself. He glanced past Henry and Robbins, over the ledge, where the Willamette, the source of such an ugly flood just months before, sparkled bright and blue and tranquil. He could see Mount Tabor from there, and the green residential neighborhoods of the east side. A freighter making its way up the river looked like a toy. A mile south, Archie noticed that the Hawthorne Bridge was up, letting a dinner cruise paddle ship called the *Portland Spirit* go under it, while a few dozen cars waited. From up there the city looked vast and pretty and bright and small. Archie thought about Susan and what she had said about the tree. That was the common denominator. He brushed off a fine mist of ash that had settled on his shoulders. "Jake Kelly was tied to a tree," he said. "Not just a tree—the tallest tree." He looked at Henry and Robbins. "This is all about heights."

Susan's purse was in a locker in the lobby. No cell phones. No cigarettes. No lighters. Basically everything in her purse was contraband. They had taken her studded skinny red belt, her long beads, and her shoulder-grazing earrings. Now she didn't have any accessories at all. She pushed a hand into her pants pockets and felt for the locker key they'd given her. It was still there. But she missed the comforting weight of the purse strap on her shoulder.

She looked over at Jim Prescott. He had met her at reception and was escorting her to the forensic psychiatric services ward currently housing the Beauty Killer. It didn't seem like a hospital. There were no intercom announcements. No cheerful art on the wall, or plaques celebrating donors. No coffee cart or gift store. And no signs of patients. If there was psychotic shouting or group counseling chatter, it was all happening behind closed, soundproofed doors.

Susan ran her hands over her goose-pimply arms.

"You okay?" Prescott said.

"Fine," Susan said. Her flip-flops flapped on the linoleum.

As they moved into more secure areas, Prescott swiped the badge on his lanyard over electronic scanners, and heavy doors opened for them.

He was nothing like she'd imagined him. She'd pictured someone older, patrician, clean-shaven with silvering hair, distinguished
wrinkles, and those half-glasses some people wear around their necks
on chains. Prescott was in his early forties, and there was nothing
patrician about him. He had a feathery beard and wild curly hair,
and he wore a creased tan sports coat instead of a white lab coat. He
wore slip-on shoes, she noticed. No laces. Shoelaces were for shrinks
who didn't have to worry about their patients strangling them to
death if they looked at them wrong.

Susan was glad she'd worn flip-flops.

"Will you be in the room?" she asked him.

He swiped his badge again. "If you want me to be."

Susan bristled. "No, I can handle it."

She followed him through the door. They were in a patient wing.
A man dressed in scrubs was sitting at a Formica counter writing in
a chart. He didn't look up.

Prescott led her to a door at the end of the hall.

"This is her room," Prescott said. "She's expecting you."

"Wait a minute," Susan said, feeling her palms start to sweat.
She had pictured Gretchen tied to a board, on the other side of bars,
with an IV of tranquilizers in her arm, surrounded by five armed
guards and a pack of growling German shepherds. "Just like that?
I'm just supposed to go in and chat with her? What if she decides to
gut me with a barrette or something?"

Prescott gave her a sympathetic, patronizing smile. "You're not
in any danger," he said.

Susan practically choked. "This is Gretchen Lowell we're talking about here. She's killed more than two hundred people."

"She *says* she killed more than two hundred people," Prescott
said. "She's delusional."

"I've seen her work," Susan said. "I've seen what she's done."

"She's disturbed."

"You're wrong, you know," Susan said. "She doesn't belong
here. I'm against the death penalty. I don't think the state should be

in the business of killing people. I think it's wrong. And it's hypo-critical. Mostly, I just think it's mean. Gretchen Lowell? She is the exception. She deserves to die. If we kill one person, one criminal in the history of the world, it should be her." Susan paused, reconsider-ing. "And Hitler. Her, and Hitler." Prescott had that shrink look on his face again, passive and unimpressed, and yet somehow judgmen-tal at the same time. Susan continued. "She removed a detective's spleen without anesthesia. She stuck a wire through an old woman's eyeball and then threaded it behind her nose and out through the other eye socket and then she stuck the wire into an outlet."

Prescott raised an eyebrow. "And you're arguing that she's sane?"

Susan decided that she didn't like him. "She knows the differ-ence between right and wrong," she said.

"You're not qualified to make that assessment," he said. He glanced at his watch and then jutted his scruffy chin in the direction of a metal switch on the wall next to the door. "That gets you in," he said. He was already moving, already hoofing it to his next psycho-path. They probably didn't like to be left waiting. "Tell a nurse when you're done," he said over his shoulder. "They can show you out."

"Wait," Susan said, not liking that she couldn't disguise the anxi-ety in her voice.

He stopped and turned back to her, and she wanted to wipe the know-it-all smile right off his face.

"I lied," Susan said. She eyed the door, imagining what was on the other side of it. No guards. No German shepherds. Just Gretchen Lowell. Would she be manacled to a dungeon wall, or maybe curled in the corner trussed up in a straitjacket? Would there be bars be-tween them? Was it a clean bright room, or a dark cell? Susan had seen Gretchen at her most vile, and at her most beguiling. And both personas scared the hell out of her. "Please don't make me be alone with her," Susan said.

15

Gretchen's room was painted pale yellow, the color of a baby's nursery, or a Klonopin. It was large, almost too big, and empty except for a twin mattress on a metal bed frame, a molded plastic chair, and a dresser. The bed was near the only window in the room. The window was covered with bars that had been painted with thick, glossy white paint. There weren't curtains. The floor was burnt-orange linoleum, blistered in places from moisture and splattered with vile-looking stains.

Gretchen was in the bed, with her head turned away from the door, so that all Susan could see were coils of dark blond hair and a gray blanket in the vague shape of a body.

"Gretchen?" Prescott said gently. "Your visitor is here."

Gretchen didn't move.

Susan could feel the hair on her arms stand up. Despite herself, she reached up to smooth down her own mangy orange hair. No one could compete with Gretchen Lowell in the looks department, but she still found herself wanting to at least make an effort. Here she was, about to meet with a megalomaniac serial killer, and she was still that geeky girl approaching the cheerleader sitting at the popular table in the cafeteria. She thought fleetingly of stepping back through the door, back into the hall, back into her Saab, where even the worst heat would be better than this. She could smell her own sweat. She could smell the oppressive floral bouquet of the Lady Speed Stick she had caked on in the car. She wasn't sure which smell was more offensive.

Prescott walked into the room, toward the bed and that tangle of blond, beckoning for Susan to follow him. She did. She thought, *This is what lambs being led into the barn on Easter weekend feel like.*

"Gretchen?" Prescott said.

Gretchen stirred this time, and then rolled on her back and slowly turned her face to them.

Susan drew back, startled.

For a second she thought there had been a mistake. That she had been taken to the wrong room. That Prescott had misunderstood somehow.

This wasn't Gretchen Lowell.

Gretchen had always been a beauty. She was the kind of woman who could silence a room when she walked through the door. It was not the only reason she had caught the public's attention—her horrific crimes would have been enough—but it helped that that lovely face of hers sold magazines. No one could grasp how someone that stunning could be capable of such merry acts of brutality. They didn't understand that her inside didn't match her outside.

Now it was closer.

Gretchen's perfect symmetrical features were blurred and bloated. Her once-pristine alabaster skin was now sallow and speckled with painful-looking blemishes. Grit clogged the corners of her eyes. Her lips were chapped, and a crust of dried saliva had collected at the corners of her mouth. Her hair, which had looked blond from across the room, was dull and brittle, almost colorless. Most notably, that thing, the unnameable quality that lit her from within, even in prison, was gone. She looked flat and blank. Susan would not have recognized her.

She was ugly.

Gretchen licked her peeling lips. "It's the medication," she said in a thick voice.

"It's an investment in your recovery," Prescott said.

Gretchen rolled her eyes.

Susan didn't know what to say. It was all she could do to muster a grim nod. Of course Gretchen was medicated. But Susan had not been prepared for the shape that she was in. She wondered if Gretchen could read the surprise on her face. But of course she could. Gretchen could read everyone.

Gretchen's bloodshot eyes went to the plastic chair next to her bed. "Let's get started," she said.

Susan took a seat in the chair. Prescott leaned against the wall and folded his arms.

"What do you want to tell me?" Susan said.

"Turn it on," Gretchen said.

It took a second for Susan to figure out what she was talking about, and then she realized what Gretchen meant and fished the tiny digital recorder from her pants pocket. An awkward moment followed as Susan realized that there was no bedside table to set it on, so she would have to hold it, which meant getting closer to Gretchen. Susan scooted the chair forward a foot, just close enough that she could pick up Gretchen's voice on the recorder, and not an inch closer.

Gretchen lifted herself up onto her elbows until she was sitting up in bed, her back resting against the wall. She moved sluggishly, like her head was heavier than normal. The threadbare gray cotton V-neck pajamas made her look even feebler.

If Gretchen Lowell hadn't murdered so many people, Susan might have felt sorry for her.

"When I was sixteen," Gretchen said, "I killed a man named James Beaton."

Susan leaned forward. Gretchen was staring off into the middle distance. Susan glanced back at Prescott. He was leaning against the wall by the window, watching Gretchen with his beady shrinky eyes. Susan glanced down to make sure the red light was flashing on her recorder.

"He was married," Gretchen said, "and I asked him to meet me in a motel room, a place called the Hamlet Inn, in St. Helens."

St. Helens was an hour west of Portland along a highway popular with bicyclists despite the fact that they were routinely flattened into roadkill by passing semis. It was a small town. They'd named it St. Helens because there was a volcano in Washington State named St. Helens and, for a few weeks a year, when the cloud cover lifted, you could see it from the town. That had always seemed kind of sad to Susan—naming a town after something that wasn't even in it.

"It was the first time I used a scalpel," Gretchen said. She slurred when she spoke and Susan had to listen hard to make sure she was making everything out correctly. "I had everything I needed in a canvas shoulder bag. I handcuffed his wrists to the headboard and his feet to the legs of the bed, so that he was spread-eagled." An angry rash crawled over Gretchen's jawbone and up her cheek. "He thought we were going to have sex," Gretchen said. "Even after I put the duct tape over his mouth, he wasn't afraid. He liked it. I was naked. I could have done anything to him. He was so hard he was grinding his hips against the sheet. Some people like it rough." Her eyelids were heavy. She smiled to herself. "Sometimes it's not the people you expect," she said.

She lifted bloodshot, bleary eyes to Susan's.

Archie. That was where Gretchen wanted Susan's mind to go. But, whatever fucked-up relationship Archie and Gretchen may or may not have had, there was no way that Susan was going there. "Continue," Susan said.

Gretchen smirked. "Like my acquaintance, James Beaton. He was married, but you and I both know how that goes." She lifted her chin toward Prescott. "Susan has daddy issues, Jim," Gretchen said. "She likes married men. Unavailable men."

Susan cut her off. "He gets it," she said.

Prescott hadn't moved. He kept up his silent vigil at the wall, his arms crossed, expression impassive. Susan couldn't decide if he was a really good psychiatrist or a spectacularly bad one.

Gretchen's gaze traveled back to Susan. "He didn't have a good heart," she said. She straightened up and folded her legs next to her on the bed. There was a little color in her face now. "He was flushed and sweating, piggish. His whole body was oozing. Sweat. Ejaculate. Like poison beading out of him. He stank with want. The smell of unwashed cock." Her words came easier now. She wiped the corner of her mouth. "I remember the sweat running into his hairy ears, a sheen of grease on his forehead, trickling down the sides of his bloated belly. He thought I'd want that? Him? I had my bag under the bed and I pulled it out and got the plastic sheeting. It was folded up, pressed into a square, and I had to give it a good shake to unfurl the thing. The plastic was thick and loud and it took me a while to lay it out on the carpet. It was only after I started to work it under him, between him and the sheet, that his eyes changed." She looked down at the blanket over her thighs and smoothed it with her hand. "Anxiety at that point, not fear. I got the plastic in place and I showed him the scalpel. His erection was gone." She leaned forward and put her mouth close to the recorder in Susan's hands, as Susan braced herself. "Just a limp little thumb of a cock in its place, bouncing around back and forth as he struggled," Gretchen said into the mike. She sat back in the bed.

Susan glanced at Prescott. He was still leaning on the wall.

Gretchen's hands readjusted the blanket over her lap. "He was trying to talk to me through the tape, shaking his head no, straining at the cuffs," she said. "I took his nose off first." She glanced up at Susan, like she wanted to make sure Susan had gotten that bit. Susan tried to steel her expression, but she must have looked green because Gretchen smiled. "I straddled him and I hooked the blade under one nostril and pressed hard," she continued. "It was easy. Like slicing an avocado. You know, that bit of resistance before the skin of an avocado splits and the knife sinks into the thick smooth flesh of the fruit? As I cut, I peeled and pulled his nose up with my other hand, slicing along the nasal fold, up one side, over the bridge, down the other side, and finally the cartilage between the nostrils. He was screaming. As much as he could, considering the tape. It was more like a high-pitched whine, a car with a bad fan belt. It came off in my hand. The nose. It didn't look like a nose. Flesh always looks so much smaller once it's been dismembered. The skin contracts. It looks small and harmless. Like nothing. But without it, his face was a bloody hole. But he was still producing mucus. It bubbled up out of his nasal aperture, this pearly gurgling snot-blood stew."

The contents of Susan's stomach pressed against her throat. She glanced behind her, looking for some reaction from Prescott, and got nothing. Susan was beginning to think he was on drugs, too.

Gretchen smiled darkly to herself. "Now he was afraid," she said. "When people are truly scared, truly in fear for their lives, the whites of their eyes go pink. I don't know why. Maybe it has something to do with their blood pressure elevating, vessels near the surface of the eyes dilating. I have always seen it, in those last moments, every single time."

Gretchen looked at Susan, and Susan felt cold all the way to the bone.

"But I didn't want him to die," Gretchen said. "I wanted him to stay alive, to see what I was doing to him for as long as possible." Gretchen took a slow, long breath. "But I had hurt him too much, too soon. I didn't have the control I would develop later. I didn't know how to pace myself."

Like when she'd tortured Archie for ten straight days.

Gretchen continued. "I cut him open. From the xiphoid process all the way to the pubic symphysis, only I didn't know the words yet. It wasn't a very clean incision. He was fat and my blade got dull. I came to regret the plastic sheeting. He shat and pissed himself and it all pooled under him on the plastic, so that I was kneeling in blood and urine and shit. I had to roll up the sides of the plastic sheeting and use towels from the bathroom to keep the blood off the carpet."

Gretchen turned over her hands and looked at them. "People just open up when you cut them. Like a big smile. Once I got through all the fat and membrane he was just all there in front of me: intestines, stomach, liver, spleen. I took my glove off before I pushed my hand inside him. I wanted to penetrate him, to feel him from the inside. He was in shock at that point, cadaverous, eyes glazed, shaking. He was suffocating, drowning in his own blood. But when I listened close, I could still hear the squealing."

She was quiet, a soft smile on her lips, and Susan wondered if she was listening for squealing at that very moment. "I put my fingers together and twisted my hand under his small intestine," she said, pantomiming the motion. "His body was so warm it sent a shudder through me. My hand in his belly made a sucking sound. He felt solid. I thought his insides would be softer, slipperier, like putting your hand in a bowlful of Jell-O."

Susan thought she might vomit. Even Prescott looked away and swallowed hard.

"It was fascinating," Gretchen said. She said, "I took him apart." Then her gaze snapped at Susan. "Have you ever prepared a Thanksgiving turkey for stuffing?" she asked.

"No," Susan said. She was never eating stuffing again. She might not eat again, period.

Gretchen continued. "I didn't even notice the exact moment when he died. I was too busy. I've always been like that. Hyperfocused." She said, "It's funny, once I realized he was gone, I lost interest in him. I folded the plastic around him, dragged him to the bathtub, and I dismembered him at the joints. It wasn't any fun. Just work."

Her face was devoid of any emotion now. She said, "It took me two hours to clean the room, and another four hours and five trips to carry the pieces of him out of there. All that luggage, I needed a porter."

She paused. Lost in thought, Susan figured. Reliving the good times. Then Gretchen looked at Susan and shrugged. "But the room was cheap," she said. "Twenty-nine dollars a night. And that included HBO. So I suppose it was worth it." She leaned closer to Susan, like a confidante. Susan braced herself, fighting the urge to recoil. "You know, they never did find his body," Gretchen said. "Or his car. His wife thought he ran off." There was something wicked in her eyes. She said, "I suppose she still hates him for that."

She stretched and settled back against the wall, like a reptile lounging in the sun. "Mr. James Beaton," she said softly. "He was the first person I killed." She lifted a hand from her lap and gave Susan a curt, dismissive wave. "You should be able to sell that. Now go away."

Susan stalled, flustered. "Why tell that story now?" she asked.

"Quid pro quo, little pigeon," Gretchen said.

"I'm not doing anything for you," Susan said.

"Yessss," Gretchen hissed. She stared straight ahead, not looking at Susan. Susan could make out a fine fuzz of hair that had grown on her cheek and upper lip. "Yes. You are. He'll know you've been here, and he'll come. He'll come soon."

Archie.

Susan's stomach hardened. "I'll tell him not to," she said. "I'll promise him I'll never come see you again."

Gretchen's eyes turned into lazy slits. "But that would be a lie, wouldn't it?"

Susan sat back in the plastic chair. She knew that Gretchen was right. Gretchen Lowell's first victim? An exclusive? Susan would sell this story. And she could sell others, as many as Gretchen wanted to tell her. She wouldn't be able to stay away.

Susan hated Gretchen for that. She flicked the recorder off with her thumb and stood up. "Someday," she said, "someone is going to surprise you."

"One more thing," Gretchen said.

The name of a good dermatologist?

"Yes?" Susan said.

"I want you to ask Archie why he's not looking for Ryan Motley," she said.

"Who is Ryan Motley?" Susan asked.

"We should go," Prescott said.

Susan had finally gotten used to his statue act. Now he was rushing her out of the room?

"Children are going to die," Gretchen said. She reached up and combed her fingers through her hair. "He's letting his personal feelings interfere with his professional judgment." She said, "You have to find the flash drive." She yanked her fist down and looked at it, a handful of hair in her fingers, tiny bits of scalp still clinging to the roots.

Susan flinched.

Gretchen laughed.

"You're not crazy," Susan said. She turned to Prescott. "She's not crazy."

Prescott stepped between them. "We're done here," he said.

"Find the flash drive, Susan," Gretchen said.

Gretchen's face looked sallow, her jowls puffy. Her chapped bottom lip had started to bleed, or maybe she had bitten it.

"Out, now," Prescott said.

Susan followed him out of the Klonopin-yellow room. Klonopin. Susan would have given anything for one of those right now.

16

Cigarettes never tasted very good in the heat. There was something counterintuitive about sucking down warm smoke when you were sweating. It was like taking a cup of coffee into a sweat lodge.

That didn't stop Susan.

She sat in her Saab, one trembling hand clawed around the steering wheel, the other clenching an American Spirit. She had left the car in the sun, and the seat was so hot she couldn't lean back without giving herself a second-degree burn. She was pretty sure she could have made a crêpe on the dashboard. So she had rolled down all the windows and opened the front doors, to let the heat out before getting back on the highway.

The nicotine had helped. She wasn't shaking as badly as when she'd first fled the hospital.

She took a last drag on the cigarette, tossed it out the window onto the parking lot pavement, and stepped on it with a flip-flop.

Then she squinted up into the sun until her eyes burned and tears formed. There was no denying it.

She had fucked up.

There was only one thing to do.

Face the music.

Her purse was on the passenger seat. She reached in and dug out her phone.

It rang four times before Archie picked up.

"What's up?" he said.

Susan closed her eyes and sank her head in her hand. "I just saw Gretchen."

There was a long pause. Finally, Archie said, "Tell me about it."

"One of her shrinks called me," Susan said, talking fast. "Said she wanted to give me an interview. She told me about a man she murdered, Archie. It's not one of the victims we know about. I have it on tape. But it's not really about that. She used me to try to get you to visit her. She thinks that when you find out I went, you'll come see her. You can't go see her."

"What else did she say to you?"

Susan took a long shaky breath. "She asked me to ask you about some guy named Ryan Motley."

"Where are you right now?" Archie asked. He gave away nothing with his voice. He was all business.

"Still in Salem."

"Bring me the tape," he said.

Susan glanced at the clock on the Saab's dash. It was eleven o'clock. She could be back in Portland within an hour. And then she mentally kicked herself. She'd been supposed to meet Archie at ten. "Shit," she said. "Our interview with Pearl. I totally forgot."

There was a pause.

Just long enough for Susan to realize that he'd forgotten, too. Archie didn't forget things like that. He'd been distracted. Something had happened.

"Maybe tomorrow," Archie said.

"I'm sorry," Susan said. "About everything."

"I know," he said with a sigh. "We'll figure it out."

Susan ended the call and dropped the phone back in her purse. Then she lit another cigarette.

She wondered sometimes which would get her first—cancer, or Gretchen Lowell. Today, the odds seemed about even.

What was that about?" Henry asked.
"Sorry," Archie said. He turned his wrist over and looked at his watch, trying to stall until he could be sure his voice wouldn't betray his emotions.

He was sitting at his desk, in his office at the Major Case Task Force headquarters. Henry was sitting in a chair opposite the desk, with his feet up on the desk's corner.

Archie knew how Henry would react to Susan's call. Henry hated Gretchen Lowell. Mostly, he hated what she had done to Archie. He would get involved. And Gretchen knew exactly how to get to Henry. She'd make him crazy. Henry didn't need that; he needed to focus on his recovery.

Henry had always protected Archie. Now it was Archie's turn.

He would take care of this without Henry needing to know.

Archie gave Henry's cowboy boots an affable tap. "Why are your feet on my desk?" he said.

"It's for circulation," Henry said, not moving. "Doctor's orders."

"I'm going to need a physician's note," Archie said.

The task force offices were in an old bank building that the city had bought and repurposed during the Beauty Killer Task Force days. Banks had once been built grandly with gilding and marble floors, to convince you that bankers knew how to handle money. Then, after a few economic collapses, banks were built simply, no frills, lots of carpet, to convince you that bankers were just like you. The task force bank was in the second category.

It was one-story, square, with a parking lot that surrounded it on all sides. The old public area of the bank was now filled with desks. They used the old vault as an interview/interrogation room. Vestiges of the bank remained: veneer desks and chairs, mauve upholstery, a path worn on the carpet leading from the door to where the deposit counter had been. A clock on the wall was printed with a slogan that read TIME TO BANK WITH FRIENDS.

Archie had been given the old bank manager's office. It was bare bones—a desk, three chairs, and a bookshelf. He had a photograph of his ex-wife and kids in a frame on the desk. But nothing else personal. He had once brought in some of his kids' artwork to hang up, but it hadn't seemed right to have his children's crayon drawings share the same space as photographs of crime scenes and autopsy reports.

Henry had Pearl Clinton's Department of Human Services report open on his lap, a pair of rectangular drugstore reading glasses perched on the end of his nose. "This kid has run away eleven times," he said.

Archie's phone rang again.

It was the landline this time. Another bank relic—it was tan, with a cordless handset and a lot of buttons. No caller ID.

"Are you going to get that?" Henry asked.

Archie hesitated. But Archie couldn't avoid taking calls, not at work, and not during a homicide investigation. He picked up the phone, hoping it would be Robbins with a positive ID of the second victim.

It wasn't.

"This is Dr. Prescott again, down at the State Hospital," a familiar voice said.

Archie stole a glance at Henry. Henry was staring at him, his forehead folded with concern. "Uh-huh," Archie said into the phone.

"I know you said not to call again," Prescott said.

Archie found a piece of paper on his desk and picked up a pen, like he might take down information. "Uh-huh," Archie said again.

"She said it was urgent," Prescott said. "Regarding the body in the park and on the rooftop. Ryan Motley. Does that name mean anything to you?"

Ryan Motley, again.

Archie glanced over at Henry, worried that he'd somehow heard the name through the phone, but Henry appeared to be engrossed in Pearl's DHS report.

Susan had only said that one of Gretchen's shrinks had set up her little tea party with Gretchen, but Archie knew exactly who it had been. "A friend of mine said she bumped into you this morning," he said. If Henry hadn't been sitting right there, Archie would have put it a lot more colorfully.

Prescott paused. "At her meeting with Ms. Lowell, yes."

"You and I," Archie said between his teeth into the phone, "are going to talk later."

Archie replaced the handset on the receiver. His face felt hot.

"Who was that?" Henry mumbled, not looking up.

Archie couldn't say, not without telling him everything. That's how it started. First the omission—then the lie. But it was worth it, if it meant keeping Henry out of the fray. "Your ex-wife," Archie said. "She wants to get back together."

"Which one?" Henry said with an eye roll.

There were two quick knocks on Archie's office door and then Detective Claire Masland breezed in. She was small, with dark pixie-cut hair, and a wardrobe that consisted mainly of jeans, sneakers, and T-shirts. Archie wondered sometimes if she tamped down her girlness to ensure that she was taken seriously as a detective. It wasn't necessary. Everyone knew she was one of the task force's toughest detectives. All those years hunting the Beauty Killer, and the only time he had seen her break down was when Henry was near death in the hospital.

Claire slapped a photograph on the desk and Archie and Henry both leaned forward to look at it. It looked like a corporate portrait. A pretty young woman in a fitted blazer smiled confidently at the camera. Her auburn hair was glossy under the photographer's studio lights. Her skin had the creamy, irradiated quality of a Photoshop makeover.

"This is Gabby Meester," Claire said, taking the chair next to Henry's. "She works at a PR firm in the Pearl District. They found her car in the lot she usually parks in. She never made it inside. Her car door was left open. I just had her dental records e-mailed to Robbins."

Archie looked at the fresh-faced young woman, whose grisly charred remains were most likely in the morgue. "She was at work early," he said.

"They were working on landing a big liquor company," Claire said. "The firm specializes in food and booze promotion."

Henry adjusted his reading glasses and picked up the photo. Archie was amazed at how much effort Henry and Claire put into remaining professional at work. It didn't matter. They all knew the two of them were sleeping together. But they remained committed to the charade.

"We're going to need a list of all her clients, past and present," Henry said. "What does her husband do?"

"Nice ring, right?" Claire said.

"It's a rock," Henry said, handing the photo to Archie.

Archie studied the picture. Gabby Meester had her arms crossed, one hand folded over the opposite elbow. The diamond on her ring finger was the size of a marble and, judging by the pose, Gabby liked to show it off.

"Lawyer," Claire said with a shrug.

It wasn't adding up. Archie glanced at the notes on his desk. "You said Kelly made a mint a few years ago selling a software start-up?"

"Yeah," Claire said. "He gave away most of the money. Everyone we've talked to thought he was a saint."

"How much are we talking about?" Archie asked.

"Ten million," Claire said. "Give or take twenty bucks."

Henry grinned. "A PR flak and a philanthropist."

"The security cameras in the parking lot are fake. But I'm trying to find any ATM footage or other cameras that cover the area between the lot and her office."

"Kids?" Henry said.

Claire held up two fingers. Archie looked down at the photo again. They were all quiet. It was always harder when there were kids. It shouldn't have been, but it was.

"Maybe it's not her," Claire said. "Might not be her."

But they all knew better.

Two dead bodies. No leads.

"What about the flower?" Archie asked.

That brought a smile to Claire's face. "I was hoping you'd ask," she said.

18

W hen they weren't eating microwave burritos at Formica tables, the task force pushed the tables together and
used the bank's old break room as their conference room. Currently
it smelled like someone had tried to microwave popcorn and had
burned it.

Martin Ngyun and Mike Flannigan sat across the table. Claire
stood next to a dry-erase board that was hung on the wall. Henry
was next to Archie, his chair pushed back so he could put his feet on
the table.

It was times like these, all of them sitting around the table,
when Archie felt the weight of Jeff Heil's death the most. He knew
that Flannigan blamed him for his partner's death. Archie had sent
Heil into the arms of a serial killer, with no backup. Heil's safety
had been Archie's responsibility, and he had failed. His guilt was
only compounded by the fact that he was so grateful that Susan had
survived, which in some way made him feel all the more culpable
for Heil's murder. If one of them had to die, he was glad it had been
Heil. And Flannigan knew it.

Claire cleared her throat.

Archie looked up from his thoughts. They were all staring at
him, waiting.

"Sorry," he said. "I'm listening."

A photograph of a lily had been printed out from the Internet and stuck to the dry-erase board with a magnet. Six white petals, with a splash of wine color at the center of the trumpet-shaped bloom. The wine hue was so delicate and precise it looked like someone had dabbed pigment at the base of each petal and then hand-drawn fine lines outward, and then repeated the process so many times that the lines together formed a color that looked almost solid.

It looked like the lilies they had found at the crime scenes.

Claire uncapped a marker and turned her back on them, and wrote something on the dry-erase board.

When she stepped back there was a word next to the photo.

Centerfold.

Archie stiffened.

Henry glanced over at him, and then looked back at Claire. "Seriously?" Henry asked.

"That's what it's called," Claire said.

"I guess *Playmate* was taken," Flannigan said with a laugh.

Gretchen had been called a lot of things. Beauty Killer. Queen of Hearts. The Serial Killer Centerfold. But Archie was feeling guilty about lying to Henry and had Gretchen on the brain.

Claire continued. "It's an Asiatic lily. As opposed to an Oriental hybrid."

"Meaning?" Archie asked. The longer he studied the lily in the photograph, the more the wine color looked like blood.

"The Asiatics bloom about a month earlier than the Orientals," Claire said. "It's August. These things bloom in late spring or midsummer. This is a specialty bulb. You're not going to find this for sale by the stem at New Seasons. We're looking into local licensed nurseries and I've been in touch with the Oregon Flower Growers Association."

The scars on Archie's chest itched. He rubbed at his shirt with his hand.

Ngyun said, "I'm working my way through online suppliers to see if this particular bulb was shipped to anyone local."

"Have we looked into getting warrants?" Archie asked.

Ngyun shrugged. "No one's asked for one."

"Should we release an image?" Claire asked the table. "Ask the public for help?"

So far they had kept the lily out of the press. It was important that they withheld a detail, something known only to the killer and the police. "Not yet," Archie said.

Henry cringed and adjusted his leg. He hadn't been to physical therapy in weeks, and Archie knew it.

"What?" Henry said.

"You okay?" Archie asked. The room was quiet.

Henry scratched his jaw and smiled. "Sure," he said. He looked at Archie for a beat and then turned back to the group. "Lilies symbolize purity and chastity," he said.

There was a beat of nervous silence, and then Ngyun said, "Look who's been on Wikipedia."

"It's the language of flowers," Henry said. "Different flowers symbolize different things." He grinned. "You learn this stuff when you've been married five times."

A flower named "Centerfold" symbolizing chastity.

"Interesting," Archie said.

Archie noticed Flannigan looking at him strangely from across the table. "Are *you* okay?" Flannigan asked.

"Yeah," Archie said. "Why?"

Flannigan hesitated.

"You're bleeding," Claire said.

Archie looked down at his chest. Spots of red stained his white shirt.

His scars were bleeding again.

"Jesus, Archie," Henry said.

"It's nothing," Archie said quickly, covering the blood with his hand. "It's the heat." He pushed his chair out and stood up. "Keep working."

Archie pulled into a no-parking zone in front of his building and put his OFFICIAL POLICE VEHICLE tag on the dash. His office was only a half dozen blocks from his apartment and he could have walked, if it hadn't been a hundred degrees, if he hadn't been expecting Susan, if he didn't have bloodstains on his shirt.

He got out of his city-issued Taurus and climbed the old loading dock stairs up to the entry door to his building. The hallway was stuffy and dark and Archie pushed the elevator button six times, even though he knew it wouldn't make the elevator go faster.

Beads of sweat ran down the inside of his shirt, mingling with the blood.

The doors to the old freight elevator opened and Archie stepped inside and pressed the button for his floor. It was a slow, creaky ride up. The elevator's metal walls were coated with a lifetime of grime. Archie could taste the dirt in the air. But it was still preferable to the stairs.

The elevator came to a stop with its usual cervical-snapping jerk.

And when the doors opened Archie found himself face-to-face with his downstairs neighbor. She was wearing a tangerine-colored bikini. Nothing else. Even her feet were bare.

Archie shrank back into the elevator. "This isn't my floor," he said.

The bikini left little to the imagination. Her breasts pressed against the orange triangles, revealing the outlines of her nipples. Her stomach was tan and flat.

Archie swallowed hard and looked at the floor, trying to find something, anything, to distract him from her young, tan body.

"Hi," she said.

Her toenails were painted light blue. She wore a small silver ring around the pinkie toe of her left foot.

She stepped into the elevator beside him. The doors creaked shut. She didn't press a button.

"Want me to hit a floor for you?" Archie asked her feet.

"You already did," she said. "I'm getting off on six."

His floor.

The elevator groaned and started moving.

He glanced up at her. She was carrying a towel and a pink plastic spray bottle.

"Did a tanning salon open on my floor?" he asked.

"Roof access," she said. Her eyes traveled down his shirt. Her brows jumped as she registered the blood. "That's a pretty ferocious cat," she said.

The elevator stopped and the doors opened. Archie allowed her to step out first, trying to avoid letting his attention drift to her almost bare backside.

The door that led to the roof was down the hall to the left, but she didn't head off that way. She waited for him, and then turned and said, "Will you tie this for me?"

She was holding the triangles of her top to her chest and she turned around to show him that the orange straps that tied together at her midback had come loose. There was no avoiding looking now. Her back was the color of butterscotch, and the bottom part of the swimsuit hugged the firmness of her, a slight shadow marking the cleft of her rear. Above the cleft, over her tailbone, was a tattoo, about the size of a sugar cube. Drawn in simple black ink, an outline of a heart.

Archie felt heat surge in his groin. He looked away, around her, down the dim hallway, his apartment doorway just ten yards away.

"I better not," he said.

She turned around to face him. "It's just a swimsuit," she said, smiling. Her eyes were blue. Her cheek dimpled on one side.

Archie cleared his throat. "It's an extraordinary swimsuit," he said.

Her smile broadened. "Thank you for noticing."

Her hand was still holding the swimsuit top in place. She had a French manicure. Between the nail care and the expensive highlights, she was spending a lot of money on upkeep, for a college student.

"Where did you say you were going to graduate school?" Archie asked.

She looked at him for a moment, and then padded forward on her bare feet, until she was right in front of him. He could smell the coconut of her suntan oil and the sweetness of her perfume. Her breasts were inches from his chest. She looked up at him, lips parted slightly, and for a second Archie thought she might lift her mouth to his. They were so close he could feel the warmth of her breath feathering his chin. "You're the detective," she said.

Archie tried to think about baseball, but nothing baseball-related came to mind. She didn't move, didn't step back. The air temperature in the few inches of space between them felt like it had gone up ten degrees. Archie felt a trickle of sweat wind its way across his forehead, behind his ear, and down the back of his neck.

"I don't have a cat," he said. "I have some old scars that get irritated by the heat. I scratch at them, and they bleed. I came home to change my shirt."

She tilted her head slightly. She had pierced ears but wasn't wearing earrings. "You should put on a blue one," she said. "You'd look nice in blue." She stepped back, and then walked off in the direction of the roof access door, the orange strings of her bikini top trailing loose behind her.

Archie exhaled.

The tattoo was still very black, he noticed. It had been a recent acquisition.

20

By the time Susan rolled up to the task force offices, she had spent an hour and a half on I-5 in heavy traffic, with no A/C, in the heat of the day. She was so sweaty she glistened, and her left arm was sunburned from having her elbow out the open window. She looked in the backseat for a hat to cover her sweaty, matted hair, and after some digging found a white Panama with a black band. This was why it paid not to clean out your car.

She still wasn't ready to go inside.

Archie was in there, and he wouldn't be happy with her. He would look all disappointed and fatherly. He was only twelve years older than she was, but had a way of making those twelve years seem like a century. She could already hear his voice, lecturing her. *I'm not angry with you, just disappointed.*

"Gathering your courage?" she heard Archie ask.

She jumped.

Archie was standing outside her window. He was wearing a blue button-down shirt and corduroy pants. The man did not know how to dress for the weather.

"How long have you been standing there?" she asked.

"I just got back from an errand," he said. "You need to get your

A/C fixed," he added, squinting up at the blindingly blue sky. "It's only going to get hotter."

He didn't seem that mad at her.

A couple of uniformed cops she didn't recognize walked by and nodded at Archie. He tapped the roof of her car with his palm. "Let's talk in my office," he said. "Now."

Susan's heart sank. He just wanted to get her alone before he laid into her.

Fine, then. She deserved it.

She got out of the car. Her skin made a Velcro sound as it peeled off the vinyl seat.

Her T-shirt was sweat-sodden and her scalp itched under the hat, but she followed Archie into the bank, past the uniformed cop at the front desk, past the detectives' desks. She was careful to keep her eyes forward, careful to avoid seeing the desk where Heil had sat. She wasn't sure if it would be worse to see it empty or to see someone else sitting at it. Just a few years before, she had only seen one dead body—her father's. And he had died of cancer. Working on the crime stories for the *Herald*, following Archie around, she had seen more. But Jeff Heil's death haunted her the most. Maybe because they had been together, and she knew that it could have been her.

It had not been easy. She'd had nightmares for two months after the flood: dark waters, creatures she couldn't see, Heil's limp corpse sinking beneath the surface. Bliss had fed her ginger tea, played Deepak Chopra audiobooks day and night, and convinced Susan to float in a sensory deprivation tank for three hours a week. Now, even with the anxiety gone, Susan still avoided that stretch of Division Street. She still kept her eyes on the bridge when she crossed the river, careful not to let her eyes wander down to the water below.

Archie didn't talk about it. She hadn't heard him mention Heil's name since the funeral. She wondered if it bothered him, living in that apartment, with all those windows looking out over the river that had almost killed them.

She was relieved when they got to Archie's office and he closed the door. Susan could take a lecture, but she never liked the bit leading up to one. She sat right down in one of the chairs facing his desk and braced herself.

Archie took his time walking around and taking a seat in his desk chair. He leaned back and folded his hands across his chest. He looked at her. "So you saw Gretchen," he said with a slow smile. "How did she look?"

There was something about the pleasure he took in the question that made Susan think he knew exactly how she looked.

"She's looked better," Susan said.

Archie's hands lifted and fell as he breathed. He'd taken the bandage off from the night before. She could barely see the scabs. He was watching her. He looked like he wanted to hear more, but Susan didn't offer. And Archie didn't ask.

After a moment he extended one hand across the desk, palm up. The smile was gone. "The tape?" he said.

"There is no tape," Susan said, rummaging in her purse for the recorder. "It's a digital file." She found the recorder and held it up for Archie. "Welcome to the twenty-first century," she said. She looked away then, her eyes shifting back to her purse, suddenly sure that she'd given away something more than she'd intended. She tried to make her question sound casual. It was reasonable enough. "Do you have a flash drive?"

"No," Archie said.

Susan glanced back at the closed door. "Perhaps one of your minions?"

Archie looked at her for a long moment. Then he said, "Okay." He gripped the arms of his chair and pushed himself up. He said, "I can get one." He walked around the desk, behind Susan, and left the office, presumably to commune with some sort of office supply cabinet.

He'd left the door ajar. The venetian blinds on the office's interior window were angled three-quarters open. Susan was already rehearsing excuses in case she was caught: *I just got my period and I was looking for a tissue to stuff in my underpants*. Men didn't question menstruation stories. Ever. You probably could get into the White House if you said you needed a tampon ASAP.

Susan scurried around to the other side of the desk and pulled open the desk drawer. It was full of crap. Pens. Papers. Rubber bands. Files. Wite-Out. (Who even used Wite-Out anymore?) There were loose staples and thumbtacks. That was so like Archie, orderly at first glance, but a mess just under the surface. It had been three months since Susan had accidentally come across the sleek silver flash drive hidden under a photograph of Gretchen, under some papers in Archie's desk. Now Susan shoved her fingers underneath the clutter until she touched something hard and smooth, the size of a pack of gum. She pulled it out.

The flash drive was still there.

Susan checked the door and then palmed the flash drive and put it in her purse. She was back in her seat a moment later when Archie returned, a brand-new flash drive in his hand. It was one of those cheap black plastic ones, nothing like the one in his desk.

Archie handed her the black flash drive and Susan focused her attention on downloading the audio file, her heart pounding in her chest. She didn't dare even glance at her purse. She felt guiltier than she thought she would. It would have been easier if he'd been mad at her.

"She talks about killing this guy named James Beaton in St. Helens when she was sixteen," Susan said. "I looked him up." She decided not to mention that she'd done this Internet research while she was zooming up I-5. "There was a James Beaton in St. Helens who disappeared eighteen years ago. They never found a body."

"What are you going to do with the interview?" Archie asked.

Wasn't it obvious? "Write a story," Susan said. Publish it. Make money. Be famous. "The *Times* magazine is interested."

Archie sat down in the chair next to her. He had never done that.

He always sat in his chair, the desk between them. Susan nudged her purse under her chair with her foot.

"Prescott set it up?" Archie asked.

Susan looked at him sideways. "Yep."

Their knees were almost touching.

"Was he in the room?" Archie asked.

"He insisted on staying," Susan lied.

Archie slumped back in the chair. "It's privileged," he said.

"What?"

"She might be able to claim that it's privileged. She was talking to her shrink. You just happened to be in the room."

"She was talking to me," Susan insisted. "He just happened to be in the room. Besides, I'm not entering it into evidence in court."

"I was talking about me," Archie said. "I can't use the confession."

Susan blinked a few times, sorting this out. "Oh."

He stood up and walked behind her, back around to his desk chair. "I need you to wait a few days before you do anything with this," he said as he sat down.

It would take her a few days to write the story anyway. "Okay," she agreed. She frowned, as if she'd just thought of something. And, trying to sound as nonchalant as possible, she asked, "Who's Ryan Motley?"

Archie reached out and adjusted the framed photograph of his family he kept on his desk. Susan knew the picture: Debbie, the two dark-haired smiling kids, Archie nowhere in sight. Archie shrugged, as if the name meant nothing to him. "A figment of Gretchen's imagination," he said.

21

B liss was waiting in the living room when Susan got home, her bare feet propped up on the industrial wire spool they had repurposed as a coffee table, a jam jar full of red wine in her hand, and naked as a jaybird. Her elbow-length peroxide-blond dreadlocks were wound on top of her head like a large bird's nest. She was pushing sixty, but her thirty years of yoga had made her body lean, and the Sauvie Island nude beach had given her a late summer tan. Bliss secured her jar of wine between her legs so she could turn the page of the book she was reading, and Susan caught a glimpse of something she was sure she would spend the next ten years trying to burn from her mind: her mother's artistically groomed pubic hair.

"What do you have going on there?" Susan asked, waving her finger at her mother's nether region. Someone at the salon Bliss worked at had started a cottage industry of "novelty" bikini waxing. Bliss, who until a few years ago had been proud of an untamed seventies-style bush the size of a salad plate, was now an enthusiast of artistic pruning.

"It's Mick Jagger's profile," Bliss said.

Sometimes Susan wished she had been born to Pentecostals. "Of course it is," she said.

Susan's laptop was on the coffee table, under Bliss's feet. "Excuse me," Susan said, kneeling before it. Her mother lifted her feet and Susan slid the laptop to a clear spot between a Tibetan skull cup full of walnuts and a ten-year-old copy of the *Whole Earth Catalog*.

Moving back in with her mother had been temporary, until Susan had lost her job. Now, on a freelancer's income, she didn't have a lot of options.

She pulled the flash drive out of her purse, opened up her laptop, and inserted the drive into the USB port.

"What's that?" Bliss asked.

"Do you have to be naked?" Susan said. "I mean, what if the UPS guy comes by?"

Bliss fanned her hand in front of her chest. "It's hot."

In fact the Victorian that Susan had grown up in was relatively bearable in the summer. As long as they remembered to keep the windows all closed and the curtains drawn during the day, and then to open the windows—at least the ones that hadn't been painted shut—at night. Sure, the indoor plants all died by August, and the open windows drew in flies and moths and the occasional panicked bird, but it worked. The house was only intolerably hot for maybe a week a year. This just happened to be that week.

"Get a place with air-conditioning," Bliss said. "If you're so concerned."

Susan barely heard her.

The flash drive had seven files on it, all PDFs.

Seven files, all with the same name:

Ryan Motley1.

Ryan Motley2.

Ryan Motley3.

Etc.

"Shit," Susan said under her breath.

What had she been hoping for? Family photographs? A secret

novel Archie was working on? (She had been hoping for the secret novel.)

Bliss took her feet off the table and sat forward, shoulder to shoulder with Susan. She smelled like patchouli and eucalyptus oil and red wine, combined with a faint hint of marijuana.

"Who's Ryan Motley?" she asked.

Susan opened her Web browser and typed *Ryan Motley* into the search field. Over eleven thousand results came up.

"I have no idea," Susan said.

But she was going to find out.

22

The Multnomah County morgue had only recently been reopened after being closed for almost three months due to flood damage. On the surface, it looked the same as it did before, but cleaner, the clutter having not yet had time enough to accumulate. But the floors had been laid with a new, gleaming white linoleum and the concrete block walls had a fresh coat of white paint. The effect made the basement facilities seem brighter, though Archie wasn't sure it was in a good way. Archie had also heard that the city had replaced the conveyor tray cadaver storage system with a walk-in refrigeration unit, the better to store more bodies.

It was dinnertime, and the morgue had a skeleton staff, but Archie found Robbins in the autopsy room, standing over the charcoaled remains of Gabby Meester. Robbins was almost entirely obscured behind his gear: a surgical gown over scrubs, shoe covers, a hairnet, a face shield in front of a surgical mask, surgical gloves.

"How'd you get in here?" Robbins asked, looking up from the steel autopsy table. Gabby was just a head and torso. With only stumps where her legs and arms should be, she looked small, like a child.

Archie walked up to the table waving a white plastic card with a magnetic strip on the back. "I have an access card," he said.

"You get that when they gave you the key to the city?" Robbins asked.

Robbins had opened Gabby up. Her charred skin was peeled back, and her ribs were removed. She was pink inside, like steak that had been burned on a high heat but remained raw in the middle. Her large intestine bulged where her belly had been.

"It's one of my perks," Archie said, putting the card back in his wallet. "They also paid for rehab."

Robbins chuckled. "I might quit my job and start catching serial killers." He cut Gabby's heart free and bagged it, then quickly removed one of her lungs. Archie was always amazed at how fast this part was. A sharp blade and a few flicks of the wrist. It only took ten minutes to cut open and disembowel a corpse.

"You do your part," Archie said. He reached into the shoulder bag he was carrying and pulled out a brown paper lunch sack. "Mind if I eat?" he asked.

Robbins raised his eyebrows. "Man, you *have* been doing this too long."

Archie pulled out the cold chicken burrito that Claire had brought back for him from a food cart. Mostly he just wanted another taste in his mouth besides burned flesh. He took a bite and chewed.

"You notify the family?" Robbins asked, snipping out another lung.

Robbins had confirmed Gabby Meester's identity through dental records just before lunch. Archie had been at the house within a half hour. "Husband and sister," Archie said, swallowing. "The kids were upstairs."

Robbins stopped what he was doing. "Hard?" he asked.

Archie could hear the kids playing upstairs, two girls, younger than Sara. They had no idea their world was about to come down on top of them. "It's always hard," he said.

"Any leads?" Robbins asked, going back to his task.

"We spent the day interviewing her coworkers, her husband, her clients, canvassing for witnesses," Archie said. "We've tracked down ex-boyfriends. Went through her cell phone and bank records, credit cards. She left the house early this morning. No one saw her after that." Archie threw the rest of the burrito back into the bag and tossed it into a red plastic biohazard bag by the table. "She didn't know her killer," he said.

"I'm not going to have anything for you until tomorrow," Robbins said.

"I know," Archie said. He looked down at Gabby Meester, her insides flaked with charcoal from the bone saw cutting through her charred rib cage, the flesh of her neck separated from the muscle and peeled up over her chin. It didn't turn his stomach. It made him feel more tenderly toward her. In the chaotic push of a homicide investigation, the victims sometimes got overlooked. Archie liked to remind himself that they were more than photographs. They were flesh and blood and meat. He rubbed his face. "I just needed to see her," he said.

"Go home," Robbins said.

Archie looked at his watch. "There's something I need to do first."

He left Robbins to do his work, stopping at an alcoholic gel dispenser on the wall at the exit to the stairway to pump a squirt into his hands.

He called Debbie as he walked up to the first floor.

"Hey, it's me," he said.

"I saw the news," his ex-wife said. She paused. "I was going to call. Rough day?"

"Yeah," he said. He didn't elaborate. She didn't ask. "Can I just say hi?" he asked.

"Hold on," she said. "I'll get them." He heard her moving through her apartment. "Kids," she called, "your dad's on the phone."

Archie heard Sara's excited squeal. He still loved that sound more than anything else in the world.

"You're worried about him again," Claire said.

Henry stared up at the ceiling fan. They were in his bed, naked and exhausted; Claire's arm was draped over his chest.

Sex took more out of him these days. He sweated more. His heart worked harder. He tried to hide it from her, but of course she could tell.

Now she had clearly picked up on the fact that his mind was someplace else. He wove his hand into hers. "Sorry," he said.

Claire sighed, settled back, and looked up at the ceiling fan with him. It had white metal blades and a light fixture that had never worked. Henry had installed it ten years ago, that first summer after he'd bought the house. The pull chain swung in slow circles. "Just talk to him," Claire said.

Henry's cat leapt onto the bed, stalked around, and then dropped and started purring.

Henry had thought about calling Debbie. But only for a second. Archie wouldn't want that. He wanted his ex-wife to have a life. And she couldn't have one if she kept getting dragged into his bullshit. That was how Archie would see it, anyway.

Claire laid her free hand flat on her bare stomach and looked down at the barely perceptible bulge. "Do you think he's noticed?"

"No," Henry said.

She bit her lip and looked away. "It's not that weird. Men are slow that way."

The ceiling fan had come loose over the years and the fan made a soft knocking sound as it rocked against the ceiling. "Not Archie," Henry said.

They were quiet for a moment, listening to the blades of the fan, the wind lifting the pages of a woodworking magazine Henry had left on the bedside table, the knocking of the fixture against the ceiling, the purring cat.

"I hate your futon," Claire said.

Henry rolled on his side and lifted her hand to his mouth and kissed her fingers. "Futons are an ancient, well-loved bed, the bed of emperors," he said.

Claire's short brown hair was spiky with sweat. Her breasts were perfect half peaches, the nipples small and dark. Everything about her was pint-sized. She got carded every time she bought beer. But she could outrun a criminal and judo his ass into next Friday. They were going to have an extraordinary kid.

Sometimes Henry wished he'd met Claire twenty years earlier.

"He's probably just focused on the case," Claire said.

It was true. They'd worked all day and turned up nothing. No connection between victims whatsoever. No evidence left behind at the crime scene. No witnesses. But Archie had seemed distanced from the case, distracted from it.

It was something else.

It was like Claire had read his mind. She said, "What, then?"

The cat stood up and stretched and then rubbed against Claire's leg, leaving a trail of gray hair on her sweaty skin. She scratched the cat's head absentmindedly.

Henry wondered sometimes how much Claire had figured out about Archie's relationship with Gretchen Lowell. It was one of the things they didn't talk about.

"Did you see his phone?" Claire asked.

The duct tape. Henry had seen it.

"And his hand?" Claire said.

It looked like he'd punched a wall. Henry had put two and two together. Archie had gotten a call he didn't like.

"Maybe he's taking pills again," Claire said.

"Maybe," Henry said.

But he had known his friend for a long time, and he had a feeling it was something worse. There was only one person who could get under Archie's skin like that, and she was locked up in the State Hospital.

Claire nuzzled against Henry's arm, the cat between them. Henry stared at the ceiling fan and tried not to think about the fact that while he was sweating his ass off, Gretchen Lowell was luxuriating in taxpayer-subsidized air-conditioning.

24

Archie watched Gretchen Lowell sleep, drinking in every inch of her.

She lay on her back, in her bed. Her hospital-issue gray cotton pajamas were the same color as the blanket that covered her from the chest down. The blanket was thin and unforgiving and Archie could make out the shape of her body underneath. Archie let his eyes drift over her wider thighs, her plump belly; the rough thickness to her arms. Weight gain in her face had made her jowls look heavy. Her skin was tinged yellow, except where acne had broken out, a red rash on her cheeks. Even closed, her eyes looked sunken. Dried blood collected at the corners of her mouth where the skin had gotten raw enough to split.

Her hair was dirty, snarled, clumped together in places by something crusty. Her face was relaxed. Her breathing was soundless and steady. She was so perfectly still—so without the twitches and small shifts of sleep—that Archie thought she might be awake.

She opened her eyes and looked at him.

He was sitting on the windowsill, leaning against the bars, and he had to consciously will himself to stay as still as she was, to not let her read him. Right now he only wanted her to see one expression on his face: satisfaction.

"Hello, sweetheart," he said.

She tried to shift her position, and then raised her head and looked down at the leather straps that bound her wrists to the sides of her bed. She dropped her head back on the pillow and smiled at him. "What are these?" she said. "Afraid I might hurt you?"

Archie got up off the windowsill and walked slowly to her bedside. He kept his hands in his pockets so he could let his fingers brush against the three Vicodin he had stashed there. He leaned close to her, slowly. He had to do everything slowly around Gretchen, because if he didn't, he'd make a mistake, show her too much.

"No," he said, in a low whisper. "I just like seeing you tied up."

Her nostrils flared and she smiled again, her once-white teeth now a pale shade of gray. "There's my boy," she said. Her eyes were bloodshot, but they were still very blue. She traveled his body with her eyes. "I thought you'd come sooner, so you could see what you've done to me," she said.

"You've used your beauty to manipulate people. It's one less tool in your toolbox."

Gretchen gave a cynical chuckle. "Is that what you tell them?"

It hadn't been hard for Archie to convince the hospital administrators to let him take a special interest in Gretchen's medication. She had killed so many people. She deserved worse. Prescott was cocky, but he was young and insecure in his position and he followed orders. He accepted that Gretchen's drug regimen was determined by his bosses. And he had no idea that Archie was involved.

Archie touched the pills in his pocket. "I don't want you seeing Susan," he said. "You need to leave her out of this."

"Out of what, darling?" Gretchen said.

He knew what she wanted to hear. But he hated saying it. "Us."

She gave him a pretend pout. "You weren't returning my calls."

"I've been seeing other serial killers," Archie said. "I knew you'd be jealous."

Gretchen raised a smug eyebrow. "I've been seeing someone else, too."

"Prescott," Archie said.

She stole a glance behind him, out the window into the night. There was no clock in her room, and he realized that she was trying to puzzle out the time. "I thought he'd be here when you came," she said. "I wanted you to meet him."

So she could manipulate them both, play them off each other. Archie was familiar with the tactic. "I didn't tell him I was coming," he said. "I'm sorry. Was that not part of your plan?"

"Who's jealous now?" Gretchen said.

There was nothing in the room. No family snapshots taped on the walls. No toiletries. No books. None of the pleasantries allowed other patients. Prescott had lobbied for that to change. Archie had read his report. Personal items, Prescott posited, would be therapeutic. Prescott had never scraped one of Gretchen's victims up off the floor.

"You don't care about Prescott," he said. "But you've done a nice job with him. Surprising." He studied her face. "Considering." Archie rolled the Vicodin in his pocket between his fingers. "He wants to reduce your meds." He took a step closer to her and saw the tendons in her arms tighten as she strained at the wrist straps. "You'd like that, wouldn't you?" he asked. "The thing is, sweetheart, I like to see you like this, that sharp brain of yours foggy, physically helpless." He was close enough now that he could smell her skin and hair. He shut his eyes and inhaled deeply through his nose, taking in her sweet stink. "I like it too much to give it up," he said, opening his eyes. "I will never let them take you off the drugs." She showed no response, no reaction. "I have to say, I don't mind you being in here as much as I thought I would. You belong in prison. We'd all be a lot safer with you manacled in maximum security. But the administrators of this place don't know quite what to do with you here. And you know who they ask?" She gazed at him blankly. "Me," Archie said. "Prescott and the rest of your team of shrinks can make all the recommendations they want. But at the end of the day, they depend on the person who knows you best to decide what privileges you can handle, what books you're allowed to read, how many hours a day you get to spend unrestrained."

"You like it, don't you?" Gretchen said.

Archie grinned. "More than you know."

"That's an awfully unkind thing to say," Gretchen said, "to someone who is suffering from mental illness."

"I'm crazier than you are," Archie said flatly.

"Prescott says that I have to be insane, to do the things I've done."

Archie nodded, drawing out the moment. Then he said, "I've gotten you a new doctor. Didn't I mention that? Because I know you like to play, and I think that Prescott wasn't enough of a challenge for you."

Gretchen's smile vanished for a second, a tiny splinter in the façade. "Ryan Motley's back."

She was a genius at redirecting.

"Let me guess," Archie said. "He's the one who's after your child?"

"He's close," Gretchen said without emotion. "If you get me out of here, I can stop him."

The drugs were making her delusional.

"Do you think motherhood might help get you out of here sooner?" He couldn't even conceive of it. "You. A mother. There's a hysterical image. Good luck with that. You think that will convince them you're cured? You know what works better?" Archie practically spat it out: "Find God."

Gretchen was watching him; with those blue eyes of hers, she always looked like she was seeing something other people couldn't. "My daughter's name was Lily," she said.

Archie's chest tightened.

She couldn't have known about the lilies.

"I'm tired," she said, rolling over. "They give me sedatives at night."

She was fishing. She was like a sideshow psychic that way, trying things out, seeing what struck a nerve. "I was leaving anyway," Archie said, heading toward the door.

"How's Henry recovering?" he heard her ask.

He stopped in his tracks. His hands were in his pockets. He pressed the pills into his thigh.

"Give him my love," she said drowsily. "It's hard for men like him to lose their physical strength. I'd keep my eye on him if I were you."

Archie spun around, took his hands out of his pockets, and walked to the side of her bed. She still had her head turned away from him when he slid his hand along her skull into her hairline and knotted her hair in his fist. He leaned in close to her. He could feel her fighting him, straining against his grip, her hair snapping at the roots, the short pants of her breaths. "Don't say his name," Archie said. He inhaled her again, the same smell, but stronger now, more intense. He saw her eyes wander to his front left pants pocket and then widen with understanding. She knew he had the pills. She recognized the shape, or saw him fingering them, or she just read him well enough to recognize when he was weak.

He waited for her to say something, to taunt him.

But she stayed silent, staring up at him as he held her.

Archie released his grip. "Get some rest," he said. His voice was hoarse. "I hear your new doctor is a son of a bitch."

25

S usan had printed out all the PDFs and sat surrounded by them in the living room. When she'd first spread them out, the fan had blown the pages into the kitchen, so now she had weighed each page down with an ad hoc paperweight: a coffee cup, an incense tray, a small statue of Shiva, her salad bowl from dinner, her ice-cream bowl from dessert, the half a bag of Pirate's Booty she'd gotten out for an after-dessert snack. The pages were on the wire-spool coffee table, the floor, even the sofa. The corners fluttered each time the fan oscillated past.

Bliss had taken a copy of *Mother Jones* to bed hours ago.

But Susan was riveted. Each PDF was a newspaper story about a different murder. All unsolved. The victims described in the articles had all been tortured to death. And they were all children. The murders all took place over a six-year period. They all took place in different states.

She had read and reread the articles, and could find no obvious connections between them beyond the torture. So she studied them again, and this time tried to think like Archie. It was only once she had absorbed the articles enough times, and was able to get past the tragedy and shock, that she began to see other similarities. The children had all disappeared and then been found dead within twenty-four hours. None had been sexually assaulted. Each had been alone when he or she was grabbed—in a bedroom, walking outside, at a park—but always alone, no witnesses.

There was no one named Ryan Motley in any of the stories. She researched each murder online, reading dozens of additional articles. She Googled Ryan Motley's name in tandem with every name and place that came up in connection to each investigation. Nothing. The cases were all cold. Memorial trees had been planted at elementary schools. Honorary diplomas had been presented to parents. No one was maintaining the remembrance Web sites anymore.

Gretchen had given the flash drive to Archie and he had stuck it in a drawer full of Wite-Out. He had his reasons. He must have seen something in the PDFs that convinced him that Gretchen's information wasn't worth following up on. Susan hadn't been able to turn up a single mention of Ryan Motley, and she was a far superior Googler than Archie. Plus Archie had access to police files on all these cases, all sorts of information that wasn't in the news stories. What had he said? Ryan Motley was a figment of Gretchen's imagination.

So what had Gretchen wanted Susan to see? *Find the flash drive*, she had said again and again.

If Gretchen had wanted to use Susan to get to Archie, she could have done it without the big confessional. She didn't need to mention James Beaton or Ryan Motley. But she had.

Susan turned to her laptop on the floor. With the keywords *James Beaton* and *St. Helens, Oregon*, she had turned up a few old newspaper stories from the *St. Helens Chronicle* on her way back from Salem. Reading them on her iPhone screen in her car going seventy miles an hour up I-5 was less than ideal. Now she opened the articles on her fourteen-inch screen. The *Chronicle* had not been online eighteen years ago, but the St. Helens Historical Society had since scanned pages of old editions of the paper and put it all on the Internet.

She grabbed a handful of Pirate's Booty and stuffed it in her mouth.

Local resident James Beaton, husband of Dinah "Dusty" Beaton, and father of two, had been reported missing a day previously. Anyone with information was asked to call the St. Helens Police Department. He was last seen in a late-model black Oldsmobile. His church was planning a vigil, blah, blah. There was a small black-and-white photograph next to the copy of a beefy-faced man in a necktie. He looked like he was in his mid-fifties. The tie had odd markings on it, and Susan zoomed in and out on the screen several times before she found a view that allowed her to make out the pattern.

Susan laughed, and almost choked on Pirate's Booty.

The tie was covered with pictures of small dogs.

If she ever vanished, she hoped they'd run a picture of her in more serious clothes.

She made a copy of the article and saved it, and then she Googled the Hamlet Inn Motel in St. Helens. The Web site was only one page, with a telephone number to call for reservations. The photographs on the site showed a highway-side two-story motel whose best feature appeared to be its large parking lot.

Susan copied down the address for later.

The mysterious Ryan Motley aside, she still had a newspaper story to write, and a little local color wouldn't hurt.

26

The fifth floor of Archie's building was much like the sixth, except for the hallway, which had been painted, inexplicably, plum. The paint had a glossy sheen that reflected the overhead fluorescent lights so that the entire hallway seemed to flicker from three sides.

Archie knocked on his neighbor's apartment door.

When Rachel opened it, he held up the plastic sandwich bag he'd found taped to his door when he got home.

"Spark plugs?" he said.

She smiled. "Now you have some," she said. "In case I need to borrow one."

He put the bag in his pocket and tapped it with his finger. "I'll keep them somewhere safe," he said, "until you need one."

She leaned against the doorjamb. It was after eleven. Too late for a social call. She didn't seem to mind.

"Do you want a glass of water?" she asked.

"I have water upstairs," he said.

"I just got a new Brita filter," she said.

Archie scratched the back of his neck. "Okay."

She opened the door and he followed her inside. She was wearing pale pink satin pajama shorts and a white tank top. No bra. Her apartment was the same layout as his, but her exposed brick wall was painted white. Her furniture all matched, like it had been purchased all at once. The sofa was butter-colored leather. The coffee table was black lacquer and glass. The two club chairs matched the sofa with a small glass end table in between that matched the coffee table. A spherical light fixture the size of a classroom globe hung over the living room. Here and there, she'd incorporated Asian touches. Framed scrolls of calligraphy, embroidered silk paints. She had a Korean wedding chest against one wall, and a six-foot print of a Chinese robe hanging on the brick wall just inside the door. Red lacquer stools lined her kitchen bar. Floor lamps, with red rice paper shades, gave everything in the room a rich crimson glow.

When Archie was in grad school, he'd had a couch from Goodwill and a bookcase built out of cinder blocks.

Rachel was at the sink on the other side of the kitchen bar.

"Have a seat," she said. He heard ice clinking against glass.

Her purse was on the floor next to one of the leather club chairs. He went to the chair and sat down. He could see her, on the other side of the bar, putting together something on a plate.

He gently lowered his hand into her purse and felt for her wallet.

When he had it, he leaned over the arm of the chair, snapped it open, and examined her driver's license. Her name was listed as Rachel Walker. The picture matched. It was a California license. Archie pulled it out of its plastic pouch and tilted it to see if the hologram was real.

If it was a fake, it was a good one.

He heard what sounded like a lacquer tray sliding off a granite counter and he slid the ID back in her wallet and dropped the wallet in her open bag.

She set the tray down on the glass table between the club chairs and took the other seat. The satin shorts sat low on her hips, and he could see the band of skin around her middle that her shirt didn't quite cover. There was a white satin robe on the back of her chair. She didn't put it on.

"Asian studies?" Archie said.

Rachel tucked her legs up under her on the chair. "Excuse me?"

"Your area of study," Archie said.

"Nope," she said. "But good guess."

"Dance?"

She tilted her head.

"You walk with your toes turned out, like someone who's taken a lot of ballet," Archie said.

"Wrong again," she said.

Archie leaned forward and picked up a glass of water and drained half the glass. She had put crackers out, and some cheese.

Who moved in at four in the morning?

He set the glass down and wiped his mouth. "You should be more careful," he said. "Inviting strange men into your apartment at night."

Rachel crossed her arms, her gaze appraising him. Her breasts shifted under the ribbed fabric of her shirt as she moved. "Is that what you are," she said, "a strange man?" Her hair was loose and tousled, like she'd been asleep when he'd knocked, but then why all the mood lighting?

"I'm not afraid of you," she added with a sly smile. "You're a cop."

"That doesn't mean I'm not dangerous," Archie said.

She blinked at him. Her legs and arms looked dark and smooth in the red glow of the lamps.

His skin itched.

"Who are you?" he asked.

"You just saw my name," she said. "It's on my driver's license."

She had seen him. Archie shifted in the chair, rattled. She had caught him going through her things. That wasn't what bothered him. What bothered him was that she should have been angrier. "It could be fake," Archie said.

"Why would I have fake ID, Archie?"

"You move in during the middle of the night. In the apartment directly below mine. You appear to be living above the means of an average grad student. You look . . ." He struggled for the words. "Like someone I know. The tattoo." It sounded ludicrous as he said it out loud, paranoid. "We keep bumping into each other."

"We live in the same building," she said.

She confused him. The way she looked at him. The way she moved. He picked up the glass of water again, drained the last of it, and set it down. Maybe he was used to Gretchen, maybe he looked for games where there weren't any.

"I just want to be neighborly," she said.

He laughed and shook his head.

"Do you want another glass of water?" she asked.

He wanted something stronger.

"I'm flirting with you, Archie," she said. "This," she said, waving a hand in front of herself, "is flirting. There is no conspiracy. I looked you up. I understand that you've been through some things. But you are searching for dark motives where there are none. Is my being interested in you so unlikely a scenario?"

"Yes," Archie said.

"What do you want me to do?" she asked with a smile. "Produce references?"

"I need to look through your things," Archie said.

Rachel cocked her head. "You don't date much, do you?"

Archie rephrased it. "I'm going to look through your things," he said.

She was very still. He fully expected her to throw him out of her apartment. She had every right to. He half hoped that she would. It was the reasonable thing to do. But she didn't.

"Put everything back where you find it," she said.

"Do you have any whiskey?" Archie asked.

She unfolded her legs and slid over the arm of her chair. "I do."

As she walked into the kitchen, Archie got up and went into her bedroom.

The bed was made. He went over to her dresser and pulled open each drawer. Everything was neatly folded. He opened her closet. Several dresses hung on hangers. Shoes were lined up on the closet floor.

There was no detritus. No crumpled receipts on the dresser top. No loose change. The three fashion magazines on the bedside table were all current issues.

It was photo-ready.

He looked in the closet again.

Four dresses, a few blouses, a single skirt.

"Where are the rest of your clothes?" he called.

"They're being shipped," she called back. "Why? Do you need to borrow something?"

He went into her bathroom. The towels were all the same color yellow as the couch. He opened the medicine cabinet. No prescriptions. Nothing with her name on it. Just cosmetics and beauty products. A toothbrush sat in a cup on the edge of the sink.

Rachel appeared in the bathroom doorway and handed him a glass of whiskey. No ice, no soda, just like he liked it.

"Find anything?" she asked.

Archie rolled a sip of the whiskey around his mouth. It tasted better than what he was used to.

She waited for him to say something.

"Where are your textbooks?" he asked.

She sighed. "Seriously?"

"You said you were a student," Archie said. "Where are your textbooks?"

"You know, I could call the cops," she said. "Tell them a strange man was in my bathroom."

He moved past her, out of the bathroom, and scanned her bedroom for the books. Nothing. He walked into the living room and didn't see them there, either.

"Hey," she said from behind him. "Sherlock."

He turned around. She tilted her head toward a book bag by the front door.

He walked over to the bag and opened it. Inside were history texts, anthologies, books of theory.

He paged through one. Then another.

"I hear you up at night, you know," she said from behind him. "I hear you walking around. I hear you talking to somebody on the phone."

Archie put the books down and stood up and turned toward her. "I can check to see if you're really a student," he said.

"I *am* a student."

"Students take notes," Archie said. "They highlight."

She stepped toward him. "Classes start next week," she said.

It was plausible, all of it. Every explanation. He imagined what his shrink would have to say about all this, what Henry would think. He was behaving like a deranged lunatic.

So why wasn't she scared?

She should be scared.

Any rational person would have insisted he leave long ago.

He looked at her. She looked at him.

"Take off your clothes," Archie said.

She raised her eyebrows, as if she hadn't heard him correctly.

He didn't repeat himself.

He waited, motionless, to see what she would do.

And then he watched as she peeled her tank top up over her head and held it out and dropped it on the floor. She didn't have a tan line. Her skin was a perfect dark honey, the color interrupted only by the soft pink circles of her nipples. Then she pushed her shorts down, stepped out of them, and stood before him, completely naked. Her tan, flat abdomen led to a wisp of dark blond pubic hair.

Her posture didn't change. She wasn't abashed; she didn't try to cover herself. She appeared perfectly comfortable.

"Okay," Archie said.

He could feel the sweat forming on his upper lip.

He hadn't thought she'd do it.

She lowered her chin and smiled up at him. He recognized this as flirting.

"Nice shirt," she said.

He looked down. The blue shirt he'd put on at her suggestion. He could feel blood rush to his face.

This was not how this was supposed to go.

She took another step toward him, put her hand on his chest, and pushed him back. He stumbled out of her apartment, into the hall. She smiled at him and sighed, before she closed the door in his face.

27

S usan had one bare foot up on the dash of the Saab, and a cigarette in her hand out the window. She was on her first smoke of the day, and her second cup of coffee. She picked at the bagel crumbs on her lap, eating some of them and tossing others out the window onto the street. All the windows were rolled down. Nothing helped. Her scalp felt sweaty. Her toenails were too long. A small white butterfly batted against the windshield, trying to get out, apparently oblivious to the four alternative escape routes.

Archie had told her specifically to wait for him in front of the Lifeworks Center for Young Women. They were supposed to meet there and then go in together. He'd told her not to go in without him four times. But she had gotten there early and he was running late and it was hot.

Archie was not someone who ran late. He was someone who had things come up. But when these things—generally dead people or homicidal maniacs—interfered with his schedule, he always called. He was conscientious that way. Susan was not. When things came up in her life—generally a good book she was reading and didn't want to put down, or a manicure—she didn't call, she just hurried.

There was no question. Archie had figured out that she'd taken the flash drive.

Susan rummaged around on the floor of the backseat until she found a plastic Dasani bottle that still had some water in it, and she took a slug. It was warm and tasted like cancer. She screwed the cap back on and tossed it back on the floor.

Her iPod battery was dead and she didn't have the charger. There was nothing on the radio.

She looked at the clock on the dash. She had only been waiting five minutes. It seemed like longer. She finished her cigarette and put it out. She wondered how many cases of emphysema could have been prevented by punctuality.

Screw it.

She slipped her feet back into her flip-flops and got out of the car. The sidewalk in front of the house was cracked and buckled from tree roots. She walked alongside the picket fence, and then up the front walk. A garden, on either side of the walk, seemed to be filled entirely with tomatoes. Susan was halfway up the peeling front porch steps when she heard Archie behind her.

"I told you to wait for me," he said.

Susan cringed and turned around. "Whoops," she said.

Archie checked his watch. "You couldn't last ten minutes?"

He walked past her on the stairs. He seemed fine. He didn't know about the flash drive. They were going to pretend that everything was fine. She could do that. She had spent the better part of high school doing that.

"Who even has a watch anymore?" Susan said, catching up with him. "I bet you still have dial-up."

He was wearing a white button-down tucked into gray pants and a pair of suede shoes with thick rubber soles. A small spiral notebook, folded open, poked out of his pants pocket. The leather gun holster on his hip matched his brown leather belt. Susan knew that Archie usually wore a jacket to cover the gun, but it was hot enough she guessed he'd given up the effort. He didn't offer any explanation for being late. But then, he was investigating two murders.

"So did you listen to it?" she asked.

"Yes," Archie said.

She was dying to know what Archie thought of her interview with Gretchen. She had hundreds of questions about the circumstances of Beaton's disappearance, the stuff that hadn't made the papers. But before Susan could ask any of them, a woman with corkscrew gray hair burst through the front door, letting the screen bang closed behind her.

She was wearing a long gray skirt, a long-sleeved white cotton shirt, and hoop earrings the size of bracelets. "She's gone," the woman said to Archie. "Pearl's split."

Archie stiffened. "What?" he said. He ran his hands through his hair and stomped inside, as Susan followed behind.

There were no introductions.

The woman appeared distressed; her earrings were swinging.

"How long has she been gone?" Archie asked.

"An hour," the woman said. "I mean, that's when she was last seen. I just went up to tell her to come down for your interview and she was gone."

No one was looking at Susan. She was trying to think back, to remember if she'd seen anyone leave the house while she was waiting in the car. Would she even recognize Pearl again if she saw her?

"She take anything?" Archie asked.

The woman wrung her hands. "Her backpack's gone."

"Does she have a cell phone?" Susan asked.

Archie and the woman turned and looked at her.

"This is Susan Ward," Archie said to the woman. "Bea Adams, the center's director," Archie said.

"Yes," the woman said. "And like any teenager, she lives and dies by it." The woman reached into a pocket in her skirt and held up a cell phone. "I found it on her bed."

"I need to see her room," Archie said.

Pearl's room looked like a college dorm that was three parts
Holly Hobbie and one part Emily the Strange. Two single beds
were pushed up against opposite walls, and a skinny girl with an orange Mohawk and a sullen expression sat listening to an iPod on one
of them. The curtains and bedspreads were gingham. An old wooden
dresser had been painted light blue and then lovingly distressed. A
strawberry and flower print had been stenciled at eye level all the way
around the room. If Susan had been forced to sleep here, she would
have run away, too.

"Our board members did some of the decorating," Bea explained.

"It's . . . nice," Susan said.

The girls had tried to Goth it up some. The corkboard on the
closet door was covered with images of screaming death-metal mu-
sicians that Susan didn't recognize. The lightbulb in the desk lamp
was a blue party bulb. All the clothing strewn on the floor was
black.

The girl with the orange Mohawk had a silver barbell through
her nose, four silver studs over each eyebrow, a ring through the
center of her lower lip, and six tiny stars tattooed in a cluster on her
right temple. She was wearing a black tank top that had been cut in
half at the seams and reassembled with safety pins, cutoff jeans, and

beaten-up motorcycle boots. Her eyes were lined with kohl and her lips were painted dark purple.

She was maybe, what, fourteen?

Susan looked closer. The girl's Mohawk was slick and sharp and as tall as a dollar bill; her head was shaved on both sides. The hair was dyed orange. But it wasn't an ordinary orange. It was a brilliant neon orange. Manic Panic Electric Lava, to be precise, in the original cream formula.

Susan knew it, because her hair was exactly the same color.

Archie started to move, but Susan put her hand out. "Let me," she said. Then she walked over and sat down on the end of the girl's bed before Archie could protest. Wasn't that why Susan was there in the first place? Because she spoke "disaffected teenese"?

The girl did one of those barely discernible eye rolls, an eye roll that said she could not even be bothered to do a full eye roll.

Susan plucked the earbuds out of the girl's ears.

The girl said, "Hey!"

"I like your hair," Susan said.

The girl gave Susan a slow once-over, ending at Susan's flaming electric tresses. "You need to condition," the girl said.

Susan thought she heard a half chuckle from behind her where Archie and Bea were standing.

"You're Pearl's roommate?" Susan said.

"No, I'm her cat," the girl said.

"Her name's Allison," Bea said.

"When did you last see Pearl, Allison?" Susan asked.

"I dunno. Like an hour ago? She came in and packed up and left. Didn't say a word."

Susan glanced down at the earbuds on the gingham bedspread. "Maybe you just didn't hear her," Susan said.

"I don't know where she went," Allison said, narrowing her eyes. "And if I did, I wouldn't say."

"She could be in danger," Archie said.

Allison gave Archie a look. Susan remembered that look. It

meant, *People like you lie.* "Whatever," Allison said. She dug her earbuds back into her ears and dialed up the volume.

Susan had done a story about the danger of earbuds, and at that decibel level Allison was looking at metabolically exhausted ear-hair cells, which would lead to hair cell death and eventual loss of inner ear functional ability. But Allison didn't look like she was up for a lecture.

"She's not going to be helpful," Bea said. She lowered her voice. "She has trust issues."

"Can I look around?" Archie asked Bea.

Susan saw Bea hesitate.

Archie took a step closer to Bea. "Let me be clear," he said. "This property belongs to your organization. So I can search this room without a warrant if you give me permission. So can I look around?"

"Yes," Bea said. "Of course."

Susan was already scanning the room for clues. "Want some help?" she asked.

"Don't touch anything," Archie said.

So Susan watched as Archie moved methodically around the room, opening drawers and scanning surfaces. When he went through the closet and dresser he called Bea over and asked her if she could tell what was missing. She couldn't.

Susan inched over to the desk next to Pearl's empty bed. The surface of the desk was flecked with colored marks, like fine-tip markers slipping off the edge of a page. Susan walked over to Allison and plucked out her earbuds.

"Hey!" Allison said again.

"Did Pearl have a diary?" Susan asked.

Allison rolled her eyes, this time the full treatment. "No one has diaries anymore," she said. "We use Facebook." She dropped her attention to the screen of her iPod. "She had a sketch pad she was always drawing in, though."

"Where did she keep it?" Archie asked.

"I don't know," Allison said. "She always worked on it in bed."

Susan, Archie, and Bea all turned toward Pearl's bed. Allison went back to killing her inner-ear hair cells.

"When I was a teenager," Susan said, "I had a diary that I kept in a sealed Ziploc bag in a frozen fish sticks box in our freezer," Susan said. She turned to Bea. "My mother would eat cat litter before she ate a fish stick," she explained. She walked over to the bed. "May I?" she asked Archie.

"Please," Archie said.

Susan flopped down on her back onto Pearl's bed. The box spring bounced and creaked. The desk was at her feet. The wall was at her left. She surveyed the room from there, looking for the ideal hiding place—someplace safe from the roommate and staff, but close enough for easy access. The desk was too public. Ditto the dresser. Then Susan slid her hand between the wall and the mattress and felt around. Nothing. "Help me," she said to Archie, and she got up and she and Archie and Bea tugged the bed a foot from the wall.

The three peered over the bed. Black scuffs marred the blue wall paint where a black hardcover sketch pad had been jammed in and pried out again and again.

Susan said, "It's gone." And then she added, to be completely clear, "She's not planning on coming back."

29

S usan leaned her head against Leo's apartment door and buzzed. Her laptop was cradled under one arm, the white cord trailing behind her down the hall like a tail.

She was attracted to Leo Reynolds for a lot of reasons. He was beautiful, in a vampire sort of way: pale and dark-haired with light eyes and the kind of nose they used to put on Roman coins. He wore clothes well, and bought suits that were worth more than Susan's car. He was elusive and guarded, which somehow made him seem mysterious and enigmatic. People thought he was a cad. His trysts, before Susan, consisted mainly of strippers and hookers. He had conquests, not girlfriends. Susan's own sexual history seemed positively puritanical by comparison. She was a virginal flower. This was a change-up; Susan was used to being the bad influence. Leo was the first boyfriend she'd ever had who thought that she was better than he was. He was also rich. At least his father was rich.

But right now the thing that appealed to her most about Leo was his air-conditioning.

She pressed her cheek against the door—even the door felt cool. She imagined the perfect sixty-eight-degree air on the other side of it, and buzzed again. Her interview with Gretchen Lowell was due in two days. And if she could just get out of the heat she could write it.

Leo looked surprised when he opened the door.

"I followed some people in downstairs," Susan explained, elbowing her way past him with her laptop.

Leo lived in a penthouse apartment in one of the new mixed-use buildings in the Pearl District. There was a designer sneaker store on the first floor next to a shop that sold ten-thousand-dollar light fixtures. His building was the tallest in the neighborhood and the view from the floor-to-ceiling windows in the living room made the urban bustle of the Pearl look faraway and irrelevant. You could see cars politely jockeying below at four-way stops and the light rail gliding by and people ambling along with gelati and bicyclists and men walking pugs and office workers on their lunch breaks sitting on sidewalk benches eating salads out of to-go boxes, but you couldn't hear anything. That's what money bought you: silence.

Before Susan had moved back in with her mother, she had sublet a loft in the Pearl from her former MFA adviser. She'd had sex with him, too. But not for his HVAC system.

She dropped her purse inside the door and flung herself on Leo's black leather sofa. "You know, people who die of hyperthermia stop sweating," she said. "They'll feel hot, but their internal cooling mechanism fails. They can't sweat. Their skin is dry to the touch. Their body can't cool itself." She pulled at her sticky, sweaty shirt. "So I know I'm not hyperthermic."

"I was on my way out," Leo said, still standing at the door.

"Please don't make me go," Susan pleaded. "I've been driving around for two hours, with no A/C, looking for this girl who is totally not my problem, but I feel like she is because she reminds me of me. I mean, she's a total hardcase. She drives Archie crazy. She Tasered him once, but that's a long story. She lives at the group home where that guy who got filleted up on Mount Tabor worked, and they think she saw him that morning. Anyway, she probably took off to avoid the hassle of having to talk to the cops and whatever, but who knows, right? Maybe she saw something more than she said she did. And she's an asshole, but she's seventeen and who isn't an asshole at that age, right? And Archie says it's a problem for Missing Persons now, but we both know they're not going to find her if she doesn't want to be found." Susan reached up and touched her scalp. "Do you think my hair needs conditioning?"

Leo didn't budge. "I really have to go," he said.

Susan put her hands behind her and stretched back on the couch. Even the leather felt cool. Leo had one of those refrigerators with the unit on the door that dispensed ice and cold water. "So, I'll see you when you get back," she said. "Do you have any sandwich stuff?"

"You can't stay here," Leo said.

"Why?"

"Because you'll snoop," he said.

Susan peeked at him over the back of the couch. "Please. I have to work. I work better with A/C and black leather furniture."

"You're unbelievable," Leo said.

His white button-down shirt was fresh from the cleaner's and still creased at the seams. His black slacks looked like he'd never sat down in them. Every piece of his dark hair was in place. He was the only person Susan knew who regularly had his shoes sent out to be shined.

She peeled off her damp shirt, unhooked her red bra, and tossed them both next to her laptop on the floor beside the couch.

"What are you doing?" Leo asked.

Susan stood up, stepped out of her flip-flops, and slid out of her skirt and underwear. "Getting comfortable," she said. She sauntered over to him, hoping that she didn't smell as bad as she thought she might.

"Really?" Leo said. "You're willing to trade sex for air-conditioning?"

Susan grinned. Then she hooked her fingers around Leo's belt and pulled him into the bedroom.

30

Leo's shower was marble and glass and it had its own light source, so you could stand bathed in light and water in an otherwise completely dark bathroom. There was a marble bench, and two showerheads, and soap that smelled, somehow, exactly like banana bread. Susan was a bath person. She had always been a bath person. Her longest bath on record was three hours and twelve minutes. Susan had dropped more books in the bathtub than most people would read in their entire lives. But she had to admit—she loved that shower. The setup reminded her of those game show booths where money blew around and you got to keep as much as you could stuff inside your pockets.

She turned off the spigot, stepped out, and dried herself with one of Leo's big black towels. She squeezed the water out of her hair and then wrapped the towel around her chest. It came down to her mid-shins. She looked at herself in the enormous mirror that covered the wall from the double sink marble vanity to the ceiling. The sun had brought out her freckles. Her wet orange hair looked like packing straw. Flat chest. Skinny limbs. Put her in braids and she'd look like Pippi Longstocking.

She touched her brittle hair.

Leo had nice hair. He had silky shiny healthy hair, hair that made you want to change shampoos.

He didn't have a conditioner in the shower. He must have some secret—a spray or leave-in ointment. Susan went to the sink he always used and opened a few drawers in the vanity. The man liked his grooming products. He used more moisturizers and cleansers than she did. She found a nail-grooming kit that had implements in it she'd never seen before. She pulled a small pair of silver scissors out of the kit and used them to trim her pubic hair. In a bottom drawer, she found old teeth-whitening trays, an electric nose hair trimmer, and a plastic bag full of a thousand cotton balls, but she didn't see any hair treatments. She even tried the drawers below the other sink, but they were empty except for a box of tampons, a toothbrush, and some nail polish remover, presumably Leo's emergency Girl Kit.

Now she was on a mission.

She looked around the bathroom and her eyes fell on the closet where Leo kept extra towels. She opened it. The towels were neatly folded and stacked on shelves. A toilet brush and a plunger sat on the floor of the closet. Behind them was a large gym bag.

Did she really think that she'd find Leo's conditioning spray in that bag? Maybe. He might use it after working out. At least that was what she was going to tell him she was thinking if he ever found out she'd opened it.

You'll snoop.

She knelt down and unzipped the bag. She did it slowly, like someone revealing the climax of a magic trick. Now you see it. Now you don't.

Unzipped, the bag fell open like a mouth. Inside, on top, was a gun.

Her brain processed it in pieces. A muzzle. A barrel. A trigger. It was the cocaine that the gun was resting on that really got her attention, a huge fucking brick of cocaine encased in plastic wrap and packing tape. Susan bought a pair of boots once that came in a box that was the same size. Those boots went up to her knees.

This was a lot of coke.

Susan sat back on her heels. Her throat felt small.

She went through the possible explanations. *He was just holding it for a friend! He'd found it on a park bench and just hadn't had time to call the cops yet!* But the most probable explanation was the one she liked least: Leo was more involved in his father's business than he'd let on.

Then Susan did something out of character—she decided it was none of her business. She zipped up the gym bag and pushed it back where she'd found it.

Archie was not where he should have been. But he hoped that if he kept the phone call short enough, Henry wouldn't ask where he was.

"There's no sign of her," Henry said.

"She's probably in Seattle by now," Archie said into his phone.

Pearl had been gone for six hours.

"How was the meeting with the mayor?" Henry asked.

"Brilliant," Archie said with a sigh. He'd had nothing to report to the mayor or Portland's chief of police. They hadn't found any trace evidence in the parking lot or on the rooftop. No trace evidence on Jake Kelly's body or at the scene or at the center's parking lot. "Canvass both the areas again," Archie said, "where they were grabbed and where they were found. He's got to have a car. See if the traffic cameras picked up anyone blowing through red lights."

Getting away with one murder was lucky. Getting away with two took talent.

"You thinking what I'm thinking?" Henry said.

Archie looked up at the midday sky. Puffy white clouds drifted overhead. "He managed to kidnap adults from public areas in daylight, murder them, and stage spectacular crime scenes, all without leaving evidence behind," Archie said. He wasn't a beginner. "This guy has killed before."

"No unsolved murders with a similar MO have turned up on the national databases," Henry said.

"Let's try looking internationally," Archie said. He was standing on the sidewalk, a few feet from his car.

"Can I go to Paris?" Henry asked.

"No."

"*C'est dommage*," Henry said with a perfect accent. "Where are you?"

Archie glanced up at the St. Helens police station. "I'm tracking down a lead," he said. "Call me if anything turns up." And he hung up.

He had listened to Susan's recording the night before. And then again, early this morning. Gretchen's honey voice sounded husky and sedated. Her speech had been intended for him. He had rewound the details and tried to puzzle it out. Why confess to killing Beaton now? Why bring up the lilies? Gretchen didn't do anything by accident. Archie made a deal with himself. It wasn't worth diverting resources from the primary investigation, but he would see what he could dig up in a few hours, and if he didn't find anything, he'd let it go.

He walked inside the small police station and pulled out his badge.

"I'm expected," he said.

James Beaton's missing person file was underwhelming. Archie scanned the report.

"Can I have a copy of this?" he asked.

Samantha Huffington, the chief of police of the small St. Helens police force, looked up from her computer. "I can send you the digital file," she said. She had been more than helpful, pulling the file, letting him use her office, not asking too many questions.

"You've digitized your files," he said. "I'm impressed."

"We have guns, too."

They were in her office, which was twice the size of Archie's and ten times as cheery. The walls were papered with local newspaper stories about various arrests her department had made, and drawings by a group of elementary school kids who'd evidently come through on a tour. A shelf displayed framed photos of a police softball team. Huffington was in the center of the last five years' worth of team photos. She was a few years younger than Archie, sturdily built, with thick arms and round shoulders. Archie guessed she was good at the plate.

She pulled a pen out of a Giants mug on her desk and held it out to him with a sticky note and he scribbled down his e-mail for her. She took it and stuck it to the side of her monitor, and he watched while she brought up a PDF of the file.

Chiefs in small departments could wear any insignia they wanted, up to five stars on each collar. Huffington only wore one. Archie liked that about her.

"Did you read this?" he asked, laying his hand on the missing person report.

She hit send. "As soon as you had me pull it."

That was what he would have done.

"Any thoughts?" he asked.

She frowned and glanced at the file. "Looks pretty perfunctory."

"That's what I was thinking," Archie said.

Huffington put her elbows on her desk. The blue sleeves of her uniform were rolled up. The brass badge over her left shirt pocket glinted under the fluorescent lights. She had a broad friendly face, no makeup. "The guy left his wife and two kids," she said. "It's a small force. My guess is they looked around a little and decided he didn't want to be found."

Behind her head, taped on the wall, was a handwritten quote by Robert Louis Stevenson. "Everyone who got to where he is has had to begin where he was."

"Pen," she said, extending her palm.

He looked in his hand and then realized that he'd inadvertently put the pen she'd lent him in his pants pocket. He handed it back. "Sorry," he said. She dropped it back in the Giants mug.

"There's a difference," she said, "between being missing and being missed."

Archie stood up. "Thanks for your help," he said.

"Just keep me in the loop," she said.

He took a step, and then turned back. "You haven't asked why I'm interested," he said.

Huffington was looking at her computer screen, her fingers tapping on the keyboard. "I know who you are, Detective," she said. She glanced over the monitor at him. "I can guess."

CHAPTER

33

Mrs. James Beaton lived in a one-story wooden house painted the color of the Caribbean, with white trim and an aluminum screen door. The yard was dead, the grass dried to a crisp. A bed of wilted white snapdragons lined the cracked concrete walkway to the porch.

Archie had barely stepped on the porch when barking exploded from inside the house. He heard a woman shout and then the door opened, and a throaty voice from the other side of the screen door said, "You the one who called?"

Archie squinted at the hunched shadow of the woman. "I'm Detective Sheridan," Archie said.

The screen door creaked as she opened it. "Careful of the dog," she said, ushering him in. "Damn thing tripped me last year and broke my hip." Archie stepped carefully inside the house. The dog, a tan and white corgi, eyed him suspiciously. "Come on, then," Mrs. Beaton said. "Before you let the air out." She was small, five-foot-one at best, though it was hard to tell because she was curled over a walker. Archie guessed her to be in her mid-seventies, which would have put her in the same age range as her husband. Her face was creased, and the skin around her arms looked like crepe paper. She was wearing a wig. A blond bob. Archie could see the soft white natural hairs poking out around her ears.

"Thanks for seeing me," Archie said.

She laughed, showing yellowed teeth. "Sure as shit wasn't doing anything else," she said. "Drink?"

"No, thanks," Archie said. It wasn't even four o'clock.

"Didn't think so," she said. She shuffled backward, pulling the walker with her, the dog weaving around her feet, until she got to a recliner, but before she could sit, the dog hopped up in her place. She made a clucking noise and the dog looked up, put its ears back, and then leapt off the chair and flopped on its side on the floor. Then Mrs. Beaton slowly lowered herself down. "Damn dog takes my place every time I get up," she said.

Archie looked for a spot to sit and settled on a low-slung couch. A snowstorm of tan dog hair lifted off the cushions and settled on Archie's pants.

The house wasn't hot. Archie could hear a window A/C unit churning somewhere. A print of a painting of Jesus Christ praying in a ray of godly light hung on the wall behind the recliner. A tapestry of several corgis curled next to each other in the wilderness hung next to it.

Mrs. Beaton picked a wineglass up off a metal TV tray. "White wine," she explained with a wink. "Doesn't count." She pulled a lever and the chair reclined with a clank. She was so small and the chair was so big that she looked like a child. "If you want something, you're going to have to get it. It takes me five minutes to get up out of this chair."

"I'm fine," Archie said.

She set her dark gaze on him. "So, you find the son of a bitch?" she asked.

"No," Archie said. "No. Nothing like that. I just had a few questions."

Her jaw set and her eyes flicked above Archie's head, but then an instant later her posture softened. She took a drink and shook her head. "Shoot," she said. "I'm just giving you shit."

The corgi started to snore.

"Can you tell me about the day your husband disappeared?" Archie asked.

"That was almost twenty years ago, son," she said. "I told the cops everything I knew back then. It's all in the report. Nothing to add." Her eyes landed above Archie's head again. Same spot.

He turned around and followed her gaze behind him, where a half dozen framed photographs hung on the wall above the couch. Studio baby pictures. High school graduation. The kind of photographs with a gold photography studio imprint in the corner. A few black-and-white shots of grim ancestors. And a photograph of a woman with a blond bob standing next to a heavy man with a yellow necktie in front of the house Archie was sitting in. Two skinny teenage girls in matching sleeveless dresses slumped between them. Two Welsh corgis sat at their feet.

"The son of a bitch took off. Left me with two kids and no income. Had to go back to work."

"Tell me about that day," Archie said.

She frowned and looked at her hands. The knuckles were swollen from arthritis. She wasn't wearing a wedding ring. "Eighteen years ago. He left the office for lunch. Didn't say where he was going. Never came back. The son of a bitch never called or wrote, all these years."

"Did he take anything?"

She snorted. "The car."

Archie searched for a way to ask the obvious. "Did he pack a bag?"

"Nope." She leaned toward him. "But he withdrew five thousand dollars from our savings account that morning."

That hadn't been in the report.

"Did it from our local branch," she continued. "I went in when I saw the money was gone, talked to the clerk. She knew us both by sight. Said he'd come in and made the withdrawal. By himself.

Signed for it and everything. No question he cleaned us out, the bastard."

"Did you tell the police?" Archie asked.

"Why would I? It was his money. He had a right to it."

Archie picked some corgi hair off his pants. This wasn't going anywhere. "Did you ever know anyone named Gretchen Lowell?"

She cackled and pointed a finger at him. "I knew it," she said, jabbing the finger in the air in triumph. "I recognized you. From that old task force. Thought this might have something to do with that. You being here." She took a sip of the wine and then set it back noisily on the table. "No. I never knew her."

"You've seen her picture?" Archie asked. Everyone had seen her picture, you couldn't avoid it, but he had to be sure.

"Sure," Mrs. Beaton said. "She was on the cover of *TV Guide* four times. I would have remembered someone who looked like that."

Archie was quiet, thinking. The A/C unit hummed. The dog snored. Mrs. Beaton cracked her knuckles.

Archie said, "Did you have any reason to think your husband might be unfaithful?"

Another snort. "You mean before he cleaned out our bank account and took off?"

Archie nodded.

"He was very loyal to his family," she said. "He didn't have any reason to leave." She fixed her eyes on Archie. "Is he dead?"

"I have no idea," Archie said. He really didn't. He didn't know what Gretchen was playing at. Had she really killed this man? Or had she just read about him in some old newspaper clipping and sent Archie off to chase his tail? She'd known that Susan would share the recording with him. She'd known that he'd investigate her claim. But as far as Archie could tell, the case was stone cold.

"Are your children still in town?" Archie asked.

Mrs. Beaton lifted her shoulders in a sad sort of shrug. "Would you stick around if you'd grown up here?"

Archie had not set foot in the town he'd grown up in since the day he'd left for college. "I'll let you get on with your day," he said, standing up and brushing the dog hair off his pants.

Mrs. Beaton's eyes narrowed and her mouth formed a crooked smile. "Why are you here, really?" she asked.

"Just following up on a tip," Archie said. "It's probably nothing."

She didn't move. She sat dwarfed in the chair, the wineglass still in her hand. The walker was still positioned in front of the chair. Two pink tennis balls had been affixed to the walker's front feet.

"I'll let myself out," Archie said. He stepped over the dog. It growled and pawed at something in its sleep.

34

Archie immediately recognized the beat-up Saab taking up two spots in the parking lot of the Hamlet Inn. He pulled up next to it. Susan was sitting on the hood eating a sandwich.

"Thought I might run into you here," she said with her mouth full. "I talked to the manager." She swallowed and licked her fingers. "The woman who ran the place back when Beaton disappeared is dead. This guy is pretty useless. He was in diapers back then." She held up half of the sandwich. "Want some?"

Archie took the sandwich and sat down next to Susan. The hood of her car was hot. Vehicles zoomed along Highway 30, the last gasp of rush hour. On the other side of the highway were train tracks and a few dilapidated buildings.

"Nice view, right?" Susan said dryly. "How was the wife?"

Susan had a way of showing up at all the wrong places. "You following me?" Archie asked.

"I looked her up when I got to town, and I saw your car in front of her house," she said with a shrug. "What's with that color, by the way?"

Archie took a bite of the sandwich and chewed it. "Didn't ask," he said.

"Did you learn anything?" Susan asked.

She was barefoot, her flip-flops on the pavement, her dirty feet on the hood of the car, and she was wearing a T-shirt from Portland's old 24 Hour Church of Elvis. The late-day sun made her orange hair look like some sort of radioactive halo.

"What?" she said.

"Are we partners now?" Archie asked.

"I gave you the recording," she said.

Archie didn't want her harassing the elderly. "Leave the woman alone," Archie said with a sigh. "She doesn't know anything."

"Think Gretchen did it?" Susan asked.

Archie peered at the sandwich in his hand. "What is this?"

"Tempeh, mustard, and sprouts on whole grain."

Archie worked his tongue on a seed caught between his teeth.

"I don't get it," Susan said. "Why go through the trouble of cutting up the body? Why not just meet him somewhere in the middle of nowhere and then leave him there? If he thought he was getting laid, she could have talked him into going anywhere. Why this place? It wasn't for the romantic ambience, believe me."

She had a point. Gretchen said it had taken five trips to get Beaton's body out of there. Where? To his car? It had disappeared with him. She had brought supplies. She had planned the murder. She would have planned the disposal of the body.

Archie heard the whistle before he saw the train. The tracks ran along all of Highway 30. They'd been there before the highway was, supporting the port towns that had grown up along the Columbia. Trains carried supplies, hauled lumber. They were lifelines.

All that luggage, I needed a porter.

The train rumbled past, a blur of primary-colored freight cars.

"I think I know how she got rid of the body," Archie said.

S usan listened as Archie laid it all out for Henry and Claire. Susan's interview with Gretchen. Her story about killing James Beaton. His visit to St. Helens. The four of them were crammed into Archie's office. Archie was in the chair at his desk, and Henry and Claire were sitting in the chairs that faced the desk. There were no more chairs, so Susan perched herself on the desk's corner. The office door was closed. The blinds were drawn. This was serious.

Henry rubbed his face. Then he dropped his hand and looked at Archie. He slowly scratched the stubble above his ear.

He didn't look pleased.

Susan squirmed. She could feel tempeh stuck between her teeth. She saw Claire glance at Henry.

Then Henry rubbed his face again, and leaned forward toward Archie. "What are you doing?" he asked. His voice was quiet, entirely calm, totally controlled. Susan could barely hear him. It was a bad sign. Susan had a feeling that the quieter Henry got, the angrier he was. "You know we have another case," Henry said to Archie. "Two murders. A. Serial. Killer."

"It's related," Archie said quickly. He nodded at Susan. "Tell him the name she gave you."

They all looked at her. She had been working on getting the

tempeh out with her tongue. Now she felt a slow bloom of heat rise from her chest to her cheekbones. The tempeh would have to wait. "Ryan Motley," she said.

She saw Henry's eyebrow twitch.

"Give him the flash drive," Archie said.

Susan froze. Her whole face felt hot now. She was perspiring. *Flop sweat.* She'd used the term, but she'd never actually experienced it.

Archie was impassive, looking at her, waiting.

"Huh?" she said.

"I'm not stupid, Susan," Archie said matter-of-factly. "Give it to him."

She could deny it. But one look at Archie's face told her she wouldn't get away with it. She slumped and dug into her purse, and then held out the silver flash drive she'd stolen from Archie's desk. "Here," she said, hanging her head.

Henry snatched it from her. "You showed her the flash drive?" he said to Archie.

"I took it," Susan mumbled.

"What?" Henry said.

She sat up straight and said, loudly, "I took it from his desk."

"So you looked at it?" Archie asked her.

Susan hesitated, confused.

"What's on it?" Henry asked.

"What do you mean, you took it from his desk?" Claire said.

Susan didn't understand. Why were they asking her what was on it? She had taken the flash drive from them. The thing had been in Archie's possession for at least three months. Then she realized that she had completely misunderstood. Archie hadn't decided the murdered children weren't worth looking into. He didn't even know about them. "You two haven't looked at it," she said in amazement. "You haven't opened the files at all."

Henry glanced at Archie. "Have you?" he asked Archie.

"No," Archie said.

"Rewind," Claire said. "Someone tell me what the fuck is going on."

At least Susan wasn't the only one in the dark.

Archie exhaled slowly, and then sat forward and folded his hands on his desk. It was quiet. Archie kept his eyes on his hands. "Gretchen gave me the flash drive a year ago. She said that she hadn't killed any of the children we'd accused her of murdering, that she had had an apprentice who'd gone rogue. He acted alone. She said his name was Ryan Motley and that I needed to find him and then she gave me that." He shot a furtive glance at Henry. "Henry and I agreed not to pursue, to not even look at it. Henry said—and I agreed—that she was trying to manipulate me. Us. That it was a game. We agreed that she was lying."

Claire shot Henry a we'll-talk-about-this-later look.

The silver flash drive glinted on the desk.

"She *is* lying," Claire said.

"That's what we thought," Archie said.

"No," Claire said. She sat up in her seat a little, and held her shoulders back. "I was at some of those crime scenes, remember?" she said. Her voice had an edge to it that Susan had never heard before. "I saw what she did to those children."

"She was never convicted of murdering a single one of those kids," Archie said. He gave Henry an I-could-use-your-help-here look, but Henry just shrugged.

Claire was sitting on the edge of her chair now. "She was never convicted of killing a lot of the people she went all Mengele on," she said. "We went for convictions on what we could prove." She pointed at Archie. "That was your idea. Get her behind bars and then get her to confess to the other murders." Archie looked back at her, composed. Susan knew that face. He could take it on and off at will. Claire crossed her arms. "If anyone had asked me, I'd have said to euthanize the bitch," she said.

Henry was studying something on the floor. Susan was hoping that Claire didn't yell at her.

Archie unfolded his hands and placed his palms on the desk. "She confessed to twenty-one more murders," Archie said calmly. "None of them children."

Claire leaned forward. "This is revisionist bullshit," she said.

Archie looked up. Henry looked up. Susan tried to take up less space on the desk.

"Some sick PR play," Claire said. *"She didn't kill any kids. She's mentally ill. Not to blame for her actions."* She squeezed Archie's hands. "So, what? We're supposed to understand? It's suddenly no big deal? There is no Ryan Motley."

Henry gave Susan a you-should-leave look, but she ignored him.

"Can we just entertain this?" Archie asked.

Claire exhaled and turned back to Henry. "Why are you just sitting there?" she asked him. "We can't trust his judgment when it comes to her."

Susan thought Henry looked tired. He crossed his legs, lifting the one that still gave him trouble and placing it on top of the other knee. "What's on the flash drive?" he said to Susan.

Finally.

Susan opened her purse, pulled out a sheaf of paper, and spread it on the desk. "News stories," she said, trying not to sound excited. "Seven murders over six years. All children. Different states. All unsolved."

Everyone leaned forward and studied the articles on Archie's desk, except for Susan—who couldn't see over everyone else's heads and knew the articles now by heart anyway. She dug at the tempeh between her teeth with her fingernail.

Archie sat back and did a quick search for a phone number on his computer. Then he picked up his phone and dialed it. "This is Detective Archie Sheridan with the Portland Police Department. I've got a question about a cold case. The detective in charge was"—he glanced at the article—"Lew Ellis."

He kept the phone in the crook of his shoulder while he continued to scan through the pages on his desk.

After a few minutes, he said, "Detective Ellis? Hi." He paused. "Yeah. That's me." Nodded. "Thank you." He picked up one of the articles. "I've got a question about an old case of yours," he said. His eyes searched the article and then stopped on a name. "Calvin Long. I'm wondering if there were any details that you didn't release to the press."

Everyone in the room leaned a millimeter closer.

"Really?" Archie said. He looked up, right at Claire. "What kind of flower?"

36

A rchie listened as Gretchen's voice filled the break room. He was used to her voice. For a long time, after she'd almost killed him, he'd heard it in his head, reassuring him, comforting him, as if his inner voice had become hers. He could conjure that voice in an instant, he knew it so well. Even muddied by the medications, he'd know her voice anywhere.

She was detailing how she'd gutted and dismembered James Beaton. He'd listened to this part seven or eight times, but it still made the hair on his arms stand up. It wasn't the content or the brutality of her words—he'd heard and seen worse—it was the way she talked about it, determinedly remorseless.

Archie looked around the conference table. They had all stayed late.

Michael Flannigan, his cap pulled low, fingers tugging on a recently grown beard; Josh Levy, back from a year working Vice, where he'd gained twenty pounds and stopped wearing a tie; Greg Fremont, who rode a recumbent bicycle to work and a button on his lapel—an outline of the state of Oregon with a green heart in it; Martin Ngyun, in his ubiquitous Blazers cap, so comfortable at a computer that when he wasn't, he drummed his fingers on a phantom keyboard. Then there were Henry and Claire, who, despite the fact that there was no one who hadn't figured out they were a couple, still sat as far apart from each another as possible.

Everyone in the room had been on the Beauty Killer Task Force except for Mike Flannigan, and he'd helped them catch four killers since. These people knew Gretchen. They had met her when she'd infiltrated the task force as a psychologist who had volunteered to work with them. They knew her murderous handiwork from scores of crime scenes. They had seen Archie consumed by her, nearly killed by her.

They listened in silence.

Henry chuckled when Gretchen brought up Susan's daddy issues. Archie saw Claire kick Henry under the table.

Then the recording ended.

No one said anything for a while. The only sound was Flannigan scratching his chin.

Archie cleared his throat. "What you don't hear on the recording is what Gretchen said after it was turned off. She told Susan that a man named Ryan Motley is behind the murders of Jake Kelly and Gabby Meester," Archie said. "Gretchen claims he was an associate of hers at one point, and she gave us these." He fanned out the stack of articles Susan had printed. "We know that lilies were left at the scene of at least three of these murders. Different varieties, but all Asiatic."

The others reached for the printouts, their heads down, scanning them.

After a few minutes, Flannigan looked up at Archie. He touched the brim of his cap. "How does this relate to James Beaton?" he asked.

The others looked up. Claire gave Archie a look as if to say, *See?*

"I have no idea," Archie said honestly. "Beaton went missing eighteen years ago. His wife thinks he ran off, and there's some evidence to support that. I have no idea if he was really murdered or, if so, that Gretchen did it. Don't focus on that. Focus on Ryan Motley. If these are all his victims, it gets us that much closer to catching him."

"But what's her game?" Levy asked. "Why confess to killing Beaton?"

"She wants him caught," Archie said. "The disappearance of James Beaton is connected to Ryan Motley somehow." He looked at Levy. "You're right," he said. "This is a game to her. She wants to make us work. But she's given us the pieces. We just have to put together the puzzle."

They didn't look convinced.

Henry took his feet off the table. "Listen," he said. "Archie can read her. If he says her information is solid, it is. Whoever killed these kids, killed our victims, or at least is trying to make it look like he did. We follow his lead. You don't have to understand it."

Archie slid over the laptop that had been playing the MP3, and brought up an image from Google Earth. He turned the laptop around to face the others. "This is the Hamlet Inn. These are train tracks. I think she cut Beaton up and carried him in pieces over here, and when the train went by, she tossed the body parts on as it went past." He looked at Ngyun. "Martin, I want you to track the lines that went past that day and see if there were any remains found in the cars or along the tracks. Those tracks run across the country, so the remains could have been discovered several states away and were never traced back."

"Okay," Ngyun said.

"We need to determine if these earlier murders were committed by our killer. Contact all the investigators who worked these cases, and review all the case files. Maybe we'll find a common suspect, or a name that keeps popping up as a witness. You don't kill this many people without making a mistake."

"On it," Levy said.

"Maybe," Flannigan said, "Gretchen knew about the lilies because she killed these kids."

Archie picked one of the printouts up off the table and slid it over to Flannigan. "The most recent one," he said. "Look at the date." A child had been murdered and left in a park in Illinois in

November, almost four years before. "She was busy carving me up," he said. He shook his head at the irony of it. "I'm her alibi." She had almost never left his side during the ten days he spent strapped to a gurney under her scalpel. She was certainly not gone long enough to get to Illinois and back. "Look," Archie said. "She's a liar. She's lying about some of this. But not everything. She didn't kill Kelly or Meester. I think she knows who did."

"She must have an angle," Flannigan said.

Archie looked at his hands. Of course there was an angle. Gretchen always had an angle. "She says that she didn't kill any of the children we've accused her of murdering," Archie said. "She says that she's never killed a child, and that Ryan Motley is behind all of those murders. That," he said, "is her angle."

Flannigan nodded. "Okay," he said.

"Okay," Archie said.

"I just wanted to know," Flannigan said. "So that I could be sure that you knew." He started stacking the printouts on the table. "I'll work with Levy on reviewing the case files."

Everyone but Archie and Henry started pushing their chairs out and packing up.

"No media on this," Archie told them. "Not until we know what we're dealing with."

Archie watched them all walk out. Except for Henry. Henry still sat at the table, his hands folded on his belly, his gaze leveled at Archie. His blue eyes were cloudy. The bristles on his shaved head were turning white. He had started to look like an old man.

Archie picked a dog hair off his pants and waited for Henry to ask.

"You went and saw her, didn't you?" Henry said.

Archie exhaled slowly. "Susan called me after the interview," he said. "I knew you wouldn't like it, so I lied to you about it. I went and saw Gretchen to tell her to stay away from Susan."

Henry's face reddened. He moved his jaw around and then pushed his chair out and stood up. He stalked back and forth for a few moments and then picked up the chair and slid it hard across the linoleum. It skidded and fell on its side. "Bullshit," Henry said.

Archie had seen Henry lose his temper only a few times. It had a way of drawing all the oxygen out of a room. Archie kept his eyes on the table. "I wanted to see her," he said. "I knew you'd stop me."

Henry leaned in close to Archie, his flushed face inches from Archie's nose. "Better," Henry said.

"She's in bad shape," Archie said. He'd meant it as an objective report, but he couldn't suppress a slight smile.

Henry saw it. He shook his head and pointed a finger in Archie's face. "I'm not doing this again," he said. "You and her." His eyes went to the ceiling in exasperation. "Your *thing*. I'm not doing it."

Archie didn't know what to say. He had lied. But he had lied about much worse, and Henry knew it. This was about something else.

"I can't take care of you right now," Henry said. "I have other responsibilities." He lowered his chin to indicate his leg. "I'm not at a hundred percent here."

Archie wanted to say the right thing. "Can I help?" he asked.

Henry chuckled. "You want to help me?" he asked. "Here's an insight. Every lie you've ever told me has something to do with Gretchen Lowell. Someday, when it matters, I want you to lie to her, and tell me the truth. Let's start there."

"Okay," Archie said.

Henry put his fists on the table and leaned on his knuckles. "Things are different now," Henry said. "I have a person. I have Claire."

"I know," Archie said.

"I would still jump in front of a bus for you," Henry said.

"I know," Archie said.

"A short bus," Henry said.

"Right."

Henry glanced behind him at the chair on the floor.

Archie hesitated. The black plastic chair lay on its side, metal legs in the air. Was this a test? "You want me to get that?" Archie asked.

"I can get my own fucking chair," Henry said. He didn't move. "But if it will make you feel better."

Archie got up and walked over and picked up the chair and carried it back to the table. Henry sat down with a groan, and started rubbing his leg. "You still have the Beauty Killer files at home?" Henry asked.

"Not everything," Archie said. "Just what I need."

Henry raised his eyebrows at him.

Archie didn't say anything.

"She killed those kids, Archie," Henry said.

Archie felt his stomach tighten. He couldn't believe he was going to say it out loud. "What if she didn't?"

I t was almost eight o'clock and Susan was on her fourth cigarette when Archie came out of the task force building. She had
been waiting an hour—rehearsing what she was going to say—when
he fled out the front door and, without even a glance at her, made a
beeline for his car.

"Hey!" she said, running after him in the parking lot. He stopped,
and she saw his shoulders slump, and then he turned around. "Susan,"
he said, making her name sound like a sigh.

The speech she'd been rehearsing went out the window. "You
played my recording for them," she said.

"You gave it to me," he said.

God, he was dense sometimes. "I gave it to *you*," Susan said.
"My *friend*. Not the Portland Police Department. You passed out
my printed copies. I didn't give those to you. I *showed* them to you.
There's a difference."

"I'll print you out more," Archie said.

"It's the principle," Susan said, exasperated. "I can't turn over
investigative material to the police. She called me as a journalist."

Archie didn't look all that impressed by her outraged reporter
act. He got his car keys out of his pocket. "She called you because
she couldn't get to me," he said. "She knew you'd give me the infor-

mation, and she knew I'd use it. She knew I would go down there. You performed your role."

Susan knew he was right, but she didn't like hearing it. She took a drag off her cigarette. "I'm writing the story," she said.

Archie shook his head. "Not Ryan Motley. You need to leave him out of it. Write about seeing her. Print every word on that tape. But do not mention Motley. You're dealing with the parents of murdered children here. We cannot make this public until we are certain. At this point he's a phantom. All we have is her say-so. And it's very likely polluted by some deranged agenda that you don't understand."

And you do? thought Susan.

Archie had said himself that Gretchen had given him the flash drive a year ago. He'd had 365 days to follow up on it. But it had been Susan who'd finally plugged the thing into a USB port. If it hadn't been for her, it would still be sitting in Archie's desk with his Wite-Out collection. And now she was being sidelined. Sometimes Susan felt like Archie didn't appreciate her at all. "Why did you wait so long to look at the flash drive?" she asked.

"We knew we couldn't trust the information," Archie said. "Henry and I agreed not to play her games."

Except that Archie had been champing at the bit to learn what was on that memory stick, once Susan had seen it. He'd known that Susan had taken the flash drive from his desk. But he hadn't been angry. He hadn't yelled at her once. "You wanted me to steal it," Susan said. "You'd promised Henry you wouldn't look at it. You were stuck. But if I opened it up, if I saw what was on the flash drive, then you could find out what was on it without breaking your promise. You left me in your office. You know I snoop. I told you over the phone that Gretchen had mentioned Ryan Motley. You knew I'd seen that flash drive, and you knew I'd take it. You set me up. You refused to play Gretchen's games. But you played me."

Archie lowered his gaze, like he was shamed or maybe just looking at his shoes or the pavement or a particularly interesting ant.

Then he lifted his head and looked right at her. "We're not friends, Susan," he said. "We don't hang out. I'm a cop. I'm not your friend."

Susan stammered. Her face burned. She took a drag of her cigarette while she tried to figure out what to say. She knew what he was doing. He was trying to push her away. He was being mean to her so she'd stalk off and leave him to wallow in whatever trap Gretchen had set for him.

Fat chance.

He wasn't telling her everything. He wasn't even telling her half of everything.

"You went and saw her, didn't you?" she said.

If she was looking for a reaction, she didn't get one. Archie didn't flinch, didn't move a muscle. When you looked at dead people and talked to psychopaths for a living, you probably got really good at masking your emotions. She watched as he gently took the cigarette from between her fingers, took a slow long drag off it, and then dropped it on the pavement and stepped on it. "You should quit," he said. "Before those kill you."

A rchie studied the picture of the dead boy.

His windows were open and a warm night air had settled in his apartment, along with a faint smell of flood-rotted foliage. Archie stretched and tried to find a more comfortable position on the floor. He settled on a slightly less uncomfortable one.

The dead boy was named Thomas, and the relevant details of his death could be stored in a cardboard file box.

Thomas had lived on Forest Street in Bellingham, Washington, a college town on Bellingham Bay, north of Seattle. It was a small, idyllic city, framed by conifer-thick hills with bald patches from decades of clear-cutting.

Archie remembered the case. He remembered all of the cases.

Thomas had set out for Forest & Cedar Park one day after school. It was a two-block walk along a street where people didn't lock their doors. That year alone the task force had attributed nineteen bodies to the Beauty Killer. But her killing ground had been south of there, and east: Seattle, Olympia, Spokane, Yakima. North of Seattle, that close to the Canadian border, the public had felt safer.

Archie unclipped the photograph from the file and gazed at it, trying to see what he had not seen the first thousand times he'd looked at it, some detail, some clue that said this wasn't the work of Gretchen.

Any physical evidence was locked up downtown. Gigabytes of data—digital photographs, reports, scanned documents—lay, password-protected, on a mainframe somewhere. But over the years, Archie had created a shadow filing system of his own—copies of originals. Gretchen had confessed to a few dozen of the hundreds of murders they suspected her of committing. Now, with her locked up, most of her presumed victims would lay in a cold-case purgatory, the cases open but half solved, forever attributed to the Beauty Killer.

In Archie's hand, in the photograph, Thomas lay dead, nestled among ferns and the velvet moss of a wooded area on the college campus, about four miles from his home. He had been posed, left on his back, arms at his sides, legs together, like a lost doll.

He was wearing the same clothes he'd been wearing when he'd left the house the afternoon before: blue jeans, a green T-shirt, sneakers.

From a distance, he could have been alive.

But the intimacy of the color photograph told another story: the telephone cord, double-knotted so tightly it cut through the flesh; the blood seeping through the chest of the green shirt; the pale lips, closed, sunken eyes; skin the color of boiled meat.

A student had found the body. The Bellingham PD had put in a call to the task force, and Archie had been in the air within an hour. It was a two-hour flight on a private plane provided by the father of another of Gretchen's victims. The local cops had been waiting for Archie as he'd departed the flight at the Bellingham airport. They had preserved the crime scene. Thirty minutes later, Archie was standing over the boy's body, his suitcase, a carry-on from a set of Debbie's, in the trunk of a squad car.

There had been no lily.

Only ants and decomp and, underneath the T-shirt, carved onto the center of the boy's undeveloped chest, a wound in the shape of a heart.

People in Bellingham locked their doors after that.

The media entered full-blown Beauty Killer hysteria. The task force had their funding doubled. The FBI sent another round of profilers. A murdered child was shocking. But no one put it past her. All of Gretchen's murders were different. She didn't have a profile or an MO. It was the key to her ability to terrorize. When serial killers only went after lanky teenage redheads, then everyone who wasn't a lanky teenage redhead didn't have to worry. But Gretchen went out of her way to kill from all segments of society, all ages, all races—she was an equal-opportunity serial killer.

She was also creative. She enjoyed her work. She looked for fresh ways to cause pain: needles, electrical cords, scalpels, poison, gardening tools, drain cleaner. Each victim's wounds were a new wicked topography. But she had also garroted her victims, suffocated them, strangled them, exsanguinated them, shot them, stabbed them, and poisoned them.

But while the MOs and victim profiles varied, Gretchen always left the same signature: a heart.

Always, a heart.

It was how she signed her work. And like any megalomaniacal artist, she always, always signed her work.

Archie extracted a copy of a second photograph from the boy's file and studied it. This one showed Thomas Vernon laid out on the brushed-steel surface of an autopsy table, the camera focused on his slight chest, the raw heart-shaped wound there. The picture would have been taken moments before the ME had cut into the boy's chest, starting at the top of each shoulder, meeting at the sternum, and extending through the rib cage, down through the abdominal wall. The top triangular flap of flesh would have then been pulled back over Thomas's face, and the ME would have used shears to tear through the chest cavity, and a bone saw to cut the boy's ribs.

Archie unbuttoned his shirt and felt for the heart-shaped scar on his own chest. He traced it with his fingertips, trying to feel if it looked the same as the wound on the boy.

He got up off the floor and went into the bathroom and he held the photo of the dead boy's chest next to his own reflection in the mirror.

"*There, darling,*" Gretchen had said after carving her signature into Archie, "*I've given you my heart.*"

Archie's hair was matted with sweat, his brow shiny. The scarring on his torso made his chest hair look scraggly and uneven. In the bright light of the bathroom he could see every nick and hash mark she'd left on him.

The hearts looked similar. The mark on Thomas had been cut with a scalpel, right-handed, the left side of the heart first, top to bottom, then the right.

It was all in the ME's report. It fit.

The heart on Archie had been cut the same way.

Archie scratched the back of his neck and looked at the photograph some more. Homicide investigation photos were shameless in their starkness. In death, there were no private moments. Bodies were picked over for trace evidence, undressed, cut open, the organs weighed and bagged. Photographs were taken at the crime scene, at the autopsy. The body became fragmented—a photograph of a chest wound, the weight of a liver, carpet fibers collected off clothing.

It was easier to see the pieces than to see the whole.

Archie looked up at his reflection. He thought for a minute.

Then he padded quickly back into his bedroom and sat back down on the floor and started sorting through Thomas Vernon's file. When he found the city map of Bellingham, he unfolded it and found the X he'd used to mark the spot where Thomas Vernon's body had been found. Then he looked for and found the other marks he had made on the map: the boy's house, the route to the park he had been heading to. Archie ran his finger from the park to the wooded area where the body had been dumped. Straight up. Thomas had disappeared on Forest Street. His body had been found the next morning on the grounds of Western Washington

University, several hundred feet in elevation up the hill from Forest Street.

He had been killed, and then carried higher.

Archie moved deftly through the boxes, sorting out the other folders of murdered children. He looked for maps, scanned notes.

His bedroom fan made the pages dance on the floor.

Every child had been left at an elevation higher than the place where he or she had disappeared. It was subtle sometimes. A child found on the second floor of an abandoned house; another vanished from a mall, then left on the fourth floor of the mall parking garage. The police had not noticed it. They had not been looking for common threads between the child victims. They had been focused on the victims as a whole, and Gretchen's victims had mainly been adults.

Archie started to bend down to pick up a photograph, then stopped. His skin prickled.

There was someone else in the room. Whether it was a sound that had given the person away, or a shadow in Archie's peripheral vision, Archie didn't know. He just went from being alone, to knowing that he was not.

Archie's hand went to his gun. It was a reflex, like lifting a hand to catch a sneeze. He had unsnapped the holster by the time he realized it was her. She was standing in his bedroom doorway, a cup of coffee in her hand, watching him. This time she was wearing the robe.

Rachel took a step back. "Easy," she said.

Archie took his hand off his gun. He tried to do it casually, and not like he had almost shot her. He took a long, careful breath, and ran his hand over his face. "What are you doing here?" he asked.

"It's five in the morning," she said. "I came up here to tell you to quiet the hell down. I keep hearing you up here walking around, dragging stuff across the floor. I knocked. You didn't hear me. Your front door was open."

Archie looked out the north window of his bedroom. The sky

was a soft pink. There were boxes all over his bedroom, files fanned out on every surface. He'd spent half the night hunched over paperwork, the other half asleep on the floor.

Rachel's eyes grazed the files. "I see you bring your work home with you," she said.

"You shouldn't sneak up on people who have guns," Archie said, still rattled.

"Your little project here has kept me awake half the night," Rachel said. Her eyes looked him up and down. "Did you sleep at all?"

"On and off," Archie said. He recognized that this wasn't normal. His room was a tornado of files, on the floor, on the bed. He sat down on the bed and started shuffling papers.

Rachel walked her cup of coffee over to him and put it in his hand. "You need this more than I do," she said. Her head moved around the room. "These are all Beauty Killer victims?"

Archie took a sip of the coffee. It was black and strong, and he kept his nose in it for a moment, letting the aroma clear his senses.

When he looked up, Rachel was sitting on the bed next to him. She had picked up a stack of evidence photos and was leafing through them. The robe was short and had slipped up, exposing almost all of her tan thighs. "I waited for you the other night," she said. "I thought you might come back."

Archie tried to concentrate on the coffee.

She peered at a photograph on her lap. "What's this?"

He took the photograph from her. It was a microscopic image of a light brown hair. He put the photo back in its proper folder and put the folder in the box.

"Dog hair," he said. They had found several dog hairs on Thomas Vernon's jeans. He didn't have a dog. It made them think he might have made it to the park before he'd been grabbed. They'd asked the public for help, thinking there might have been a potential witness, a dog owner who'd come in contact with the boy before he'd disappeared. No one came forward. But it could have been anything. Hair like that traveled. It came off the dog, was passed from person to person.

"What kind of dog?" Rachel asked.

"Welsh corgi," Archie said.

"They're cute," Rachel said.

Archie barely heard her. "Shit," he said.

A lot of people have corgis," Henry said.

It was a point he had made several times that morning on the drive to St. Helens. Archie wasn't hearing any of it. He knocked again on the door of the aquamarine-colored house. The peeling paint crumbled under his knuckles and fell as lead-tainted dust to the porch. "It's not a coincidence," Archie said.

Henry leaned in conspiratorially and said, "Do you think the Queen of England is involved?"

Archie ignored him, listening instead for some sound of movement from within. The Beatons had a corgi. Judging by the family photograph over the couch, they'd had corgis for years. Gretchen knew if she confessed to murdering James Beaton that Archie would look into it. She knew he'd connect the dots back to Thomas Vernon. She was leading him . . . somewhere. "Mrs. Beaton?" Archie called for the fourth time. "It's Detective Sheridan again. I just had a few more questions for you." He imagined her up from the recliner now, shuffling toward the door, her weight on her walker, the dog cutting back and forth in front of her legs. He willed her to move faster.

"You called first, right?" Henry said. A fly landed on his arm and he batted it away.

"She doesn't always pick up," Archie said.

"Maybe she's not home," Henry said.

Archie remembered the bubble-gum-pink tennis balls jammed on the walker's feet, their pristine condition. Those tennis balls had never touched a sidewalk. "I got the impression that she doesn't get out much," he said.

"Maybe she's napping," Henry said. "Maybe she's watching TV." Henry shifted his weight—Archie could tell his leg was starting to bother him. "Or maybe," Henry said, "she's tired of people digging up a bunch of shit that happened almost twenty years ago."

Archie knocked harder and then let the screen door snap shut and took a step back. Something was nagging at him. She should have answered the door by now. The gold Lincoln was still in the driveway. The grass in the yard was so dead he could smell it. "Something's wrong," he said.

He could hear the air-conditioning unit rasping from around the side of the house. A light breeze whispered through the trees. The wooden porch creaked under the weight of their feet. A dozen flies buzzed in circles in front of the door.

Archie said, "I don't hear the dog."

There was no barking. That dog had gone ballistic the moment Archie had stepped onto the porch during his first visit. Another fly tried to land on Henry. This time Henry slapped his arm and then flicked the wings and flattened fly carcass onto the porch.

Archie's right hand found the butt of his gun. With his left, he opened the screen door again, secured it with his foot, and tried the doorknob. The house was unlocked. He glanced at Henry.

"You're back to the corgi again?" Henry said. "Really?"

"Watch the flies," Archie said. He kept his hand on his gun. The flies continued to swarm around the porch. Archie turned the knob and pushed the door open a crack.

"What the hell?" Henry said.

"Wait for it," Archie said.

Nothing happened.

Then, one by one, the flies flew inside the house.

Henry raised his eyebrows at Archie. "Mrs. Beaton?" Henry called through the crack of the door. "It's the police. Everything all right in there?"

Refrigerated air from inside the house seeped outside into the heat.

"Mrs. Beaton?" Archie called. "It's Detective Sheridan." He looked over at Henry. "I'm here with Detective Sobol. We're going to come on in and check on you, okay?"

Archie opened the door and stepped inside. Henry followed him. There was no discussion. They would figure out probable cause later.

Now Archie blinked, trying to adjust to the dim indoor light and thirty-degree drop in temperature. It hadn't been this cold the first time Archie had been in the Beaton house. Goose bumps rose on his forearms. He reached for the wall and turned on a light switch. The change in illumination barely registered.

His eyes ached as he strained to focus.

The chair in the living room was empty. Mrs. Beaton's walker stood alone on the other side of the end table, out of reach from any sitting place.

Inside the house, the drone of the A/C unit was fainter than outside. Archie listened. And then there it was: the sound of flies. As his vision finally adjusted, he could see them—a cloud of black spots where the flies had regathered in the Beaton living room.

The flies hovered briefly there, and then, as if from some collective decision-making process, they hung a left and disappeared down the hall toward the back of the house.

The pit of Archie's stomach twisted.

"Mrs. Beaton?" he called again. Archie checked in on Henry. Henry's face was grim, his gun out. Sweat stains already darkened his charcoal T-shirt where his shoulder holster crossed at his upper back. He wasn't limping now; too much adrenaline.

Archie squinted through the living room down the hall. The

hall had a door on either side of it, and ended at a linen cabinet. One of the doors was ajar and Archie could see, behind it, part of a bathroom vanity and medicine chest.

The flies were in front of the second door.

The bedroom.

"Police," Archie called out. "Anyone there?"

He saw Henry switch the safety off on his weapon.

The most dangerous places in a building were called "fatal funnels." Doorways, narrow hallways, windows—any place that limited your ability to move or take cover.

They could call it in and wait for backup. Archie imagined how that call would go. Probable cause? "Flies," Archie would say. "And it's too quiet."

No.

He and Henry crept forward, into the fatal funnel, hugging opposite walls. When they reached the bathroom, Archie gave the door a push and then stepped back. The door creaked, bounced off a doorstop, and then settled open. He heard the flop of a towel slipping off a towel rack onto the floor. They waited a moment. Archie listened to his pulse throb.

Then, weapons raised, he and Henry edged in front of the open door.

The bathroom was small: a toilet, vanity sink, and shower. Metal handrails had been installed next to the toilet and in the shower. Someone had covered up old wallpaper with a coat of cheery yellow paint, but the paper had started to blister where water had leaked through the ceiling. The back of the toilet and the vanity counter were crammed with dozens of jewel-colored glass perfume bottles and makeup containers. A dark green towel lay in a heap on the linoleum.

They stepped across the hall and stood near the doorknob of the other door. Archie watched as Henry soft-checked it. The door was unlocked. The flies flitted around Archie's head.

Archie gave Henry a go-ahead nod, and Henry pounded on the

door. Focused like that, his muscles tensed, face flushed with adrenaline, Henry looked like his old self.

"Mrs. Beaton?" Archie called again. "This is the police. We're coming in."

If she was in there taking a nap, she was in for a surprise.

Archie readied his weapon as Henry turned the doorknob and gave the door a hard push. The door swung open, banged against the interior wall, and then came to a stop.

The walls were stacked with framed photographs, prints of stately landscapes, paint-by-numbers mountains, and needlepoint portraits of stoic-looking corgis. Clothing littered the carpet. The bedside tables were stacked with greasy water glasses, paperbacks, magazines, and empty tissue boxes. Two twin beds sat side by side. One was crisply made, its surface the most immaculate thing in the room— the other, abuzz with berserk, happy flies, held the bloody, butchered remains of Mrs. James Beaton.

All except for her nose, which, as far as Archie could tell, was the small chunk of flesh on the carpet in the middle of the room next to a blood-matted platinum wig.

40

A rchie turned his head away from the flash of the digital camera. The Columbia County ME had sent out two crime scene investigators, who were busily documenting the surroundings. Archie watched them work.

The flies were multiplying.

St. Helens averaged about one homicide every ten years, which meant that statistically the Beatons had met nearly a quarter century's worth of the town's quota. A murder was big news, and everyone wanted in on it. The entire St. Helens PD—all nineteen officers, plus five volunteers—had shown up, and every time one of them came in or out of the house more flies would find their way inside. The house had been full of cops, poking around with latex gloves and putting evidence markers next to each other's footprints. It hadn't taken Chief Huffington long to throw everyone who wasn't essential out of the house. Now most of her force was standing in the yard getting sunburned necks while the local press took their pictures.

Archie stayed in the bedroom. It wasn't his case, but old habits died hard. Huffington didn't ask him to leave. She stayed in the bedroom, too. He wasn't sure if she was keeping an eye on the crime scene techs or if she was keeping an eye on him.

The flash went off again.

Huffington rocked back and forth on her heels. If the smell of decomp was bothering her, she wasn't showing it. "Funny that you show up asking questions about her husband and she ends up dead the next day," she said to Archie.

A fly wandered through Archie's peripheral vision.

"Yeah," Archie said.

Huffington got a hair band out of her uniform pants pocket and put her hair in a ponytail with a few quick movements of her hands. She adjusted her St. Helens PD cap. Then she went back into her pocket for a penlight, pulled it out, and aimed it on what was left of Dusty Beaton's hands. "No defensive wounds," she said to Archie. Her mouth was tight. She moved the point of light to the dead woman's abdomen, where seashell-pink entrails spilled from a jagged fist-sized wound. "Last big crime we had around here," she said, "was when Troy Schmiedeknecht drove his dad's F-150 into the bookstore down on Columbia."

Archie glanced over at her. Huffington's expression looked tense, but not particularly distressed. Archie had seen dozens of cops lose their lunch at crime scenes like this. Huffington hadn't blanched. Her mouth was set, her gaze focused. Archie knew the expression. It was the mask that people in authority put on when they needed to be in control. Archie had a mask just like it.

Huffington continued her penlight tour of the corpse: the bloody cave in the middle of Dusty Beaton's face where her nose had been gouged out, her shoulders and hips, where her arms and legs had been partially severed, revealing ball joints and bone. The bed was soaked with blood. Projectile blood spatter dotted the walls.

"This kind of intensity," Huffington said. "It's personal."

"Yep," Archie said.

"Give me a hand," she said. She put the penlight away and took a tape measure out of her pocket and gave it to Archie. Then she took hold of the end of the flexible metal strip and walked it across the length of the room, sidestepping Dusty Beaton's nose. She checked the measurement and recorded it in her notebook, and then she and Archie repeated the process across the width of the room.

When she was done she let go of the measuring tape and it retracted back into Archie's hand with a metallic snap.

Huffington said, "Tell me about this thing with Gretchen Lowell."

The camera flashed again as the crime techs took another shot. Huffington waited. With her brown hair back, her face looked especially broad. There was something about the roundness of her cheek and her sturdy physique that gave her a certain owlish quality. Archie got the feeling that she picked up a lot by watching and keeping quiet.

"I never said there was a thing with Gretchen Lowell," Archie said.

"Why else would you come out here, poking around a cold case?" Huffington continued. "Either that or you think Dusty was connected to those two murders in Portland, and I'm not seeing how she managed to kidnap and kill those people, what with her walker and all."

She extended her hand and Archie tossed her the tape measure. She caught it easily.

"Recently, Gretchen Lowell gave a very detailed account of James Beaton's murder," Archie said. "She said she tied him to a bed, disemboweled him, lopped off his nose, and then severed his arms and legs before disposing of the body."

Huffington's expression didn't change. "Gretchen Lowell is locked up," she said.

"Yes, she is."

One of the crime scene techs squatted down and nudged Dusty Beaton's nose into a plastic evidence bag. He shook the bag and a fly flew out before he sealed it.

"So if she killed James Beaton, who did this?" Huffington asked.

Archie catalogued the possibilities in his head. Maybe Gretchen had had help when she'd killed James Beaton. She'd used men before, men she'd called her "apprentices." She was an expert at manipulating a certain kind of man into doing what she wanted. Or she had killed Beaton alone, and had later told someone how she'd done it, and that person had killed Beaton's widow. Or she had arranged the killing from the State Hospital, instructing it to be done in the same manner in which she'd killed James Beaton, or at least had said she had. She could have been lying about killing him, and had somehow arranged this murder to back up her story. But then there was the dog hair. The path to the truth was somehow wrapped up in that family, that house. If Archie was going to figure any of this out, he was going to have to unravel what had happened eighteen years ago.

"Where are her daughters now?" he asked Huffington.

"She only had one daughter," Huffington said.

But that wasn't right. The photograph above the couch showed the Beatons with two dogs and two teenage girls. "The file said she had two kids," Archie said.

"Two kids," Huffington said. "One girl, one boy."

There hadn't been any photographs of a boy.

Archie hurried out of the bedroom.

"What?" Huffington said, following him.

Archie jostled past three St. Helens cops in the hallway and raced for the living room. Henry was on his cell phone on the couch, his bad leg up on the coffee table. Archie headed straight for him. Henry glanced up and saw him, and said, "Huh?"

The photographs were still there, in their cheap frames, arranged at seemingly random heights and intervals. But as Archie got close, he realized that something was different.

He took one of the photographs off the wall and examined it. It was not the same picture he'd seen yesterday of the Beatons with two teenage girls.

From the distance, it had looked the same. It was hung in the same spot. It was from the same era, roughly twenty years ago. It was the same composition. Mr. and Mrs. Beaton stood in front of the house. They were wearing the same clothes. She had on the same yellow dress. He was wearing a suit. The dogs sat at their feet. Two teenagers stood side by side between the adults. But in this photograph, one of the teenagers was a boy. He was wearing belted tan slacks and a short-sleeved white button-down shirt, tucked in. A flop of brown hair hung in his eyes. He was as skinny as the girl, the same height; they had the same sharp elbows and sloped shoulders. They were all looking at the camera. Dusty Beaton was the only one who was smiling.

Archie blinked, confused. He said, "This isn't the picture that was here yesterday."

No one answered. Archie looked up. Everyone in the room was eyeing him with a sort of benign mistrust. Archie recognized the expression from when he'd first come back from medical leave. It said, *We think you might be a little bit crazy.*

Huffington was at his shoulder. She took the photograph and looked at it. Archie pointed at the picture. "This isn't the picture that was here yesterday," he said again. He looked at Henry for support.

Henry scratched his neck. "Are you sure?" he said from the couch.

"Yes, I'm sure," Archie said, trying to sound sure, trying to sound not a little bit crazy. "There was another picture," he said to Huffington. "It was similar, from the same series. But the Beatons were standing with two teenage *girls*. The boy wasn't in it."

Huffington frowned. "So you're saying there was another picture that looked exactly like this picture but with a girl instead of a boy."

"Yes."

"You saw this other photograph for how long?" Huffington asked.

Archie knew where she was headed. "I glanced at it," he said. "I gave it a long, hard glance."

She nodded slowly, still frowning. "Could it be that you just thought you saw two girls?"

Archie looked down at Henry. Henry shrugged.

This wasn't going the way it was supposed to. "It's a different picture," Archie said.

Huffington ran a finger along the top of the frame. Then she leaned over Henry and peered at the top of the other pictures. "It's dusty," she said. "Like the other ones."

"It's not a new *frame*," Archie said. "It's a new *picture*."

"Maybe she changed it," Huffington theorized. "After you left." She was humoring him, and they both knew it.

"I need to talk to the son and daughter," Archie said.

"They both left town after high school," Huffington said. "Melissa Beaton moved to California, I think. Died of cancer about ten years ago. Colin Beaton came and went for a while. But he hasn't been in town for a few years. I think he lives in Nebraska. We'll try to track him down. Tell him what's happened. I'll let you know when we locate him."

She seemed to know a lot about the Beatons. Archie wondered where all this information was when he'd visited her at her office.

"There are ten thousand people in this town," Huffington said, before he could ask. "We know each other. And when cops come poking around in our business, I make an effort to ask around and get up to speed."

Archie wasn't sure how far he could push it with Huffington, but he decided to try. "I want all the photographs from this house," Archie said. "And any old letters or diaries."

The corners of Huffington's mouth tightened. "It's not your investigation, Detective."

Archie hoped he didn't look as desperate as he felt. "Please," he said. "I will turn over anything that seems related to the investigation. I need to find out more about the girl I saw in the photograph."

She looked at him for a long moment. There was the mask again.

Someone sneezed.

One of the three cops said, "Sorry. Allergies. It's the dog hair."

The dog.

Huffington's shoulders dropped. "Shit," she said, looking around. They had all forgotten about the dog.

"It must have gotten out when the killer came in or left," Archie said.

Huffington raised her voice. "We need to fan out and find the dog," she said. "You three," she said, pointing to the three officers, "you're not doing anything. Search the neighborhood."

She took a few steps away from Archie and then turned back. "You find anything in those pictures, you tell me," she said.

"Absolutely," Archie said.

"This is a small town," she said. "Full of nosy neighbors. So far, no one my guys have talked to says they saw anything, but someone will. We notice stuff that doesn't belong. Strange cars. Strange people."

"It's a man," Archie said. "If it's connected to Gretchen Lowell, you're looking for a man."

She handed the framed picture back to Archie. "I'm reopening the James Beaton case," she said. "I'll be needing any information you have on that."

Archie hesitated. "My task force is already on it," he said with a nod in Henry's direction.

Huffington smiled curtly at both of them. "Then you won't mind the help."

It was her jurisdiction. And she knew the town. It was possible she'd see something that they didn't. "Okay," Archie said.

Huffington said, "I'll be in touch."

She went back into the bedroom and Archie sank down on the couch next to Henry, immediately creating a dust storm of corgi hair. Archie could hear the three cops calling for the dog outside. More flies had gotten in when they'd gone out. The flies floated in the living room, trying to orient themselves to the source of the smell of rotting flesh. Archie looked down at the photograph he held in his lap. "I need to see her again," he said.

Henry sighed. But he didn't look surprised. "I'm coming with you this time," he said.

Archie didn't protest. Henry hadn't seen Gretchen since the hearing. He was in for a pleasant surprise.

The Beaton family stared up from the strange family portrait. Three people in that photograph were already dead. Archie handled it gently, careful not to destroy any salvageable prints.

Henry hunched forward and gave the picture a long look. "You think the girl in the photograph you saw was Gretchen," he said quietly.

Archie nodded. He could barely breathe. He had never been this close to her, to who she really was. The first record of Gretchen Lowell had been a bad-check-writing bust when she was nineteen. Before that, nothing. No birth certificate. They had no idea where she'd come from, who her family was, or even how old she really was. He didn't even know if Gretchen was her real name.

"So where is she?" asked Henry.

Archie's finger hovered above an image at the bottom of the photograph, a dark shape on the grass—the shadow of a teenage girl holding a camera to her face. He said, "She's the one taking the picture."

CHAPTER

41

Bliss offered the bong to Susan. "Do you want a hit off this?" she asked. "It's Northern Lights."

The bong was hand-blown glass. One of Bliss's boyfriends had made it several years before. He called himself a "functional glass" artist, but everyone knew what he meant.

"I'm working, Mom," Susan said.

Bliss held a lighter to the bowl and took a long drag, and Susan heard the familiar babbling-brook gurgle of bong water. When Bliss finally exhaled, the sweet-smelling smoke drifted up and joined the marijuana smog that hung over the living room. "You shouldn't have that on your lap," Bliss said. "It'll give you cancer."

Susan looked down at her laptop. She was sitting cross-legged on the sofa, the laptop balanced on her bare thighs. "It's a laptop," she said. "They wouldn't call it that if it wasn't supposed to go on your lap."

"It's not called a laptop," Bliss said. "It's called a notebook. They're careful not to call it a lap *top*, so you can't sue them when you get lap *cancer.*"

The sun had set and it was finally cool enough to open the curtains, pry open the windows that weren't painted shut, and revel in the feeble current of fresh evening air that moved through the house. Bliss had lit candles, but the fan kept blowing them out.

Susan took her computer off her lap and set it beside her on the sofa. She'd never heard of lap cancer, but why risk it?

Bliss stood up and stretched. She was wearing a teal and red Jazzercise bodysuit that she liked to wear the nights she taught yoga at the Arlington Club. It was a one-piece unitard; sleeveless, with a teal-and-white-striped top, a red band around the middle where a belt would be, and teal leggings with stirrups. Bliss wasn't wearing a bra, or probably any underwear at all. Susan's mother hadn't worn a bra since the night Ronald Reagan was elected. Some sort of personal protest. Susan was pretty sure that Bliss wore the unitard to scandalize the society ladies at the Arlington, but it was hard to tell with Bliss; she might think of it as dressing up.

Susan was wearing her Pixies T-shirt and underpants. It was too stuffy for pants. Though pants probably provided at least some protection from lap cancer.

Her mother took another hit off the bong, and used the lighter to relight a candle.

Susan squinted at her computer screen.

The editor at *The New York Times Magazine* had given her two days to get him copy. She had transcribed the interview with Gretchen and pasted the quotes she wanted to use into her document. She wondered which quotes they would make her cut. She guessed the *Times*' style guide might have a thing or two to say about Gretchen's gift for graphic detail. Grossing out readers first thing in the morning couldn't be good for business. But then again, they put starving babies on the front page all the time. . . .

"I'm thinking of taking a masonry class," Bliss said, bending her left leg, opening her hips, and resting her left foot on the inside of her right thigh, and then balancing in "tree" pose. "I'd like to build a rock wall. I've always been interested in rocks." She put her hands in prayer position in front of her chest and then slowly raised them above her head until her arms were straight. "Do you remember when we used to go tubing on the White Salmon River and I'd pick up river rocks? I knew a man who had a rock collection. He spent summers on the East Coast as a kid, and he would go to this particular beach he loved, his secret beach, and he always came back with a rock. He was in his sixties when I knew him, and he had a whole shelf full of these rocks. He'd stopped traveling years before and he hadn't been back to that beach since he was a kid, but he'd held on to these rocks. One day an acquaintance of his came over and saw the rocks and she said that she had a similar collection. It turned out that she had spent summers as a kid on the East Coast, too, in the same town that he had. She had gone to the exact same beach, his secret beach, and she had brought back her own rocks."

"You're high," Susan said.

Bliss reached down and grabbed her left big toe, and then leaned forward and lifted her left foot up behind her above her head. She held it here.

Susan had done what Archie had wanted. She had left Ryan Motley out of the story. If Archie brought it up, she would tell him she'd done it for him, but the truth was that she hadn't made a copy of the flash drive before she'd had to unexpectedly return it.

She wondered if it hadn't been an accident that he'd taken all her printouts. Maybe he'd known exactly what he was doing. Now, without the flash drive or the printouts, she had nothing.

Her phone rang. It was sitting next to her laptop on the couch and Bliss glanced at it, her foot still behind her head.

"It's Leo," Bliss said.

Susan had recognized the ringtone. "I'll call him back," she said.

Who had closets in their bathrooms anyway? Rich people, that's who. What did she expect? She had known what she was getting into. Archie had warned her outright. Told her what Leo's father did for a living. Maybe Leo had a perfectly reasonable explanation for why he had a brick of cocaine the size of a toaster oven in his gym bag.

She listened for the tone that would alert her to a voice mail. But Leo didn't leave one.

Archie was probably working.

She wondered if he'd even call her if he found something. In the old days, when she'd worked at the *Herald*, she'd know right away when news broke.

Now she had to make an effort.

She opened the KGW local news page on her laptop. Star anchor Charlene Wood smiled from the banner at the top of the page. Charlene's arms were crossed jauntily, and she was winking, as if to say, *I'm a serious journalist, but still a lot of fun in the sack.*

SECOND MURDER! screamed the headline. PORTLAND LANDMARK DAMAGED! SERIAL KILLER AFOOT? KGW IS THERE AT 11!

That was the thing with local news: too many exclamation points. Susan thought that exclamation points should only be used ironically. Or when someone was actually screaming.

If Susan hadn't glanced at the sidebar of stories, she would have missed it altogether: WOMAN MURDERED IN HOME IN ST. HELENS. She clicked on the link and read the story. Dusty Beaton had been found dead. Her death was attributed to "homicidal violence." Her body had been discovered that morning by two Portland detectives. The story was four paragraphs. There was no mention that her husband had disappeared eighteen years earlier. "Homicidal violence" wasn't as sexy as "burned to a crisp on the Portland, Oregon, sign."

Susan looked at the time on her screen. It was minutes before eleven. "Can we watch the news?" she asked her mother.

"Kill your television," Bliss said loudly. "The medium is the message. Television is chewing gum for the eyes."

Sometimes Bliss talked like that; in bumper stickers.

"Please, Mom," Susan said.

Bliss rolled her eyes, sighed deeply, and waved her hand in a sort of grand acquiescence, like she'd just allowed her sons to go off to war.

"I'll get it," Susan said.

She got up and went into the kitchen, opened the cabinet under the sink, and pulled out the nine-inch black-and-white TV that Bliss kept behind the Dr. Bronner's all-purpose peppermint liquid soap and the unbleached paper towels. Bliss only had the TV for emergencies: congressional hearings, or special episodes of *Masterpiece Theater*. Susan heaved it to the living room, plugged it in, turned it on, and switched the dial to channel eight. But no matter where she directed the antennae, she wasn't getting any reception.

Once when Susan was a kid she'd twisted a whole roll of aluminum foil into an elaborate system of antennae that had allowed her to watch an episode of Scooby-Doo.

She smacked the side of the TV. "This isn't working," she said.

"That's because there's no more free TV," Bliss said. She had changed legs when Susan was getting the TV, and was now standing with her right leg wrestled up behind her. "They offered me a free digital converter box, but I said I didn't want it."

Susan had forgotten about this. Had it really been that long since she'd tried to watch TV at Bliss's house? The transition to digital TV had meant that Bliss's analog TV was useless without a converter. "Why didn't you take the free converter?" Susan asked.

"On principle," Bliss said.

"Why do you still have the TV if you can't watch it?" Susan asked.

Bliss sighed and wrenched her foot up over her head another inch. "For emergencies."

"What are you going to do, throw it at someone?"

Bliss raised an eyebrow. "I may throw it at you in a minute," she said.

Susan let out a frustrated groan and flopped back down on the couch. "If you had faster Wi-Fi I could stream it," she said.

"If I had faster Wi-Fi, we'd both have brain tumors."

Susan clicked on the live video button on the KGW home page. It started buffering.

"What's so important?" Bliss asked.

"I want to check on something."

"What?"

"The wife of someone I'm writing about was murdered this morning," Susan said. "Plus, there's that guy they found in the park. And that woman who was torched on the rooftop downtown. Do you keep up on the news at all?"

"I don't want to think about that kind of stuff," Bliss said. "It attracts negative energy."

"Here." Charlene Wood's image stuttered on screen. She was standing in the studio in front of a photographic background of the city. "Gabrielle Meester. Murdered." An image of a dark-haired smiling woman appeared in a graphic on the side of the screen. There were no leads. They were asking for people with information to come forward.

Susan heard an intake of breath and turned to see her mother lose her balance. Bliss toppled onto the couch, and immediately sat up and pointed at the screen. "I know her," she said.

"That's Charlene Wood," Susan said. "There's a poster of her on all the bus shelters in town."

"Not her," Bliss said. She pointed at the image of Gabrielle Meester. "*Her.*"

"What do you mean, you know her?" Susan asked.

"She looks familiar," Bliss said.

"She looks familiar?" Susan asked. "Or you *know her*?"

"I've seen her before," Bliss said.

"From the salon, or a yoga class?"

Bliss pulled her legs into lotus position. Then she picked up the bong and took another hit. The bong water gurgled.

Susan waited.

Bliss exhaled an impressive lungful of smoke. "No," she said. "Somewhere else."

The video on the Web site was buffering. "I hate this Web site," Susan grumbled.

"Why don't you go to the *Herald* site?" Bliss asked.

Because they'd fired her. "On principle," Susan said.

Bliss stood up and stretched again. "I'm going to meditate," she said.

That was code for going to bed.

"Don't let the bedbugs bite," Susan said.

Bliss patted Susan's head. "He'll come around," she said. She took a few steps, returned for the bong, and left again.

He'll come around.

Susan realized that she didn't know which man in her life her mom meant—Leo, or Archie?

She closed the Web site and searched for information on Mrs. Beaton's murder online. Nothing useful came up. Archie wasn't picking up his phone. So Susan focused on the story, rereading what she had so far and then editing the first few paragraphs. She'd work in Mrs. Beaton's murder at the end—it would make a great close. Susan had to admit this story just got better. It was a special pleasure to describe Gretchen's physical deterioration. They'd run a photo of Gretchen that was as glamorous as ever, of course. It was her beauty that drew people. If she hadn't been such a centerfold, she wouldn't have become a media icon in the first place. Ugly people killed people all the time. But when pretty people did, it got attention.

The goat was baying at the back door. Bliss let the thing roam free back there. It had already eaten the better part of a hundred-year-old rosebush, and a pair of faux-crocodile-skin clogs that Susan had outside the back door.

Now she stamped her hooves on the back stoop.

She wanted something.

What did goats want?

Grapes?

Hay?

Antidepressants?

The goat stamped again.

"Okay," Susan called. "I'm coming." She got up and made her way through the kitchen to the back door. The door was open to let the air in, and the wooden screen door knocked gently in the breeze.

She didn't see the goat.

Maybe she'd heard the door.

"Goat?" she called.

She turned on the back porch light, and a circle of the yard was illuminated, but it just made the area outside the circle look even darker.

Susan peered at the goat's house in the far corner of the yard.

She took a few tentative steps, down the back porch stairs, into the lawn. The dry grass was brittle under her bare feet. She stepped gingerly, feeling for goat turds. The thirty-foot bamboo privacy hedge that ringed the backyard created a dark wall against the star-filled sky.

She cleared the compost pile and the fire pit, and when she got to the goat house, she looked inside, and she saw blackness.

"Goat?" she called.

A rustle made the hair on her arms stand up.

Something came forward, out of the dark.

A flash of two glowing eyes. And then a white muzzle.

Susan gave a sigh of relief as the goat pranced forward, baying. She gave the goat's head a rub. It nuzzled up against her.

The goat was lonely. That's all. It was the case of the lonely goat, and Susan had solved it.

She petted the goat for a few more minutes and then retraced her steps back inside. It was almost chilly being outside with bare legs.

When she stepped back into the house and closed the screen door behind her, this time she locked it.

"Back so soon?" Gretchen asked.

She was out of bed; sitting up, strapped into a wheelchair, her wrists and ankles bound with leather restraints. A larger leather strap circled her chest just under her breasts, harnessing her to the back of the chair. Her breasts pressed against the gray fabric of her institutional pajamas. Sweat beaded on her neck and darkened the neckline of the shirt. Her knees fell apart. The gray pajama pants were too long, and spilled several inches past the leather ankle straps, making her bare feet look especially small.

It was easier seeing Gretchen at night. The hospital was quieter. There were fewer questions. Archie wondered if she had been roused out of bed and put in the chair when he'd told the staff he was coming, or if she had been left upright like that for the night.

"I brought a friend," Archie said.

Gretchen was sitting in profile and when she turned her head Archie could hear Henry's breathing change at the sight of her bloated face.

"Oh, good," she said flatly. "Henry."

"Hello, Gretchen," Henry said. His delight at her physical condition was palpable. He walked right up to her, a bounce in his step, and looked her up and down like she was a used car he was going to pass on purchasing. A huge grin spread across his face. "You're looking well," he said.

He was enjoying this way too much.

Gretchen glared at Henry.

Henry was beaming. He clutched his hands in front of his chest. "Isn't Gretchen looking well this evening?" he asked Archie. "Isn't she beautiful?"

"Was this necessary?" Gretchen asked Archie.

Archie stood inside the closed door to Gretchen's room. He watched them for a moment. Henry, practically doubled over with glee, pink-faced and bright-eyed; Gretchen, seething in her chair. Henry needed that moment. He needed to see Gretchen suffering, robbed of her loveliness and power. Gretchen had taken something important from Henry. She had taken Archie, his best friend, his partner. And there was a part of Henry that could never forgive either of them for that. So he needed this moment. And Archie let him have it.

Henry laughed at her, and Archie let him. And after a while, Henry straightened up and wiped the tears from his eyes. He looked down at Gretchen and he kicked the wheel of her chair. "We need to talk, hot stuff," he said.

She tried to look over at Archie.

"Me," Henry said, leaning over her and gripping the sides of her chair. His voice was humorless now. "Not him. You and I need to have a talk."

"I don't find you very interesting to talk to," Gretchen said.

"James Beaton's widow was murdered yesterday," Archie said from the door. Cut to the chase. Henry and Gretchen would go around and around like a couple of territorial dogs all day.

Gretchen nodded. Dusty Beaton's murder had been on the news, but Archie could tell that this was the first Gretchen had heard of it. There was no verbal comeback. She was off her game.

Even Henry could tell. "Does the pretty girl want her boyfriend to come sit next to her?" Henry asked.

Gretchen didn't move. "The pretty girl won't say fuck without him," she said.

"This is how it's going to work," Henry said, rotating the wheelchair around to face the chair by the bed. "You and I are going to have a talk, and if you're good, I'll let Archie come sit on the bed." Henry folded his large frame in the plastic chair opposite Gretchen, and then he looked at Archie and patted the mattress. Archie walked over and took a seat on the edge of Gretchen's bed, so that the three of them were sitting practically knee to knee.

"I start electroshock therapy this evening," Gretchen said. She raised a skeptical eyebrow in Archie's direction. "The new doctor you arranged to lead my team feels it's in my best interest."

"Hey, it's like the electric chair," Henry said, slapping his knee with a grin, "but in small doses."

Archie looked away, at the white wall behind Gretchen's head. Even across the room, Archie could make out the graffiti that had been carved into the wall and then layered with paint over the years. *Kill me. They're listening.*

Let Henry do the talking. That was the agreement.

"I have an alibi," Gretchen said. "I was here when Mrs. Beaton was murdered."

"See, the thing is," Henry said, "the Widow Beaton was gutted and mutilated. Seems someone dug her nose out of her face and left it on the carpet."

Archie looked at Gretchen.

She smiled at him. "That sounds familiar," she said.

Henry leaned between them. "Who killed her?" he asked.

Gretchen settled back in her chair. Her reactions were a half beat off, like someone who'd had three cocktails too many. "It wouldn't be my place to speculate," she said. She licked a flake of dried saliva from the corner of her mouth. "That's your job."

Henry hunched farther forward in his chair, his back muscles tightening under his shirt. "Just give it a go," he said.

A lock of blond hair fell in front of one of Gretchen's blue eyes.

She looked at Archie with the other one. "If I were to hazard a guess," she said in a mock whisper, "I would presume that it was Ryan Motley."

Henry's upper lip tightened. He glanced over at Archie. Archie gave him a look that said, *If you strangle her, she wins.*

Henry exhaled slowly, working his jaw. Then he fixed his gaze back on Gretchen. "You want us to believe that he's been out there killing all this time and we've never noticed?" he said. "What is he, invisible?" Henry clawed his hands in the air. "Does he sneak into children's bedrooms at night?"

"No," Gretchen said coolly. "That's the tooth fairy."

Henry's big hands tightened into fists. He was close to her, closer than Archie dared. The veins pressed against the skin of his forehead. She was Henry's weakness as much as she was Archie's. Henry could always control his emotions, except when it came to her. Archie wondered sometimes what bothered Henry most—the fact that Gretchen had nearly killed Archie, or the fact that they'd had an affair. "You're making shit up," Henry said.

Gretchen didn't flinch, didn't blink. Her beauty may have been marred, but when she comported herself, she looked as regal as a queen. Henry didn't like that. Archie could see it in his face. He wanted her defeated.

"There are a lot of people out there killing other people," she said. "There are serial killers you don't know about, and that you will never catch. They will die natural deaths surrounded by their grandchildren, and no one will ever know what ghoulish trophies grandpa kept in the jars hidden under the shed."

"Why would Ryan Motley want Dusty Beaton dead?" Henry asked.

Gretchen turned to Archie. "Because you were getting close, darling," she said.

"Talk to me," Henry said, tapping his chest. "I'm the one asking the questions."

Archie couldn't help it. "Close to what?" he asked.

Gretchen batted her crusty eyelashes at him. "Are you ready to talk to me now?"

Henry got up, stepped in front of Archie, put his hands around Gretchen's forearms, and pushed her chair back a few feet.

Archie was now staring at Henry's back.

"It's not like the others, princess," Henry said. "He didn't leave a flower. He didn't move the body up."

"He's copying me," Gretchen said. "He copies me sometimes."

Archie could see the stubble on the back of Henry's shaved head, and, if he craned his neck, he could see Gretchen around Henry's shoulder. Her hair covered half her face now. A piece was stuck to the crust at the corner of her mouth. Behind her, on the white wall, Archie could see more scratched messages. *She's trying to kill me.*

"Like with all the kids you're accused of killing," Henry said. "Like how he's the real child killer and you're falsely accused."

"Yes," Gretchen said. She shrugged. "I mean, I killed all the others. I just feel it uncharitable to take credit for actions not my own."

"I see," Henry said. "So he copies you sometimes, and sometimes he kills kids his own sicko way, with the torture and the lilies, and then sometimes he kills grown-ups with the torture and the lilies." He craned his head back toward Archie. "This guy, he likes to change it up."

"He was always a self-starter," Gretchen said.

"You've known him awhile," Archie said.

Gretchen craned around Henry and looked Archie in the eye. "Longer than I've known you," she said.

Henry leaned to the side, blocking Gretchen's view. "When was the last time you saw him?" he asked her. He leaned his weight on his good leg. He did that late in the day, when his leg bothered him more. Archie hoped that Gretchen wouldn't see it.

"Just a few days ago," Gretchen said.

"Now, see there, angel face, you're fucking with me," Henry said. "That makes it very hard for me to take you seriously."

"I heard you almost died," Gretchen said. "It must be hard for you. A man so invested in being strong, reduced to a lesser version of himself. Did they tell you that you'd recover fully?" She leaned around Henry's shoulder again and shot Archie a devious smile. "They were lying."

Henry's head was down.

Archie put a hand on his friend's back and stood. "That's enough," he told Gretchen. He walked around behind Gretchen's wheelchair. The photograph was in his inside jacket pocket. Now he slid it out and squatted next to Gretchen. He showed her the picture. "I think that this is you," he said.

Her eyes traveled slowly down his face and chest, and then fixed on the photograph. She didn't move. Archie could hear her breathing. "That's a shadow," she said.

"I saw another photograph," Archie said gently. He put his finger on the teenage boy in the picture. "One where he is taking the picture." That girl had been skinny, with a flat chest and dark hair; shoulders slumped, trying to take up less space. Nothing like the Serial Killer Centerfold. "You must have worked hard to reinvent yourself," Archie said.

"And look at you now," Henry said dryly. "Such a looker."

Archie studied Gretchen. Scrutinizing her for answers, some hint of recognition, a flicker of emotion. "What were they to you?" he asked.

Her eyes moved back up to meet his. Her head swayed a little. He realized how much effort she was putting into this, appearing functional with all those drugs in her system. But the clues were there—swollen eyelids, slack jowls, heavy limbs. She was exhausted. The hair stuck to the crust at the corner of her mouth fluttered as she exhaled.

"Will you get my hair out of my eyes?" she asked.

Archie hesitated only for a second, and then he reached out and touched her hair with his fingers, brushing it back across her cheek, and then tucking it behind her ear. His fingertips grazed her earlobe and the touch reverberated up his arm.

The hair gone, her full face was revealed. Even with the added weight, inflamed skin, crud stuck to the roots of eyelashes, sores at the corners of her mouth—he could still find something lovely about her. He wondered how long that would last. How many years in this place it would take before he could face her and not feel that physical draw.

"Give us a minute," Archie told Henry.

Henry didn't move.

Archie turned around. He could do this. He just needed Henry to trust him. "It's okay," Archie said. "She's tied to a chair. I think I can handle this."

Henry snorted. He took a step, cringing only slightly as he put weight on his bad leg. "I'll be right outside," he said. He paused and leaned back in front of Gretchen. "You look great, sugar lips," he said. "Keep doing what you're doing."

Gretchen stared straight ahead.

Henry chuckled. "This was fun," he said. He was still smiling as he left the room.

When the door was closed, the two of them sat there. The leather straps that held Gretchen's wrists to the arms of the chair were lined with sheepskin. They buckled like belts. Her arms were pale and spotted with bruises. Archie didn't know how much weight she had gained. Her body had changed. Her thighs spread wider on the seat. Her hips looked bigger. Her once-flat belly was now rounded. Even her neck and face looked filled out. Her breasts were fuller than before. Her angles had softened. But her figure was still there. It still pulled at him.

He wanted her to look worse. He wanted to look at her and feel nothing.

"Thinking up new ways to hurt me?" Gretchen said.

"You're the expert," Archie said. "You taught me everything I know."

"I didn't think you'd like it so much," she said.

Archie didn't answer. He looked outside, through the bars, at the brick wall.

She said, "If we're just going to sit here, I'd like another Lorazepam."

Archie glanced at the closed door. It was soundproof. No one was listening.

"I killed a man a few months ago," Archie said.

Gretchen stared at him.

He studied his shoes, the laces confiscated downstairs. "That man who kidnapped the boy and killed those people during the flood. He killed Jeff Heil, a detective I worked with."

"The one who poisoned Henry."

Archie nodded.

"Was it self-defense?" Gretchen asked.

Archie scratched the back of his head. "At first." He glanced up at her. Her face was absent of emotion. "He came at me," Archie explained. "We fought." He touched his forehead, above the eyebrow. "He had a skull fracture. A piece of the bone was missing. His brain was exposed." Archie rubbed his eyes. "He was subdued. He was probably dying. He was certainly not a threat." Archie looked at his hands again. They were soft hands, the hands of an academic, not big like Henry's. He was not a fighter. As his apartment wall could attest. "I punched him," Archie said. "I jammed my fist through the hole in his skull." These hands, his hands, had done this. He still couldn't quite believe it. "The bone fragments gave way." He turned his hands up, studying the palms. "His brain was warm Jell-O. It just slid out between my fingers."

"Did you like it?" Gretchen asked.

Archie folded his hands and looked up at her. "I'm not like you."

Her brow furrowed. "But you don't regret it."

"I'm glad he's dead," Archie said. "It makes things easier for the boy."

"You got away with it," Gretchen said.

"They never found the body," Archie said with a shrug. "They accepted my version of events." He glanced back at Gretchen's bed, where he had left the photograph of the Beaton family. He had Gretchen's full attention now. If there was one thing she loved, it was seeing Archie turn himself inside out. "You know that's how my mother died," he said.

Gretchen licked her lips. "In the car accident?" she said.

"She had a skull fracture," Archie said. "No air bags. No shoulder strap. Her head hit the dashboard." It had been almost twenty-five years, and his chest still tightened when he thought about that day. "It took her ten minutes to die. I tried to hold her skull together, but by the time the ambulance got there it was too late. I could feel her brain pulsing under my fingers; I thought she was alive. But it turned out that it was just my own pulse I was feeling." His hands betraying him again. He was sitting close to Gretchen, their knees almost touching. He leaned forward, his elbows on his knees. "I was seventeen," he said. He let that hang in the air for a moment, and then he rocked his chair back and grabbed the photograph off the bed from behind him. When he had it, he scooted the chair back right in front of her, the feet of the chair against the feet of her wheelchair. Her knees were open slightly, and he sat with his knees open, too, just a little bit wider, so that the outside of her knees rested against the inside of his. He laid the photograph on her lap between them.

He felt her stiffen. He might not have noticed it if they hadn't been touching. But she reacted to the contact of the photograph against her body. It meant something to her.

He was on the right track.

"That's about how old you were here, isn't it?" he said, touching the shadow of the girl. His hand was on the photograph; the photograph was on her upper thighs. Touching the girl in the photograph was like touching Gretchen. He was aware of her breasts, rising and falling with her breaths; her breathing quickening. He said, "That day, when I went through that stop sign, it changed everything. My life is before that day, and after that day." He could feel the burn where their knees made contact. She was pressing her knees out against his, or the other way around. "Just as there is my life before you, and after you."

He traced his fingertips over the girl's shadow, her long limbs exaggerated by the angle of the sun, her elbows, the silhouette of her skirt. "This girl"—he tapped his finger on the photograph—"hadn't killed anyone yet." Archie moved his finger to the image of James Beaton. "You said that he was your first victim." Archie held the photograph up, showing it to her. "What was the thing that changed? What happened to her?"

"She's dead," Gretchen said. "You couldn't have saved her." Her fingers curled around the arms of the wheelchair. "There's a stream that runs next to a red barn off Gilman Road on Sauvie Island, past the pumpkin patch—I buried what remained of her there under a grove of oak trees."

He saw her then. Archie had only caught a glimpse of her a few times. He didn't know who it was. Something changed in her posture, behind her eyes. It was as if, for a moment, she let the mask fall. He didn't know who was on the other side. But he was willing to take advantage of it.

He pointed to the teenage boy in the photograph of the Beaton family. "Is he Ryan Motley?"

Gretchen fixed her eyes on the boy and nodded slowly.

"I need to hear you say it," Archie said.

She looked at Archie. "Yes."

Archie pushed the chair back, brought his knees together, and stood. His head was already out the door, ready to get back to the investigation, ready to find Colin Beaton.

He heard Gretchen ask, "How is the dog?"

He turned. She was still where he'd left her. Strapped to the chair—unable to move. Her head was twisted in his direction.

"The dog is missing," Archie said.

A warm sweet smell filled the room, and Gretchen turned away from him.

"You can go," she said.

There was something wet on the floor.

Archie walked back around to her chair. A dark stain was growing on the lap of her gray pajama bottoms. The seat of the chair was slick with wet, something dribbling along the metal frame and down her pants leg.

"Are you okay?" Archie asked.

Gretchen's eyelids fluttered, her nostrils flared. Her hair was back in her face again. "It's the medication," she muttered. For a moment he didn't recognize her. She looked helpless. "I'm peeing myself," she said.

A stream of urine ran under her chair and formed a scribble of dark yellow on the linoleum.

CHAPTER

43

"Don't panic," Bliss said. She held an earthenware mug, and was wearing drawstring tie-dyed pants and a T-shirt with the slogan THIS IS WHAT A FEMINIST LOOKS LIKE across the chest. Her thick blond dreadlocks hung loose over her shoulders. The sunlight was streaming in behind her, illuminating every stray fuzzy hair so that her head looked like a bundle of frayed ropes.

Susan roused herself. She had finally invested in a futon, so she didn't have to sleep in the hammock her mother had installed in Susan's old bedroom the day after Susan had left for college. It was now a meditation/yoga room. The hammock was for guests.

Bliss wasn't leaving. Whatever she had in the cup smelled like the compost pile.

Susan sat up on the futon. It wasn't one of those fancy futons with the natural wood frames. This futon sat directly on the floor. With futons, you got what you paid for.

Susan's neck hurt.

"Promise me you won't freak out," Bliss said.

Susan's mother had a habit of overreacting. When Verizon had tried to put in a cell tower in their neighborhood, Bliss had protested by chaining herself to the front door of the building where the rooftop tower was supposed to be erected. Never mind that it was a retirement home. Bliss got on the evening news, and Verizon relented. Susan reminded her mother of that every time Susan's cell phone dropped a call because of bad reception. "Were you reading *The New Yorker* again?" Susan asked. *The New Yorker* always sent Bliss on a terror. Some people clipped coupons or funny comics. Bliss clipped stories she read about famine or child trafficking or household items that could kill you.

One time, after reading a story about the dangers of BPA in plastic products, she threw away all the plastic in the house, including toothbrushes, the produce drawers and shelves from the fridge, all the Tupperware, and Susan's brand-new professional featherweight ceramic ionic hair dryer.

Bliss still wore gloves to the ATM machine so she could avoid touching the BPA-coated ATM receipts with her bare hands.

In normal circumstances, Susan was the kook—in the presence of her mother, Susan was the voice of reason.

"Don't overreact," Bliss said. "Until you know the whole story."

"Did you throw away something of mine again?" Susan asked, feeling her lip start to curl.

"We have a guest," Bliss said. She squatted and put the mug in Susan's hands. It was hot and smelled even ranker close up. "Drink this."

Susan held the mug as far away from her face as possible. "What is it?"

"Kindness tea. It's calming."

Wait a minute. Susan narrowed her eyes at her mother. She could be sneaky sometimes. "A guest?"

Bliss was wearing her serene look now, the one she wore when she was charging people fifty bucks an hour to teach them how to meditate. Her forehead was smooth, she had a dippy smile on her face, and her eyes looked sparkly and spacey, like an anesthetized rabbit. "She spent the night on the couch," Bliss said in a calming tone. "She's scared, and I've told her she can stay."

None of this was making any sense to Susan. "What is it, like a cat or something?"

"Noooo," Bliss said. She fiddled with the sash of the black kimono she was wearing as a robe. "Not a cat."

The screen door had been unlocked, banging in the wind. It had been that way for hours before Susan had locked it. She was wide-awake now. "You found someone asleep in our living room?" she said, incredulous.

"My living room," Bliss said lightly. "My house. You're a guest."

Susan was looking around the room for something she could use to bludgeon an intruder to death, but everything there was too goddamn tranquil. Soft pillows. Tapestries on the walls. A poster of some freaky Indian guru.

"What are you looking for?" Bliss asked.

"This person's down there now?" Susan asked. Where was her phone? Downstairs on the couch where she'd left it, that's where. How many people had been murdered in their homes because they couldn't get to the room where'd they'd left their cell phone? Bliss's landline was in the kitchen.

"You're not being calm at all," Bliss pointed out.

Susan looked down at her hands. The mug. She smacked the mug against the wall. It exploded into pieces and smelly golden tea splashed everywhere. It dripped down the wall, splattered their feet, and scalded Susan's bare thighs.

Bliss stammered something about vintage pottery.

"Stay here," Susan said.

She took a good-sized piece of broken ceramic and held it in her hand like a shiv, or at least how she imagined people held shivs.

She had one goal: get to the landline.

She peered out of her bedroom into the hall. No intruders. Only the hardwood floor and the open doors to the bathroom and to her mother's room. George McGovern smiled at her from a framed campaign poster across the hall from her room. COME HOME, AMER-ICA, 1972. She could see her reflection in the glass, superimposed over George McGovern's huge head as she tiptoed past toward the stairs. Susan could smell blueberry pancakes.

"She's not dangerous," Bliss said from behind her.

Susan jumped and nearly shivved her mother in the gut. "Shh!" she said.

Bliss said, "She says she knows you."

Susan stopped. Her thighs stung where the tea had burned them. *She says she knows you.* Bliss had a habit of burying the lead. Susan lowered the shiv. George McGovern looked at her wisely. Susan groaned. The landline. She had given it out one time. She had written it on the back of her business card. In case of an emergency. If you Googled a landline number, you could get the street address that went with it pretty easily. Any teenager would know that.

"Pearl?" Susan called.

It was quiet.

Then a small voice from downstairs answered, "Yes?"

"Un-fucking-believable," Susan said.

"She told me everything," Bliss said. "Over breakfast."

"You made blueberry pancakes for our home invader?" They were Susan's favorite.

"I didn't want to wake you up," Bliss said.

"I'm calling Archie," Susan said. She stormed back into her room and pulled on a pair of sweatpants from the pile in front of the closet. "The police are looking for her. She ran away from a halfway house. She's a witness to a murder. We're turning her in."

Bliss knelt down and started picking up shards of the mug. "Just talk to her," she said.

Susan pushed her hair behind her ears and, very purposefully not helping deal with the mug, headed down the hall. She would call Archie, and then she would give this kid a piece of her mind.

Bliss was a pushover. Susan knew that. But if Pearl thought that she could sell Susan a bill of goods, she had another thing coming. Because telling-lies-as-a-teenager-to-get-out-of-trouble? Susan had invented that.

But before Susan could storm downstairs, Pearl appeared at the end of the hall, her mouth stained with blueberries.

Susan froze, stunned by the sight of her.

Archie had told Susan that Pearl looked different. When Susan had last seen her, she had been a pierced, angry steampunk moppet. Now the facial jewelry was gone. She was taller. Prettier. She looked like a street hippie, long hair, gypsy skirt; like those girls who sell beads off of blankets on Hawthorne Boulevard while their boyfriends play guitars for change.

"Someone's trying to kill me," Pearl said.

Susan took a sip of Stumptown organic Holler Mountain Blend black coffee, collected her thoughts, and looked gravely over at Pearl. The table was cluttered with the remnants of the breakfast that they had enjoyed without her. Bliss started clearing dirty dishes.

"So tell me what happened," Susan said.

Pearl's lips flattened into a little frown and her eyes darted toward Bliss.

"Just tell her what you told me," Bliss told Pearl.

Susan took another sip of coffee. She didn't need this. Pearl was lucky she hadn't called the police already. In fact, she was lucky Susan hadn't stabbed her with a mug handle.

"He said he was a cop," Pearl said.

Susan put down her coffee cup.

Pearl ran her finger along the lip of the glass in front of her. The glass was coated with the last of the orange juice. A few sips remained at the bottom of the glass. A fruit fly was drowning in it. "He had a badge," Pearl said. "I was smoking outside, and he said he was there to take me to talk to Sheridan." Her eyebrows twitched together. "He didn't look like a cop. He was wearing jeans and a dark T-shirt. And he didn't have a gun or anything." She stopped moving her finger along the glass, but kept it there, touching the lip. The fruit fly had stopped moving. "And he didn't have a cop face." She looked up at Susan for affirmation. "You know, that face cops put on when they're pushing you around. Even Archie has it. I had a foster dad who was a cop, so I know." She was quiet. Then the finger started again, around and around the glass.

"He didn't have the face of a cop," Pearl said again. "So I said I had to go ask Miss Bea. He said, 'Get the fuck in the car, Margaux.'" She looked up at Susan, like she expected a reaction.

Susan didn't know what to say.

Pearl blinked. "He called me Margaux," she said, emphasizing the name. "No one calls me that."

"Oh," Susan said.

"Then he grabbed me by the arm." She put her left hand over her right upper arm to illustrate, and said, "I socked him in the balls."

"Way to go, girl," Bliss said with a fist pump from the sink.

"Mother," Susan said. "Let her talk."

"I guess I got him good," Pearl said, "because he let go and I pulled away and ran inside. I went straight upstairs, got a few things from my room, and split out the side door."

"Why did you leave your phone?" Susan asked.

"They can find you with those things," Pearl said. "I didn't want him to triangulate me."

Susan didn't know whether to believe Pearl or not, but she knew enough to know that if she was telling the truth, it was serious. "You have to go to the police, Pearl," Susan said. "You saw this guy. What if he's the killer? They can catch him."

Pearl looked stricken. "You don't get it," she said. "Margaux is my legal name. It's the only place I use it. I'm registered at the center as Margaux Clinton. My juvie record is under Margaux Clinton. The police reports would have used that name. What if he was a cop and he knew my name because he had access to those records?"

"You said he didn't have a cop face," Susan reminded her.

Pearl leaned forward, eyes wide, suddenly looking like a scared teenager. "Maybe he's a bad cop."

"Two people have been murdered," Susan said, and that wasn't even counting the widow Beaton and who knew what the hell had happened to her. Then she realized that Pearl might not even know about Gabby Meester. Susan tried to sit up straight, to channel her inner grown-up. "A woman was murdered after Jake Kelly. Burned to a crisp. They think it's the work of a serial killer. You might be able to help find the killer before he strikes again." *Before he strikes again?* Had she really said that?

"I didn't see anything that morning," Pearl whined. "I barely knew Jake Kelly."

"You might have seen something and not known it," Susan said. It sounded like something that Archie might say. "You certainly were a witness to your own attempted kidnapping. Unless," Susan added, "you're making that up."

Pearl looked authentically offended. "I slept on the street the night before last," she said. "Under a bridge."

Bliss gasped and came around behind Pearl and put her hands on Pearl's shoulders. "Poor thing," Bliss gushed.

This, from a woman who had lived on a beach for three months in the sixties.

"Oh, please," Susan said, groaning. "It was seventy-five degrees last night. It's like camping."

Bliss gave Susan a scathing look.

"You said it," Pearl said to Susan. "This guy killed two people. And now he's after me. It doesn't matter if I saw something or not now, does it? I've seen him. Now he has to kill me." She looked up at Bliss, her eyes all wide and Bambi-like. "Please let me stay here."

"Mother," Susan said sternly.

Bliss patted Pearl's shoulders. Her dishwater hands had left suds on Pearl's T-shirt, but neither of them seemed to notice it. "You go upstairs and take a long bath and clean up," Bliss told Pearl, "and then we'll get you into some of Susan's clothes. We'll figure things out down here."

Pearl nodded and, with one last pitiful gaze at Susan, got up, grabbed a last piece of toast for the walk, and then trudged off upstairs.

"She's not some Bosnian war orphan," Susan said, crossing her arms. "She's a teenage hustler. She Tasered Archie so her boyfriend could hang him from meat hooks."

"Ex-boyfriend," Pearl called from halfway up the stairs. "And I said I was sorry."

"You did some foolish things when you were that age, too," Bliss said.

"I never Tasered a cop!" Susan said, exasperated.

Bliss sat down in the chair Pearl had been in. "She's safe here," she said.

"I'm pretty sure this is illegal," Susan said, hunching forward. "Harboring a fugitive. Custodial interference." She searched her brain for other scary-sounding charges, but couldn't come up with any.

"She's not a fugitive," Bliss said. "She's wanted as a witness, not a material witness, and she's not a suspect. She's an emancipated minor. That's how she got out of the foster care system. She elected to stay at the center as a transition to independent living, and she can elect to leave. She says she didn't see anything the morning this dishwasher was murdered, and I believe her."

"She saw something two days later," Susan pointed out, "when a man came to *murder* her. Assuming her story's even true."

Bliss nodded sagely. Susan knew what she was trying to do. Bliss was trying to play the responsible adult. She even dabbed her mouth with her cloth napkin, which she *never* did. "And she is safe from that man here," Bliss said. She sat up straight and tightened her kimono sash. "End of discussion."

"Excuse me?" Susan said, barely able to contain her sudden urge to break another cup. "No. If she's telling the truth, the guy who came after her is probably the guy who killed those people.

Those articles I printed out the other night, about all the child murders, Archie thinks it's the same guy." She said it again, in case Bliss didn't get it: "Archie thinks the guy who killed those two people killed all those kids. This guy is a serial killer—if Pearl's telling the truth about this man attacking her, that means she can identify him. She needs to work with a sketch artist. If the cops have his picture, they can find out who he is. They can catch him."

"And what if this freak is a cop?" Bliss said.

Then they were in big, big trouble. Then they would trade Pearl for their lives and move to Norway. "I'll work it out," Susan said.

Bliss stared into a coffee cup. She didn't use it for coffee. She used it for tea. It had a picture of a moose on it. "She stays here," Bliss said.

Susan had bought her mother the moose cup for Mother's Day about a hundred years ago. It was a stupid cup, but Bliss used it most mornings.

"For now," Susan said.

Bliss closed her eyes, exhaled, and nodded. Then she stood up and started gathering the brown sugar and organic honey and homemade raspberry jam off the breakfast table.

"I know why you're doing this," Susan said.

"She reminds me of someone," Bliss said.

Susan said, "I was never that irritating."

The room still smelled like blueberry pancakes. Susan plucked a crumb off the table and ate it. "Mom?" she called. "Will you make me a pancake, please?"

Bliss was drying dishes. "You know where the stove is," she said.

Susan got up to use the phone. There was a glass with a little bit of orange juice left in it still on the table and she took it with her to the couch. By the time she realized that she had a dead fruit fly in her throat, her only option was to swallow it.

Archie had all the Beaton photographs and documents that Huffington had boxed up delivered to his apartment. He and Henry unpacked the boxes without talking and spread the contents out on the floor of Archie's living room.

The dead children were in the bedroom.

A dead woman's personal papers filled the living room.

That was about right.

"Gretchen could be lying," Henry said. "About this whole thing. She could be lying about all of it."

"We need to organize the photographs by subject," Archie said. "If you think it's the boy, put it here." He paused. "I want to see any picture of a teenage girl."

There was a knock at the door, and then the knob immediately started to jiggle. Archie walked over, unlocked the door, and opened it.

Susan walked in.

"I need your help," she said. She walked past him into the kitchen and opened the refrigerator. "Claire said you were here," she said, pulling an apple out of his produce drawer. "I'm not mad at you anymore."

"Help yourself," Archie said.

Susan carried the apple into the living room. "Oh, hi, Henry," she said.

"Hi," Henry said.

Susan shuffled up a stack of photographs that Henry had just sorted and moved them over so she could take their place on the sofa. Henry stared, dumbfounded at what she had done. Susan didn't seem to notice.

"I know where Pearl is," Susan said.

She paused, like she expected climactic organ music. Archie didn't have time for this. He had other leads to follow. He lingered near the door, hoping Susan would take the hint. "Pearl didn't see anything," he said.

"What if she did?" Susan said.

"We're working here," Henry said from the floor. He snapped the pile of photographs Susan had displaced and began re-sorting it.

Susan took a bite of the apple, chewed, and swallowed it. Then she wiped some juice from her mouth with the back of her hand. "She says she ran away because some cop tried to grab her," Susan said.

Archie couldn't help but be interested and Susan knew it. "A cop?" he said.

"Well," Susan said, waving the apple in the air, "a guy pretending to be a cop."

It was a good story. But Archie didn't believe it.

"Teenage girls say a lot of things to get out of trouble," Archie said.

Susan arched her brows at him. "You're willing to give a psychopathic serial killer the benefit of the doubt and you don't trust a seventeen-year-old kid? What if this guy tried to bump her off because he thought she saw something that could connect him to the crime?"

Bump her off? Where did Susan get this stuff? "Can she identify him?" Archie asked.

"Yes," Susan said.

It was worth following up on. Pearl was trouble, but she was also only seventeen. She'd age out of the system in a few months, and then she'd be lost to them. In the meantime, the system owed her every effort.

"Where is she?" Archie asked.

"I'm not saying." She took a bite of the apple.

Susan could be a real pain in the ass sometimes.

"Is she at your mother's house?" Archie asked.

Susan looked to the right. "No."

Pearl was at Susan's mother's house.

"She's a minor," Archie said. "I need to call child services. You know that."

"She's an emancipated minor," Susan said.

Henry laughed out loud.

"Do you even know what that means?" Archie asked Susan.

"She's been declared an adult," Susan said.

"She's emancipated from her guardians," Archie said. "She can sign business contracts and work long hours. She's still a minor as far as the law."

Susan bit her lip. "Shit."

"Do you want to call CPS, or shall I?" Archie asked.

Susan pointed at him. "You owe me."

Archie was at a loss. "How do you figure that?"

"You took my flash drive," she said.

"You took *my* flash drive," Archie said. "I required that you return it." This wasn't worth arguing about. "If she was attacked, we need to investigate that."

"Send Claire to talk to her," Susan said. "Send a sketch artist. But give me twenty-four hours to call child services. In the meantime, she stays with me."

Henry chuckled some more from the floor. "*Send* Claire," he said. "I'm gonna tell her you said that. She loves it when people do that. She loves to be *sent* places."

Susan blew away some hair from her face. "You know what I mean," she said to Henry. "Pearl doesn't hate her."

Archie felt the need to point out the obvious. "What if she's actually in danger?"

"He doesn't know where she is," Susan said. "She's safe."

Archie looked around at the files on the floor. It wasn't like he didn't have enough to deal with already. "Okay," he said. "For now."

Susan eyed all the boxes, like she'd just noticed them. "Are you moving?"

"It's evidence from the Beaton house," Archie said.

He'd had fifteen e-mails from Susan since last night asking questions about Dusty Beaton's murder. He'd given her statements when he could, and forwarded the e-mails to the right people when he couldn't. Sometimes the only way to get Susan to stop was to give in.

"I'll say one thing for Gretchen, she knows how to create narrative," Susan said. "I couldn't have asked for a better ending to my *Times* story. Widow slaughtered eighteen years after Beauty Killer murders hubby." Susan paled and gave Archie an anxious look. "Hey, you don't think she had that woman killed for my story, do you?"

"No," Archie said.

Susan seemed satisfied. "I should get back," she said. She stepped over the stack of Beaton family photos that Henry had just finished sorting, nearly sending them cascading with her flip-flop. Henry got his hand out just in time to secure them. Susan looked down at the pictures and frowned. "I wonder if they made it," she said.

"Where?" Archie asked.

"Heaven," Susan said, like it was self-explanatory. "Look at them. What a bunch of Jesus freaks."

Archie still didn't understand.

Susan reached down and fanned some of Henry's neatly stacked snapshots out on the floor. They were all taken in the Beaton house.

"Look," she said. She pointed to the walls in the background, the bookshelves. Archie noticed, for the first time, all of the crucifixes. She handed him an apple core. "Crosses," she said. "Every picture."

46

Pearl was wearing Susan's favorite Decemberists T-shirt and a pair of red cutoff corduroys that Susan hadn't been able to zip up since high school. Susan was on deadline, but she couldn't take her eyes off her. Pearl was curvier up top than she'd been a year ago. She filled out the T-shirt and then some. Susan hated to admit it, but Pearl had cleaned up well. While Susan was at Archie's, Bliss had trimmed and colored Pearl's hair over the sink. When Bliss did Susan's hair, they used colors like Atomic Turquoise and Vampire Red. Pearl's dye job looked more like "prom queen." Bliss had transformed Pearl's mangy hippie mane into a glossy mix of dark blond and buttery gold highlights. It swung and shimmered and gleamed. Susan hadn't known that Bliss had that kind of hair in her. If Susan's mother had done that for her in high school, Susan's whole life might have turned out differently.

Pearl was lounging like a cat, stretched along the back of the sofa. She rolled from her side onto her back without missing a beat on her handheld video game.

Since the couch was taken, Susan was relegated to a nearby chair constructed out of driftwood and sheepskin. It had been a gift from an ex-boyfriend of Bliss's who'd turned a nice profit making driftwood grizzlies for tourists in Newport. The chair was more comfortable than it looked, but still not ideal.

The video game sounded like a car alarm that was going off a half block away. It wasn't exactly loud; it was just annoying and persistent.

Susan glanced at Bliss, who was in the kitchen rolling out flaxseed pizza dough for their lunch. Susan hadn't seen Bliss cook this much since she'd volunteered to provide craft services for a community theater production of *The Vagina Monologues*. Bliss didn't seem too concerned about Pearl's video game. Apparently Susan's mother hadn't told Pearl about her "magnetic field free zone" policy. Or warned her about the correlation between electronic handheld devices and lap cancer.

"I'm on deadline," Susan said to Pearl. "Can you do that upstairs or something?"

Pearl's eyes stayed on her screen as her thumbs danced furiously. "It's too hot upstairs."

That was true enough.

Susan went back to writing.

Pearl kept playing.

Soon the smell of pizza filled the room. It wasn't real pizza. It was some vegan flaxseed version of it. But it smelled like pizza.

After a while, Pearl put down her video game, rolled down the back of the couch, wound herself in Susan's direction, and flung her arms and legs over the couch arm. Teenagers didn't have bones, Susan decided.

Susan waited. Her cursor blinked.

Pearl crossed her arms over her legs and rested her chin on the space inside of her elbows. Her hair looked perfect. "So what's Archie like, in person?" she asked.

Seriously? "You've met him," Susan said. "Just before you electrocuted him."

Pearl shrugged that last bit off. "He seemed nice," she said. She gave Susan a conspiratorial smile. "Do you like him?"

"I have a boyfriend," Susan said quickly. "A person. A person of interest. That I'm interested in."

"Where is he?"

Who the hell knew? He hadn't called. He was somewhere selling a gym bag full of coke, that's where he was. Drug runners worked strange hours, like surgeons. They didn't have time to call people. "He knows I'm on deadline," Susan said.

"Is he hot?" Pearl asked.

Susan craned her neck. Where was her mother?

"I don't have a boyfriend," Pearl said.

Susan was finding Chatty Pearl a lot more annoying than Sullen Pearl. "I think I'll go work upstairs," she said.

"Can I come with you?" Pearl asked, blinking hopefully.

"Don't you have a car to steal or something?" Susan asked.

There was a knock at the door and Susan bounced up to get it. "It's Claire!" she said when she saw Claire Masland. "Come in, Claire."

"Uh, hey," Claire said. "It's me. Here I am. Hurray." She was with some guy with a goatee and a laptop.

Susan opened the door and let them in, as Bliss came bounding over from the kitchen.

"This is L.B., our composite artist," Claire said, jabbing a thumb toward the guy with the laptop. She looked peeved, like she had better things to be doing. Susan knew the feeling.

Bliss threw her arms around Claire, while Susan gave Claire an apologetic shrug from over her mother's shoulder.

"Pearl's over there," Susan said, pointing to where Pearl had rolled herself into a sullen ball on the couch.

"Okay," Claire said. "We're going to need to take her statement." She waited a beat. No one moved. "Is there somewhere we can talk to her privately?"

Susan glanced at Pearl sulking on the couch and then, knowing full well that it was a hundred degrees upstairs, smiled. "You can use my room," she said.

The Church of Living Christ was a one-story brick building with a marquee out front that read FREE COFFEE, EVERY SUN-DAY. Archie parked in the church parking lot. The grass around the church was dark green, right up to the property lines, where the irrigation stopped and the grass turned the color of hay. The paved path from the parking lot was lined with white flowers. Snapdragons. There was a big double door at the end of the walk. About ten feet over was another door with a sign on it that read OFFICE. Archie walked to that door and knocked on it.

After a minute, a woman about Archie's age opened the door.

She smiled. Her dark hair was threaded with gray and wound back in a tight bun that looked like it required a lot of muscle and hair spray. She had a long face, with a lot of forehead and chin, and three brown moles on one cheek. Her eyes were joyful; her smile beatific; and her laugh lines were deep. She was someone who smiled a lot.

She said, "I'm glad you're here."

That caught Archie off guard. He assumed she thought he was someone else. He said, "Excuse me?"

Her lips were frosted pink. She said, "Jesus is in your heart."

Archie fumbled for his badge. "I'm not here about Jesus," he said. He showed her the badge. "I'm here about Dusty Beaton."

The smile remained locked into place, but her posture shifted. Her eyes darted to the side, back inside the office. Then she frowned sadly. "We were so sorry to hear of her passing," she said. She gave him a helpless shrug. "But she had not been a church member here for many years."

Archie got the feeling that she wasn't going to let him in. "Did you know her?" Archie asked.

She adjusted the shoulder pad of her silk blouse. "No, not well. Not to speak of. I remember her. But I couldn't tell you anything personal about her."

Someone was taking care of things at the Beaton house. Someone was helping keep up the exterior of the house, cutting the grass. Someone had planted white snapdragons in Dusty Beaton's front yard. Archie looked back along the snapdragon-lined path where he'd just walked.

"You've got some nice flowers," Archie said. "Who planted them?"

"We have volunteers," she said. "Church members."

The door opened wider and an elderly man appeared next to the woman. He was wearing a clerical collar. The woman immediately dropped her head submissively. He patted the woman on the arm and said, "It's okay, Nancy."

She stepped back into the office, and the reverend stepped outside into the light. He had thick white hair and the eyebrows to match. His face was cobwebbed with wrinkles, and he had ears the size of coasters. He held a hand out to Archie.

"I'm Reverend Lewis," he said. "Let's go find someplace to talk. I'm all ears."

✧

Someplace to talk turned out to be a park bench behind the church. The bench overlooked a Dumpster, and beyond that a pasture, and beyond the pasture a mobile home park. The afternoon sun was hot, but the bench was under a tree, in the shade. There was a vague vinegar smell from the Dumpster, and Archie could hear crows fighting in the tree.

"How long have you been reverend here?" Archie asked.

"Long enough to be the one you're looking for," the reverend said.

"You knew Mr. Beaton?" Archie asked.

"I knew the whole family," the reverend said.

A crow swept down and picked up something that was lying on the pavement next to the Dumpster and flew off with it.

"Are you a religious man?" the reverend asked.

Archie hesitated. "Will my answer affect what you're willing to tell me?" he said.

The reverend smiled. "I'll answer your questions as truthfully as I can, regardless of your eternal salvation."

"I think that my eternal salvation is a lost cause," Archie said with a rueful smile.

"We're all sinners," the reverend said. "That's why we seek forgiveness."

"I've worked too many homicides to put much stock in forgiveness," Archie said.

The reverend nodded thoughtfully. "Human beings are capable of great evil."

"That's your word, not mine," Archie said.

"You don't believe in evil, either, eh?"

"It presumes a lack of biology or experience," Archie said. "People don't kill because they're evil. They usually kill because they want money or sex."

"Ah, a moral relativist." He cocked his head at Archie. "What about Gretchen Lowell?"

Archie looked out over the pasture. "You know who I am."

"We get newspapers. Even in St. Helens."

The pasture was spotted with green—weeds were always the last to die in the summer. Archie looked back at the reverend. "I haven't figured her out yet," Archie said.

Reverend Lewis reached behind his neck and loosened his clerical collar. "It's been a hot few months," he said.

"Yes, it has," Archie said.

They both looked at the view. Two more crows landed near the Dumpster.

"I have a theory that James Beaton was murdered," Archie said.

The reverend nodded solemnly. "Do you think Mrs. Beaton's murder is connected to her husband's murder?"

"Well, it's a hell of a coincidence," Archie said. "Excuse my language."

"Oh, we use the word *hell* here quite a bit," the reverend said with a soft smile.

"Right," Archie said. "So what can you tell me about the Beatons?"

"James grew up in St. Helens, attended church," the reverend said. "He left to attend college. He met Dusty at school and brought her home when he graduated. Dusty joined the church, and I officiated at their wedding. James took over his father's accounting business not long after that. He and Dusty had the two kids. Colin and Melissa were both teenagers when James disappeared."

"How did they all react?" Archie asked.

"Dusty was angry, mostly," the reverend said. "She truly loved him."

"He cheated on her," Archie said.

"She forgave him."

There was a warm breeze. It rattled the leaves overhead. Archie felt a drop of sweat snake down the side of his neck into his shirt.

"The children went in opposite directions after their father's disappearance," the reverend continued. "Colin became very focused on the church, very devout. Melissa strayed. They both left town after high school. A lot of young people do. I didn't hear from Melissa for several years, until the day she called and told me that she'd been diagnosed with cancer. She asked for us to pray for her." He tugged on one of his huge ears. "She would have been about twenty-five then. I know she was married. We got a letter from her husband telling us that she had died."

"Do you have a copy of the letter?"

"No, I'm sorry. The return address was somewhere in Northern California."

"What about Colin?" Archie asked.

"Gone," the reverend said. "I know Mrs. Beaton received cash from him on an irregular basis, and the occasional postcard. She said he moved around a lot. I'm not even sure what he did for a living."

"Did you ever see any photographs of him, as an adult?" Archie asked.

Reverend Lewis shook his head. "No, I don't think so."

"Mrs. Beaton left the church."

"That's right," the reverend said. "She had a crisis of faith after Melissa died. We believe in a literal interpretation of the Scripture. We rely on faith healing through prayer and the laying on of hands."

"You don't go to doctors?"

"We do not," the reverend said.

"Ever?"

"To do so would be to express doubt in God."

"But you took care of Mrs. Beaton, even after she left."

"Just because she wasn't a congregant anymore doesn't mean she isn't one of God's children."

Archie slid the photograph out of the envelope and showed it to the reverend. "When I was at the Beaton house a few days ago, there was a photograph on the wall," Archie said. "It was just like this, but there was a girl in it, in Colin's place. Does that sound familiar?"

"A girl?"

"Did Melissa have a close friend or cousin?"

"This was almost twenty years ago. Have you checked with the high school? There might be some of her old teachers still on staff. They might remember someone."

Archie kept pushing. "Were there any girls Melissa's age in the congregation at the time?"

"It's a small congregation."

"Are there photographs I could look at?" Archie asked. "Church picnics or celebrations?"

"I can have Nancy look through the archives and see what we can pull together. Can't promise anything. We were in a building up the hill until about five years ago. We lost a lot of our records in the fire."

Archie kept his voice steady. "What caused the fire?"

The old man chuckled. "I think the insurance company called it an 'act of God.' You probably passed by the old foundation. It's right up the hill. On Lowell Street."

D o you know how many Lowell Streets there are? There's probably one in every town." Huffington was sitting at her desk eating tuna fish from a plastic freezer bag. It was after five, but Huffington didn't look like she was planning on heading home anytime soon.

"I know," Archie said.

"And if Gretchen was from St. Helens, don't you think someone would have recognized her by now?" Huffington asked. "Her face has been plastered all over the news for three years."

Huffington's light brown hair was pulled back. There were new kids' drawings up in her office, Archie noticed. Another tour must have gone through.

"I think she's changed her appearance," Archie said.

"People don't change that much," Huffington said. She took another pinch of tuna out of the bag and put it in her mouth. "You think she was close enough to the Beatons to be included in a family photo—but only one—which has since disappeared. You think she killed Papa Beaton. Perhaps with the help of the son, Colin. And the two of them began serial killing sprees. With him sometimes using her signature. And now he's killed Mama."

It sounded even crazier when she said it. "I just need you to help me prove it," Archie said.

"So Gretchen Lowell isn't talking."

"Not really," Archie said.

"She got you this far," Huffington pointed out.

"She wants Ryan Motley caught."

"And Ryan Motley is Colin," Huffington said.

"That's my theory," Archie said.

Huffington sorted through some papers on her desk. "Last anyone heard of Colin he was getting a traffic ticket in Boise eight years ago," she said, scanning a report. "He had a Nebraska driver's license at the time, but that's expired, and after that he's not in the system."

Archie copied down the date of the speeding ticket and the address on the driver's license. One of the children murdered with Gretchen's signature had been killed in Boise about that time.

"What about Melissa?" he asked. "The reverend over at their old church said that she was married. Can we track down her husband? Maybe he knows where Colin is."

"I'll see what I can do," Huffington said. "And I'll send someone over to the high school. In the meantime, we turned up something interesting on the Dusty Beaton case."

"What did you find?"

"Tears," Huffington said. "On the pillow. And they aren't Mrs. Beaton's."

DNA testing required cells. Tears didn't have cells. "I thought you couldn't get DNA from tears," Archie said.

"You can't. But apparently if you have ocular herpes they can see the virus in your tears. Mrs. Beaton didn't have ocular herpes. But her killer does."

Colin had cried when he'd killed his mother. "Nice work, Huffington," Archie said.

She held the freezer bag of canned fish across the desk. "Tuna?" she said.

49

Henry was in bed by the time Claire came over. She had worked late. Archie had the entire team following leads attempting to tie Colin Beaton with Ryan Motley and prove him responsible for the murders. Henry had left Claire at the office an hour before, sitting in front of a computer, with barely a cursory good-bye glance. Now he listened as she let herself into his house with her key. One of the cats got off the bed to go and greet her. She didn't come in right away. She made tea. He heard the familiar sound of her fumbling around his kitchen, the water running into the kettle, the mug on the countertop, the foraging through tea boxes in the cupboard. He read through James Beaton's missing person report while he waited for her tea water to boil. After a few minutes he heard the whistle, and a few minutes after that Claire came into the bedroom, followed by the cat.

She put the tea on the bedside table and sat down and started taking off her shoes.

Henry took off his reading glasses and waited.

When she had her shoes off she leaned over and kissed him lightly on the lips. She smelled like Thai food.

"I've barely seen you since yesterday," she said. She tucked her legs up under her on the bed. "I missed you last night."

They spent most nights together. It had happened organically, after he'd gotten out of the hospital. Nearly dying had a way of putting a spark in a relationship. "I didn't get home until after one," Henry said.

She reached for her tea and blew on it. "So you missed physical therapy?" she asked. The cat curled up next to her and started purring.

"I'll reschedule tomorrow," Henry said.

He liked that she didn't ask where he'd gone. She had every right to know. Even though Henry knew she wouldn't like it. "I went down to Salem with Archie," he said. Salem could only mean one thing in that context. Henry didn't have to elaborate.

He could tell by her body language that she'd figured it out already. There was no jolt of surprise. She took a sip of tea and lifted an eyebrow. "I thought he'd agreed not to see her anymore," she said.

"I couldn't let him go alone," Henry said. "He thinks she's connected to this Beaton thing somehow." What was he supposed to say? *Archie thinks he can see Gretchen's shadow in the grass?*

Claire's face was over her tea, the mug cupped in her hands. "What's his deal with her?" she asked.

It was a rhetorical question. There were things Henry had learned about Archie and Gretchen that he would never tell Claire, and she knew it. Maybe someday—when they were old and dying side by side in futuristic recliners—but not now, not today. "We don't know what he went through," Henry said.

"Yeah, we do," Claire said. "She nearly killed him. You know the appropriate emotional response to that?" She glanced over at him, and he saw her eyes flash. "Anger."

Henry didn't know where this was coming from. Claire had been on the Beauty Killer Task Force. They'd all worked together for years. "What's your problem with Archie all of a sudden?" he asked.

She set the mug back on the table and looked at him. "I love you," she said. "And Archie does, too." She exhaled a long, troubled-sounding breath. "But . . ."

Henry saw, then, where she was headed. "She gets in his head," he said. "But he comes out of it when it counts."

Claire lifted her knees in front of her stomach and wrapped her arms around them. "If he gets you killed because of her, I'll shoot him," she said. "I seriously will."

Henry had been with Archie after Heil's funeral. When it was all over and they were back at his apartment, Archie had let the mask drop.

"If he ever gets me killed," Henry said, "he'll do it himself."

Claire put her hands over her face. "What is wrong with me?" she said. She peeked through her fingers. "I'm sorry," she said. "It's hormones."

Henry held the Beaton file off the side of the bed and dropped it. It hit the wood floor with a thud. Then he opened his bedside table drawer and pulled out a folded catalogue page and handed it to Claire.

"What's this?" she asked.

"I ordered it," Henry said.

She narrowed her eyes at him for a moment and then slowly unfolded the paper. Her eyes widened and brightened when she saw the catalogue picture of a king-sized bed.

"You're giving up the futon?" she asked.

Henry nodded.

She climbed on top of him, straddling his waist, and threw her arms around him. For Claire Masland, he could get used to sleeping on a mattress. He kissed her hair. "Will you be my domestic partner?" he asked.

She lifted her head and looked at him and beamed. And then she nodded, her eyes glassy with tears. "But the dream catcher has to go," she said.

Henry looked over at the far corner of the ceiling, where his twenty-two-inch diameter authentic Native American, Alaskan birch, mink-fur-lined dream catcher hung, dripping with beads and eagle feathers. He patted her shoulder. "Baby steps," he said.

A rchie had been the last person to leave the office. It was late, but he didn't want to go home.

Instead, he got out of the elevator on the fifth floor and walked down the plum hallway to Rachel's apartment. He had barely knocked when she answered the door.

"Hi," he said. "I was wondering if I could borrow an Allen wrench."

She looked back into her apartment. "I think I might actually have an Allen wrench," she said.

"Well, that would be awkward, because I was just using that as an excuse to knock on your door."

She was wearing a short black cotton dress. She smiled at him. "Have you come to interrogate me some more?"

"No," Archie said.

Rachel looked up at him intently. "I'm starting over," she said. "That's my story. That's all I'm going to tell you. Can you handle that? Or do you need to figure me out?"

"I can handle that," Archie said.

"Do you want to come in?" she asked.

The last woman Archie had had sex with was a serial killer. Before that, his wife. He had met Debbie in college. There hadn't been that many women. "I think so," he said.

She held his gaze. He could see the outline of her nipples through the cotton of the dress. She moved her hand forward and pressed it against his abdomen and then slid her fingers inside his shirt against his skin. His breath caught and she smiled and untucked his shirttails and slid her fingers deeper, moving them through his pubic hair, teasing him with her fingertips. Then she smiled. He was already hard. He had been hard since she'd come to the door. She wrapped her hand around his cock. He tried not to whimper as she pulled him inside.

✧

Archie heard his phone and fumbled for it in the dark before he remembered where he was and that his phone was in his pants on the floor next to Rachel's bed. He slipped out from under the sheet and felt around on the floor. He was naked on his hands and knees when Rachel turned on the bedside light.

"What are you doing?" she asked sleepily.

He saw his pants then, discarded at the foot of the bed. "Phone," he said. He pulled his phone out of the pocket, glanced at it, and hesitated only for a second before lifting it to his ear.

"Hello, Patrick," he said.

"What are you doing?" Patrick asked.

Archie leaned back against the side of the mattress and stretched his bare legs out on the floor. The bedside lamp sent long shadows across the room. "Just sleeping."

"Do you want to watch TV?" Patrick asked.

Archie scratched the back of his neck. "Right now?"

"Yeah. We both turn on the same channel and watch the same thing. That way we can do it together."

Archie turned around to Rachel. She was sitting up on her elbows, looking at him. "Do you have a TV?" he asked.

She nodded.

"Okay," Archie said into the phone. "Give me a minute."

"There's a *Simpsons* marathon on Fox."

"Do your parents let you watch that?"

"All the time," Patrick said.

Archie was too tired to argue. "Okay," he said. The kid had seen people murdered. He could handle *The Simpsons*. "Just a second." He put his phone on mute and stood up. "This is hard to explain," he said to Rachel. "But there's this kid. He's having a tough time. And he can't sleep. And I need to watch TV with him."

Rachel slid out of bed. For a moment Archie lost himself in her body. He had to take a deep breath as he followed her into the living room. The room was dark except for the moonlight coming in the paned factory windows that overlooked the city. She picked a remote off her coffee table and aimed it at a flat-screen TV that hung on an interior wall. The screen went blue, bathing her body in a watery glow. Then she picked up a second remote and looked at him.

"Fox," Archie said.

The Simpsons sprang to life on the TV screen.

Archie took his phone off mute. "I'm here," he said.

He sank down on her sofa, the leather buttery soft against the backs of his legs.

"I've seen this episode," Patrick said.

"Do you want to watch something else?"

"No," Patrick said. "I like knowing what happens."

"Okay," Archie said. "I'm here. I'll be here as long as you need me."

Rachel was still standing with the remote in her hand. He watched her set it down. He put his hand over the phone. "You can go back to bed," he said. She gave him a strange, tender smile. Then she crawled onto the sofa next to him and laid her head against his chest.

Patrick laughed at something Bart Simpson said.

Archie put his arm around Rachel.

For the first time in a long time, he felt at home in his body. Holding her like that, he couldn't see his scars.

51

Archie had the boxes from his apartment brought to the office—all of them. The Beauty Killer case files formed a floor-to-ceiling wall, three boxes deep, on one side of the break room. The personal papers from the Beaton house were unpacked and laid out on tables. The dead children they thought Gretchen had murdered were on one wall. The dead children they thought Colin had murdered were on another wall. The photograph of the Beatons standing in their front yard was attached, with a magnet, to the dry-erase board.

It was lunchtime, but no one was eating.

"You were right," Claire said. "Colin Beaton's traffic ticket puts him in Boise at the same time that Taylor King was murdered. He had a Nebraska driver's license with an address in Lincoln. Hannah Fielding was killed in Lincoln, Nebraska. The first time any record of Gretchen Lowell shows up was a bad-check-writing bust in Lincoln, Nebraska, a few months after Beaton's license was issued at a Lincoln DMV. Then Beaton falls off the face of the earth. We think this is when he started going by 'Ryan Motley.'"

"We're going through all U.S. licenses issued in the name of Ryan Motley that match his general age and description," Levy said. "But nothing has turned up yet."

Archie turned to Robbins. "You've reviewed the autopsies?" he asked.

"All of them," Robbins said. "There's a progression of violence. The killings overlap. But if we look at the children that were left with lilies and the children who were left with the heart signature and we lay them out consecutively, the pattern fits. Each murder ups the ante. Also, Gretchen never killed the same way twice. But if we remove her child victims and look at them as a group, there's a pattern—no defense wounds, nothing under the fingernails. No signs that the kids were restrained. Our theory at the time was that Gretchen drugged them. We found traces of a paralytic in two of them. The others were all found too late. It would have worked its way through their systems. You wouldn't find a paralytic unless you were specifically looking for it. It wouldn't show up on a standard tox screen. The six children left with lilies fit this same pattern. No defense wounds, no signs of restraint. I think they were drugged, too."

"So whoever killed them, killed the others," Archie said.

Robbins looked around the table. "It looks like it."

Archie gazed back and forth from one wall to the other. There was another element all the child murders shared. "They were all left somewhere higher than where they were taken," Archie said. "We didn't notice it then."

"Maybe Gretchen killed them all," Henry said.

"She didn't kill him," Archie said, pointing to the photo of Calvin Long. "She was with me."

"No offense," Robbins said, "but you were dying, and, might I add, high on the same paralytic that we're saying was used on these kids. We can't rely on your sense of time."

But Archie could rely on what he knew about Gretchen. And he knew that she wouldn't leave him for that long. She enjoyed hurting him way too much. Archie's eyes wandered over the crime scene photos on the wall. "He drugged them, killed them slowly, and then moved the bodies to a higher place, always a higher place." He thought of the Church of Living Christ and the crucifixes throughout Colin Beaton's childhood home. And then it dawned on him. "He wanted to leave them closer to God," Archie said.

"Well, that's fucked up," Claire said.

"Now he's moved on to adults," Archie said. "Any traces of the paralytic in those screens?"

"Jake Kelly was just outside the window when it would have been detectable," Robbins said. "Gabby Meester was positive."

"What about Mrs. Beaton?" Archie asked.

"Jackpot," Robbins said. "I suggested to the Columbia County ME that he might want to run an expanded tox screen. It came up positive."

"This whole theory is based on the word of a woman who is sitting in the state mental hospital," Levy said. "There's no proof that James Beaton is even dead. He could be in Cancún right now sucking on a margarita with some hot tamale and watching his half-Mexican kids play in the surf."

Ngyun walked into the break room with a folder under his arm. "He's not in Cancún," Ngyun said. "He's in New Jersey."

He had their attention.

"They couldn't identify him at the time," Ngyun said. "The body was too degraded. Nothing like a train ride across country in a freight car to accelerate decomp. A hobo found him. They're not called hobos anymore. But the modern equivalent. Some local cops caught the case, and didn't try very hard. ME's office kept the bones in a box." Ngyun pulled a photograph out of the folder and stuck it to the board. "This is his skull," he said. "A few years ago some anthropology student at Princeton did a reconstruction for a class." He pulled another photograph from the folder and put it on the board next to the skull. "Look familiar?"

A plaster cast of the skull had been filled out with modeling clay and prosthetic eyes. It looked just like James Beaton.

"Why didn't anyone match it to the missing person report?" Archie asked.

"It was for a class," Ngyun said with a shrug. "I guess they thought they couldn't rely on the work, because no one asked for a copy of his finished project. I had to track down the student to get a copy. He's using his Ivy League anthropology degree to work as a barista in New York, by the way." Ngyun looked at the doorway. "You need something?" he asked.

Archie turned to see a man standing in the doorway with a laptop under his arm. He was in his twenties, goateed, with a ponytail, wearing a T-shirt and tight plaid shorts. Archie guessed he wasn't a cop.

"That's L.B.," Claire said. "The composite guy."

"Good," Archie said. He leaned behind Ngyun and snapped the Beaton family photo off the dry-erase board and held it out to L.B. "Can you age him?" Archie asked. L.B. inched into the room and took the photo.

He looked at it, and then he looked up at Archie. "Is this a test?" he asked.

"What?" Archie said.

L.B. opened his laptop and clicked on an icon on his screen. A digital composite of a man's face materialized. "This is the composite I worked on with that kid yesterday," he said. The image on his laptop showed a disembodied head and neck floating at the center of a white screen. Composites were created by assembling photographic splinters of facial features until the correct combination matched the image in a witness's mind. The effect was unnervingly real-looking. The head on L.B.'s screen was a man in his mid-thirties, with dark hair and a hollow face. L.B. held the family snapshot up next to the screen and put his finger next to Colin Beaton's teenage face. "It's the same guy. Look at the bone structure."

The room was silent.

Archie looked at the teenage Colin Beaton in the snapshot, and then at the laptop composite image of the man who Pearl claimed had tried to attack her. He could see the resemblance.

Pearl had been telling the truth about the man she'd seen. If Colin Beaton had tried to grab her, it implicated him in Jake Kelly's murder, which led then to Gaby Meester's murder, and the six child murders on the flash drive, which led to the child murders they had attributed to Gretchen.

Colin Beaton had killed them all.

CHAPTER

52

S he can't stay here," Archie said.

Susan stood in her front door. Archie stood on the porch with a Child Protective Services caseworker named Peggy.

Susan shrugged and opened the door for them to come in. "Fine," she said.

Archie had thought she would take it harder.

He walked inside the house. Peggy followed him. Peggy had smooth brown skin, dark hair ironed so straight it looked wet, and the poise of someone who'd seen her share of chaos. The house smelled like marijuana. Peggy arched an eyebrow at him. He shrugged.

"They're outside with the goat," Susan said. "Come on." She led them through the kitchen, past the kitchen table, where Archie saw her laptop set up next to a collection of coffee cups and empty water glasses, and out the back door.

The yard stretched back a good quarter acre and was framed with English ivy and bamboo that walled it off from the neighbors. Every inch of space was utilized. A huge tree, its branches festooned with Tibetan prayer flags, shaded the back half of the yard. A fire pit was surrounded by old wooden dining room chairs, bleached gray by the elements. An overgrown garden gleamed red with tomatoes. Sheets fluttered on a laundry line next to a pair of drawstring tie-dyed pants. In the far corner of the yard, a mattress-sized compost pile constructed out of wire mesh and snow fence baked in the sun under a black tarp. Archie counted three birdbaths.

Beyond the garden, under the tree, near the wall of ivy, was a rickety wooden shed that looked like a large doghouse. Between the back porch and the shed stood a brown and white goat. Squatted on either side of the goat were Bliss and Pearl.

They both looked up.

Archie walked toward them, flanked by Peggy and Susan.

Bliss looked at the goat and then at Archie. "I have a permit," she said, in a way that made Archie think that she didn't have a permit.

The goat's muzzle was stained with tomato juice. It nuzzled against Pearl's shoulder.

"Pearl needs to come with me," Archie said.

Pearl looked stricken. She put her arm around the goat. "No," she said. Her eyes darted to Peggy, and Archie saw recognition on her face. Kids in the system knew social workers at a glance.

Bliss stood up, brushed the dirt off her hands, and put her hands on her hips. She was wearing a T-shirt that read FUCK THE MAN.

Peggy said, "Take it easy, ma'am."

"I'm a member of the NAACP," Bliss told Peggy.

"Excuse me?" Peggy said, crossing her arms.

Susan sighed.

Archie focused on Pearl. "The man who tried to attack you?" he said. "He killed Jake Kelly. He murders children. He burns people alive. He thinks you can identify him, and he wants to kill you."

Bliss wiped her mouth with the back of her hand, smearing her red lipstick. Then she lifted her chin defiantly. "He doesn't know where she is," Bliss said.

"She should be in protective custody," Archie said.

Pearl shook her head. "I'll run away."

"I was thinking of a more secure environment than the center," Archie said.

Pearl's jaw dropped. "You want to put me in juvie? I didn't *do* anything."

"You'll be safe there," Archie said.

"She's safe *here*," Bliss said.

"She's a ward of the state. She needs to be in a state-sanctioned facility or with a foster parent. It's the law."

"I am a registered foster parent. You can place her here with me."

Susan did a double-take. "You're a foster parent?"

"Remember Luther?" Bliss asked.

Archie looked questioningly at Susan. "Luther?"

"They dated," Susan explained.

"He taught weekend seminars to prospective foster parents," Bliss said. "I completed my training at the Eugene Holiday Inn Express. I had a home study and everything."

"And you passed it?" Susan asked, incredulous.

Bliss looked a little offended. "Yes. Why wouldn't I?"

Peggy lowered her chin and raised her eyebrows.

"They can smell it, Mom," Susan said.

Archie tried to suppress a smile.

"I have a medical marijuana card," Bliss said with a hapless shrug. "For my anxiety."

"She's doing well here," Susan said to Archie. "Pearl hasn't electrocuted anyone yet." It was a begrudging endorsement.

Archie sighed. He didn't really want to put Pearl in lockup, and he knew what a crapshoot the foster system was. He could put her in danger trying to protect her.

Peggy said, "If she completed the training, she might be eligible. We could do an emergency placement. Something temporary." She leaned in close to Archie. "She does seem to really love the goat."

They were all staring at him.

Even the goat.

Archie ran his hand through his hair. Then he turned to Susan. "You call or text me every two waking hours," he said.

When Archie got back to the office he had a message that Huffington had called, so he called her back.

"Anything?" he said.

"I sent my guys over to the high school," Huffington said. "Some of the teachers remember Melissa. But no one could think of any close friends. She was a bit of a loner. No luck on locating Colin Beaton, either. The church is taking care of his mother's funeral expenses."

Someone had made a color xerox of the photograph of the Beaton family standing in their yard and left it on Archie's desk. He picked it up and looked at it. "When's the funeral?" he asked.

"Tomorrow. Ten A.M. There's a service at the church and then they're burying her at Mountain View Cemetery."

Colin Beaton had murdered his mother. But he had also cried on her pillow. Archie wondered if he would find a way to be at her funeral. "I want to send some of my people out, to mingle with the guests, maybe set up some surveillance."

"You think junior's going to show?"

Archie squinted at the teenage Colin Beaton, unsmiling, his eyes fixed on the camera. "I want to be there if he does."

✧

After he got off the phone, Archie did an Internet search on the Church of Living Christ. Several church children had died over the years, because their parents had chosen their faith over seeking medical care. Juvenile diabetes. Strep. The kids had died of treatable conditions, while their parents and other followers of Reverend Lewis knelt in prayer around their beds.

"How'd it go with Pearl?" Claire asked.

Archie glanced up from his desk to see Claire at his office door. "I let her stay," Archie said.

"Softie."

"She's bounced around foster care for years," Archie said. "She deserves a break."

"She gamed you. Admit it," Claire said.

She left and Archie looked at his desk, where Pearl Clinton's file lay open. She had rotated through foster homes almost her whole life. In and out of people's lives. A member of the family, until she wasn't anymore.

Then he picked up the xerox of the Beaton family again. Colin wasn't looking at the camera. He was looking at the person holding the camera. The girl casting the shadow.

Archie closed his eyes and tried to conjure the alternate image he'd seen on the Beatons' wall. Colin had stepped out of that picture, behind the camera. And the girl had taken his place.

Why include a teenage girl in a family photograph?

Unless she was part of the family. Sort of.

Archie opened his eyes.

He pulled a business card from his pocket and punched in the number for Peggy at Child Protective Services. He could feel his heart racing and he put his elbows on his desk and rested his forehead on his free hand. He listened to the phone ring. He checked his watch. She'd said she was going back to the office, but that didn't mean she was at her desk. After seven rings, she picked up.

"Peggy Holbrook," she said.

"It's Detective Sheridan," Archie said. "Can you tell me if someone was a registered foster parent about twenty years ago?"

"Is this about Bliss Mountain?" Peggy asked. "I looked her up. Her foster parent status is legit."

"No," Archie said. "James and Dusty Beaton. St. Helens, Oregon." He scratched his head. "Is that enough?"

"Hold on."

He could hear her typing on a keyboard. She had acrylic nails and they clicked on the keys.

He pressed his forehead harder into his palm.

"I've got their file right here," Peggy said. "Looks like they had one placement. Didn't last long. A few months. She ran away. Happens sometimes."

Archie's throat tightened. "What was her name?"

"Gretchen Stevens. But that may have been an alias. She walked into a hospital in St. Helens, Oregon, with a few shattered ribs. Says here she was bloody and covered in mud. No ID. Claimed her parents were dead." He heard her typing again. "This is strange. There's no photo in the file."

"Didn't they try to find her family?" Archie asked.

"The file's incomplete. They would have had to run her name through the system before they placed her. But not all runaways get reported missing."

Archie picked up a pen. "Who was the caseworker?"

"Tena Tahirih." There was a pause, and Peggy made a sympathetic clucking noise. "I knew her. She died a few years ago."

"Great," Archie said.

"I can send over what I have."

Archie leaned back in his chair. *Nice to meet you, Gretchen Stevens.* "E-mail it to me," he said.

When he got off the phone he immediately called Huffington.

"I think the girl in the photograph was a foster kid named Gretchen Stevens. I'm going to send you what we know about her. Ask around. See if she was registered at the school. And send someone over to the hospital. She was a patient there. They might have her medical records."

"Medical records are confidential," Huffington said.

"Use your charm."

"It is considerable," Huffington said.

54

Archie put on his one dark suit to wear to the funeral. It was dark blue, but passed for black. He wore it for funerals and for court appearances. Considering the wear the suit had gotten the past few years, he was going to have to buy a second one. He loosened his tie. He could already feel the heat collecting around his collar, and he didn't even have the jacket on yet.

He drank his second cup of coffee leaning over the sink so he wouldn't stain his white dress shirt.

Henry didn't knock. He walked in and said, "I feel like a jackass." He was wearing a short-sleeved gray button-down shirt and dark gray pants with black cowboy boots.

For Henry, it was evening attire.

"You look fine," Archie said, slurping down the rest of his coffee. He set the mug in the sink and grabbed his suit jacket off the back of the chair. When he turned back to Henry, Henry was staring slack-jawed at Rachel, who had just come out of Archie's bedroom wearing his robe and drying her wet hair with one of his towels.

"Hi," Henry said.

"Oh, good," Archie said to Henry. "You can see her, too."

Rachel grinned.

"There's coffee in the pot," Archie said. "I've got to go to work."

Archie had to practically push Henry out of his apartment. Henry's cheeks still glowed with amusement when they got down to the car. "So, who is she?" Henry asked.

"My neighbor," Archie said.

They were quiet as Henry pulled onto I-5, and then over the Fremont Bridge and onto Highway 30 through the Northwest Industrial District.

"She looks like you-know-who," Henry said.

Archie looked out the window at the faceless buildings and acres of parking lots. "Gretchen Stevens," he said. They had pored over the DCS file together. Henry still wasn't convinced.

"It's just sex," Archie said.

Henry glanced over at Archie. "And she's never murdered anyone?"

"Not that I know of."

"I think this is a big step forward for you."

"Thanks," Archie said.

The highway narrowed and the loading bays gave way to trees and feed stores. Henry was still beaming, tapping out a tune on the steering wheel that only he could hear. "You're going to tell Claire, aren't you?" Archie said.

Henry's grin grew wider and he nodded. "Oh, yeah," he said. Then he chuckled happily to himself.

"What?" Archie said.

"Susan's gonna hate her," Henry said.

F reeze," Susan said.

"What?" Pearl said.

"That's my Pixies T-shirt."

Pearl poked her finger through the hem and wiggled it. "It's got a hole in it."

"Yes," Susan said. "Yes, it does. That's because it's old. Like me. Now take it off."

"I don't have any clothes," Pearl pouted. "Bliss said I could borrow yours. What am I supposed to do? Go around naked?" She flipped her hair over her shoulder. "I don't even like half your clothes."

Sometimes Susan could see why people committed murder. "I have terrific clothes," she said.

Pearl pulled at the shirt over her breasts. Susan had to admit, puberty had done well by Pearl. "They don't fit me right," Pearl said. "Your boobs are smaller."

"Then borrow something of Bliss's," Susan said.

"All of her clothes smell funny," Pearl said, wrinkling her nose.

Patchouli. It was true.

I'll be nice. That's what Susan had promised her mother before Bliss had left for work. She had a deadline. She didn't have time to argue with a teenager. "That's my favorite T-shirt," Susan said, "and if you stain or damage it I will kill you."

Pearl rolled her eyes. "Oooh, I'm so scared," she said, heading for the back door.

"Where are you going?" Susan asked.

"I'm going to hang out with Baby," Pearl said.

"The goat is not named Baby," Susan said.

"That's what I call her," Pearl said, letting the screen door slam behind her on her way out.

Susan sat down at her laptop at the kitchen table. There was a note on her keyboard. She knew it was from Bliss because she'd written it on the back of a scrap of wrapping paper.

Susan read the note: *REMEMBERED WHERE I KNEW THAT WOMAN FROM. HEROES COLUMN.*

What woman? Susan looked at the note for a few minutes before she realized that Bliss must be talking about Gabby Meester, the rooftop fire victim.

The Heroes column ran in the *Portland Tribune*, a free commuter paper. Her mother refused to buy the *Herald*, the paper that Susan used to write for, but she'd occasionally pick up the *Trib*. Susan brought up the *Trib*'s Web site on her laptop and then searched Gabby Meester's name. Several stories came up about the murder, and then, farther down, from about five years ago there was another story about Gabby Meester and several other people participating in one of those kidney donation arrangements, where if you have a friend who needs a kidney but you're not a match, you can give your kidney to someone else who has a friend who isn't a match to their person but is a match to your person and who then gives a kidney to your person in exchange. Or something. This particular donation required six people, three of whom had kidneys removed, and three who got new ones.

Susan heard Pearl say her name. There was a terror in her voice that made Susan look up instantly. Pearl was standing at the back door, her shirt and hands covered with blood. Her face was ashen. "Something happened to Baby," Pearl said.

Susan didn't understand. What was Pearl talking about? The goat?

Pearl gasped and tears streamed from her eyes. She put her bloody hands over her face. "I think the coyotes got her."

Coyotes? There weren't coyotes in Portland. Susan leapt up and pushed past Pearl into the backyard. She scanned the yard for the goat's friendly face, and didn't see it. Then she ran for the shed. She knelt at the door to the shed. The goat was on her side, her fur slashed open and darkened with blood. Her mouth was full of even darker blood, almost black. Flies had already started to circle and Susan batted them away. She could hear Pearl behind her, sobbing, and she didn't want to turn around, didn't want Pearl to see her own tears. Susan touched the goat's coat. She was still warm. The wounds were frenzied. Why hadn't they heard her cry out?

Susan looked around the backyard, the privacy fence, the impenetrable wall of bamboo.

Fear prickled the back of her neck. "This wasn't coyotes," she said.

She'd left her phone inside on the kitchen table. Pearl was still blubbering. Susan took her by each shoulder. "When I say, 'Go,'" Susan said, "I want you to run to the back porch as fast as you can."

56

They were praying again.

The Mountain View Cemetery did, indeed, have a view of Mount St. Helens. But no budget to water the grass. The pile of earth next to Dusty Beaton's open grave looked hard and dry. The grass was bleached. Even the trees looked thirsty.

Archie sat in one of the folding chairs next to the grave.

Henry stood on the other side of the grave, hands folded, head down.

Josh Levy was somewhere squatting behind a gravestone with a telephoto lens.

A few polite congregants from the Church of Living Christ had shown up, and Archie saw Huffington leaning against her parked squad car. But Colin Beaton had yet to make an appearance.

Archie took off his suit jacket and then laid it across his lap to cover the weapon clipped to his belt.

He could see the sweat glistening on Henry's bent head.

Reverend Lewis said some closing words and tossed some of the parched earth into the open grave. It bounced and skidded on the wooden coffin.

Everyone started to pack up.

No one tossed a rose into the grave or broke down in tears.

Archie scanned the cemetery. Some of the gravestones were old, their engravings worn, weeds grown high around them. The newer, slick marble slabs blinked like mirrors reflecting the sun. The trees in the cemetery were as old as the town. Their grizzled branches, heavy with leaves, bowed over the graves. Archie could hear the hypnotic whirring of the cicadas in their branches, singing happily in the heat.

He turned around in his chair and took in the three-sixty view.

The congregants headed for their cars, their feet crunching the dead grass. Henry came and sat down next to Archie.

"I am so fucking hot," Henry said.

"Give it a few more minutes," Archie said.

Henry got a handkerchief out of his pocket and swabbed his forehead.

Two grave diggers stood ready with shovels next to the hill of dry dirt.

Reverend Lewis walked over to Archie. "They want to get her underground as quickly as possible." He looked up at the sky. "The heat."

Archie nodded, and the men started to heave shovels of dirt onto the coffin. Archie watched it drop into the deep rectangular grave. They used a backhoe to dig graves, but they filled it in with shovels. No one wanted to see a dead loved one buried by a John Deere.

Archie leaned forward. The sides of the grave were dark. The earth on top was drier, sun-parched.

"Wait," Archie said.

The men with the shovels stopped and looked at him.

"When was this grave dug?" Archie asked.

One of the men said, "Last night."

Archie stood up, put his hands behind his neck, and stared down at the final resting place of Dusty Beaton. He could feel the grease of sweat soaking through his shirt. The grave had been empty all night. Beaton had wept over his mother's corpse. If he had decided to stay away from the funeral, he'd find another way to say his good-byes. Archie loosened his tie. It couldn't be helped. "We need to dig her up," he said.

The back door was open, and Susan could see her phone sitting on the table in the kitchen.

It was eight steps from the back door to that table.

Pearl was hunched on the back porch, sniveling.

"I'm going to go in and get my phone," Susan said.

Pearl grabbed on to Susan's arm. "I'm going with you," she said.

Susan took a couple of breaths. They should stick together. Susan shouldn't leave Pearl alone. She nodded. Pearl released Susan's arms, leaving behind a perfect set of bloody fingerprints.

Ushering Pearl behind her, Susan crept through the back door into the kitchen. It looked just as they had left it, but it felt stiller somehow, like the dead air that fills a house whose owners have been away on a long vacation. All the little noises were magnified. The flap of Susan's flip-flops on the kitchen floor. Pearl's sniffles. The whir of the fans. The faucet dripping in the sink. Susan got to her phone and snatched it up and immediately felt something was wrong. It was wet. She looked at the phone. It glistened with water. The screen was black. There was a puddle on the table where the phone had been.

"What is it?" Pearl asked.

Susan turned to the landline. The phone line had been cut. She could see it dangling uselessly against the wall.

She tried to turn on her iPhone. It was dead. Waterlogged.

Pearl whimpered. Susan took her hand. *Front door,* Susan mouthed.

Wait.

Susan squeezed Pearl's hand, signaling to be still. The steady thrum of the fan in the living room was slowing. Susan knew that sound. It was the sound that fan made when someone turned it off.

The man stepped from behind the open pocket door, like a performer taking the stage. He was about forty, with a friendly clean-shaven face and short brown hair, and he was tall, and dressed like a missionary in black pants and a white button-down. Blood splattered the shirt and dripped off the machete he held in his right hand. His eyes gleamed. "Pray with me," he said.

Susan stepped in front of Pearl.

The man with the machete was between them and the front door. The backyard offered no escape. They had to buy time.

"You're Colin Beaton," Susan said.

He smiled. "I'm the guy who has come to kill you," he said.

"It's him," Pearl said. "He's the one who tried to grab me."

No shit, thought Susan. "She didn't see you," Susan told the man. "She can't testify that you were there. This is a mistake."

"No," he said. "It's not a mistake. It's God's plan."

He lifted the machete, and Susan pulled Pearl toward the stairs and pushed Pearl up ahead of her.

She could hear Beaton behind her, laughing.

They scrambled up the stairs and down the hall into the bathroom, which was the only room on that floor with a lock on it.

It was a stupid lock, not suitable for keeping a machete-wielding madman out, but it was the only lock they had.

Pearl crouched next to the Guatemalan basket that Bliss used for a laundry hamper. The cast-iron claw-foot bathtub was lined with candles. Bliss had painted the wooden floor light blue and the walls indigo. A framed picture of Che Guevara hung over the toilet. *Hasta la victoria siempre.*

"Now what?" Pearl asked.

The tiny muslin-covered window was too small for either of them to crawl out of.

"What time is it?" Susan asked.

Pearl looked around helplessly. "I don't know." She flapped her hand at Susan. "What's wrong with your phone?"

Susan hadn't even realized she still had it in her hand. "He dipped it in water or something." You could drop an iPhone off a building and still make a call. Get the thing wet, and you had an expensive hockey puck.

The doorknob rattled.

Pearl and Susan froze.

They heard him moving on the other side of the door. Then he said, "I see you."

Susan grabbed a towel, lunged forward, and began stuffing it under the sizable crack under the door. She saw a glint of metal and heard Pearl wail. She managed to jump back just as the machete sliced underneath the towel.

She scampered back to Pearl.

"Look," Susan whispered. "If I don't call, Archie will get worried. I texted him an hour or two ago."

"An hour or two?" Pearl said through tears. "Which was it?"

"I'm bad with time," Susan growled.

Pearl sobbed. "We're going to be macheted to death," she said.

Susan stood up. "That's not even a word," she said. She opened the medicine cabinet above the sink and began sorting through it.

"What are you doing?" Pearl asked.

"Looking for anything we can use."

"What?" Pearl said. "Like bandages for when he chops off our arms?"

Susan squatted in front of Pearl. She touched the eraser-sized scar on her own cheek. "Your boyfriend did this."

"Ex-boyfriend," Pearl said. "Dead ex-boyfriend."

"He pierced my fucking face with a needle while you watched."

"I said I was sorry."

"I don't want sorry," Susan said. "I want hard as nails. I want headstrong. Fierce. I want the little bitch who Tasered a cop. So get your shit together and help me stop this motherfucker."

Pearl was nodding. Her face was streaked with blood and tears. She sniffed.

"I don't hear you praying," Beaton said through the door.

Pearl reached up and slowly pulled a hand towel off the rack above her head. Then she stood up at the sink. Susan thought she was going to wash her face, but she didn't. She looked in the mirror.

"Stand back," she said.

Susan took a step back.

Pearl dumped the toothbrushes out of the earthenware toothbrush cup and then tapped the cup hard on the center of the mirror.

The mirror splintered, and wedges slipped out of the frame and dropped into the sink. Pearl fished out a knife-shaped piece and wrapped the bottom of it in the hand towel. She handed it to Susan by the towel hilt, and started to make another one.

"Where did you learn that?" Susan asked.

"Juvie," Pearl said. She opened one of the built-in cabinets. "Do you have any drain cleaner? If you throw it in someone's face it really burns."

By the time they got the coffin out of the grave, Henry had his shirt off and they were all coated with soil, except for Reverend Lewis, who had bent his head in prayer at the moment of the first whisper of the impromptu grave digging.

They had used straps to lift the coffin out, along with some creative gymnastics on behalf of Henry and the larger grave digger, a man named José.

Henry and José sat by the coffin, breathing hard. Guillermo, the other grave digger, made the sign of the cross.

José said, "You sure this is legal, man?"

Archie looked at Huffington, who had come over from her car at the first sight of the dirt coming *out* of the grave.

"It's not an exhumation," she said. "We're just burying her a little slower." Her large aviators made her expression hard to read. "This isn't going to be for nothing, right?" she said to Archie.

Archie sat down on the board on the edge of the grave and dangled his feet below. Without the coffin, the six-foot-deep rectangular pit looked especially deep and dark. He slid in. It was a farther jump than he thought and he landed in a crouch.

"What are you doing?" Henry called.

"Give me a minute," Archie said.

It felt fifteen degrees cooler down here and the damp earthy smell tasted sharp in his mouth. He stood up. The top of his head was just about level with the surface. When he craned his neck back, he could see his friends' feet.

"Huffington," Archie said. "Toss me a flashlight."

She knelt down and held out a long black flashlight and Archie took it, turned it on, and ran the beam in a search pattern along the bottom of the grave.

"See anything?" Huffington asked from above.

Archie didn't answer. He was hunched over, focused on the soil at his feet. The heat and sun and sky felt very far away right now. Worms wiggled soft and pink in the soil. Tiny black beetles crawled over his shoe. Archie made a mental note to make sure his will called for cremation. Then the light caught the edge of something bright white. He stopped, and looked closer. It was a corner of paper, half covered in dirt. Archie squatted and brushed aside the soil and then very carefully extracted the paper. It was about the size of an index card, torn from a larger piece.

"I need an evidence bag," he called.

Huffington lowered one down to him and he slid the paper into the plastic bag and zipped it closed. Archie handed the bag up to an outstretched hand, and then two more hands lowered and then, with a lot of grunting, Henry and José pulled Archie roughly from the grave.

Archie rolled over into a sitting position, squinting in the sun. His suit was filthy; he had dirt in his hair, and he had rocks in his shoes.

Huffington held the evidence bag up and read what was written.

"'The Lord saw how great the wickedness of the human race had become on the earth, and that every inclination of the thoughts of the human heart was only evil all the time.'"

Reverend Lewis said, "Genesis 6:5."

Archie reached for the evidence bag and studied the note. It was handwritten in careful print letters, hard to analyze or match. He'd used a black felt-tip marker.

Under the biblical quote, in the same black ink, he'd drawn a heart.

Archie felt a chill settle on his shoulders.

Reverend Lewis was standing next to the head of the coffin, his hand resting lightly on it, as if he were communicating with the dead.

"Gretchen Stevens," Archie said.

The reverend looked up at Archie.

"She was a foster kid that the Beatons took in right before James Beaton was murdered. Ring a bell?"

Huffington stepped beside the reverend and laid a gentle hand on his arm. "If you've got something to say, Reverend, you better say it."

"It was a long time ago," the reverend said. "She wasn't with them long."

"You met her?" Archie asked.

"They would have brought her to church," the reverend said.

"Did they?" Huffington asked.

Reverend Lewis looked at Huffington. "Yes."

"Why didn't this occur to you when I asked yesterday if you remembered any teenage girls being around?" Archie asked.

"I barely knew her," the reverend said.

There was more the reverend wasn't telling them. And they all knew it. But anything that had come up during spiritual counseling was protected. Whatever secrets the reverend had, they were his to dole out. "What happened to that family?" Archie asked.

Reverend Lewis glanced back at the coffin, then at Huffington, before finally fixing his blue eyes on Archie. "They were tested by God."

Archie inspected the note in his hand.

Beaton had left it in the grave at some point during the night. He cried when he killed her. He wanted to be at her funeral. Instead, he'd settled for a scrawled biblical quote on a piece of scrap paper.

"He knew we'd be here," Archie said.

"He couldn't risk getting caught, even for Mama," Huffington said.

If they were all here, where was he?

Archie brushed the dirt off the face of his watch. It was after noon. "Susan should have checked in fifteen minutes ago," Archie said.

"She's not exactly a slave to time," Henry said.

Archie punched in Susan's cell phone number. It went straight to voice mail. Then he dialed her mother's landline. It was disconnected.

The door shook in its frame as Beaton threw his body against it again and again. The Victorians made good doors, and this one had lasted a long time, but it was starting to splinter.

"It won't be long," Susan said.

They gripped their little homemade shivs and waited. Bliss did not have any drain cleaner. The most toxic thing they'd found in the bathroom was tea tree oil. They'd poured it in a squirt bottle and Susan was going to go for his eyes, on the off chance it might sting.

"Susan," Pearl said.

He heaved himself at the door again and the wood made a cracking sound.

"What?" Susan said.

Pearl glanced down at the bloodstained Pixies T-shirt. "I'm sorry about your shirt."

"Find me another one," Susan said.

One more good slam, and he'd be upon them.

Susan looked at Pearl.

Pearl nodded.

Susan reached for the lock on the door, and, as quietly as she could, she turned it.

They squeezed against the wall, just inside the door, and waited.

"'For whatsoever a man soweth, that shall he also reap,'" Beaton hollered through the door. Then he slammed into the door, only this time the door was unlocked, and it flew open, sending Beaton stumbling forward, the machete at his side.

Susan was ready with the squirt bottle and she squeezed it and a stream of golden tea tree oil went right into his eyes.

He howled and squeezed his eyes shut and flailed the machete in the air. They couldn't get past him out of the bathroom; the blade's reach was too far. They had one shot. Susan waited for the machete to swing away and then struck him in the thigh with her shiv. He hollered and dropped the machete and his hand went to his leg, where the shard of glass was wedged in his flesh.

At the same time she felt a tiny stab in the muscle of her own thigh.

Beaton's eyes fell on her. His eyelids were raw and the whites of his eyes were dark red and wet with tears. She was backed into a corner.

She heard Pearl say, "What did you do to her?" She had picked up the machete and was holding it like a baseball bat. "Let her go."

Susan looked down at her leg, where a hypodermic was jammed into her thigh like a meat thermometer. She slid it out and looked at it. The hypodermic was empty. The plunger all the way in. Whatever it was, it was now in her system. She was feeling woozy. She stumbled, and caught herself on the edge of the tub. A candle tumbled onto the floor. Susan's vision was getting blotchy. Was she dying? She looked for Pearl. She had to help Pearl.

Pearl's eyes were frantic. The machete gleamed and trembled in her hands.

"Cut off his fucking head," Susan slurred.

Beaton lifted his palms. Susan dropped to the floor. The light blue paint was the color of the sky.

Beaton said, "Pearl, have you accepted the Lord?"

It was the last thing Susan heard before the world went black.

S he's still out cold," Claire said. She was sitting at Susan's bedside. The ambulance had taken her to Providence, which was
located on the central east side. It was a relief to Archie. They had all
spent too much time at Emanuel Hospital over the past few years.

Claire looked Archie and Henry up and down. "What happened to you two?"

Archie and Henry had driven straight there from St. Helens,
nearly breaking the sound barrier going through Scappoose. They
were both still covered with dirt. The cuffs of Archie's pants were
caked with mud. Henry had streaks of soil on his arms and neck, and
a dirty handprint on the front of his shirt. They had both left dirty
footprints behind them down the hospital hall. Archie's socks felt
slimy. One of his shirt buttons was missing. He had lost his jacket.

"We had to do some digging," Archie said.

Susan was in a private room in the ER. She was wearing a hospital gown, a white cotton blanket tucked in up to her chest. Archie
went to the side of the bed, rubbed a dirty palm on his pants, and
took Susan's hand. Dirt fell off his knuckles onto the blanket and he
brushed it away, onto the floor. This was his fault. He never should
have agreed to let Pearl stay there.

"Do you want to sit?" Claire asked, offering her seat. Archie nodded and sat down, still holding Susan's hand in his. Claire walked over to Henry and licked her thumb and wiped some mud off the side of his nose.

"Thanks," Henry said.

Archie's skin itched from the dirt and the sweat. The mud on his pants had dried to a stiff shell. He could smell the graveyard soil, and the stink of his own body where he'd sweated through his shirt.

Susan was in REM, her eyes darting back and forth underneath her eyelids. The side of her mouth twitched.

Beaton had drugged her with a heavy sedative. The hypo had been on the floor when Claire found her unconscious in the bathroom.

"They put up a real fight," Claire said. "There's blood and broken glass all over the bathroom. His blood," she clarified. "Not Pearl's type."

Susan stirred and said something in her sleep.

Archie knew what he had to do.

"I need to talk to her doctor," he said.

"I'll find him," Claire said. She hurried out of the room. Henry leaned against the wall, not saying anything. Susan looked younger when she was asleep, all the attitude faded from her face. Every freckle was visible against her pale skin. Even her neck and shoulders had freckles, something Archie wasn't sure he'd ever noticed before. Archie prided himself on noticing details, but when it came to Susan, for some reason, he missed things. There was something about her that distracted that part of his brain.

Claire returned with the doctor. He was young, probably a resident. His eyes widened when he saw Henry and Archie. Archie didn't bother explaining the mud. He pulled out his badge and opened it, and the doctor nodded a few too many times. He was nervous. Sometimes people who were used to being in positions of authority didn't like it when someone else with authority showed up. That was good. Archie could use that. With the right approach, the doctor could be pushed around.

"We need you to give her something to wake her up," Archie said. He could feel Henry's and Claire's eyes on him. They weren't going to like this.

The doctor had a name tag that read DR. CLOOP on his white medical coat. The name tag was engraved silver—probably a gift for graduating from medical school. Cloop took a pen out of his chest pocket. He didn't do anything with it. He just held it in his hand. "What's your interest here?" he asked.

Susan's hand was warm and limp. Archie closed his fingers around it. "I'm her friend," he said. He cleared his throat. "I'm also the lead detective on this case. She witnessed a kidnapping. A girl is still out there, in great danger."

"She'll wake up naturally in a few hours," Cloop said.

"We don't have that much time," Archie said. "She was drugged with a sedative." He waited a beat. "So give her an amphetamine."

Henry straightened up off the wall, leaving a streak of dirt where his shoulder had been. "You sure that's a good idea?" he said.

Cloop worried the pen in his hand and shook his head. "It's not that simple. I can give her Flumazenil. But it's controversial. If she's got any health issues, it can cause seizures, cardiac issues, even death. The risks outweigh any potential benefits."

Susan slept peacefully in the bed. Archie had risked his life to save hers on more than one occasion. Now he was considering risking her life to save Pearl's. He didn't know if Susan would understand. He was sure that her mother wouldn't. "Susan doesn't have health issues," Archie said. He moved his eyes to Cloop. "Give her the shot."

"I need to talk to an attending," Cloop said.

"Look, Doctor," Archie said. He knew that Cloop would like the honorific. "A serial killer has a seventeen-year-old girl and he is going to kill her. He is probably hurting her right now. And Susan may have information that can help us find them."

Cloop was caving. Archie could see his eyes moving, already

computing the dosage. "Depending on how she reacts to the benzodiazepine, she might not remember much," Cloop said.

"She'll remember," Archie said. He squeezed Susan's hand. He believed in her.

Cloop took a breath and slowly exhaled. He put the pen back in his chest pocket. That was when Archie knew he had him. "I'll be right back," Cloop said.

"Bliss is on her way," Claire said as soon as Cloop was gone. "What is wrong with you? We should wait for her."

"If we wait for her, she won't let us do it," Archie said simply. "She'll want to protect Susan."

Henry rubbed his forehead. "What do *you* want?" he asked Archie.

"I want to help Susan save Pearl's life," Archie said. He took a moment. And then he turned his attention from Susan to Henry and Claire. "She can do this," he said.

Claire hesitated. She was studying him. She sometimes looked at Archie like he was a very hard math problem. Then she threaded one arm under Henry's elbow and nodded.

Cloop returned with a vial of clear fluid and a hypodermic. He pierced the foil top of the vial and drew fluid into the hypodermic. Then he tapped it. "If this is going to work, it's going to work fast," he said. And he injected the medicine into Susan's IV.

Archie held her hand between both of his, his eyes fixed on her closed lids. The sounds of the ER—the flap of nurses' clogs on linoleum, the hushed chatter, the soft cries, and the steady electronic heartbeat of the machines—all faded away. There was only Susan.

They waited.

Archie tightened his grip on her hand. *Come on*, he thought. *You can do this.*

Her eyelids fluttered.

Archie held his breath.

Then Susan opened her eyes. Her freckles faded as color rushed back into her face. She looked at Archie and said, "Where's Pearl?"

Archie was flooded with such relief that he almost felt sick. He had to look down and clear his throat before he could answer. "She's gone," he said.

Claire was tucked under Henry's arm, a rare display of public affection. Archie saw her pull away as Susan came to and the tension dissipated, but he also saw that Henry still had a hand on the small of her back.

Susan's eyes were wide, her gaze darting around the room. "He had a machete," she said. "He killed our goat."

"I know," Archie said.

Susan turned to Archie, blinking back tears. "I loved that goat. I know I said terrible things about her. But I swear to God, I really did love her. I didn't want her to die."

"I know," Archie said.

"He took her?" Susan said. She was gripping Archie's hand so hard it hurt, like she might fall if she let go.

Archie nodded. "You need to tell me everything that happened."

He saw Susan's brain working, her eyes searching for details. "Pearl went outside to play with Baby," she said. "That what she calls the goat. I have no idea why. It's not her name." Susan's nostrils flared and tears slid down her cheeks. Then she drew in a long, halting breath. "She came back all upset. Said something had happened to the goat, so I went out to see. I think he must have slipped in the back door then." She swallowed hard. "It didn't look like coyotes or raccoons." Susan's face blanched at the memory. "I was going to call you," she said to Archie, "but I'd left my phone inside. So we went back into the house, just to get the phone. I could see it on the kitchen table. But when I got to it, it was wet. He'd dunked it in water or something, so it didn't work. And the landline was cut." Archie's stomach twisted, but he forced his expression to remain neutral. She was already upset. She didn't need to see his fear. "And then he was just there," Susan said. "He had the machete. And he was covered in goat blood. And we couldn't get past him, so we ran upstairs and locked ourselves in the bathroom." Susan wiped her nose with her free wrist and muttered, "We really need to get some real drain cleaner."

Archie squeezed her hand. "What else do you remember?" he asked.

Susan looked at their intertwined fingers; and then at Henry. "Why are you so dirty?" she asked.

"Gardening," Henry said.

"Focus on remembering," Archie said.

She nodded and looked off at something Archie couldn't see. "He was laughing and spewing Bible quotes," she said. "'We reap what we sow,' and stuff like that. We made these weapons out of broken mirror pieces and towels and he was about to smash in the door, so we unlocked it, and when he body-slammed it, he fell through and we squirted tea tree oil in his eyes and I stabbed him in the leg with the mirror. He dropped the machete and Pearl picked it up. But he'd already stabbed me with the hypodermic." She touched her leg. "Right here. What was it?"

"A sedative," Archie said, with a glance at Cloop.

"It worked right away," Susan said. "I couldn't help her. But she had the machete. I told her to use it."

Archie looked questioningly at Claire.

"We didn't find a machete," Claire said. "And I don't think she used it. There's not enough blood."

Bliss blew into the room and froze, her red lips a round circle. "I shouldn't have left," she wailed.

"I'm okay, Mom," Susan said as Bliss swept to her bedside, elbowing Cloop out of the way and taking Susan in her arms. Susan's hand slid from Archie's grasp as she reached around her mother's shoulders.

Archie's hand throbbed as his circulation returned.

"I tried to keep her safe," Susan said.

Bliss held on to Susan. When she lifted her head, there was a bright ring of red lipstick on Susan's neck.

Susan's mouth was small, the way it got when she was troubled. "What is it?" Archie asked her.

"He said, 'Pearl, have you accepted the Lord?'" Susan said. "He called her Margaux when he tried to grab her at the center."

Henry said, "Maybe he heard you call her Pearl."

Susan shook her head, her expression dead certain. "I didn't say her name. Not once."

It was not the only thing that bothered Archie. If Colin Beaton had hunted Pearl down because he thought she had seen him at the scene of Jake Kelly's kidnapping, then why leave Susan alive?

He needed to get out of there, to get looking. But as he stood up, Susan caught his hand.

"You have to find her," she said. "Promise me."

"Everyone is mobilized," Archie said. "We've issued a three-state Amber Alert. The FBI is coming in. State cops. Everyone. We'll get him."

"Promise me," Susan said. She looked him in the eye. "Because if you promise me, I'll believe you."

Archie hesitated. He looked down at their hands. His hand was grimy with soil, black under his fingernails and caked into his knuckles. Susan's hand. The white blanket. It was all dirty. Everything he'd touched. Susan reached her other hand and folded it around the first, so that his hand was tucked in hers.

He looked up at her. And he had to fight the urge to lean forward and put his lips on her forehead. Because if he did that, he would want more. "I'll find her," he said. "I promise you."

Her eyes darted to the left, over his shoulder, in the direction of the door into the room. "Leo," she said. "Who called you?"

Archie looked over his shoulder as Leo Reynolds walked into the room.

"I did," Archie said. He pulled his hand away from Susan's. "You and your mother need somewhere safe to stay."

62

The cocaine was gone. It had been the first thing Susan had checked, in the guise of taking a shower. The whole gym bag was gone. Like it had never existed.

Now she sat, wet-haired, on Leo's couch, wearing his robe, pondering the irony of Archie sending Bliss and her to stay with a drug dealer to keep them safe.

Bliss had the TV on. All the local channels were live with coverage. Bliss flipped through them, as if one might offer some new information, some glimmer of hope; but it was all the same images, over and over again. Pearl, represented by a series of DCS mug shots, the digital composite of Colin Beaton, and video of an earlier press conference—the chief of police, the mayor, and Archie, freshly scrubbed and in a clean suit. Footage of their house, lit up by TV news lights, cops going in and out. Beaton was still at large. Pearl was still missing.

Bliss changed the channel again. She looked pale, her mouth a tight, small line.

"Archie will find her," Susan said.

"Archie could have killed you," Bliss said, not moving her eyes from the TV.

Ever since the doctor had told them about the call Archie had made to force her out of sedation, Bliss had been seething. Maybe if her mother could have had the opportunity to scream at Archie, she would have gotten it out of her system. But Archie had gone by the time she found out, so Bliss was reduced to angry grumbling.

"He knew what he was doing," Susan said, though she wasn't sure she believed it.

Bliss turned and looked at Susan. The muscles in Bliss's neck were taut. When she put her hand on Susan's leg, Susan could feel it tremble. "Don't waste your time on him," Bliss said quietly. "There's a reason his marriage didn't work out."

Little did she know, thought Susan.

"I'm going to get some water," Susan said. She stood up and went into the kitchen. Leo's kitchen was all steel appliances and sharp angles. He was making tea. His gleaming white dress shirt was rolled up at the sleeves and his black pants were crisply pressed. He looked up at her and smiled. "Chamomile," he said.

Susan lifted herself up to sit on the black granite counter, next to the two matching white ceramic mugs that Leo had ready for the tea. "Do you have any blow?" she asked.

Leo raised his eyebrows. He picked up the electric kettle and poured steaming water into the two cups. "Do you think that's a good idea right now?"

"I think it's the perfect idea right now," Susan said. "I need a boost."

He picked up a spoon and stirred the tea bag in one cup, then the other. Susan could smell the chamomile, pungent and floral. "All out," Leo said.

She poked him in the arm with her index finger. "You're lying."

"You just got out of the hospital, Susan."

Susan pushed herself off the counter. "So let's celebrate," she said. She headed for his bedroom, and he followed her. She knew where he kept a gram now and again. It wasn't like she didn't know he did coke occasionally. She wasn't stupid. She opened the top drawer of his dresser, and he closed the bedroom door. Inside the drawer was a leather toiletry bag. Susan pulled it out and unzipped it. The coke was in a little plastic bag, the kind you get at bead stores. There was also a black straw, about two inches long.

"Good news," Susan said. "Looks like you've got some left."

Leo stood just inside the bedroom door with his hands in his pockets.

She tapped some white powder out of the bag onto the smooth dark wood of his dresser.

"You don't want to do much of that," Leo said.

Susan ignored him, put her hair behind her ears, plugged one nostril, and snorted.

She recoiled immediately—her nose burned and her eyes watered. She rubbed at her nose and jumped up and down. "Fuck, that's strong," she said.

"It's uncut," Leo said quietly.

"Get me a tissue," Susan said, flailing a hand.

He laid a handkerchief in her palm. He was that kind of guy, the guy with the cloth handkerchief.

Susan blew her nose and handed him back the handkerchief.

She actually felt great. Her arms tickled. Her brain felt warm. She felt like she was getting more oxygen, like a veil of haze had been lifted. "That's really good shit," she said.

"Archie's going to fucking kill me," Leo said.

"Why do you care so much what Archie thinks?" Susan asked.

"Why do you?" Leo countered.

Susan shrugged and turned away. She felt like moving.

"He caught my sister's killer," Leo said. "We have a relationship. I've known him forever."

"He doesn't even like you," Susan said. Did she say that aloud? She put her hand over her mouth. "Sorry."

"He likes me," Leo said. "He just doesn't like me with you."

"Why?"

"He could probably foresee this moment," Leo said.

"I found the gym bag." She had said it. It had come right out.

That's what a bump of cocaine gave you—courage. She put her hands on her hips for emphasis.

Leo blinked at her, then exhaled like someone had socked him in the belly. He threaded his hands behind his head. "Fuck," he said. He was sputtering, shaking his head. He looked angry, even angrier than she thought he'd be. "Fucking Christ, Susan. I told you not to snoop."

His reaction made Susan feel defensive. "You're a drug dealer," she said, "just like your father."

"Did you touch it?" Leo asked. He was pacing, looking at the floor. "Shit, they're going to print it." He walked over to her and took her by the arms. "Did you touch the plastic?"

Susan was confused. "Print it? What? No."

He let go of her and backed away.

"What did you do with it?" Susan asked him.

He turned away from her and started pacing again. "Shit, we cannot be having this conversation. Not now."

The seriousness of this was settling on her. "What are you?" she asked.

His look was sharp. "What did you think I was?"

"A lawyer."

He leveled a skeptical gaze at her. "With one client?"

Susan's nose was running. She didn't want to ask for the handkerchief again. She sniffled and wiped it with her hand. "That was a lot of coke, Leo."

His eyes widened slightly. It was quick, but she caught it. "Yeahhh," he said.

It wasn't coke. It had looked like coke. "What was it?" Susan asked. She didn't feel euphoric anymore, just jittery. "Was it heroin?"

Heroin. Hero. It was weird the way the brain worked. Maybe it was the cocaine. Maybe it was free association. All Susan knew was that up until that moment she had forgotten about the note that her mother had left her, about Gabby Meester and the *Trib*'s Heroes column. And now she remembered. And what's more, she remembered that when she and Bliss went back into the house, the note was gone. It had been next to her laptop, next to the phone. And then it wasn't there. Beaton had taken it. Because it was important.

"I need your computer," Susan said.

Archie stared into the darkness of Gretchen's room. The hall lights made a door-shaped rectangle of light on the floor. The room was cold.

"Are you awake?" Archie asked.

"Yes," Gretchen said.

The light switch was in the hall, just outside the door. Archie flipped it on, and the door on the floor disappeared as the room sprang into sick institutional color. Gretchen was lying on her back in bed. He had the feeling that she'd been lying there a long time awake in the dark.

"Gretchen Stevens," Archie said. "It's a pleasure."

She didn't react visibly to that. But then he wasn't close enough to see any minute shifts of expression play on her face. "What a busy bee you've been," she said. She turned her head and looked at him. "I wasn't expecting you. No one came in to tie me up."

"I've had a long day," Archie said from the doorway. "I didn't call ahead."

She beckoned him with a hand. "Come and fill me in. I'm a little out of the loop."

Archie walked to her. She scooted a little over in the bed and propped herself up on her elbows and he sat down on the edge of the bed. He could feel his closeness to her.

Her hand ran up his back and threaded into the short hairs at the base of his neck. "Tell me about your day," she said.

His shoulders relaxed under her touch and he let his head drop forward. "Your old friend Colin Beaton put Susan Ward in the hospital and he kidnapped a kid named Margaux Clinton. Seventeen. A foster kid, like you."

He stole a sideways glance at her.

She gave him a small smile. "He doesn't like that name now."

"Sorry, Ryan Motley."

She looked different. Her skin was clearer, and her eyes seemed sharper. The slowness of her speech was gone. Or was he imagining it?

Her fingers moved deeper into his hairline, caressing his scalp.

"The Beatons took you in," he said. "And you murdered James Beaton. Was it Colin's idea? Did you do it together?"

"That's sweet," she cooed. "You want to blame it on him. He was the psychopath and I was the innocent flower, caught up in the carnage." Her lips spread into a wicked smile. "Sorry, darling. Daddy Beaton was all me."

"You turned Colin into a killer," Archie said.

"I showed him how to survive—I didn't know he was insane."

Archie chuckled dryly. "Now he's the insane one?"

Gretchen sat up so that she was directly behind him, and she put her head over his shoulder and her lips to his ears. Her warm breath fluttered against his neck. "He's testing God," she whispered.

The Church of Living Christ. Scriptural purists. "He believes in faith healing," Archie said, understanding. Gretchen tortured her victims for her own amusement. Beaton tortured his victims to make dying last longer, to give them as much time as possible for God to step in. "He tries to save them."

Gretchen's face lit up with delight. "With *prayer*. And they die anyway, of course." She arched an eyebrow. "You'd think he'd catch on."

"Why did he carve the hearts on some of the children?"

"It's a private joke."

"It's not very funny."

She shrugged and settled back onto her elbows again.

Archie looked around the sad, dank room. "Is this better than prison?" he asked.

"It's better than lethal injection."

"Worried that the angels won't be there to greet you?"

She blinked, and looked away, and Archie couldn't tell if she was really feeling something or if she was just faking it. When she looked back at him, her eyes were soft. "Lie next to me," she said.

Archie glanced at the door. This was going too far. He scratched the back of his head. He could feel the weight of her stare. He took off his shoes, slowly, and lined them up side by side on the floor. Then he stretched out next to her on the bed, so that they were shoulder to shoulder, hip to hip.

"Does it help, seeing me like this?" she asked.

Archie tried not to think about the heat in his groin. "Not really," he said.

"You're seeing someone." She said it casually.

He knew she was just guessing, reading him somehow, but it still threw him. "Am I?" he said.

"Does she look like me?" She hesitated at the end of the sentence, and the correction was clear: *How I used to look?*

"Henry thinks so," Archie said.

"Good. I want you to be happy."

Archie laughed. "No, you don't."

She smiled and ran the tip of her finger along the scar she'd left across his neck. "You should have had me restrained," she said. "I could kill you. You never know when I might have a razor blade tucked up my sleeve."

"Why kill me now?" Archie said. "It would seem anticlimactic."

She moved her finger from his neck down the buttons of his shirt to the front of his pants and then settled her palm over his pelvis. He strained for her.

She grinned. "You still like me."

He knew it was what she wanted. Power. To know she still wielded it over him.

She moved her hand to her mouth and sucked on her fingers, then danced her fingers back down his shirt and slid her fingers into his pants. The rush of blood in his body made him feel light-headed. The heat of her hand, the stickiness of her saliva.

He put his hand on her wrist.

"No," he said.

He could smell the sex between them. Both of them breathing heavily, sweating in that cold room.

She pulled her hand out of his pants and curled next to him, her head on his shoulder. "I didn't plan it," she said. "Our affair. I just wanted to get inside the investigation."

"Is that supposed to make me feel better?" he asked.

"It should probably make you feel worse. If I'd planned it, you'd be a victim of my wiles."

"This way I'm a guilty shit," Archie said.

"We're all guilty."

"Yeah, well, some of us more than others," he said. He yawned and rubbed his face. "I don't know why I came here."

She lifted her head and looked at him. "I do. You want to save the girl. You think I might know where they are, and you think that if you're nice to me I might tell you."

This was it.

"Do you know where they are?" Archie asked.

Her chin was on his shoulder, their faces close. He could see the threads of blood vessels in the whites of her eyes. "I need you to kill Colin," she said. "I don't want him caught. I want him killed."

"I'm a cop, Gretchen," he said. "I couldn't even kill you when I had the chance."

Her nostrils flared. "You think I'm dangerous? He is twice as dangerous as I ever was. He has done worse things. He will do worse things."

He cupped her head in his hands and looked her in the eye, searching for some tell, some spark of humanity. "Do you know where he is?"

Her gaze didn't waver. "Tell me you'll kill him," she said.

"If I catch him, the state will do that for us."

"The state didn't kill me," she said.

Archie brushed her cheek with his thumb. "You're a fucking aberration, sweetheart."

"Promise me you'll kill him."

He squinted at her, still searching for her angle. "We lie to each other all the time. Whatever we say, it doesn't mean anything."

"I'll believe you," she said. There was an urgent quality to her voice that he had never heard before. It unnerved him.

"I'll kill him," he said.

She closed her eyes. And he dropped his hands.

Her lids lifted. And she fixed her blue eyes on him. "Where do you go, when God fails you?"

And then he knew. Lowell Street. "The church," Archie said. The husk of the burned-out building was still there. What better place to hide? He swung his legs off the bed and pushed his feet into his shoes.

"Darling?" she said. "I'm not crazy."

Archie was already headed for the door. He looked back at her as he closed it behind him. She was still on her elbows, still watching him. "I know," he said. And then he flipped off the light and sent her back into darkness.

Henry was waiting in the hall. "Did it work?" he asked.

Susan sat on the edge of Leo's bed, his black laptop bobbing on her jiggling knees. Leo was sitting next to her, watching her like she might have a heart attack at any minute. She had Googled every name she could think of in conjunction with the Heroes column. Jake Kelly. Ryan Motley. All the Beatons. In fact, she had never typed faster. But nobody but Gabby Meester came up.

Then she had borrowed Leo's phone to call Lucy Trotter, the *Trib* staffer who put together the Heroes column every week. Lucy had said that a friend of Gabby's had called her a few months ago to ask some questions for a form she was working on, nominating Gabby for some award that paid 10K and had been advertised in the classifieds of the *Oregon Herald*. So then Susan had looked up the call for nominations in the classifieds of the *Herald*, and there it was. "Nominations Wanted for the Good News Award. 10K to local person with most charitable heart. Reap what you sow."

"Motherfucker," Susan said.

The *Herald* classified system provided a third-party e-mail to protect the privacy of the person listing the ad. But you had to provide bona fide contact info in order to get that third-party e-mail.

Susan called Derek Rogers. With the cutbacks at the paper, he'd be working late, covering the crime beat she'd once hoped to inherit.

He was one of those people who worried about his job, which was probably why he still had one and she didn't. He probably had on a tie right now. She hoped he'd pick up. She drummed her fingers on her legs while she waited. He picked up after four rings.

"*Herald,*" he said, wearily.

"It's me," Susan said.

"Where are you?" Derek asked, his voice dropping. "Are you okay?"

"I'm calling to give you an exclusive interview on everything that happened today."

There was a long pause.

"What's in it for you?" he asked.

He'd been suspicious of her intentions ever since she'd stopped sleeping with him.

"I need a favor," she said. "I have the third-party e-mail for a *Herald* classified and I need you to e-mail me the guy's real contact information."

"Why are you talking so fast?" Derek asked.

"I'm excited," Susan said.

She saw Leo roll his eyes.

"I'll have to go down to classifieds," Derek said. "It'll take a few minutes. The number you're calling from is blocked. Give it to me so I can call you back."

Susan glanced over at Leo. "It's not my phone. I'll call you when you e-mail me the contact info."

There was another pause.

Susan groaned. "Cross my heart and hope to die," she said.

"Okay," Derek said, and he hung up.

Susan slid the computer off her lap and jumped up and headed for the dresser.

"No," Leo said. "Not a chance."

"I'm on to something," Susan said, picking up the small black straw. "I don't want to get tired."

"That's not going to help you find her," Leo said.

"You're pretty self-righteous for someone with a gym bag full of heroin," Susan said.

Leo picked up the little bag of cocaine, pinched it between his fingers, and emptied it on the floor. "Whoops," he said.

The bedroom door opened and Bliss popped her head in. "What are you two doing?" she asked.

"Mom!" Susan said, dropping the straw. "Knock first." She moved away from the dresser, from the mirror, from the white powder on the floor. "What if we'd been having sex?"

"Sexuality is nothing to be embarrassed about, honey."

Susan cringed internally. "Any news on TV?" she asked.

"Nothing," Bliss said.

"Do you want some tea?" Leo asked.

"I want some wine," Bliss said.

Leo leveled his gaze at Susan. "I'll be right back," he said. He plucked his cell phone from her hands and led Bliss to the kitchen.

Susan sat back down on the bed and hit refresh until Derek's e-mail came through. The ad had been placed by Ryan Motley. There was a telephone number listed and an address in St. Helens. The telephone number was bogus: 503-555-1212. Crack security at the *Herald*, as usual. Susan Googled the address. It was some church in St. Helens. The Church of Living Christ.

By the time Leo walked back into the bedroom, Susan was dressed and had her shoes on.

"What's going on?" Leo asked.

"There was a gun in that gym bag, do you still have it?" Susan asked.

"No," Leo said.

Susan raised her eyebrows. "Do you have another gun?"

Leo didn't answer.

"Do you?" she asked.

He nodded.

"Get it," Susan said.

"I'm wearing it," Leo said.

She looked him up and down. She didn't see a gun.

He scratched the back of his ear. "It's around my ankle," he said.

Sure, that wasn't weird. Carrying a concealed weapon. Susan twisted her wet hair into a ponytail. "We need to go," she said.

Leo was between her and the door. "Where?"

"There's something I want to check out," she said, trying to slide past him.

He put his hands on her shoulders. "I'm supposed to keep you safe," he said. "Detective Sheridan's orders."

She looked up at him. She didn't know who he was. Or what he was involved in. Right now it didn't matter. What mattered was that he had a gun, and she was beginning to suspect that he knew how to use it. She looked at him hard. "You want me to trust you? You trust me."

"What about your mother?" Leo asked.

Susan lifted each of Leo's hands off her shoulders, and then motioned for him to follow her. She went to the kitchen, pulled a butcher knife out of the knife block by the Viking range, and carried the knife to the living room where her mother had just lifted a large pinot glass of red wine to her mouth.

"Mom, we're going out," Susan said. She held the knife out, hilt first, and her mother took it. "If anyone comes to the door, stab them with this."

The land around what remained of the Church of Living Christ was treacherous. The moon was full, and the spotlights from the patrol cars threw blinding light and cast strange shadows. Archie watched with Henry from behind the car as Columbia County SWAT crept forward slowly, their flashlights navigating the overgrown weeds and strewn two-by-fours that littered the ground.

Archie tried the megaphone again. "Colin Beaton, this is the police. Come out of the building with your hands behind your head."

There was no response.

The frame of the structure was still standing. They had all studied a photograph of it. A hundred-year-old wooden building, windows and door blown out, ceiling caved in. The white paint job was still visible, darkened with soot.

"It looks haunted," one of the SWAT guys had said. And no one laughed.

Archie hated this part. Waiting in the back with his Kevlar vest, as the SWAT radio in his hand crackled with hushed communications.

"Approaching."

"In position."

"Entering east window."

Archie peered over the hood of the car and saw the flashlight beams slicing the darkness inside the house.

Henry pulled back the slide on his weapon and released it.

"Clear."

"Clear."

"Clear."

"Shit," Archie said.

"Sir, we don't see anyone in here."

Archie stood up.

He grabbed a flashlight from a nearby officer and started walking toward the church, stumbling over the debris in the yard. He still had the megaphone in his hand. He lifted it to his mouth and said, "Don't shoot, I'm coming in."

The SWAT commander was waiting at the front door.

"Bad info," the commander said.

"Keep looking," Archie said.

The commander stepped aside so Archie could walk inside the church. Archie could see stars through the ceiling and the flashlights of the SWAT team spread throughout the building.

The commander shone his flashlight clockwise around the church. The interior walls had been stripped to their studs. It was basically all one room. There was nowhere to hide.

"Is there a basement?" Archie asked.

"Brick-and-fieldstone foundation. He's not here, sir."

Archie hurled the megaphone on the floor. "Goddamn it," he said.

The flashlight beams froze.

A shadow stepped behind Archie, and he felt a hand on his shoulder. It was Henry. "You're in a fucking church, Archie," Henry said.

Archie looked up at the night sky, the stars, the moon. "Sorry," he said.

✧

Huffington arrived just as SWAT was clearing out. Archie was in the passenger seat of Henry's car and Huffington pulled up next to him in her patrol car, her window down.

She said, "Next time you stage a raid in my town, give me a heads-up."

"There wasn't time," Archie said.

"It took you an hour to get here," she said.

She had him there.

"We had a lead that he was in the old church," Archie explained. "He wasn't."

"Keep me in the loop, Detective," Huffington said. She pressed a button somewhere and her window went up, and then she rolled off down the street.

Henry got into the driver's seat. "She pissed?" he asked.

"She reminds me of Susan," Archie said. He glanced at the time on the dash. "Let's go," he said.

Henry pulled the car away from the curb and headed down the hill toward the highway, while Archie gazed out the window.

"There's something Claire and I have been meaning to tell you," Henry said.

The houses they passed were dark, except for the occasional flickering blue light of a TV screen. "She's pregnant," Archie said. "I've been meaning to congratulate you." He was going to give his friend a slap on the back, or a handshake, or one of those other physical gestures men give each other at times like this, but Archie got distracted by something he saw out the window.

"First trimester," Henry said. "Wait a minute, you knew?"

"Stop the car," Archie said.

"What?"

"Stop the car," Archie said.

Henry stepped on the brakes. They were in front of the new Church of Living Christ.

Archie peered out the window. The church was dark, except for the stained-glass windows in the main chapel, which glowed in an abstract pattern of red and gold. "Looks like somebody's home," Archie said quietly.

"Maybe they're burning the midnight oil."

Archie opened the car door. "Maybe we went to the wrong church," he said, stepping out.

"Hey," Henry said, struggling to get unbuckled.

Archie was halfway up the walk when Henry caught up with him.

Their Kevlar vests were in the trunk.

Archie tried the knob on the main doors to the church. They were locked. The large double doors were oak, with expensive hardware. Archie went to the office door. As he remembered, the door was cheaper, with a standard cheap brass doorknob. He tried the doorknob. It was locked. He got his wallet out and rifled through his cards for the right flexibility, and then settled on a Starbucks gift card. He pulled it out and slid it next to the doorknob between the door and the frame.

"What are you doing?" Henry hissed.

Archie bent the part of the card that was still exposed toward the doorknob and said, "Breaking into a church." He pushed until he felt the card slide in past the mechanism. Then he leaned against the door and bent the card the opposite direction, until the lock popped and the door swung open.

"I'm pretty sure you just violated a commandment," Henry said.

They both stared into the still, dark office.

"I'm going in to check it out," Archie said, unholstering his weapon.

"You want me to get SWAT back?" Henry asked.

"If I find something," Archie said, stepping through the door.

Henry drew his own weapon and stepped through the door behind Archie.

"You don't have to come with me," Archie said.

"You think I'm going to let you burn in hell alone?" Henry said. "Just don't shoot the janitor."

The office was dark, but there was a slice of light under an interior door in the back left corner. Archie motioned to it, and they headed toward it, past inky shadows of desks and filing cabinets.

"How do you know how to do that thing with the door?" Henry whispered.

"I looked it up on the Internet once," Archie said.

They had reached the inside door. Archie tried the knob. It was unlocked.

Archie looked at Henry.

They readied their weapons.

Then the door opened.

Reverend Lewis stood in the doorway, his white hair backlit by the chapel lights, holding a sweater to his chest, like he'd been caught in the middle of folding laundry. "Yes, gentlemen?" he said.

"Jesus Christ," Henry said, lowering his gun.

Archie didn't lower his gun. The hair on the back of his neck bristled. "Everything okay, Reverend?" he asked.

"I'm praying for that girl," Reverend Lewis said. "How did you get in here?"

"We'll get out of your hair, Reverend," Henry said.

Archie didn't move. "Can we come in and look around?"

The reverend's lips were thin and pale. "That's not a good idea," he said.

Archie raised his gun so that it was level with Reverend Lewis's forehead. "Step to the side and let us in," Archie said.

"Archie," Henry said in a low, incredulous voice. "What the fuck?"

The reverend swung the door all the way open and for a moment he was surrounded by light. Archie squinted as the reverend stepped out of the way to let them pass. Archie walked through the door, gun level in front of him.

The church interior was modern and airy, with beige wall-to-wall carpet and white walls. Gleaming blond wood pews faced the front of the church. A carpeted aisle led between the pews and up three beige carpeted steps to the sanctuary up front. The carpet was marbled with bloodstains, like someone had been dragged, bleeding, down the aisle. On the altar of the sanctuary, Archie could see Pearl, laid out like a human sacrifice. She wasn't moving.

A dark-haired man in his thirties stood at the pulpit. He hadn't shaved in days, and his hair was wild. But Archie recognized the long limbs and vulpine features of the teenage Colin Beaton. There was a trembling desperation about him, an almost tangible anxiety. If Archie had seen him on the street, he would have assumed he was mentally ill.

In the room, saturating everything, was the overpowering scent of lilies. Huge bouquets of white blooms were gathered in brass urns at the front of the church and along the backs of the pews. That was where Colin had gotten the lilies. He had stolen them from churches. A missing lily here and there, a congregation wasn't likely to even notice it.

Colin waved Archie in as he leaned close to a microphone and said, "Come and pray with us." The words echoed in the church, and Colin smiled.

"We're the police, Colin," Archie said. "You're under arrest."

"Reverend Lewis," Colin said into the microphone, deepening his voice in a parody of authority. "You need to resume your spiritual duties." He spread his arms wide. "'For I will restore health unto you,'" he bellowed into the mike, "'and I will heal you of your wounds, saith the Lord.'"

"Stay where you are, Reverend," Archie barked.

"Archie," Henry said.

Archie stole a glance to the left. Reverend Lewis had dropped the sweater. His torso was swaddled in duct tape that held some device to his chest.

No one said anything. Colin was so close to the microphone

that it amplified his breathing. It was the only sound in the room. Archie had never seen a real bomb up close. But he was pretty sure that he was seeing one now. He could feel sweat forming on his upper lip as he counted to five. *One.* Stay calm. *Two.* Keep your voice measured. *Three.* Project authority. *Four.* Build a rapport. *Five.* Be firm. "What have you done, Colin?" Archie said.

Colin laughed, and the microphone squealed with a blast of feedback that made Archie flinch. "There a phone on the pulpit," Colin said. "I hit one button and that bomb goes off."

Archie couldn't see Colin's hands or the phone. But that didn't mean it wasn't there. These days anyone with an Internet connection could find out how to build a bomb with a cell phone detonator. Archie leveled his weapon, centering the sights on Colin's forehead. How long did it take to press one button on a cell phone? A second? Half a second? He could feel the trigger under his finger. Archie's legs were shoulder-width apart; his elbow was locked; his breathing was steady. All he had to do was squeeze.

"Do you think you can kill me with one shot?" Colin asked, his amplified voice reverberating through the church.

Archie exhaled slowly. He was fifty feet away from Colin, and Colin was a twitchy, fidgeting target. Archie wasn't that good a shot. Even if Archie did manage to shoot him in the head, Colin's hand might clench reflexively. Archie looked over at Henry, hoping that he had a better shot, but Henry shook his head. They needed to get closer.

"Reverend," Colin said. "Pray for our sister."

Reverend Lewis glanced back at Archie, and their eyes met. Archie searched the old man's eyes for some sign of serenity or faith, something that the reverend could hold on to, but all Archie saw was fear. The reverend's eyes looked up at the ceiling, or heaven, or God, and then he lowered his head and hurried down the aisle and up the stairs, where he knelt before Pearl.

She was so still up there, it made Archie's chest hurt. She hadn't made an effort to move since they'd come in. She wasn't restrained.

She was unconscious. One arm hung limply off the altar, her fingers grazing the carpet. Archie couldn't tell if the dark stains he saw on her body were shadows or blood. "Pearl?" Archie hollered. "Can you hear me?"

Reverend Lewis's white head was bent in prayer, one of his hands on Pearl's forehead. She didn't respond to Archie's voice or the reverend's touch. Archie hoped she knew the reverend was there, that she wasn't alone.

He lifted his weapon an inch, refocusing his aim. Archie had to get Pearl out of there. He had to do it for Susan.

Colin was looking at the Bible open on the pulpit, flipping frantically through the gold-edged pages. Archie glanced back at Henry, who was digging in his pocket for his phone.

Henry mouthed the word, *Backup*.

"Wait," Archie said. Colin looked up from the Bible. Henry had his phone in his hand. "Don't," Archie said. Archie didn't know anything about bombs. But he knew a little bit about cell phones. He knew they shared frequencies.

"If I were you," Colin said, "I'd turn off your cell phones. Any incoming or outgoing calls on the wrong frequency and the reverend goes boom."

It wasn't worth the risk. Archie kept his weapon raised and slid his free hand in his pocket, pulled out his phone, and turned it off. "Do it," Archie told Henry.

Henry hesitated and then scowled and hit the off button.

Archie took another step forward, staring down the barrel of his gun. Maybe he couldn't kill Colin with one shot; but Colin didn't need to know that. "This isn't going to work, Colin," Archie said. "She needs medical attention. Not faith healing."

Colin left the pulpit, and Archie followed him with his weapon. Colin's phone was in his fist. The reverend was still praying over Pearl. If the bomb detonated, the reverend would take Pearl with him. Colin stalked over to the altar, raised his arms in the air, and said, "'Behold, I will bring you health and cure, and I will cure you, and will reveal unto you the abundance of peace and truth.'"

Maybe if Colin Beaton had never met Gretchen Lowell, or been introduced to the Church of Living Christ, or had a different father, he wouldn't have killed anyone. But Archie was pretty sure he still would have been nuts. They needed to end this. Archie saw Henry start to creep right, around the back of the pews, so he could move forward along the wall to get a better shot. Archie had to keep Colin distracted, keep him talking; draw his focus away from Henry. Archie bent his elbow a little, to keep circulation flowing to his hand. He could feel his palm sweating around the grip of his gun. His arm ached. "If she dies, it's on you, not God," Archie said.

Colin's face contorted. "He said the spirit dwelled in me," he said. "He lied." Colin was breathing hard, his face red. He glared down at the kneeling reverend. "'Forgive him,' you said. You knew what he was doing to us, and you did nothing."

His pain was so raw it made Archie want to look away.

"Please let me take her to a hospital," Archie said, taking another step, his gun still leveled at Colin. "She's a kid. A foster kid, like Gretchen Stevens."

Colin straightened up and wiped the tears off his face with his sleeve. "Is Gretchen here?" he asked with a sniff, peering out into the empty pews.

"She sent me," Archie said. "That's how we knew where you were."

Colin frowned and gazed down at the phone in his hand. "I thought she would come," he said with a sad shake of his head. "I looked for her for so long. I sent her messages."

Archie could see Henry in the periphery of his vision, edging up to the front of the church. "You mean the hearts you carved on the children you murdered," Archie said. "And the lilies."

"I thought she'd come this time," Colin said.

"She sent me," Archie said. He locked his elbow and fixed his gaze down the barrel of his gun. "Instead."

Colin pointed at him and a light seemed to go on. "I know who you are," he said. He cocked his head and his eyebrows shot up hopefully. "Did she say anything about me?"

Archie squinted and lined up his shot. "She asked me to kill you," he said.

66

T his is it," Susan said, looking out the car window at the low brick building that was the Church of Living Christ. "There's a light on."

Leo had a black Volvo and its wood veneer accents gleamed purple from the dash lights. He turned the headlights off and the car went dark.

"Stay here," he said, opening his door.

Susan unbuckled her seat belt to go after him. "I'm going with you."

Leo turned around and leaned back into the car. His face was dead serious. "You just got out of the hospital," he said. "I'll check it out. Wait here."

Susan stiffened and nodded. She felt a shot of fear run down her back. The idea of running into Colin Beaton again had not actually occurred to her. Now she couldn't get the image of his machete out of her mind.

Leo closed the driver's-side door and Susan watched him walk around the hood of the car, illuminated by a streetlight. She rolled down her window. "Wait," she called.

He turned back.

"Give me your phone," she said, reaching out the window. "In case something happens."

He tossed her the phone and she caught it. "Don't download anything," he said. "And no smoking in my car. I'm going to walk the perimeter, and then I'll be back."

"Listen to you," Susan said. "'Walk the perimeter.' Who's been watching TV cop shows?"

Leo ignored her and she watched him walk toward the church until he was far enough away from the streetlight that he disappeared into the darkness.

It was at that moment, sitting there alone in Leo's dark car, that she remembered Derek. Shit. She had never called him back. She punched his cell phone number into Leo's phone. It rang a few times and then went to voice mail. He was probably asleep. "It's me," she said. "I'm an asshole, I know. Sorry. Listen, my phone isn't working, but you can call me on this one." She rattled off Leo's number. "Later."

She settled back in the seat, watched out the window, and waited.

And waited.

She picked up the phone and had almost finished punching in Leo's number before she realized that he didn't have his phone, she did, so he wouldn't get the call.

Crap, she thought. How long did it take to walk a perimeter, anyway?

She got out of the car and was closing the door behind her when she saw the Crown Vic parked a dozen feet ahead of them under the streetlight. The make, model, dark color. The whip antenna. It looked like Henry's car.

Susan called Archie. It went straight to voice mail.

She looked back at the church.

Then she walked around to the driver's side of the Volvo, popped the trunk, and got out a tire iron.

She couldn't call Henry or Claire or anyone else on the task force because she didn't have any numbers memorized but Archie's. Bliss didn't have a cell phone. If she called 911, what would she tell them? *There's a light on in a church and my heroin-dealing boyfriend is taking too long to walk the perimeter?*

It was up to her.

She had to find out what was going on.

She headed for the church, gripping the tire iron. As she got close she noticed that a door to the side of the main double doors was ajar.

"Leo?" she whispered.

She readied the tire iron and pushed open the door with her foot. The office was dark, but she could see light coming from another door, farther in. There were voices, too. Someone ranting.

She was inching toward the noise, straining to make out the voices, when she heard a woman behind her say, "Don't move."

Susan's stomach dropped.

The voice said, "Turn around."

Susan slowly turned and found herself blinking into a flashlight beam.

The beam lowered, illuminating the woman behind it enough that Susan could see that she was a cop.

A cop! Susan almost laughed, she was so relieved. Then she remembered she had just broken into a church and was holding a tire iron.

"Who are you?" the cop asked.

"I'm a journalist," Susan said quickly. "I came here looking for Pearl Clinton. I think my friends are in there. With a serial killer."

The cop nodded at the tire iron. "Put that down," she said. "And we'll go take a look."

S he doesn't want me dead," Colin said. He shook his head defiantly, but Archie could see the despair in his eyes.

"She thinks you're insane, Colin," Archie said.

"Liar!" Colin bellowed.

Colin lifted the phone, as if he were going to make a call.

"Wait!" Archie cried.

"Archie!" Susan yelled.

Susan's voice made Archie's stomach drop. What was she doing here? He couldn't turn around, couldn't take his eyes off Colin. It was all he could do not to run to her. "Susan?" he asked.

"I'm with a cop," she said. "I've brought help."

"Colin," a stern female voice said. "You need to let them take that girl out of here. You hear me?"

It was Huffington. Archie felt flooded with relief. She would have radioed her location in before she came inside. If she failed to check back in, her dispatch would send in reinforcements. Now all they had to do was stall.

"I saw the light," Huffington said. "Decided to check it out."

Colin was fixated on Huffington, his mouth open.

"He's got the reverend wired to some kind of bomb," Archie

said. He kept Colin in his sights. He might not be able to kill him, but he could hurt him.

Colin was growing more distressed. His thumb hovered over his phone's keypad. Huffington's presence had rattled him. He knew he was outnumbered. "Drop the gun," he ordered Archie. "Or I make the call."

"You'll blow yourself up, too, Colin," Archie said. The reverend. Pearl. Colin. They were too close together.

Now Colin was shaking uncontrollably, like something long coiled inside him had finally come loose. "Gretchen took care of us," he protested. He looked frantically at Huffington. "She protected us."

"By killing your father?" Archie said. "You had other options. Whatever was going on, there were ways to get help."

"The church told us to forgive," Colin wailed in Huffington's direction. "You know how many kids have died because their parents didn't pray hard enough, didn't love God enough?" he asked Archie. "Where were the police then?"

"We're here now," Huffington said from behind Archie.

Colin blinked sorrowfully out at Huffington. The twitching stopped. His body went still. Something had gone dead in his expression. His arms went slack. His eyes fixed. Only his lips were moving. Archie realized he was praying. He was going to do it. He was going to detonate the bomb.

There was no more time.

"Look at me, Colin," Archie said quickly. "Watch. I'm going to put down my gun." Colin's lips stopped moving and he eyed Archie warily. Archie could only hope that Henry was getting close enough to line up a shot, and that Colin had, for now, forgotten about him. Keeping his eyes locked on Colin's, Archie knelt down, hit the thumb safety on his weapon, and slowly set it on the carpet. Huffington was behind him. She was armed. She could cover him. "See?" Archie told Colin. "There it is. I've set down my gun. I'm going to stand up now, okay? Okay, Colin?"

"Is Pearl all right?" Susan cried from behind him.

"Susan, get out of here now," Archie said. "Huffington, get her out of here."

"I just want to see how she's doing," Susan said.

"Colin!" Huffington cried, and he turned in the direction of her voice, just as Henry fired. Henry hit him in the shoulder, and Colin fell back and his phone hopped from his hand onto the carpet. Colin shrieked like an animal and then reached for something under the altar and came up with a machete.

Henry was already scrambling up the steps after him, his gun raised. "I can kill you from here, Colin," Henry yelled. "You hear me? Drop the machete or I will fucking drop you."

Archie was crouching back to reach for his gun on the floor, when he felt the muzzle of a gun pressed against the back of his head.

The reverend was still praying. Pearl was still on the altar. Henry's gun was aimed at Colin. Colin was on his feet, bleeding, holding the machete like a baseball bat.

Huffington had called Colin's name, warned him in time for him to turn away from the kill shot.

"Sorry, Detective," she said.

Archie was inches from his gun. Huffington kicked it and it skidded under the pews. He turned around, very slowly, feeling the muzzle of her gun draw a band around his head until it settled on his forehead. Then he looked up at her. Weight gain had changed the quality of her features. She had changed her hair. But now that he knew to look, he could see the traces of the girl.

"You don't want to do this, Melissa," he said.

Susan was frantic. The cop she had brought to rescue everyone was now holding a gun to Archie's head. She could see Pearl, but she couldn't get to her. She needed to get to her. Colin had the machete, but he was wounded, she could see blood seeping down his arm. Archie and Huffington were in the center of the congregation pews. Susan needed to get up there. She pressed her back against the wall that she had seen Henry creep along, and she started inching sideways.

"Keep me, Melissa," Archie said to Huffington. "Keep your brother. But let Susan and Henry get the girl and the reverend out of here."

Susan kept moving. Trying not to audibly sob. Trying not to draw attention to herself. Archie had called the cop Melissa. *Melissa Beaton.*

"Tell your partner to holster his weapon, Detective," Huffington said.

Susan could see Henry's back, his gun raised defiantly at Colin, whose bloody machete flashed in the light.

She was even, now, with Huffington and Archie, him kneeling in front of her, her gun pressed to his head. It looked like an execution.

"You're not going to kill me," Archie said, looking straight ahead. "You're a good person, Melissa. You put the past behind you. You became a cop so you could protect people. Even after everything that happened to you here, you came back to this town to keep an eye on things."

"I can't let you hurt him," Huffington said. "It's not his fault. He shoots Colin, I shoot you."

Susan's legs felt weak. She couldn't move. She was frozen, watching the scene unfold in front of her.

Archie said, "Shoot him, Henry."

"No!" Susan said, forgetting her plan to be stealthy.

"That girl's dying, Melissa," Archie said. "Pearl will die if we don't get her help."

Susan didn't know where Leo came from. Suddenly he was just there, in the room. He was holding a bloody handkerchief to the back of his head with one hand, and in the other he had a gun. He didn't break stride. Didn't show any surprise or horror at the scene. His gun was raised at eye level. He was looking down the barrel. He was aiming at Huffington.

"No one's shooting anyone," Leo said.

Huffington glanced back at him and said, "I'm a cop."

"So am I," Leo said. He fired into Huffington's shoulder.

Huffington dropped to her knees, and then slumped forward onto the carpet. Susan's ears rang from the gunshot. She could smell gunpowder. She had her hands over her face and was half crouched against the wall, peering out between her fingers.

Colin was screaming. Henry lunged for him and tackled him to the ground. The podium toppled over, and the microphone bounced down the steps with a sustained mechanical screech. Colin let go of the machete, sending it slicing through the air. It impaled a pillar-shaped plant stand, which tumbled to the floor, sending a brass urn full of lilies on its side. The flowers spilled out of the urn and the urn rolled down the sanctuary steps after the microphone. The plant stand lay on its side, the machete still sticking out of it.

Susan stood up out of her crouch and ran alongside the wall up the stairs to the sanctuary, lilies flattening under her feet. Her vision was blurry from tears. Henry had Colin facedown, his arms twisted behind him—still wailing. The reverend hadn't budged. Susan had to scramble around him to get to the other side of the altar, nearly tripping on his calves.

She reached Pearl just as Archie did.

When Susan saw Pearl, she was nearly overcome with relief. Pearl's eyes were closed, and her body looked boneless and blood-less. They had gotten there just in time. They didn't have minutes to spare. She was hurt. She was so pale and limp. The Pixies T-shirt was soaked with blood. There was blood everywhere.

"She's dead," Archie said. His face contracted in pain for a moment and then he looked away. Susan didn't understand. They were there now. They could rescue her. "I'm sorry," Archie said.

Dead? But Pearl couldn't be dead. The reverend was still praying, still babbling about Jesus. He hadn't given up. Why was Archie giving up?

Susan shook her head. This wasn't happening. Archie had it wrong. "She's not dead," Susan said. "You can save her." She grabbed on to his arm and made him look at her. She could make him understand, if she pleaded hard enough. Archie had brought her back from the dead. She had drowned. Her heart had stopped. She had been clinically dead. And he had saved her. He had brought her back. "Like you saved me," she said.

He could barely look at her. She could see how hard it was for him, how much he was struggling. "She's been dead for hours," Archie said.

The weight went out from under Susan's legs. She fell to her knees, and Archie caught her and lowered her gently to the carpet, and she folded her hand around Pearl's. It felt cool and dry, and not like a real person at all.

Henry had his knee on Colin's back and was holding him to the floor.

The reverend was still praying. Susan wanted him to stop. Didn't he know? Didn't he understand that it was useless?

"Reverend Lewis," Archie said gently. "It's over. We need to get that vest off of you."

The reverend looked up. His eyes were red. His hands were covered with Pearl's blood. "Forgive me," he said to no one in particular.

"This way, Reverend," Henry called. "I can cut you out of that."

Susan couldn't stop shaking. "I'm sorry," she whispered to Pearl. "I'm so sorry." She said it over and over again. Then she felt Leo's phone vibrating in her pocket. It was reflex that she even pulled the thing out. It was Derek. He'd send help. She lifted it to her ear.

"No," Archie yelled.

But she had already hit the green button to take the call.

She saw a flash of light before she heard the explosion. A burst of orange and black fire followed by an eardrum-splitting blast of sound. The floor shook. She heard glass cracking and the sound of wet splatter on wood. Something hot and soft seared Susan's neck. She found herself on the carpet, eyes squeezed closed, trembling, choking on smoke. She kept her eyes closed, terrified to look. She could feel bits of things, terrible warm squishy human things, against her skin and on her clothes. The smell of burned flesh and hair made her stomach twist. When she had mentally catalogued her body and was sure that all of her parts were still there, she opened her eyes. The beige carpet was blackened and sticky with blood. She lifted her hands off it, sat up, and looked around, dazed, her head thumping, at the slick pieces of flesh and hair and bone that seemed to cover everything. It was still smoking.

Henry was wiping body goop from his eyes. His clothes were bloody. His eyebrows were singed. He had been knocked on his back by the blast.

Colin was gone. The explosion had been just the opportunity he needed to escape.

Susan looked up at Archie, his forehead covered with a fine mist of red.

She didn't know what to say. Somehow "sorry" didn't seem to cover it.

Archie lifted his arm and wiped the blood off his face. "Are you okay?" he asked her.

Susan nodded.

Archie looked back at Henry.

Henry was pulling himself to his feet. "Me?" he said. "I'm fucking perfect."

Susan tended to Pearl. Her body was spattered with tiny bits of the reverend's flesh and blood, like someone had combined shrimp and tomato soup and then forgot to put the lid on the blender. Susan picked some of the larger pieces off while Archie called 911.

Susan was wrapped in a blanket and curled up on a church pew, where she had been instructed to wait until a crime scene investigator could collect the evidence that stuck to her clothes.

There were, by her estimates, a hundred cops now on the scene. City cops. State cops. County cops. FBI. The Coast Guard would probably be there in a minute.

"Anything?" she heard one of them ask.

"He must have had a car," someone else said.

Pearl was still lying up there, right out in the open, while strangers took pictures of her. It made Susan sick.

Archie walked up to her. He had cleaned most of the blood off his face, though he still had something vile-looking spattered on his shirt.

"Where's Leo?" she asked.

Archie sat next to her and leaned in close. She thought, for a moment, that he was being affectionate, offering solace or something. But his eyes were too serious for that. "Leo was never here," he whispered. "They're going to take your statement. You borrowed his car. You came alone. Got it?"

Susan managed a minuscule nod.

✧

The EMTs beckoned Archie over. Huffington had been loaded onto a gurney and stabilized for transport. She was weak, but she wanted to talk.

"She kept asking for you," one of the EMTs said.

Huffington turned her head, looking for Archie.

"I'm right here," Archie said. He could tell she was having trouble seeing. He knew what it meant—her blood pressure was tanking. It wasn't good.

Huffington turned toward the sound of his voice. "I owed her," she said haltingly.

Her. The pit of Archie's stomach tightened. "What did you do?"

He felt Henry's firm grip on his shoulder. "We need to talk," Henry said. "Now."

"Melissa," Archie said, "what did you do?"

Her head lolled and she lost consciousness. "We've got to go," one of the EMTs said, and they lifted her and began rolling her to the ambulance waiting outside.

Henry's hand was still on Archie's shoulder.

The church was crawling with crime scene techs. There was blood and body matter everywhere. Everything smelled like death.

"Gretchen," Archie said softly. He wanted Henry to tell him he was wrong, that Gretchen was still locked up, but he could see the truth in Henry's face as Henry stepped beside him.

"She got out," Henry said. "Apparently her new doctor took her off most of the meds. Cleared the bitch's head. She cut his throat with a razor blade, killed a nurse, and got out with her clothes and ID."

Archie lifted his hand to his throat and ran his fingers over the scar there. "A razor blade?"

"I had them check the visitor log," Henry said. "The only people allowed in to see her are hospital staff and cops."

He could hear the wail of the siren as the ambulance left the church parking lot. "Let me guess," Archie said. "Huffington."

"She was there to see her just before we were," Henry said.

You never know when I might have a razor blade tucked up my sleeve.

She had let him live. Again.

Susan was in another emergency room with a new plastic hospital bracelet. She had been swabbed, scraped, and combed, picked clean and washed off, had her clothes taken into evidence. The hospital was freezing. She hadn't been that cold since Archie had fished her out of the Willamette River. She was sitting on the bed wrapped in two thick white cotton blankets, wondering when someone was going to come in and tell her what to do next, when Leo walked in.

His clothes were spotless. Except for the blood in the hair on the back of his head, he didn't appear to be injured. He'd left before the explosion. He had left right after he'd shot Huffington.

"Who are you?" Susan asked.

Leo took a breath and put his hands on Susan's shoulders. He was looking at her like Archie did sometimes. Like she was innocent. She wasn't innocent.

"I want to get you home," Leo said. "Your mother will be here in a minute. She brought clothes."

Susan pulled away from him, scooting back farther onto the bed. She could feel the tears coming, but she couldn't stop them. "A kid I was supposed to keep safe is dead," she said. She tugged at her wet hair. "I just had two men with tweezers and magnifying glasses pick brain matter out of my hair." Then she tapped her chest with her hand. "A man died because of me."

She was not innocent.

"That's not your fault," Leo said. "Colin Beaton built that bomb."

Susan's lips were trembling. Snot was dripping from her nose. She needed someone to give her the hug of a lifetime. She just wasn't sure that someone was Leo. She leveled her gaze at him. "Who are you?"

He glanced at the door.

"Are you a cop?" Susan asked.

He looked at her. His hands were in his pockets. He was perfectly still for several minutes. She didn't say anything. She just waited.

"DEA," Leo said quietly, motionless. "I'm inside my father's operation. He has cops on his payroll. I can't be on any of the reports."

"Archie knew?" Susan asked.

Leo looked at the floor. "He introduced me to my recruiter."

Susan shook her head. None of this was making sense. "But he doesn't like you."

Leo looked up. "He's trying to protect you," he said. "From me."

The door to the room flew open, and Bliss rushed in, kicked off her clogs, and climbed into bed next to Susan. Bliss didn't have on any makeup. Her platinum dreadlocks looked like a mop of fuzzy ropes. She was wearing a T-shirt with the word ATHEIST printed across the chest. She laid her head on Susan's shoulder and took her hand. Susan looked at their hands together—so much the same. Square palms, and thin stubby fingers with nails bitten to the quick.

"He killed her," Susan said, squeezing her eyes shut, still not quite believing it.

Bliss started to say something, but had to stop, and Susan realized her mother was crying. Bliss was an epic bawler, capable of clearing out a movie theater with her caterwauling. She dissolved into tears every year on John Lennon's birthday. She wept during Joni Mitchell songs and blubbered when she saw lobsters scrambling in their aquarium at the fish counter. This time she didn't make a sound.

Susan fell apart. Sobbing wracked her body. She couldn't speak; she could barely breathe. She gasped and mewled while her mother held her tight. Finally, exhausted, Susan was able to catch her breath and lift her head.

Leo was still standing there, waiting to take her home.

Bliss peeled the stray wet hair off Susan's cheeks with that hand that looked so much like Susan's own. At that moment, Susan was filled with love for her mother. Bliss was maddening sometimes, but when it came down to it, she was always there when Susan really needed her.

"I heard you blew up a reverend," Bliss said in an excited, conspiratorial tone.

Susan blinked at her mother, astonished. Then she looked at Leo. He gave her a sympathetic shrug. They both had embarrassing parents.

"What?" Bliss asked.

Susan sighed and leaned her head back in the crook of her mother's warm neck. "Nothing," she said.

Archie had been up all night helping to direct the manhunt for Colin Beaton. The small St. Helens police station had been taken over as the base of operations. The low white building looked like a dentist's office that had been taken over by eminent domain. The hunt for Gretchen Lowell had diverted resources, but it was still crowded in there. Huffington had died in surgery at the hospital. She had returned to town five years ago, with a new name. She had married and divorced in California, and kept his last name, and then started using her middle name, Samantha, as a first name. As identity changes went, it had been easy. No one had thought to connect her to the skinny teenage Beaton girl who had left so many years before only to succumb to cancer.

Sixty cops crowded in that building, and not one had thought to take her photograph down off the wall below the brass label engraved with the title CHIEF OF POLICE.

I owed her, Huffington had said.

Archie got a cup of bad coffee and walked outside and leaned against the four-foot concrete slab that read POLICE above the city seal. There was a residential house right next door. The neighbors stood on their parking strip, gawking.

It was cooler that it had been. The flag above the precinct was flapping in the wind.

Henry's car pulled to a stop in the middle of the street in front of the station. "Get in," Henry said. "They found him."

Archie left his coffee cup sitting on the concrete slab and climbed into the car.

✦

Ninety armed officers searching for Colin Beaton, and it had been a maid who had found him.

Room Six. The Hamlet Inn.

Archie kicked himself for not thinking of it.

Two patrol cars had arrived when Henry pulled into the motel parking lot, and they could hear sirens approaching from all sides behind them.

One of the uniformed cops on the scene was vomiting over the second-floor hall railing.

Archie and Henry galloped up the steps, taking them two at a time. The door to the room was swung open. A maid's cart was parked out front. Neat stacks of toilet paper. Freshly cleaned towels. Archie had a feeling that Colin wouldn't be needing any of it.

The vomiting patrol cop looked up, his face gray, and said, "Don't go in there."

"It's okay," Archie told him. "I've done this before."

Archie stepped into the doorway.

Henry stepped beside him.

They didn't say anything for a few minutes. They just took in the scene. There was a protocol to surveying a crime scene that was drilled into all cops. Start left; scan right. Look up; look down. Don't miss the details. But sometimes the thing in the middle was so distracting that you couldn't pull your eyes from it.

The king-sized bed had been stripped of its top sheet and

polyester floral bedspread, which lay discarded on the floor. The bottom sheet, still on the bed, was so soaked with blood it could have been red.

Colin Beaton was bound, naked, spread-eagled, to the headboard and footboard with an industrial-looking black twine. His torso gaped open, split from his ribs to his pelvic bone. His abdomen was sunken, its contents extracted and then strewn next to him by the bed, like refuse from a butcher shop. A slither of intestines. A chunk of liver. Handfuls of fat and muscle. Blood and bile soaked into the sheet. The stink was powerful. His feces had been squeezed out of his large intestine and smeared on his face. Flies crawled in and out of him, along his hairline, around his mouth.

She hadn't just killed him, she'd slaughtered him.

On the wall, above the headboard of the bed, using his blood, she had drawn a heart.

Archie could hear voices behind him, people jogging up the stairs. There'd be dozens of cops here in a minute. He turned back to the gray-faced patrolman. "Secure the scene," he said.

The cop was young, in a St. Helens uniform. He had vomit on his chin. "On whose authority?" he asked.

"Mine," Archie said.

"This is a Beauty Killer case," Henry explained. He handed him a task force business card. "It's ours now. No one gets in but our people."

The cop nodded and wiped his chin. He looked glad to have an important job, a way to redeem himself.

As Archie and Henry entered the room, Archie could hear the cop's voice rising with authority. *Beauty Killer. Restricted. Task force.* They watched where they stepped. Archie scanned the room. There was something on the dresser. As he got closer he saw that it was a dirty red wallet. Archie plucked a pen out of his pocket and nudged it open. It was empty.

"What is it?" Henry asked.

"Toss me an evidence bag," Archie said.

Henry did and Archie slid the wallet into the bag and sealed it. Underneath the caked dirt, he could barely make out a faint gold monogram. GS.

When Archie had asked Gretchen about the name Gretchen Stevens, she had said that Stevens was dead. She had buried her on Sauvie Island, she said. According to the DCS file, when Gretchen had turned up in St. Helens, she had been both bloody and dirty. She had come from the island, where she had buried her past. And now she had gone back, and she had dug it up.

"It's something she buried a long time ago," Archie said.

Archie carried the wallet over to where Henry stood next to the bed. Colin's mouth was taped shut. His eyes were pushed open unnaturally wide, the upper lid folded over the lashes. She'd used superglue, Archie realized, to keep Colin's eyes open, so he wouldn't miss a minute. Then used a triangular incision to carve out Colin's nose, in the style of a Halloween jack-o'-lantern.

"He got what he wanted," Archie said. "He got to see her again."

Henry grunted. "He doesn't look very happy about it."

"True," Archie said.

Henry paused and then looked around. "Where is it?"

"What, his nose?" Archie said. They hadn't seen it on the carpet.

"Yeah." Henry bent down to look under the bed.

Archie studied Colin's face, his cheek, where the flesh bulged out on one side, like a squirrel with a nut. "I think it's in his mouth," Archie said.

"Archie."

Archie recognized that tone. It was never good. He looked up and Henry nodded at Colin Beaton's chest.

It was pale, and scattered with brown hair. And over his left nipple was a heart-shaped scar, just like Archie's. Archie was intimately familiar with the life span of scars. He knew what they looked like when they were raw and sore and fresh; he knew what they looked like months later, when they were dark pink and tender; and he knew what they looked like after years had passed and they healed to a thick thread of pearly pink tissue. Colin Beaton had had this scar for years. If Gretchen had carved it on him, she had done it long before she had ever taken a scalpel to Archie.

"You want protection?" Henry asked quietly.

Archie sighed and glanced up at the heart she'd drawn in blood on the wall. He could see her fingerprints in it, the path of her delicate hands as she lovingly painted in blood. "If she wanted to kill me," he said. "I'd be dead."

When Archie got out of the elevator, he could see Susan sitting on the floor in front of his apartment door. She stood up when she saw him, and gave him a little wave.

"Henry said you'd be home soon," she said. "I texted you." She held up an iPhone. "I got a new phone. Same number. And I got an extension on my story. The editor wants five thousand more words."

He could tell that she'd been crying. Her eyes were red. She wasn't wearing makeup. Her orange hair was pulled back into a tight ponytail. She was wearing a short black dress and silver Doc Martens. Even at the end of the summer, her legs were still pale.

He got to his door and leaned against it. "Colin is dead," he said. "You and your mom can go back to the house."

She nodded. "I heard."

She looked at him, like she wanted him to say something.

"Yes?" he said.

"Leo told me," she said. "Some."

At least she knew now. He wanted to tell her how much he'd struggled with it, how often he'd considered jeopardizing the DEA's entire operation. He wanted her to understand that it hadn't been a casual decision, not telling her. But, of course, he couldn't say any of that. "I can't talk about that with you. I'm sorry."

He fumbled for his keys. "I need to sleep," he said.

Susan leaned the side of her head against his door and looked at him. "How did Colin find Pearl at our house, do you think?"

"I don't know," Archie said. "We may never know. He might have been following her there to begin with."

"They're saying that Gretchen killed Colin," Susan said. She narrowed her green eyes, studying him. "Why did she do that, Archie?"

Archie rubbed his face, his keys still in his hand. "I think she had her reasons."

"Is she going to kill you?" Susan asked. Her eyes were glassy, filled with tears. He could see her struggling not to blink.

Archie was filled with tenderness for her. That was why she had come. She was worried about him. He lifted his hand and touched her cheek. "No."

Her eyes widened and then she blinked and tears ran down her freckled cheeks.

Archie moved his hand from her cheek into her wet orange hair and pulled her to him, and she lifted her mouth to his. He could feel her tears against his face, the warmth of her mouth, her tongue. Her damp hair was thick under his fingers. He moved his arm around the small of her back, and she reached her arms around the back of his neck. He kissed her gently. It took self-control. His body was hungry for her, and finally being there, tasting her cigarettes and coffee, the smell of her sweet shampoo and peppermint soap, he had to consciously hold himself back. He didn't want to be rough with her. He didn't want it to be like it had been with Gretchen.

But Susan seemed to have other ideas. She lifted herself up onto her toes, pushing her tongue deeper into his mouth, circling his tongue and tickling his throat. Her fingertips scratched the back of his scalp, and neck, and then along the edges of his ears. He moved his hands down her body to her hips and backed her up against the wall, and then lifted her and pressed his body against hers, so that she was supported between him and the wall. He could feel her under him, the slightness of her, her hip bones and pelvis, her dress bunched up under his hands, barely covering her. His brain felt like it was buzzing, his hands heavy and clumsy.

His whole body was trembling. He kissed her deeper, willing himself to compose himself. Her hands glided under his earlobes along his jaw, her fingers against his cheeks.

He wasn't shaking; Susan was.

He let himself forget sometimes how vulnerable she was.

He pulled his mouth from hers, and stepped back, and lowered her to the floor.

She looked at him, confused, cheeks flushed, her lips still parted.

He wiped his mouth. What had he done?

"I'm sorry," he said. He hadn't meant to do that. He was exhausted. He wasn't himself. He wasn't strong.

"Why?" she asked.

He pressed his forehead into the door and tried to figure out a way to say it, how to explain it to her. He took a deep breath and then turned to look at her, face-to-face. "Because I care about you," he said. "And this is not a good idea."

But she was happy. She was glowing. She laid a hand on the front of his shirt. "I know how fucked up you are. I don't care."

"Thanks," Archie said.

She blushed. "You know what I mean."

"This isn't a good idea," Archie said. "It shouldn't have happened."

"I'm an adult, Archie," Susan said.

"I'm not over her yet," Archie said.

He waited.

Susan's face fell. But she nodded. She seemed to understand. "Your wife," she said.

Archie gave her a look.

Susan's eyes widened. Then she looked away. "Oh," she said.

"Yeah," Archie said.

✧

Archie was standing at the kitchen counter drinking a double shot of whiskey when there was a knock at his door. He smiled. He had told himself, if Susan came back, even after what he'd told her, that he would let her in, that he could take a chance. But when he opened the door, it was Rachel, not Susan, who stared back at him.

She was wearing her white satin robe, and he got the feeling that she wasn't wearing anything else.

"You're all over the TV," Rachel said. "A big hero. I came here as a citizen, to express my gratitude."

"Really," Archie said.

Rachel slipped past him into the apartment. "I thought I'd start with your cock," she said.

Archie nearly choked on a sip of whiskey. "I usually just get some sort of commendation."

He closed the door and when he turned back into the apartment, Rachel had dropped the robe and was standing naked in his living room. Every time Archie saw her body, it made him weak in the knees.

"I was planning on just going to bed," Archie said.

Rachel smiled and wetted her bottom lip with her tongue. "I'll meet you there," she said, and she turned and walked into the bedroom.

Archie looked at the empty glass in his hand, and then walked to the kitchen counter again and poured himself some more whiskey. Then he took his holster off his hip and laid it on the counter next to the bottle. And then he took his phone out of his pants pocket. He had a text message from Susan, just as she'd said: *Coming over. Need to see you.*

He scanned through all the previous texts from her, all of them checking in, letting him know that Pearl was fine; everything was fine.

Archie lifted the whiskey glass to his lips.

Rachel put her arms around his waist from behind. "What's taking you so long?"

Archie took another swig of whiskey. "Just finishing some stuff up," he said.

She turned him around so they were facing each other and then she spun slowly around for him.

"Tell me the story of the heart tattoo again," he said.

She put her finger on his mouth. "Don't ask so many questions. Do you want to fuck me, or not?"

He let his eyes graze over her. Her blond hair, blue eyes, the cheekbones and chin, the dip of her collarbone and curve of her breasts and hips. "You look like someone I know, have I told you that?" he said.

"Yes," she said. "But you didn't say if that was good or bad."

Archie considered this. "A little of both."

Rachel grinned and lifted her hand to her mouth, and pushed three fingers deeply into her mouth and slowly pulled them out. Then she walked them down Archie's shirt and slid them into his pants.

"You like that?" she whispered.

Archie took another sip of whiskey.

"Very much," he said.

Archie awoke to Rachel's gentle prodding. "Your phone's ringing," she said.

He pulled it off the bedside table, looked at it, and sat up in bed in the dark. Then he lifted the phone to his ear. "Hello, Patrick," he said.

"Are you all right?" Patrick asked.

The kid had seen the news. He sounded panicked. Archie swung his bare feet on the floor and stood up and walked to his north bedroom window. "I'm fine," Archie assured him.

The bedroom was dark. The red IKEA gooseneck lamp was off.

Archie looked out the window, at the stars in the sky and the bridge lights over the dark scar of the Willamette River. The city's buildings glowed. The interstate stretched north and south. Streetlights twinkled. From this view, standing in the dark room, the city looked brighter.

"I'm ready to tell you my secret," Patrick said.

"I'm here."

Patrick exhaled a long, sad breath. "Sometimes I miss him," he said. Archie heard the words catch in Patrick's throat. "Sometimes I want him to come back for me."

"I know," Archie said. "It's okay. I promise," he said. "You'll be okay."

Archie wanted to believe that it was true.

73

W hen Archie woke up in the morning, Rachel was gone, and he had a headache from the whiskey. He took a shower, drank some coffee, got dressed, and drove to Sauvie Island.

It was a beautiful day. The sky was high and bright. It was so clear that Archie could see the Cascade Range from the bridge to the island. Most Portlanders loved Sauvie Island. Situated between the Columbia River, the Multnomah Channel, and the Willamette, it was just ten miles north of Portland; but it was its own ecosystem of trees, fields, wildlife areas, beaches, farms, houses, rivers, and slough. People went there to pick raspberries, swim in the river, hike, hunt, bird-watch, and cycle. They also went there to dump bodies. Children drowned in the currents off the beach. A few years before, a woman had tossed her two small children off the bridge to the island. One died, the other was rescued by someone in one of the houseboats who heard what sounded like an animal crying.

Archie felt that he could never quite see the island the way other people did. But he could still appreciate it. Once you crossed that bridge, it felt like someplace else, and he liked the way the fields looked and the horses and the old farms.

After a nice talk with Pennie at the Sauvie Island Community Association, the creek with the oak trees next to the red barn wasn't hard to find. Archie took a left off the bridge and followed Gilman Road around back under the bridge and along the south side of the island. He knew this road from taking his kids to the pumpkin patch and the corn maze.

He pulled over at the milepost marker that Pennie had given him and parked the car. The creek was on farm property, behind a house. Archie could see a small grove of trees and a large red barn in the distance. It didn't look like anyone was home at the farm. The lights were off and there were no cars in the gravel driveway. Archie climbed over the barbed-wire fence and started walking. As he got close, the grass got higher. It was above his waist, green from the wet soil. He waded through it under the trees. It was quiet. No birds. The creek was more of a swamp. The water looked gloomy and stagnant. Small white wildflowers sprang up in the places where the grass didn't grow. The ground was soft and wet, easy to dig.

He couldn't see his car from here. A few sheep grazed in a nearby meadow. Nothing else moved.

Archie sat down at the base of a tree and waited.

It was three hours before she showed up.

She still surprised him.

He was staring at a piece of grass he had picked, twisting it in his fingers, and then he looked up and she was standing there. Her legs were bare. The green cotton dress she was wearing was the same color as the grass. He wondered if she'd planned that.

"Have you been waiting long?" Gretchen asked.

"Just a few hours," Archie said.

Her hair was dark now, and pulled back. Makeup covered whatever blemishes remained on her face. Out of the institutional pajamas, in the green dress, her body curved and flattened in all the right places.

She took off a pair of large dark sunglasses and arched an eyebrow. "I had to make sure it wasn't a trap."

"Don't think I didn't consider it," Archie said.

Gretchen pulled on a leash and a corgi sauntered through the grass and flopped down next to Archie.

"I think of you more as a cat person," Archie said.

"Colin had him," Gretchen said. She squatted daintily on the other side of the dog and ran her hand down the length of the dog's back. "He could kill his mother, but he couldn't kill the fucking corgi."

"You killed Colin," Archie pointed out. "And not the corgi."

Gretchen shrugged. "Colin's been trying to get me to kill him for years." The corgi rolled over on its back and gazed up at Gretchen with adoring brown eyes. "The corgi wanted to live," she said, rubbing its belly.

"What happened between you and Colin?" Archie asked.

Gretchen was quiet for a moment. The wind moved the leaves in the trees above them. "We were together for a few years," she said. "And then I left him." She frowned. "He took it rather hard."

"I'll say," Archie said. She could have killed Colin back then, left him dead, as she had so many of her other apprentices. Or she could have killed him when he'd started the copycat routine. "What took you so long?" he asked.

She leveled her gaze at him. "Some people are harder to kill than others," she said.

He wound the blade of grass around his finger. "You heard about Melissa?" he asked.

Gretchen stopped petting the dog. "Yes."

The trees formed a canopy of pale green. Sunlight dappled the still creek. Archie could smell the fecund sweetness of the dirt and grass.

"I tried to save her," Archie said.

"She would have been arrested," Gretchen said. "It's probably for the best. She would not have done well in prison."

"No," he said.

She lifted her eyes to his, daring him to say it.

All the pieces fit together. The reason Colin thought that Gretchen would come for Pearl. This time, he had said. *I thought she'd come this time.* Gretchen hadn't had her tubes tied until she was nineteen. *She says her child is in danger,* the shrink had said.

"Not Melissa," Archie said. "*Pearl.* I tried to save your daughter." Her face didn't change. There was no sign of grief, or regret.

"People die," she said. "You and I know that more than most."

Archie rubbed his eyes. "The thing about your child being in danger, I thought it was one of your games. But this was always about Pearl. The lilies he left at the crime scenes. Lily. The name you gave her. He moved on to killing adults. But he wanted pure adults, who would be worthy enough to be saved. Susan found an ad he was running in the *Trib.* That's how he found Gabby Meester. Someone nominated her for her good citizenry. But he killed Jake Kelly because he was close to Pearl."

"Well done, Detective," Gretchen said.

The dog rolled back on its belly and laid its head on Archie's thigh.

"You must feel something," Archie said. He wanted her to feel something. "I saw what you did to him in that motel room. You cared for him, but you slaughtered him for what he did to her."

"I gave her up a long time ago," Gretchen said.

Yet, when Archie had his first run-in with Pearl, Gretchen had kept showing up. Archie had thought she was watching him.

"You've been looking out for her, though, in your own fucked-up way," Archie said. He picked another blade of grass and looked at it. "Which Beaton was her father?"

Gretchen looked at him askance. "Neither," she said. "I arrived in St. Helens with that little project already under way." She snorted. "Though the elder Beaton did try to pray it out of me. Sort of a faith abortion." Her expression steeled. "The world got a little brighter the day I threw him piece by piece on that train."

"You should have told me," Archie said. "I could have done more to protect her."

She looked away, toward the sheep meadow.

Archie balled up the blade of grass and tossed it into the creek. "She Tasered me last year."

Gretchen turned back, smiling. "I guess she had a little of me in her after all."

The dog whined and pawed at Archie's leg and he reached down and scratched its head.

"She likes you," Gretchen said.

"I like dogs," Archie said. "They're relatively uncomplicated."

"If I had told you, and you'd saved her, then everyone would have known," she said. "She would have known. Imagine that life."

Archie studied her face. Empathy. It was the thing that psychopaths weren't supposed to have. But some of them got very skilled at faking it. He couldn't trust himself with her. He saw things that weren't there. And she knew him well enough to give him what he wanted.

"I can't tell," he said. "What's real for you."

"Maybe that's why you keep coming back. Maybe I'm the one person you can't figure out."

Archie thought of Dusty Beaton, and how many times, during the Beauty Killer media mania of the past few years, she'd probably seen a photograph of Gretchen Lowell. Had she ever connected that serial killer centerfold with the gawky foster child she'd taken in so many years before?

"Did Mrs. Beaton know what you became?" Archie asked Gretchen.

"I spent two months with her," Gretchen said. "And blossomed considerably after leaving," she added. "But the truth is, I think the old bitch didn't want to recognize me. Melissa was the chief of police of that little town. She wasn't exactly in hiding. I saw her photograph in a newspaper four years ago and I knew exactly who she was. Dusty saw those same newspaper photos; she watched the local news. She didn't know her own daughter. That woman was always very good at not seeing what was in front of her. In my experience, people who lie to themselves long enough don't even know when they're blind."

It wasn't until Gretchen said Melissa's name that Archie finally put the last piece of the puzzle in place. "This was about Melissa," he said. He had to give Gretchen credit. She had set in motion a complex set of events, and played each of them perfectly. But Archie had not been her target. "You sent me digging into Beaton's past, knowing what carnage would follow, knowing how Melissa would react. Pearl's fate was incidental. You needed Melissa to get you out. You used the rest of us to drive her to it."

"Melissa owed me," Gretchen said. "She knew it. I helped her see it."

"And Pearl?" Had she truly meant something to Gretchen, or had she just been bait?

"I didn't love her," Gretchen said. She said it matter-of-factly, without malice or regret. "She was two." She was looking past him at something far away. "And I couldn't love her. So I gave her away." She tilted her head and turned back to him. "I wanted her to have a life."

He searched for some quality of Pearl in her, and he could see something in the jaw and cheekbones, the regal nose and full mouth. A year ago, when he'd first met Pearl, she had been sixteen, skinny and boyish and angry. At seventeen, Pearl had grown several inches, developed curves, and inhabited her body completely differently. She had, like her mother, "blossomed considerably."

"You didn't kill any of the children?" Archie asked. "The ones we accused you of murdering, the children left dead with your signature carved on their torsos, those were all Colin trying to get your attention."

"Is that a question?"

"Yes," Archie said.

"We lie to each other all the time, remember?" she said with an amused smile.

"Tell me," Archie said, "and I'll believe you."

She looked him in the eyes. "I didn't kill any of those children."

Her gaze was unwavering. Her voice was steady. There was no rise in vocal pitch, no fidgeting, no extended pauses or rapid blinking. None of the usual telltale signs.

Wait a minute. "Any of *those* children?" Archie said. "So have you killed *other* children?"

She wrinkled her forehead. "Do teenagers count?"

"Let's say no," Archie said evenly.

She leaned forward, until her face was centimeters from his, her lips almost touching his lips, and she widened her eyes. Archie loved her eyes. They were so blue they almost glowed. "Then I'm as innocent as a rose," she said.

He believed her.

It was, he thought, the first time he could remember ever believing anything she had ever said about anything.

Her breath tickled his lips. "How did you know I was sleeping with someone?" he asked. He wondered what he would do if she pressed her mouth against his. He tried not to move.

"Lucky guess," she said. She lifted her hand and caressed his cheek with the backs of her fingers. "Like I said, I want you to be happy."

She stood up, gave the leash a tug, and the corgi hopped up and looked at her, its tail nubbin wagging furiously. Archie could see Gretchen's shadow on the grass, the outline of a human, the girl she had been.

"Lovely chatting with you, darling, but I've got to run. Face it, you're always more content when you're chasing me than when you have me locked up. I think we're going to have a lot of fun."

"Gretchen?" Archie said. She turned back. The breeze made the grass vibrate and the green dress hug her thighs. Archie unbuttoned the top three buttons of his shirt and pushed his hand under the cloth, along the heart-shaped scar until his fingers found the short pieces of tape that held the tiny microphone to his chest. Then he peeled back his shirt so she could see it. "I have a confession," he said, holding his shirt open so she could see the wire he was wearing.

Her eyes lifted from his and grazed the perimeter. They had been here for hours: FBI, state police, Archie's task force, SWAT. They had snipers in the trees. Beyond the quarter-mile radius that Archie had insisted on, the area was surrounded. All the nearby farms had been evacuated. The barn, the dark farmhouse—each teemed with law enforcement. At that moment, Gretchen was in the scope of at least ten high-powered rifles. *Don't think I didn't think about it.*

For a moment he felt a tinge of regret. Not because he had set a trap for her—she was a killer, she deserved to be caught—but because he had lied to her. Then she turned back to Archie, and winked.

The explosion knocked him back hard against the tree. Whatever the device was, she must have buried it when she'd dug up her wallet and other belongings. The ground in front of them exploded, sending dirt and rocks and mud spraying in all directions. The shock wave rippled underneath Archie like an earthquake. Birds shot off squawking into the sky. The slough sloshed. Leaves and twigs rained down from the trees. Archie fumbled for his weapon. He couldn't see her. There was a wall of pain in his head where he'd slammed his skull against the tree trunk behind him. His ears rang. His clothes and face were splattered with mud. He tried to get up and fell back down; then tried again. The air was so full of leaves he couldn't see. He felt someone next to him, holding him up. It was Henry.

"You're bleeding," Henry said. "Sit still."

"Where is she?" Archie said. His legs were jelly. The soles of his shoes slid in the mud. He could see people all around him then. Uniforms. FBI windbreakers. Flak jackets. Radios crackled. His vision wavered and he let Henry move his hand from his holster and lower him back safely to the ground. Archie's teeth hurt. He could taste his own blood in his mouth where he'd bitten his tongue.

"We'll find her," Henry said.

She was gone.

Colin had not taught himself how to make the bomb he'd strapped to the reverend; he'd learned how to make that bomb from Gretchen. And now she had made one herself.

Archie pushed himself to his feet. "I'm okay," he said to Henry. He held himself upright by keeping a hand on the tree trunk and he scanned the meadows, the stream, the farm.

There was one bridge from the island to the mainland, and it had been secured immediately. But there was water on all sides, and a boat could get someone far fast.

A helicopter took off from behind the barn and started a search pattern overhead, flattening the long grass and sending more leaves spiraling off the trees. Archie's knees buckled again and Henry helped him back to the ground.

"They won't find her," Archie heard himself mumble.

Henry wiped a clot of mud off Archie's cheek. "An ambulance will be here in ten minutes," he said.

"I don't need an ambulance," Archie said. The leaves in the air were dizzying. They whirled around like confetti. Archie watched one float, gliding gently side to side until it hung in the air next to him, and then he caught it in his dirty hand. "I'm fine," he said.

He heard a dog bark, and looked up. Then he shook his head and laughed.

"What's wrong with you?" Henry asked.

"She left me the dog," Archie said.

A red-haired patrol cop named Whatley jogged up with the corgi on a leash.

"We found her in the backseat of your car, sir," Whatley said to Archie. "The windows were cracked," he said. "And we found this." He held a folded note out to Archie.

Archie opened the note. It was handwritten in Gretchen's perfect script.

Darling—something to remember me by.

Archie showed the note to Henry. Claire came up next to Henry while he was reading it and slipped her arm through his. It was a tender casual gesture, but for them it was a brazen display of public affection. Archie couldn't help but smile. "Congratulations," he said.

"Really?" she said. "Right now?"

The corgi barked again. Archie held his hand up and Whatley laid the end of the leash across his palm. The dog walked over and stretched along the length of Archie's thigh and laid her head on his knee. Her fur was splattered with mud, too, and one of her ears had blood in it. She whined and Archie stroked her head. Archie could feel the sun on his face. The leaves that had rained down from the trees had blanketed everything with a layer of gleaming green.

"We're better off without her," he said.

ACKNOWLEDGMENTS

My mother, Mary Cain, gave me a great gift when I was a kid. She didn't raise an eyebrow when I announced that I was writing a book. I wrote a lot of "novels" in my room growing up. And I probably would have given up if she had ever pointed out the obvious fact that I was a child and needed to get a clue and take up sports. These days it is my writing group who humors me: Chuck Palahniuk, Lidia Yuknavitch, Monica Drake, Cheryl Strayed, Mary Wysong-Haeri, Suzy Vitello, Diana Jordan, and Erin Leonard. Yes, we still meet every week. My editor, Kelley Ragland, always makes my books better. And my husband, Marc Mohan, is always the first person to read a manuscript from start to finish. I think, Marc, I am finally learning the difference between *steel* and *steal*. Our daughter, Eliza Fantastic, is already writing books of her own, although "author" is several slots below "restaurant owner" on her aspiration list. Eliza, this is the book I was working on up in the attic the summer before first grade. Thanks also to my agent, Joy Harris, and her excellent crew at the Joy Harris Literary Agency, and to everyone at St. Martin's Minotaur, with special thanks to Andrew Martin, George Witte, Sally Richardson, Matthew Shear, Matt Baldacci, Matt Martz, Hector

DeJean, and Nancy Trypuc. Also, Ryan O'Neill, consider this your acknowledgment redux. Sorry I left off one of your "L's" in the last book. Last, thanks to all the people who read the acknowledgments. You know who you are.